P9-CBX-333

"Tantalizing . . . a complex, riveting plot with engaging characters."
—*Mystery News*

Suspicion of Deceit

"Combines believable characters, local color, and politics with a gripping plot about friendship, family, and betrayal . . . [takes] the legal thriller to a new level."
—*The Blade* (Toledo, OH)

"Parker knows how to steam up the pages."
—*Montgomery Advertiser*

Suspicion of Guilt

"A breathlessly paced legal thriller with a powerful punch."
—*Publishers Weekly*

"The author deftly shifts puzzle pieces . . . while building tension to a slam-bang conclusion."
—*Booklist*

Suspicion of Innocence

"Barbara Parker's prose is as swift and clean as the Gulf Stream, and just as powerful."
—James W. Hall

"This sizzling page-turner will keep lamps lit late into the night."
—*Publishers Weekly*

"Parker unleashes a resplendent cavalcade of multiethnic tanginess and richly drawn characters with . . . stylish flair. . . . Superbly plotted, with a sense of pacing to kill for."
—*Boston Herald*

ALSO BY BARBARA PARKER

THE
PERFECT
FAKE

BARBARA PARKER

AN ONYX BOOK

ONYX
Published by New American Library, a division of
Penguin Group (USA) Inc., 375 Hudson Street,
New York, New York 10014, USA
Penguin Group (Canada), 90 Eglinton Avenue East, Suite 700, Toronto,
Ontario M4P 2Y3, Canada (a division of Pearson Penguin Canada Inc.)
Penguin Books Ltd., 80 Strand, London WC2R 0RL, England
Penguin Ireland, 25 St. Stephen's Green, Dublin 2,
Ireland (a division of Penguin Books Ltd.)
Penguin Group (Australia), 250 Camberwell Road, Camberwell, Victoria 3124,
Australia (a division of Pearson Australia Group Pty. Ltd.)
Penguin Books India Pvt. Ltd., 11 Community Centre, Panchsheel Park,
New Delhi - 110 017, India
Penguin Group (NZ), 67 Apollo Drive, Rosedale, North Shore 0632,
New Zealand (a division of Pearson New Zealand Ltd.)
Penguin Books (South Africa) (Pty.) Ltd., 24 Sturdee Avenue,
Rosebank, Johannesburg 2196, South Africa

Penguin Books Ltd., Registered Offices:
80 Strand, London WC2R 0RL, England

Published by Onyx, an imprint of New American Library, a division of Penguin Group
(USA) Inc. Previously published in a Dutton edition.

First Onyx Printing, November 2007
10 9 8 7 6 5 4 3 2 1

For James

CHAPTER 1

Through the tinted windows, the Miami club district slid away—purple neon, stucco colonnades, people jamming the sidewalks. In the backseat of the Escalade, Larry looked over at Carla. Her shoulders moved with the heavy beat of the music on the stereo, and a curve of blond hair swung across her face. She thought they were on their way to score some cocaine.

Joe turned his SUV south through downtown, which was dead this time of night. The headlights shone on a soda can rolling across the street and metal gates over the stores. The temperature would drop below fifty by dawn. In the passenger seat, Marek turned around to watch Carla. He laughed and snapped his fingers to the music and watched the hem of her dress sliding up her bare legs.

They went under the low overpasses of the expressways, a forest of concrete columns. Behind the chain-link fences, homeless men slept under tattered plastic tarps. Cigarettes winked in the darkness. A short bridge went over the river and came down on West Flagler

Street. The big tires hummed on the grid. Marek craned his neck to watch two women staggering out of a Nicaraguan nightclub.

Marek worked for the Russian, who had sent him over here. The first thing Marek had asked for when Larry picked him up at the airport was stone crab claws. After that, "Take me to South Beach. I want to buy a shirt at Tommy Bahama." He had bought a dozen shirts and some silk pants, but he still looked like he'd just walked off a farm in Bulgaria.

When Joe turned right into the industrial district along the river, Carla asked Joe if he was lost or what. He turned off the stereo and told her it was just around the corner. Silent now, the Escalade went through the open gate of a chain-link fence topped with razor wire and then past stacks of lobster traps. The guard at the gate vanished into the darkness. Joe parked in the shadow of a two-story building, a former fish market. A hooded security light shone on faded red letters.

Carla put her face to the window. "Where the hell are we?" Larry grabbed her purse and passed it between the front seats. She yelled, but Larry held her down. Joe said there was nothing in the purse. Marek turned around and told Larry to look for a wire.

"She's not wearing a wire."

"Be sure."

Carla's cursing got louder when Larry felt down her back, around her waist. Larry said, "No wire. Satisfied now?"

Carla leaned over and grabbed her purse from Joe. "I'm out of here." She pulled on the door handle. "Joe, unlock the door!"

Larry said, "Calm down, baby. We just want to ask

you something." The security light at the gate didn't reach this far, but floods on the electrical transformers down the river gave enough light. She was shaking. He said, "I'm not going to hurt you. Just tell me the truth. Last Tuesday Joe walked into the Second Street Diner for lunch, and he saw you in the back with someone, a black-haired Hispanic guy, late thirties. Do you remember that?"

She put on a blank look. "Tuesday?"

"That's right. Four days ago. Who was he?"

"Tuesday. . . . Oh . . . him. He just . . . he comes in to eat. I guess he lives in the neighborhood or something."

"What's his name?" Larry asked.

"I don't remember."

Larry slapped her twice before she could get her hands up. "Joe says you got in his car. What was his name?"

Her voice was shrill. "I don't know. . . . Wait! Let me think! Manny!"

"Manny what?"

She peered out from behind her arms. "Suarez."

"Okay. Manny Suarez."

Carla's tongue came out to touch her upper lip. "Son of a bitch." She started crying.

"Where did Manny Suarez take you?"

"Nowhere. I had walked to lunch, so he dropped me at my apartment. Why are you asking me this? Who is he?"

"He's a cop. He's with the ATF."

"What is that?"

"Alcohol, Tobacco and Firearms." She still looked blank. He said, "That's the U.S. government. He's a federal agent."

"Well, he didn't, like, walk up to me and say, 'Hi, I'm a cop!' " She laughed and looked at the others in the front seat. "Why would he talk to me? I don't know anything."

"You only saw him that one time?"

"Yes. I mean, except when he came in the diner sometimes, like I said."

Larry wanted to believe her. Carla wasn't that smart, and he didn't think the ATF would use a bimbo like this as an informant. On the other hand, the Miami Beach Police had arrested her for possession, and the case had gone away. But that didn't necessarily mean they had given her to the feds.

Turning around, Marek put his chin on the seat back, and his small, brown eyes studied her. "I think she is lying."

"Stay out of this," Larry said.

Marek raised his eyebrows. "Ask her again."

Carla laughed. "Larry, come on. I didn't know who he was. What am I supposed to do, ask every guy who talks to me if he's a cop?"

"What did you talk about, you and Manny?"

"Nothing. You know. Just . . . like, 'Can I buy you a drink sometime?' And I said I had a boyfriend. It was nothing."

"Did he ask you about Oscar Contreras?"

"No."

Larry tried to get through the arms she held over her face. "Lying bitch." He could see Marek watching, and it made him angry. She clawed at him. He pushed her arms away and put a slap across her face. She kicked wildly, scraping the leather seat with the heel of her shoe.

"Hey! Hey!" Joe turned around. "Don't mess up the car, man. Take her outside."

"Then unlock the fucking doors."

"I am! Get out!"

Larry shoved the door open with his foot and dragged Carla across the seat. She landed on the ground and tried to twist away, but he had a good grip on her. The interior lights fell on the broken asphalt paving. Carla fought him, but he put a knee in her back.

The wind brought a stink from the river: diesel oil, seaweed, rotting fish. Marek lit a cigarette.

Larry leaned down close. "I gave you a chance to tell me the truth. I could throw you in the river. Nobody would look for you. Nobody would care. A piece of garbage, another whore, and Miami's full of them."

She was crying.

"Joe, get that rope out of the back."

"Okay! He asked me about Oscar, but I didn't say anything, I told him I didn't know anybody named Oscar."

"Did he ask you about anybody else?"

"No. Only Oscar. Please. Please let me go." She was begging now, tears dripping off her face. "I'll leave. I'll go back to L.A. I swear."

"You've been saying that for a long time."

"I'll leave tomorrow. I'll be on the first plane. I want to go home. Please."

"I don't know, baby. I just don't know." Larry stood up and took his money clip out of his pocket, peeled off some hundreds. "All right. You're leaving tomorrow, and if I ever, *ever*, see your face again, we are going to have problems."

Carla grabbed for the money, scraping it together quickly.

Marek was behind her. When she stood up, he put an

arm around her throat and lifted quickly. He jerked his arm right, then left. There was a dull cracking sound. As she fell, Marek caught her around the waist, and a sigh hissed out of her mouth. Urine flowed down her legs and splattered. Marek shifted his feet.

"*Coño,*" Joe said.

Larry stared. "Are you out of your fucking mind?"

"She was going to talk to them," Marek said. "Maybe already she was talking."

"She would have been gone tomorrow."

"Now is better. Now we are sure."

Exhaling a held breath, Larry turned away and ran a hand over his hair. His forehead was sweaty. Upriver the drawbridge at Northwest Twelfth began to clang, and lights flashed. A freighter was coming through.

Marek picked up Carla's arms and dragged her to the rear of the SUV. "I watch *CSI: Miami* on the satellite. I saw one show where they put a body in the Everglades, and it's gone in a week. Amazing. You take her there. Burn the ID."

"I'm not taking my Escalade to the fucking swamp," Joe said.

"Open the door. Don't worry, no blood to mess your Cadillac." Marek laughed around his cigarette.

Larry gave Joe a nod, and Joe opened the back door. Marek lifted Carla inside and folded her legs. Her hair was across her face. Marek threw a beach towel over her and closed the door. He looked around at Larry. "You said no one is looking for her. She was living alone?"

Larry said, "With another girl. A roommate."

Smoke drifted through the mustache. "We should talk to this girl."

"Forget it. This isn't East Romania."

"Croatia. She is working for you also, this other girl?"

"I said leave her alone. You'll be back in Europe in a few days, but I have to live here, and I don't want the cops on my ass."

Joe kept his eyes on Marek but shifted closer to Larry, like he didn't know what to do next. Joe had a pistol under the front seat, but against a lunatic like Marek, it wouldn't be enough.

Larry said, "Listen to me, Marek. There are some negotiations going on, a lot of money on the table. I myself have an interest, not directly, but an interest. So I'm telling you. Do not go after the roommate."

"She is your girlfriend?"

"No, but if she disappears, questions will be asked. She works part-time for a judge. A judge has connections. Do you understand? She won't be a problem unless you make her one."

The mustache shifted like Marek was smiling under there, like what assholes he had to deal with. He shrugged. "Okay."

"Okay, then." Larry picked up the bills that Carla had dropped.

Turning around, Marek scanned the parking lot. He found a high heel and threw it toward the water. It floated, a small black dot moving slowly toward the bay. He put a foot on the seawall and smoked his cigarette. The ship came nearer, gradually filling the narrow river like a wall of rusty steel. One of the men on deck raised a hand toward the parking lot below them, and Marek waved back. The propellers splashed, and gradually the throb of the engines faded.

CHAPTER 2

When his number flashed over the check-in desk, Tom Fairchild folded the sports section, picked up his motorcycle jacket, and made his way through the rows of molded plastic chairs. He stepped over a man's bare, skinny legs and swerved around a little kid banging an empty soda can on the grimy tile floor. His mother grabbed the can away, swatted the kid, and went back to her cell phone.

Tom slid the numbered receipt under the glass divider. "*Hola*, Daniela."

"*Hola*, Tomás." She drew a line through his name.

"What's up, girl?"

"Not much."

"You're looking good. Got a new boyfriend?"

A smile put dimples in her round cheeks. "I wish."

She buzzed him in, only half an hour after he had arrived—a record. Several turns in the narrow, dirt-smudged corridor led him to Keesha Smith's door, which was open. He stepped inside and saw bare walls and cardboard packing boxes.

"What's this?"

Keesha turned around from the file cabinet with her arms full. She dumped the folders on her desk. She was a big woman, old enough to be his mother, with hair processed straight and swooping gold frames on her pink-tinted glasses. "Morning, Tom. Move that box out of the way and sit down, if you want to."

He tossed his jacket over it. "They finally fired you?"

She laughed. "No, I got myself transferred to the Tampa office."

"You're kidding."

"Well, my mom's having heart trouble, and she's old. She needs me close. I didn't want to just leave and have you asking, 'What happened to Ms. Smith?' You've been assigned to another probation officer starting today."

"I don't want another PO."

"Don't play like you'll miss me. You kept sayin' how I always had my spurs in your ribs."

"You do. You don't let me get away with anything."

"Remember now, it's the straight and narrow path that leads to freedom. Stay on it. You'll be all right."

"So . . . who has the pleasure of my company from now on?"

She hesitated before she said, "George Weems."

"Not the Weasel."

She pointed at him. "You listen to me. He might be tough, but he wants his clients to succeed. You do your best for him, and watch your mouth. He'll slap you down if you show an attitude."

"What attitude?"

She shook her head. "Don't you disappoint me."

"I promise not to." They shook hands, and Tom held on. "I'm going to miss you," he said. "You believed in me, Keesha, when nobody else in the system did. You kept me out of prison."

"Good luck, Tom. And good luck with that sailboat! If you ever get around to Tampa Bay, I want a ride."

"Absolutely."

She sent him back to the waiting room, where he pulled another number off the roll. Fifty-one. He checked the display, which said twenty-four. He rolled the number into a ball.

"Hey, Daniela." He leaned close to the smudged glass of the check-in window and waited for her to smile. "Ms. Smith wants me to go right in and see George Weems. Would you find out if he's available?"

She lifted the phone while Tom leaned an elbow on the counter and ran his hand over his buzz-cut hair, silently cursing. Bad news, getting George Weems. They had a history, going back to Tom's first arrest, at age thirteen, busted at the mall for shoplifting He-Man and Battle Cat in full armor. Tom's father had just died, not that it was an excuse, but Weems had kept him on probation for a year by writing up bad reports for the judge. When Tom and a friend had been caught smoking grass on school grounds, Weems had insisted on a residential facility. That was where Tom had learned the basics of street fighting, which later had served him well in the county lockup. Weems hated all his clients, but he particularly hated anybody who could insult him in complete sentences.

Tom had been out of serious trouble for four years before this latest stumble, which wasn't even his fault. If not for a good lawyer, a judge with some brains, and Keesha Smith's vouching for him, Tom would have been looking at eight to ten years. The judge had given him a year in county and eight on probation. Two years down, six to go. Any major fuckup, they would ship him to state prison to serve the remainder of his sentence.

Being only marginally incompetent, George Weems had been promoted to the adult division. He hadn't forgotten Tom Fairchild. The first time they'd crossed in the hall, the Weasel's eyes had gleamed with anticipation. *Lookee who's here. My, my.*

Keesha was right: Walk the straight and narrow. There was no choice.

A tap on the glass drew his attention.

Daniela said, "He says you need to wait. Sorry." She wrote Tom's name at the bottom of Weems's page.

Tom checked his watch: a quarter past ten. He rode the elevator down. Standing on the sidewalk in front of the shabby probation office, gazing at the Miami Police Department a block away, a building more familiar to him than any church, Tom flipped open his cell phone and called his sister, Rose, to let her know he'd be late. Rose owned a shop that sold antique maps and prints. Tom did the framing and archival coloring. He took next to nothing for this because it was all she could pay him. Rose's husband had been a drunk, and the only downside to his early departure, a result of rolling his car into a canal, was that Rose had inherited a pile of bills and two kids to raise on her own.

When the rings flipped over to voice mail, Tom left a message. "Rose, it's me. I'm stuck at my PO's office, but don't worry about that map for Royce Herron. It's almost done, and I can take it to him by this afternoon, no problem."

Tom had chained his motorcycle to a utility pole in the reserved-parking area, rather than leave it in the main lot.

The bike was a 1988 Kawasaki he had paid only five hundred bucks for, but a roving meth-head might steal it for the tires. Tom unlocked the storage box and took out a notebook and a mechanical pencil. The notebook contained sketches of the forward hatch on the sailboat he'd been restoring. Ten years ago, he and a buddy had dragged it out of the mangroves, and Tom had been working on it—off and on—ever since. Tom had set himself a deadline. By the end of February, a month from now, the boat would be dropped into the Miami River. Tom would motor it out to Biscayne Bay for its first water test—if he could find the money for engine repairs.

By the time his number was called an hour and twenty minutes later, Tom had sketched both forward and aft hatches, embellished the gunwales with carved teak, and made a masthead with bare breasts and flowing hair.

He flipped the notebook closed.

The Weasel's office had been decorated in gray-steel file cabinets and brown carpet, all the warmth of a strip-mall insurance office. Weems had cranked up the seat of his chair to put him eye-to-eye with his clients. If he stood more than five-four, it was on the days he wore lifts in his shoes. He had light brown skin and eyes a weird shade of gray. A receding hairline and large front teeth made his narrow face even more rodentlike. He knitted his claws together on the wood-grain Formica surface of his desk. "Mr. Fairchild, it seems that fate rejoins us."

"It seems so."

"I'm gonna tell you first off that whatever your deal was with Ms. Smith, you don't have it with me."

"We had no deals. If Keesha asked me to do something, I did it."

"I've reviewed your file." A slight nod indicated the

thick folder on the desk. "There's been a lot of slip-sliding on your part. Example: Alcoholics Anonymous. Have you been attending meetings regularly?"

"Not anymore. I don't have a problem with alcohol. Ms. Smith wrote that in the file."

"I don't care what she wrote in the file. The judge ordered you to attend AA."

"It was a total waste of time. I'm not an alcoholic."

"Denial, Mr. Fairchild. Denial. It's how you got here, and it's what's gonna keep you here until you own up to it." He let the silence hang there while Tom looked at him across the desk. "You've been flaunting the terms of your probation. I could write you up right now."

The heat in Tom's neck was starting to make him sweat. He smiled. "You want me back in AA? Fine." After which he would go out and have a beer. A psychologist in the distant past had written "alcohol abuse" in his file, and it had dogged him ever since.

"Before you leave, pick up the paperwork. Ask your sponsor to fill it out." Weems clicked his black ballpoint pen a few times, then began filling out the monthly report form. "Have you made your payment this month?"

"I just mailed a money order," Tom said.

"Uh-huh. The check is in the mail. Your payment is due the first of the month, and today is February the second." *Click-click-click.* "It appears to me like you're consistently late on your payments to the court."

"Not always. Not by more than a day or two."

"We have a pattern here, Mr. Fairchild. What it is, is a lack of respect for the court. You need to accept your responsibility to pay restitution to the victim."

"The so-called victim is the one who ought to be sitting here. He padded the damages by about five grand."

"That is not my concern. The judge ordered you to pay, and my job is to make sure you do." Slowly, Weems turned the pages in the file. "The last financial affidavit is from six months ago. Fill out a new one before you leave. I want to know the sources of your income, and how you spend it."

"Fine."

"Do you own a vehicle?"

"I own a motorcycle."

"Do you carry liability insurance?"

"Yes."

"You still earn about two thousand a month?"

"More or less. It varies."

"Do you believe you're working up to the level of your ability, Mr. Fairchild?"

Tom tapped the toes of his sneakers together to let off some energy. "I'm building my business. It takes time."

Weems clicked his pen. "And what is your business?"

"I'm a freelance graphic designer. It's in there. I also work for my sister in her map shop."

"Catch as catch can. Are you registered with our job placement service?"

"I have a job."

"Register anyway, and make sure I receive proof that you've done so."

"Fine."

Weems tapped his finger on the page. "Is your rent still eight hundred a month?"

"Yes, it is."

"That's a lot of money."

"Not in this market," Tom said.

"You live alone?"

"Yes."

"A lot of my single probationers rent a room to save money."

"My place isn't big enough for a roommate," Tom said.

"No, *you* find a room to rent," Weems said. "Why can't you do that?"

Tom stared at him. Explaining anything to Weems was like talking to a dish of potato salad. Tom lived in a garage apartment ten minutes from Rose's shop. He kept his tools and his bike in the garage, and the owner let him work on his sailboat in the backyard.

He said, "I like the neighborhood."

Lifting the cover with his pen, Weems let it fall shut.

"Here's what we're going to do, Mr. Fairchild. Heretofore, you've skated by on the minimum of effort. No longer. You will pay your two hundred and sixty dollars and nineteen cents on the *first* of every month, and not a day later. If the first falls on a weekend, you will pay by the preceding Friday. You will attend regular AA meetings, and you will sign up for a course in anger management."

"Anger management?"

"Did I not speak clearly enough for you?"

"Wait a minute." Tom held up his hands. "When I was released from jail, Keesha said I should take that course, and I did. The certificate's in the file. Take a look."

"You might have taken the course, but it doesn't seem to have done you much good. I want you to take it again."

"I don't have the money right now."

"That's not my concern. Within a week I want you enrolled in anger management, *and* on Friday morning, *this* Friday, I'm going to check the registry of the court to see if your monthly payment arrived. You said you mailed it today? You weren't lying to your probation officer, were you?"

"This is fucking ridiculous."

The Weasel's eyes glittered. "You are this close, Mr. Fairchild, to being violated."

Tom shifted his gaze toward the ceiling and smiled.

"Is something funny?"

"No, Mr. Weems. There's nothing funny at all."

The Weasel's quiet voice stopped him at the door. "Mr. Fairchild. You might have charmed your way past some people, but not me. We're going to get you straightened out, one way or another."

Clamping his teeth on a reply, Tom went to the main office to fill out the forms. Half an hour later, he pushed through the glass door of the probation office and thudded down four flights of concrete stairs to the emergency exit, which he opened by kicking the push bar.

He put on his sunglasses and unlocked his bike. Looking up, he calculated which window belonged to George Weems. He pushed his bike under it, swung a leg over the saddle, and jumped on the starter. He gave it some gas. The scream of the 600-cc engine bounced off the building next door, and smoke poured from the exhaust.

Double-glazed windows muffled the traffic noise. The porch roof and dense banyan trees down the middle of the street blotted out the buildings on the other side. Tom could walk into The Compass Rose, with its dark pine floors, its walls hung with antique maps in gold or mahogany frames, and one of his sister's classical music

CDs playing softly on the stereo, and time would roll backward to when he'd sat under the display table with his crayons and a coloring book. He could almost—not quite—forget about wanting to break the Weasel's jaw.

The building had once been their grandfather Fairchild's house, built in the twenties. The shop was on the ground floor; Rose and the girls lived in the converted apartment upstairs. It was rare to have more than a few customers a day. There were better markets for antique maps than Miami, but their grandfather had founded the shop, and he'd left it to Rose because she loved maps. They were all she knew.

Coming in through the workroom a little while ago, Tom had found his sister in the front, pulling maps for the Miami International Map Fair, an annual event at the historical museum downtown. Rose always rented a booth and somehow sold enough to survive.

"Rose, I hate like hell to ask you, but I'm about three hundred dollars short of what I need. If you could lend me the money, I'll have it back to you by Friday. If I don't mail the money order today, Weems will be on my ass for sure. He's looking for an excuse to write me up."

The crease between her brows deepened. "Oh, no. Tom, I'm sorry, I just paid some bills, and I don't have— Wait. Yes, I do." She went around to her desk and shuffled through envelopes in the outgoing mail. She pulled one out. "This can wait a few days."

"What's that, the bank? No, I'm not going to let you—"

"It's all right. Really it is . . . as long as you're sure you can get the money back into my account by the end of the week."

He nodded. "I'm sure. Absolutely."

"Good." She smiled at him. "Problem solved."

Tom could see himself in her green eyes and sandy blond hair. A pretty woman, but worry had sketched lines on her face. She was thirty-eight, the sensible older sister. The rock; the one who had put a $75,000 mortgage on the building to pay for a lawyer who could get her younger brother a year in county plus probation, instead of eight to ten in a state penitentiary. Tom sometimes wondered if he should have saved her the trouble. If he could go back to the moment the cops put the handcuffs on, would he even let her pay his bail? Rose had already given or lent him so much he'd lost track. He had tried to pay it back, but his bike blew a tire, or a tooth had to be filled, or the landlord wanted a security deposit. That Rose still trusted him made him want to scream at her: *You fool, don't do it!*

He unhappily watched her write out a check. When she gave it to him, he said, "I swear to have the money on Friday. I'd go back to prison before I'd take bread out of the kids' mouths."

"Oh, don't be so dramatic. It's fine." Her eyes searched his. "And you're fine, too, Tom. Don't forget that. I know it's hard for you right now, but just put your head down and plow through it. My advice about Mr. Weems? Ignore him. He can't hurt you unless you do something wrong, and you won't. You *won't*."

Tom managed to fake a reassuring smile. Rose had no idea. There were fifty ways of falling off the straight and narrow. Keesha Smith had been a god-sent piece of luck. He was afraid it had just run out.

He snapped his fingers. "Hey, I almost forgot. I want to show you something."

The workroom was at the back of the house, converted years ago from a kitchen and enclosed porch. Coming in, Tom had tossed his jacket and a brown mailing envelope on the table he used for framing maps and prints. He opened the envelope and slid something halfway out.

"I'm going to let you see this," he told Rose, "but just look. Don't pick it up."

On the carpeted surface of the table he set a small map about ten inches by seven and turned on a gooseneck lamp. Then he crossed his arms and waited. Rose bent over the map, studying it intently, twirling the end of her sandy blond ponytail.

She was looking at the Gulf of Mexico, Florida, and Cuba, surrounded by a narrow border of ocher. Tattered corners. A small stain near the top. Pale pink land; rivers meandering through; settlements as small red forts; tiny script for the place names. The ocean was shaded with thousands of black dots, denser at the shores. A cartouche contained the words *La Florida,* and underneath that, *Hieron. Chiavez, Antwerp 1584.* Off the Atlantic coast sailed an inch-long wooden caravel with banners flying, sails puffed out, the bow dipping into a wave.

"What do you think?"

"Oh, my God."

"You like it?"

"Ha. What a question. I've got goose bumps!" She slowly straightened and looked at him. "Where'd you get this?"

"Not so fast," he said. "Can you name the cartographer?"

"Hieronimo Chiavez. It's on the cartouche."

"And the publisher?"

Her eyes shifted back to the map. "Oh, my God. It can't be an Ortelius. Can it?"

"Maybe. Maybe not. You tell me."

"Tom, where did you *get* this?" She gave him a little punch on the shoulder. "Where?"

"Turn it over."

"Oh, for heaven's sake. You!"

On the reverse was the shop's logo, a pink and green compass rose, with directions, the phone number, Web site. And in old-fashioned script, her name: Rose Ervin, Proprietress. Tom said, "You wanted something to give out at the map fair next weekend."

She reached for a magnifying glass and held the map to the light. "Ahhhh. Cotton rag paper, the right color and weight, more or less, but . . . there it is. A watermark from Eaton. Busted!"

"Yeah, but it took you a while," he countered.

"Where did you find this particular Ortelius to copy? I've never seen it anywhere."

"I made it up. I combined three others I saw in the catalogues and put them together on Photoshop. You could say it's an original Fairchild. I can take the disk to the printer this afternoon. How many should we get? Five hundred?"

"None." Rose laid the map on the table. "We can't use this."

"Why not?"

"Because . . . it looks so *real*."

"It's supposed to. That's the fun of it," Tom said.

"Tell me how much fun it's going to be when somebody buys a framed one and starts complaining they were ripped off. I can't afford that risk."

"Oh, I see. People will think you conspired with your brother, the convicted felon, the ex-con. Are you *sure* you want me at your booth at the map fair?"

Her face colored. "Stop it, Tom. I wasn't thinking of you."

"Of course not." Hands knitted on top of his head, Tom crossed to the back door and stared out at the enclosed backyard, the shade trees and cracked concrete where Rose parked her old minivan. He stared at his battered motorcycle chained to the porch railing. He saw the next six years stretching ahead of him like a hike across the Arctic.

"I was thinking of Eddie." Rose came to stand beside him. When Tom looked at her, she dropped her eyes.

"First time you've mentioned his name in about a century," he said.

She shrugged. "Out of sight, out of mind."

Eddie Ferraro, their former neighbor two doors down: ex-marine, Chicago Cubs fan, fisherman, a pressman at Kopy King. He'd fallen hard for Rose, and her daughters liked him so much that Rose started thinking she might have a future with Eddie. He moved in and quickly learned the antique map and print business. And then, to help Rose through a lean season, sold some phony botanicals and bird prints that he himself had forged. Rose managed to buy them all back, but there were whispers about her integrity. Eddie promised he'd never do it again, but Rose threw him out. A week later the Treasury Department arrested Eddie Ferraro on an old warrant for counterfeiting. He posted bail and skipped to Italy. That had been four years ago. Eddie had sent letters to Rose, but as far as Tom knew, she'd never answered them.

She put an arm around Tom's waist. "It's a good map." She laughed. "It's scary-good. We'll order a thousand. But you have to put our logo on the front. And your name. People should know who the artist is." She gave him a squeeze. "Everything's going to be just fine."

CHAPTER 3

Before going to the door, Royce Herron glanced through the living room window to see who had rung the bell. A minivan was parked under the jacaranda tree near his gate. On the front steps stood a muscular young fellow with short blond hair, wearing a faded black T-shirt. He held a large, flat package wrapped in brown paper.

"Ah, marvelous!" Herron opened the door and held the screen. "Tom, come in."

"Hello, Judge Herron. I have your map."

"Carry it out to the back porch for me, will you? I can't wait to see what you've done with it."

In clear, crisp weather like this, Herron liked to spend the afternoons on his screened porch. A week ago he had set a piece of plywood on two sawhorses, a place to work on his exhibit for the Miami International Map Fair. The makeshift table was now covered with large rectangles of ivory-colored paper and parchment mounted on acid-free cardboard and encased in Mylar. Herron had hired a girl to help out. She watched their visitor unwrap the package.

"Hi, Tom."

"Hey, Jen. What's up?" He held the framed map so Herron could see it. "I shaded the ocean a little darker near the shore. It's subtle, but it adds some depth."

Herron adjusted his bifocals on his nose. *The Counties of Florida*, 1825, previously black-and-white, had been transformed by a delicate, four-color pastel wash, and the ocean had turned blue. "Oh my, yes. It's perfect. A beautiful job." He picked up the frame and turned it to get the reflection of the backyard off the glass. "Perfect."

Tom pulled an envelope from the back pocket of his jeans. "This is an invoice for the balance due. If it's no trouble, could you bring a check by the shop tomorrow? Rose needs to cover some expenses for the map fair."

"All right. Be happy to."

"I'm glad you like the map," Tom said. "See you next weekend." He smiled and tossed off a wave. "Excuse me, but I have to get to the post office before five."

"Tell your lovely sister I said hello."

"I'll see him out," Jenny said as she went inside. The curve of her hips showed between the low waist of her pants and a tight yellow top. An orchid tattoo decorated the smooth caramel skin of her shoulder.

She took her time, and when she came back, Herron said, "Are you aware of his history?" When she looked at him blankly, he said, "His artistic talents aside, young Mr. Fairchild has quite a rap sheet. He's on probation for burglary. I was a good friend of his grandfather, William Fairchild, who endowed the Caribbean map collection at the museum. Tom's sister is a terrific gal, but you should be careful with Tom."

"He's all right," Jenny said. Her remarkable cinnamon eyes slanted up, like a kitten's. "I'm going to work at their booth at the map fair on Saturday."

"Oh?"

"I'm good with maps. You said so. It would be fun."

"Yes, you might learn something. You listen to Rose. She knows her stuff." Herron set the framed map on one of the rattan sofas, out of the way. Shadows reached across the lawn; the sun would be gone soon. "Jenny, may I trouble you to turn on the light?"

She stepped just inside the Florida room. The light in the ceiling fan came on, and the blades rotated slowly beneath the open beams of the porch roof. Bamboo wind chimes swung and clinked. Jenny Gray had been born in Brixton, a rough area of London, to a white nurse's aide and a drummer in a reggae band who had died in a way that Jenny didn't want to talk about. Her beauty had been her escape. Herron could guess how, but it didn't matter. Nor did it matter that her upper-class British accent sometimes slipped, revealing her origins. It pleased him to think he had inspired her.

He had hired Jenny Gray three months ago. She shopped for groceries, fixed his drinks, tidied the kitchen, and helped him catalogue the maps. When there was nothing to do, he paid her for being available. It was like having fresh flowers in the house. Inevitably his friends had noticed, a young woman like that, coming and going at all hours, running errands for the bald, fat old fool. So what? He had no public image to uphold anymore. He had retired from the bench, his wife was gone, and his son and daughter-in-law rarely visited.

Clapping his hands together, he said, "All right, then. Let's get back to work." He pulled a map off the stack he'd brought from his study. "Take a look at this one."

"It's quite old, isn't it?" A zigzag of curly, blond-streaked hair fell across her cheek.

"Nearly as old as I am," he said. "Published in 1597. Cornelius Wytfliet. He was Flemish. Notice anything unusual about it?"

"Florida is square on the bottom."

"Come around and take a closer look."

She came around. The black-and-white map showed the southeastern portion of what would later become the United States. The entire area had been labeled FLO-RI-DA. The syllables fell between rivers snaking southward into the gulf. The peninsula had the shape of a serrated brick, and Cuba was a fat oval.

Through the Mylar, she touched the row of triangles that indicated the hills of the Appalachian chain. "Florida used to come up to here?"

"According to the mapmaker."

"You'll show this one, I should think."

"Indeed. Put it on the 'yes' stack." The cat leaped onto the table, a lithe curve of orange. Herron pulled him back from the maps and draped him over his forearm. "Bring that stool over here, would you?" When Jenny placed the bar stool alongside, Herron eased a hip onto it. He let go of the cat. "Get down. And stay off the table." He brushed fur from his paunch, pulled more maps from the stack, and stopped at a sudden flash of blue.

"Judge Herron? I need to ask you a favor," Jenny said.

He picked up the map, a trapezoidal shape wide at the bottom, sloping toward the top, as if the piece had been cut from a globe. Deep-blue ocean, creamy land, delicate traceries of red, bright as blood. The text was in Latin. The slanting orange borders contained the medieval equivalent of longitude and latitude numbers.

"What favor is that, Jenny?"

"Could you lend me some money? I'm sorry to ask you, but my landlord said if I don't pay the rent by tomorrow, he'd evict me."

"Well. Sounds serious."

"You know I'll work it off. I did last time."

Last time, she hadn't needed to ask. He had heard her car wheezing and offered a loan to get it fixed. Now she assumed he was an easy touch. Well, he was, and she knew it. It was his own fault. Herron turned the map toward her. "These islands should be familiar. *Albion Insula Britannica.*"

"You're not putting Britain in the exhibit, are you?"

"No, but it's an interesting map, don't you think?"

She tucked a curl into the clip at the nape of her neck. "The N's are backward."

"A quirk of the times. Can you guess what century?"

"Sixteenth."

"Late fifteenth. Fourteen eighty-two. Copper plate or woodblock?"

"Woodblock."

"Very good. This is a Ptolemaic map. The Ulm edition. Printed in the city of Ulm, in what is now Germany. The cartography was based on the writings of Ptolemy, a Greek mathematician and astronomer residing in Egypt."

Her face lit up. "Ptolemy! Like in the movie. He was Alexander the Great's general, and he founded the library at Alexandria."

Herron looked at her several seconds, then said,

"That's a different Ptolemy. I am speaking of Claudius Ptolemaeus, who lived two centuries later."

She shrugged. "Is it worth a lot, that map?"

"Not so much. I think I paid a few hundred dollars." Which had been forty years ago. Herron was starting to feel like a skinflint. "How much do you need, Jenny?"

She made a playful grimace. "A thousand. *Eeeek*."

"Good Lord."

"Well, I had to pay my car insurance . . . and the phone bill was outrageous this month, you know. My mum . . . I told you, she's been sick."

Herron studied the ornate lettering of the cartouche. The island of Malta, 1680, in the *Mare Mediterraneum*. To the north, *Sicilia Pars*, part of Sicily, and to the south, *Barbaria*—Africa. The engraver had created ships under full sail, a sea battle, clouds of smoke, one ship sinking, a rowboat of sailors frantically pulling away.

"What about your roommate? Carla, is that her name? Where's her share of the rent?"

A shadow passed over Jenny's face. "Carla's gone."

"Gone? What, into thin air?"

"Yes." It took Jenny some time to explain. "She went out last Saturday night, and I haven't seen her since then. I don't know where she is."

"People don't just vanish. Who was she with?"

"I don't know. She didn't tell me."

"But surely you know her friends." She shook her head. Herron found this highly unlikely, but he said, "Have you called the police?"

"No. Maybe she just went back to Los Angeles. Carla was sort of irresponsible that way." Jenny gave a pointed sigh. "Anyway, she stuck me with the rent. If I don't pay it, I'll be out in the street."

"Highly unlikely, a young lady as clever as you."

A flicker of irritation showed before she gazed past him into the yard, her eyes picking up the green of the foliage. "Are you suggesting I should get the money from Stuart? He'd probably give me a lot more than a thousand."

"Oh, for pity's sake, don't even think it."

"Well, he would."

"What he would do, Jenny, is to make a couple of phone calls to Immigration, and you'd be on your way back to Britain. Stay away from Mr. Barlowe. He's a fake."

"A rich one," she replied testily.

"But a fake nonetheless. I'll tell you a story about him. I sold him an atlas last year, a marvelous vellum-bound edition of Tommaso Porcacchi's *L'Isole più famose del Mondo*, 1572, and do you know what he did with it? He cut out the pages and gave the pieces as business gifts. And he calls himself a collector. I was horrified."

Jenny Gray crossed her arms and continued to stare past the screen, where the late afternoon sun glittered on the canal. A flock of parrots in a palm tree screeched and took off in a whir of green wings.

"Of course I'll lend you the money," he said.

She turned and smiled at him, the witch. "Thank you, Judge Herron."

He had to go upstairs to his bedroom for the cash, which he kept in a strongbox in his closet under some extra blankets. Perhaps she knew this. He had noticed small things out of place, the fringe on the rug twisted, the hint of perfume in the air. Closing the box, hiding the key in a drawer, he chided himself for distrusting her. Jenny had paid him back last time, hadn't she? Herron had first noticed Jenny pouring champagne at a museum fund-raiser at Stuart Barlowe's house. She had agreed to help Herron with his maps at twenty dollars an hour, cash.

When he came back onto the porch she was studying a Mercator map of North Africa. He was missing a couple of small maps. He hadn't asked if she had taken them. He didn't want to know.

He gave her the money, which vanished into a pocket of her jeans. "I want you to come at nine o'clock tomorrow morning. We have to finish the maps and take them to the museum this week without fail. Can you roust yourself out of bed that early?"

"I'll bring Cuban bread if you make some *café con leche*," she said.

"*Sí, señorita*." He snapped his fingers tango-style.

She kissed him lightly, impetuously, on his lips, and his heart sank. "See you tomorrow."

"Run along." He heard her quick footsteps receding. The front door closed. "See you tomorrow," he said.

In the kitchen he opened a cabinet over the sink for his bottle of pain pills. "Oh, Royce, what a supreme idiot you are." He glanced down at the cat, who looked back at him. "I suppose you agree, don't you?"

By 8:30 PM Herron had set aside a dozen maps for his exhibit, "The History of Cartography in Florida." Bracing himself on the plywood table, he bent slowly to retrieve a paper plate from the floor. The cat had eaten the remains of his ham sandwich, and now lay belly-up on the couch. "You're getting chubby, aren't you, old man? Ha. I know what you're thinking: Boss, you're a fine one to talk."

The telephone rang. Herron picked up the handset, said hello. When he recognized the voice he cursed himself for not having checked caller ID.

"Royce, it's me."

Meaning Martha Framm. Martha owned a marina on the river but spent more of her time volunteering for the Neighborhood Action Committee. She was sixty-seven, bleached blond, darkly tanned, and wiry as a feral dog. They'd gone out to dinner or the opera since his wife died, but Martha's conversations inevitably turned toward venal politicians, the real estate developers who paid them off, corrupt lobbyists, and kiss-ass Cuban radio. Even while making enemies at the Chamber of Commerce, her group had shot down five condo projects, a Home Depot, and three gas stations.

"Martha," he said cheerily. "How are you?"

"I left a message. Didn't you get it?"

"Yes, I'm sorry. I've been up to my elbows preparing for the map fair this weekend. Everything going well for you?"

"Peachy, except for the fact that Moreno just announced that he's reconsidering his stand on The Metropolis."

There was a pause, into which Herron murmured, "Is that so?" He played with a loose button on his cardigan sweater. Martha Framm's current target was a condominium-and-retail development to be built on the west bank of the Miami River. City commissioner Paul Moreno had been against it—until now.

"Something happened. They got to him. He's been bribed or threatened."

"Oh, don't listen to rumors, Martha."

"It's the *truth*. If they turn one more vote, we're

screwed. We're having a rally on Friday before the vote at city hall, and I want you to speak."

On their last date, after too many glasses of wine, Herron had agreed to support Martha's campaign against The Metropolis, and the next day he'd found his name splashed across her group's Web site. This had gone against his vow to stay out of local politics. After forty years as a lawyer and judge, he'd had enough. The idea of massive, glass-and-steel towers looming over the river made him as angry as anyone, but he didn't want to be lumped in with the antidevelopment fanatics at the NAC.

"Friday? No, I'm afraid not. I'll be tied up with the map fair."

"We *need* you, Royce. I told everyone you'd be there."

"Martha, it was a mistake, my becoming involved with a partisan organization. I'm on the circuit court mediation board, and I have to stay neutral."

"Oh, really. Have you accepted even *one* case? I'm holding you to your promise. You gave me your word you'd help defeat this monstrosity."

"I can't be there. I'm sorry—"

"What's going on? Stuart Barlowe? Has he threatened to take back his contribution to the goddamned museum?"

"I won't discuss this any further, Ms. Framm."

"*Ms. Framm?* Oh, for Chrissake, Royce. Wake up. It's Stuart Barlowe's money behind that damned project. He would drain the Everglades if he thought he could make a buck. Your family and mine go way back in this city. Don't you care what's happening to it? Where is your integrity? Where are your balls?"

He pressed the heel of his hand against his forehead and closed his eyes. "Martha, please."

"Forgive me, Royce. This is driving me insane."

He took a long breath to calm his nerves. "I can't be at the rally, but trust me, I have already done my part."

"What do you mean?"

"Never mind."

"Royce, tell me."

"Oh, just a wee bit of persuasion. A way to bring Stuart Barlowe around to our point of view. That's all I'm going to say about it. You have to swear not to repeat this to a soul. Martha?"

"Repeat *what*? You haven't told me anything. But all right, I swear."

Over Martha's demands to know what the hell was going on, Herron managed to end the call. When his heart missed a beat, he sucked in some air and rubbed his chest. "Sweet Jesus." With shaking hands he quickly stacked the maps and carried them into the house, nearly stumbling over the threshold.

A brass lamp shone at one end of the L-shaped sofa, putting a glow on faded green upholstery, a closed baby grand in the corner, and a worn oriental carpet. A mantel clock ticked over the coral-rock fireplace. He crossed the dining room, with its clutter of books, papers, and boxes, then went down the hall to his study. He hit the light switch with an elbow and dropped the armload of maps onto a metal map cabinet for Jenny to sort through in the morning.

Swiveling his desk chair around, he sank into it, forehead in his palm. The cat rubbed against Herron's leg. He leaned over and patted its head. "I know what you're thinking, Ptolemy. I'm gutless. I should have the courage to speak out."

Herron slammed his hands on the arms of the chair, went back to the kitchen, fixed a martini on the rocks, and returned to his study to work on the exhibit guide. He turned on his computer, sat down, stared at the screen, then spun his chair around to face the opposite wall, which, like the others, was covered with framed photographs. He got up and crossed the room.

Tilting his head to focus his glasses, he gazed at a black-and-white photo in a metal frame, taken at the International Map Fair in Toronto, 1968. The group included various dignitaries—the president of the International Map Society, the governor of Ontario, et cetera—and a thinner version of himself, along with his fishing buddy and fellow map aficionado Bill Fairchild. He and Bill had just traded their British sea charts for some choice Caribbean maps to be donated to the museum in Miami. Dead center, Frederick Barlowe, who had organized the event. Off to the side, almost out of the picture, Frederick's wife, whose name Herron could not recall, and his two teenage sons, Stuart and Nigel.

Herron studied the photograph for a while longer. Little Miss Gray had giggled when she realized it was him under all that dark, wavy hair. Everyone in the picture had changed. Some dead. Others closing in on terra incognita. And one astounding fake.

The cat jumped onto a table at the window, settled onto a cushion, and licked his paws. Through the window Herron could see his low coral-rock wall, the porch light of his neighbor's house, and the empty street. He tried to remember if he had closed the glass doors. Surely he had. Yes, he was positive. He hadn't turned on the alarm. He never did, except for his trips out of town.

An illogical sensation of being watched came over him, and he drew the curtains. A yellow legal pad lay on his map cabinet with two pages flipped back. Herron picked up the map on top of his cabinet, an Italian Renaissance map of the world, 1511, on loan from Stuart Barlowe. Truly a wonderful map. Florida floated at a crazy angle in the western Atlantic.

Gradually he became conscious of a low growl. He glanced over to see the cat with his yellow eyes fixed on something across the room.

Still holding the map, Herron turned toward the open door. In an instant his mind grasped that someone had come into his house, but he couldn't understand why. He saw the gun. Then a flash and a pop no louder than a hand clap, and at the same instant felt the jolt in his chest. Then another like a punch to his stomach.

Bewildered, confused, he ducked his head and raised his hands. A bullet tore through his palm. Scorching heat filled his eye. He formed the words *Stop, stop it, please* but his lips wouldn't move.

Herron staggered against the cabinet and went down, plummeting into a dark and endless void.

CHAPTER 4

Banyans and jacarandas dimmed the morning sunlight on the three short blocks of Judge Herron's street, which came to a dead end at Biscayne Bay. The house itself, squeezed between two recently built Mediterranean-style mansions, looked at least sixty years old, with a carport on one side, a metal flamingo decorating the screen door, and crank-out windows across the living room. Air plants sprouted from the low coral-rock wall, which was nearly obscured by the line of police vehicles.

Neighbors had gathered on the sidewalk. Allison Barlowe, making her way through them, realized with a sudden jolt of recognition that she'd been here before. It had been a party, probably something to do with maps, since that had been the only interest her father and Royce Herron had shared. She'd been . . . fifteen? She remembered something else: At the party Judge Herron had given her a 1927 pocket-size road atlas of Canada, the country of her birth. That same night, after a nasty argument with her stepmother, Allison had stolen her father's Mercedes and had driven a thousand miles before being stopped by a Virginia state trooper. Two years after that, she fled to college in New York, hoping never to see Miami again.

But she had come back, and the city was both familiar and strange to her. At a fund-raiser last week for the museum, Royce Herron had put an arm around her shoulders and said, "Welcome home." A nice man. And some remorseless animal had shot him dead.

She walked quickly toward the front gate, where a uniformed officer had been posted. The wind pushed her long hair across her face, and she tossed it back. "My client is inside—Jenny Gray. She called me, and I'd like to speak to her."

The officer said to go in and ask for Sergeant Martinez.

Allison didn't consider it too much of a stretch to say "my client." She hadn't yet taken the Florida bar exam, but she had been practicing law for five years in Boston and now was working full-time as a paralegal until she was sworn in. She had already advised Jenny on a minor landlord-tenant dispute, a favor for her stepbrother, for whom Jenny worked. Half an hour ago, in a frantic phone call, Jenny said she had arrived at Royce Herron's house at nine o'clock. When he didn't respond to the doorbell, she went around back and through the unlocked sliding glass door on the porch. He was dead in his study. Allison told her not to make any statements; she was on her way.

Putting on her glasses and snapping her prescription sunglasses into their case, Allison stepped into the living room. From the activity in the hall to her right, she guessed that Judge Herron's body lay in that direction. She told a plainclothes officer what she wanted, and he went through a wide opening that led, Allison remembered, to the kitchen. A minute later he came back with a gray-haired man in a plaid polo shirt who said his name was Detective Martinez.

Allison asked where she could find her client, Jenny Gray.

"Are you an attorney, Miss Barlowe?"

"Yes, I am."

"Can I see your bar card?" He looked at her over the top of his steel-rimmed bifocals.

"Why?"

"Anybody could come in here claiming to be a lawyer."

"I don't usually carry my bar card with me," she said, "and unfortunately, I don't yet have a card from my office. I was just hired. I work for Marks and Connor, P.A. Our client, Ms. Gray, called me a little while ago. She says she wants to leave, and you can't force her to stay—unless you've arrested her, which I don't believe is the case."

"Uh-huh." Martinez exchanged a look with his partner, then said, "Ms. Barlowe, we're talking to Ms. Gray in the kitchen right now. Why don't you have a seat and relax?"

"You won't get anywhere with Jenny. I told her not to talk to you." Allison gave them a sigh and a regretful smile. "I'm sorry. I want to know what happened as much as you do. Judge Herron was a family friend. He and my father, Stuart Barlowe, have known each other for years. You might have heard of Stuart Barlowe? He's on the Miami Development Council."

"I don't care who your daddy is."

The younger detective nudged his arm. "Barlowe. La

Gorce Island. I do off-duty security work for his parties out there."

Allison said, "I'm not asking for special favors, Sergeant. I'm sure I can arrange for Ms. Gray to answer your questions. Right now, though, I am requesting—very politely—that you let me see my client."

Martinez thought about it, then said, "Let me ask you something first. We found a bunch of antique maps in Judge Herron's study. Ms. Gray told us that she and the judge had been out on the back porch all day working on them. Are they valuable?"

"Some of them are."

"What kind of valuable are we talking about?"

"It depends. A few hundred dollars or several thousand. Some of them may belong to my father. He lent them to Judge Herron for an exhibit at the map fair." Allison turned her gaze toward the hall. "Are they missing?"

"We don't know. The killer could have had that in mind, but we just don't know. You might be able to tell us. The judge's body is still in there. He's been shot. Just walk over to the map cabinet. If this is going to cause you any distress, don't do it."

"No, it's all right. I mean . . . if I can help."

They entered the hall, passing someone dressed in white disposable overalls and booties going the other way with a small vacuum cleaner. Martinez led Allison to the second door on the right. Every inch of the now too-small room was being examined by the crime scene technicians. A woman with a camera took pictures.

Allison's eyes swept the perimeter of the room—an old oak desk, reclining lounge chair, framed photographs and maps, metal cabinets with shallow drawers—before she saw the man lying on the floor. The curve of his stomach, clad in a white shirt, rose from a brown cardigan sweater. Then she saw the red holes in the shirt, and the blood that obliterated one eye. It had flowed out to make an irregular stain in the pale carpet under his head. Unframed maps lay around him, under him, crumpled and spattered with blood.

Allison leaned against the door frame.

"Miss Barlowe?"

Her breath caught in her throat. "Someone should die for this. Have his family been notified? I think he has a son who lives out of state."

"We're working on it."

"Didn't anyone hear gunshots?"

"We're asking the neighbors, but so far, nothing. The windows are heavy hurricane glass, which muffles the sound." Martinez nodded toward the map cabinet. "Do you recognize any of those? Don't touch them. We're going to dust for prints. Most of them are wrapped in plastic, so if anything's there, we might get some good results."

Allison noticed that some of the map drawers were open. "Did you open the drawers?"

"We haven't touched them," the detective replied.

Allison went over to see. "I can't tell what's missing without a list, but some of the folders appear to be empty. There were some maps stacked on top of this cabinet, you see? And they slid off. He . . . he was probably holding that one when . . . Oh. It's the Corelli. It belongs to my father." Allison noticed the fringe of soft gray hair above Royce Herron's ear. His pale cheek, a broken vein. She turned away. "The Corelli map is worth a lot. I don't know how much. It's ruined now. That one on the cabinet belongs to my father, too. It's a John Speed, worth . . . I'm not sure. Five thousand? I don't know what else is here."

Martinez said, "How would we get a list of the maps?"

"My father has one—the maps he loaned for the exhibit. I'm sure Judge Herron would have had an inventory."

"How hard would it be to track them down? Pawnshops? Art dealers?"

"Not pawnshops. The map fair is in town this weekend, but you won't find any of these maps for sale. Reputable dealers won't touch stolen goods. I'll put you in touch with the organizers if you want. They'll be able to tell you how to publicize a theft. May I go now?" In the hall, when she was able to breathe, she said, "He was a good man. Find out who did this."

Allison took Jenny out the back door, and they went along the seawall, then through the next yard to avoid reporters. When they reached the street, they cut behind a satellite news truck and crossed to the sidewalk on the opposite side.

No one paid any attention to them, one woman in a suit and dark glasses, the other with a wild mane of gold-streaked brown hair. If anyone had noticed, Allison thought, it would have been Jenny they looked at, a gorgeous mixed-race girl with a tiny waist and perfect boobs that most other girls would have had to pay for. Allison's stepbrother had seen Jenny Gray lying on a towel on South Beach and offered her a job as a hostess in his restaurant at the top of a Brickell Avenue bank building.

When Jenny reached her car, a flashy little Nissan

with a dented fender, she dug into her purse, finally slamming its contents onto the hood to find her car keys.

"Can you follow me to my office?" Allison asked.

"I can't. I have to go."

"Wait a minute. I just got you out of there, the least you can do—"

"Thank you for coming to the rescue," Jenny said, throwing things back into her purse. "Send me the bill, all right?"

"Jenny, we need to talk about this. Would you stop for a minute?"

She leaned against her car and wiped away sudden tears with her fingers. "He's dead. They shot him dead!"

Allison gave her a tissue. "Jenny? Do you have any idea who did it?"

"No. I don't know anything about it. I told the police. I just came in and found him like that!"

"All right. Now listen. They'll want to talk to you again, and I'm going to refer this case to the senior partner at my law firm, who knows her way around criminal law."

"Why do I need a lawyer? They don't suspect me!"

"Not at the moment, but they think somebody might have come in to steal the maps. They know that you were working on them for Judge Herron, and they could wonder whom you might have told."

"Nobody! I had nothing to do with this!" Indignation colored her cheeks. "Everybody knows he was a collector."

"But he didn't keep the most valuable maps at his house until he started working on the exhibit for the map fair. Who knew about it? I mean, besides the people connected to the map fair?"

"I wouldn't trust that lot. They're all mad."

"That may be true, but a collector wouldn't kill for one. A collector wouldn't shoot a man through a Corelli worth tens of thousands of dollars."

Jenny's mouth fell open. "How much?"

Allison shook her head. "Never mind. Just think. Did you talk to anyone about the maps? Maybe Larry? Or any of his friends?"

"No! Larry knew I was working part-time for Royce—I mean Judge Herron—but your brother doesn't like maps, does he?"

"Larry is only my stepbrother," Allison said. "Do you know if the judge had any appointments later in the evening? The police might find something in his desk diary, but they're not likely to tell me."

Jenny wiped her nose. "He didn't mention anyone coming over. He said he had to finish the catalogue."

"Did anyone come during the day?"

"While I was there? Only this one guy who dropped off a map."

"Who?"

"The delivery man for the map shop."

"What map shop?"

"The Compass Rose."

"I see." Allison's mind supplied the answer before she asked: "Who was the deliveryman?"

"His name is Tom Fairchild. He was only there like five minutes, and he didn't see anything. He didn't go into the study."

"Did he go out to the back porch? The police said you were working there."

"He knew about the maps, but he wouldn't . . . he isn't the sort who would *kill* someone. He's a great guy, really he is."

"Where did you meet him, at the shop?"

"Yes, and then we went out a couple of times." Jenny laughed. "He took me to an AA meeting, if you must know. But he doesn't drink, I mean, not like that. He used to go because it was part of his probation. I didn't like it. All those depressing stories."

Allison raised her brows. "What's he on probation for?"

"It wasn't anything *serious*. Burglary, but Tom was breaking into a house to take back his own stuff, which his roommate had stolen when he moved out—"

"All right." Allison held up her hands. "We'll talk later. When can you come by my office?"

Jenny aimed her key ring at the car to unlock it. "Maybe tomorrow. I'll call you."

"I want a better answer than that," Allison said, holding the door.

Jenny jerked on it. "I'll call you. Let go of the door."

Allison watched the car do the turnaround at the end of the street, then take a fast right, leaves swirling as it vanished past the houses.

A face appeared in her memory, one she hadn't seen in twelve years.

"Tom Fairchild. Oh, great."

CHAPTER 5

L eaving the office that afternoon, Allison put the convertible top down and let the wind swirl through her hair. On the causeway from Miami to the beach, she checked for police cars, then gunned her roadster to ninety-five miles an hour. She had bought it just last weekend, a black BMW Z4 that could run like a cat with its tail on fire. She braked at the exit and headed north.

At the entrance to La Gorce Island, she gave her name to the guard. He checked a list on his computer and wrote down her tag number while Allison fumed. The electronic gate opener that her father had promised to send hadn't arrived yet. Allison was certain he'd left it up to Rhonda, who conveniently forgot anything she didn't want to do.

The gate arm rose. Allison flexed her hands on the steering wheel and took a deep breath. She had promised herself to take a new approach with her father's wife: no confrontations, no anger, no sarcasm.

The twenty-room house, designed like an Italian

villa, sat on a triple lot overlooking the bay. Allison
drove through the open gate, between a double row of
royal palms, past the guesthouse, then the tennis court.
Every stray leaf had been swept from the lawn, and two
men in valet parking uniforms were setting up a kiosk
under the portico. Allison noticed a catering truck from
The Biscayne Grille, her stepbrother's restaurant downtown. Nobody had told her about a party tonight.

She swung the wheel and scooted around the truck to
park under a bougainvillea arbor. She grabbed her purse
and went into the kitchen, where servers in white shirts
and bow ties were unwrapping trays of food and setting
rows of wineglasses on the granite countertops.

Coming up behind the housekeeper, Allison gave her
a squeeze. Fernanda was a short, round woman with
curly gray hair. She had been with the family for twenty
years. "*Hola*, Fernandita."

With a smile, Fernanda patted her cheek. "*Niña,
¿cómo andas?* We don't see you enough."

"I've been working twenty-five hours a day. What's
going on?"

"It's a party for the Heart Association. Should I tell
Mrs. Barlowe that you're here?"

"No, thanks. Is my father home yet?"

"Not yet. Do you want a glass of wine or a soda,
maybe?"

"I'll get it. You're busy." Allison made her way
through the caterers to the bar, where she found a cocktail glass, then searched in the freezer among the various
bottles of vodka, looking for something drinkable. "Oh,
yummy." She opened the Armadale and poured some
over ice.

She was cutting a curl of lemon when Rhonda came

through the open French doors from the terrace in a jade-green silk suit and a pair of leopard-print Manolo Blahnik pumps that Allison had seen at Neiman for five hundred dollars. Rhonda's hair had been sculpted into a froth of blond waves. She was trailed by her Pekingese dog and a slender man in black shirt and pants, with a diamond stud in his ear and black-framed eyeglasses exactly like Allison's. He was explaining why he liked mustard sauce instead of butter for the stone crab claws.

Allison dropped the lemon peel into her drink. "Hello, Rhonda."

Rhonda noticed her, noticed the Armadale, then the crystal tumbler, as though Allison ought to be drinking Smirnoff out of a paper cup. Then the bright smile. "Allison, how nice to see you. I can't chat just now. Your father and I are going to be busy tonight, I'm afraid."

"I won't be staying long," Allison said. "He expects me."

"Oh?" When Allison supplied no details, Rhonda said, "He should be home any minute. You're welcome to wait."

Allison said, "Did you hear about Royce Herron?"

"God, yes. How absolutely terrible. We're all in shock." Rhonda put a hand to her throat, and her gold bracelets gleamed. "They don't have any idea who did it. That's the latest I heard on the news, coming home."

"He was such a sweet guy. I liked him," Allison said.

"So did I. It's just tragic. Well. I have a million things to finish. You should come back when we can spend more time." She draped the dog over her arm and resumed the conversation with the party planner. She preferred drawn butter to mustard sauce.

Allison took a deep swallow of her drink. She reminded herself not to let Rhonda get to her. Somewhere under that reptilian skin there had to be a heart, even a two-chambered heart.

She told Fernanda she would be out back, and to tell Stuart, when he came home. On the covered terrace the caterers had set up two dozen round tables and chairs with red bows in the backs, like little girls' Sunday dresses. Standing propane heaters had been placed near the periphery, just in case. As night fell, the air would be cool, but not the bone-rattling cold of Boston, where nobody dined al fresco in February.

Allison followed the walkway around the pool, then down some steps to the dock, where the bay lapped softly against the pilings. It hadn't been the icy gray skies of Boston that had sent her south. Allison had been lonely for the friends she'd once had, and lonely for her family, or at least the idea of family. Sliding past thirty, she had realized that she didn't want to work eighty hours a week in a monstrous law firm. She wanted to come home.

Stuart had offered to have his lawyer find her a job, but Allison had found one through friends, a general practice south of the city run by two women. Of course they'd known whose daughter she was, and they hoped she could bring them some business. Allison couldn't appear in court yet, but she researched cases, interviewed witnesses, and drafted legal papers. Assuming the bar exam went well, she would be admitted to practice sometime in the summer and resume a normal life. That included reestablishing her relationship with Stuart.

She corrected herself: "Dad."

She had started calling him by his first name when

she was about thirteen and decided he'd become impossibly remote and dismissive. He hadn't always been that way. When Allison was very small, Stuart traveled for the family's export company, and each time he came back to Toronto he brought her a special gift; just one. He told stories about the places he had seen and the people he'd met—magical to the ears of a child. Then he married Rhonda and they all moved to Miami. Allison couldn't remember her real mother, who had died before Allison could walk. Her father was all she had. That same man who used to tell her stories, and said one day he would bring her a box full of stars, couldn't have disappeared entirely. He had to be there, even now, and Allison wanted to find him.

She stretched out on one of the padded chaise longues, dropped her purse to the deck, and kicked off her pumps. Looking across the flat, blue plain of the bay, she could see past the causeway to the buildings downtown, everything turning a little rosy in the setting sun. She closed her eyes. Here on this gated island, lulled by the hum of boats going back to port and the faint clink of silverware from the caterers, she could almost pretend that violence and death didn't exist. But then the image would come back: an old man lying dead in his own blood.

Allison welcomed the burn of vodka in her throat. Today she had paid the law firm's private investigator a hundred dollars to fax her a report on Tom Fairchild. She had been dismayed, but not completely surprised, to see the wreck Tom had made of his life: currently on probation for burglary and grand theft. Previously convicted for DUI, drunk and disorderly, battery on a police officer, trespassing, carrying a concealed weapon. Credit rating near the bottom of the scale. No house, no vehicle except for an old motorcycle.

There had been a time, in her idiot teenage period, when she'd thought that a few minor felonies were exciting, even sexy. In the years post–Tom Fairchild, she had heard, through the grapevine of her friends, that he'd been arrested again, but reports had become further apart until nobody said his name anymore. Allison had purged him from the list of topics in which she had even the remotest interest.

She raised her knees and held her drink on them. Her skirt slid down her thighs, but nobody was out there to catch a view of anything interesting.

Tom Fairchild had showed her how to do tequila shots: bite into a lime, then suck the salt off her fist and toss back the José Cuervo. He'd laughed at her when she asked where the worm was. Her first nude swim in the ocean, the first time going over a hundred miles an hour on a motorcycle without a helmet, and her first time having sex had all been with Tom.

Allison sipped the vodka. "Idiot."

Her father had never known any of this, of course. Or that Allison had engineered Tom's enrollment at an art school in New York. She'd been accepted to Barnard, and in her monumental naïveté had thought that Tom would do something worthwhile with himself.

"Sad, sad, sad." She pulled her BlackBerry out of her purse, clicked to the organizer, and saw that tonight she would review Florida constitutional law. She clicked forward to the weekend and saw the Miami International Map Fair. She had never been to the map fair in Miami, though it always attracted some of the best dealers in the world. Friday: the cocktail reception. Dinner afterward. Saturday: study. Do the fair on Sunday. Avoid The Compass Rose.

There was a chance that she and Tom Fairchild would run into each other. Allison would look at him as if puzzled, then smile and say, "Oh, yes. Tom. How nice to see you again."

Ten years ago, he'd been attractive, in an unpolished way. Shaggy blond hair, jeans hanging off his hips, a tattoo around his upper arm, a smile that started slow and danced around his green eyes. He'd shown some gentleness and intelligence. But he was older now. Thirty-two. Hardened by his experiences. Allison could imagine him bulked up by weight lifting with the other inmates in the yard, tattoos on his chest and down his arms. Bitter. Wanting to even the score with the system. She had to admit: He could have done it. Could have broken into Judge Herron's house, shot him dead, and stolen whatever maps he could grab. If Jenny Gray had told him about the maps.

No call from Jenny Gray yet. Allison doubted there would be one. Jenny was hiding something; that was clear enough. Allison could not, however, talk to Detective Martinez about Tom without betraying a client. She was thinking of how to get around this when she heard the growl of engines and splash of water. She lowered her knees and tugged on her hem.

A boat was edging close to the seawall, a cruiser on whose bow sat three tanned girls in swimsuits. One was putting a sweater on, and another held on to the low stainless steel railing and gawked at the house. The men were in the cockpit getting drunk. Allison recognized the captain. Her stepbrother. Laurence Gerard, thirty-three, son of a rich restaurateur in Montreal. Larry's father had died last year, and the inheritance had finally come through. Now Larry was pretending to be a real estate mogul.

One of the girls threw the bowline to the dock, and a mustached man in a Hawaiian shirt jumped off to wrap the rope around the cleat.

The engines went silent, but reggae blared from the speakers. Larry opened the little gate and stepped off the stern, a husky man in a Florida Marlins cap and a blue Windbreaker. Allison knew why he wore the cap: The Rogaine wasn't working. He went to fix the rope that the other guy had cleated wrong.

Allison said, "Is that your new boat?"

"Like it? I'll take you for a ride."

"No, thanks. I'm busy."

He looked around at his friend with the mustache. The man's cheeks, his hairy forearms, and his legs were burned tourist-pink, right down to his brown socks. "Marek, this charming young lady is my sister, Allison."

"Stepsister," she said. "How do you do."

Larry sat on the arm of her chaise. "Let me run this by you. 'Chez Gerard.' What do you think?"

"Chez Gerard? Too pretentious."

"For my signature restaurant at The Metropolis? Forty-ninth floor. The deal is in the works. I'm getting all the restaurants and bars, plus an apartment. Sweet."

"Sweet for you. How much did Stuart have to guarantee the developer?"

"Jealousy doesn't become you, Al," Larry said.

"Believe me, it isn't jealousy."

The man in the Hawaiian shirt lit a cigarette, and she saw that the nail on his left thumb was missing. His wavy black hair frizzed into graying sideburns, and his nose, with its flaring nostrils, curved toward his big mustache and beard-stubbled chin. He was utterly fascinating.

"Excuse me. What was your name again?"

"Marek." The cigarette bounced as he put away his pack.

"Is that Polish?"

"Croatian. You know where Croatia is?"

"Yes, it's across the Adriatic from Italy. It used to be part of Yugoslavia."

"Your sister is very smart girl."

"Stepsister," Allison said.

Larry said, "Marek's last name is Vuksinic, rhymes with 'itch.' The root word means 'wolf.' Interesting, isn't it?"

The big man stood over Allison, grinning down at her, his moist brown eyes moving up her bare legs.

She said, "Back off."

Nicotine-stained teeth appeared under his mustache. "Come with us on the boat."

She pivoted off the chaise, slipped into her shoes, and caught up with Larry. The music faded as they walked up the slope to the house. "Your friend gives me the creeps. Who is he?"

"Marek works for a good customer of mine at the restaurant," Larry said. "I'm showing him around, doing the tourist thing. I got roped into putting him up at my place, but he'll be gone next week, praise God. Are you here for the party?"

"No, I have to talk to my dad. Have you heard about Judge Herron?"

"On the news. I can't believe it. Poor old guy."

"Jenny Gray found his body."

"Who?"

"Come on, Larry. She went over there to work this morning and found him shot to death. Have you seen her? She was supposed to call me." When Larry shook his head, she stopped him at the edge of the terrace. "I want to ask you something. You knew Jenny Gray was working for Judge Herron on Stuart's maps, didn't you?"

"I guess so."

"Did you tell anyone about it?"

"Not that I remember. Why?"

"A bunch of maps were stolen. Are you sure you didn't mention this to anyone?"

"I said no. What's your problem?"

"Frankly, Larry, you have some questionable friends."

As he folded his sunglasses, Allison followed him through the linen-draped tables. He said, "This might surprise you, Allison, but not everyone gives a rat's ass about antique maps."

When they reached the kitchen, Larry opened the door of the wine cooler and pulled out four bottles of Cristal champagne. Fernanda hurried over and told him to put them back; they were for the party. He told her there was some Dom Pérignon in the pantry; use that. Fernanda said the Dom wasn't chilled. With a roll of his eyes Larry said, "Just put it in the cooler, Fernanda. How hard can it be?"

The idea of her father subsidizing this creature made Allison want to scream. She stepped far enough into the hall to watch Larry go out. She said a prayer his boat would run into a sandbar. When she turned around, she noticed a tall, thin figure in a dark suit heading for the stairs. "Dad!"

He waited with one hand on the bannister.

"Do you have a few minutes?" she said.

"Yes. Come up."

It had shocked Allison, returning to Miami, to see how old her father had become. Shadows darkened his eyes, and gray streaked his neatly trimmed beard. He wasn't ill; he went skiing with Rhonda several times a year. More accurate to say, Rhonda went to collect another black-diamond lapel pin, and Stuart went for the view, sitting alone in a ski lodge watching the fireplace. He had confided to Allison that he preferred solitude. He hated parties but endured them for Rhonda, who seemed to shine, the more he waned.

"Forgive me for being late," he said, glancing over his shoulder as they went up the stairs. He had just come from a meeting with the developer of The Metropolis. An issue with the zoning permits. Not to worry.

Having been out of her father's life for so long, Allison had only a vague idea what he did. The family wealth had come from his father, Frederick Barlowe, an exporter of Canadian beef and wheat based in Whitby, Ontario, a town on the rail line east of Toronto. Her uncle Nigel had died in his twenties, leaving only Stuart to inherit. Luckily Grandfather Barlowe had established a trust for Allison. It had given her the courage to leave home. And the independence to come back. She did not need her father's money. She didn't even want it.

Their reflections went in and out of the gilded floor-to-ceiling mirrors in the upper hall. Stuart and Rhonda had separate adjoining suites. He opened the door to his study and let Allison enter first. The decor was English hunt club—mahogany paneling, leather furniture, and oil paintings of horses. Allison expected to open the curtains and see meadows and forests instead of turquoise water and palm trees.

He tossed his suit coat over the back of a chair and went to the bar in a corner. "Would you like a drink?"

"Please. Vodka and soda, very light. I'm cutting back."

His smile made long creases in his face. "Shouldn't we all? Terrible news about Royce Herron, eh? I'd wager a dozen people from the museum phoned me today wanting to know if I'd heard."

"That's what I sort of wanted to talk to you about. Your maps, the ones you loaned to Judge Herron."

He gave her the drink and a monogrammed napkin. "What about them?"

"I was at his house this morning. Do you remember that exotic-looking British girl who works for Larry? Jenny Gray? Her father was Jamaican, I think. She came to some parties here as a server."

"Can't say I recall."

"Well, she was also working part-time for Royce Herron, and she's the one who discovered his body. I did a minor landlord-tenant case for her last month as a favor for Larry, so this morning she called me to extricate her from the Miami Police, who wanted to keep her at the scene. I had a talk with the detectives. They asked me to tell them if any maps were missing. They're looking for a motive for murder. Dad, it's possible—no, it's likely—that quite a few of the maps were stolen by the person who shot him. The police want a list."

Stuart, in the middle of pouring Glenfiddich over ice, slowly set the bottle on the bar. "Are you saying that some of my maps were stolen?"

"I'm not sure yet, but . . . at least two of yours were damaged. One of them was the Corelli map of the world."

He stared at her, then quietly said, "Damaged? In what way?"

"Bullet holes. And when Judge Herron fell, the map was underneath him. He bled on the map. The paper is creased. Perhaps it could be restored, but . . . I don't think so."

"God *damn* it!"

The violence of this outcry made Allison jerk, and she dropped her glass on the oriental rug. She grabbed some napkins, scooped up the ice cubes, and blotted the liquid. "Dad, I'm sorry." As she said it, she wondered what she could be sorry for. "It's just a map."

"Just a map?" He stood over her. "It isn't *my* map, Allison. I've already promised it to someone else! It's the centerpiece of his collection! I swore he could have it, he expects it, and what in hell am I supposed to do about that?"

She scrambled to her feet. "Stop screaming at me."

Rhonda's dog had gotten into the room somehow, yapping and snarling, jumping onto the furniture.

"Stuart?" Rhonda stood by the door to her room in a red chiffon dress, fastening one of her earrings. "What on earth is going on? Zhou-Zhou, be quiet!"

"One of my maps was just shot to pieces. Whoever killed Royce Herron destroyed the Corelli map. Bang, bang, bang. Gone."

"Wasn't it insured?"

The dog was still barking. Stuart picked it up, pitched it into Rhonda's room, and slammed the door.

"Stuart!"

"Keep that damned dog out of here!" He took a deep breath and came back to Allison. "You say the map can't be repaired?"

"I— I don't know. Perhaps it can."

"We need to find out. We have to get it back immediately."

"The police might want to hold it for evidence, but . . . shall I call the detective for you? I have his card."

"Would you, Allison?" He pressed his knuckles against his lips, then said, "If you have any trouble, let me know, and I'll ask my lawyers to contact the mayor or the chief of police. I must have that map."

"Darling, calm down. Please." Rhonda pulled him over to the sofa. "I should have said something. I thought it was a foolish idea when she suggested it."

"What are you talking about?" Allison said.

"You insisted that we lend the maps to Royce Herron. They should have gone directly to the museum. He should have worked on the exhibit there."

"Are you saying it was *my fault*? As if I *knew* someone was going to put bullet holes in it? That's totally unfair of you, Rhonda."

"I am *saying*, if you would listen, that there was no security at his house. It was negligent to risk them in that way. And you see what happened."

Allison turned her back. "I can't talk to you."

Her father said, "Go finish dressing, Rhonda. It wasn't her fault."

Rhonda smoothed his hair off his forehead. "Are you all right?"

"I'm fine. Go on." He kissed her hand.

"You need to get ready, Stuart. Our guests will be here soon. Red cummerbund tonight, don't forget."

"Yes, yes."

Rhonda crossed the room and closed the door behind her.

Trembling from confusion and uncertainty, Allison sat on the other end of the sofa. "Dad? I'm so sorry about the map."

"Can't blame yourself." He put his elbows on his knees and entwined his long, thin fingers. "Sorry for yelling at you, dear."

"Was the Corelli so special? There are other maps, better than that one."

He murmured, "People have their obsessions."

"Who is he? Dad? Who did you sell the map to?"

He looked up at her. "A fellow in Europe. A Russian. A map fancier. One of my investors, actually. He wanted the Corelli because a member of his family once owned it. There are no others like it. I may have a devil of a time explaining."

"I'll get it back," Allison said. "I'll get it, and we'll see. There are people who do restorations. You'll just have to tell him what happened and offer to give him something even more wonderful if this one can't be fixed."

"Yes. Perhaps."

She heard the soft tick of his wristwatch and, through the double-glazed window, the faraway noise of a jet airplane. "I'm glad to be home."

He nodded. "We're happy you're with us again."

She said, "I want very much to be a part of your life. We had our disagreements, and I used to blame you, but I can't do that anymore. I wasn't exactly a perfect kid, was I? Remember the time I stole your car?"

He smiled and nodded. "Twice."

"But you forgave me," she said.

"Yes. We're a family. All of us." He reached over and squeezed her hand. "Don't worry about the map. I'll take care of it. Well, now." He pushed himself up. "I'd better get dressed or Rhonda will have my head."

When she hugged him, he patted her shoulder. She had the feeling that he was embarrassed by the emotion, and it made her want to cry. She stepped away and said, "Enjoy the party. Maybe we could get together for dinner sometime. Just us."

"Yes. Why not? See you later, then, Allison."

Chapter 6

Jenny Gray opened her shoulder bag, took out a folded envelope, and gave it to Tom. Sunglasses hid her eyes; bright points of light shone in the lenses. "This is a hundred and fifty dollars. I don't think it will cost more than that. I put my mother's address in there, too."

"I'll send the boxes tomorrow." Tom slid the extra key off his key ring. "Just turn the lock and leave this in the kitchen when you go."

"Thanks, Tom. Please tell Rose I'm sorry I couldn't be at the booth this weekend. Is she mad at me?"

"Not at all. In fact, we're not that busy."

Jenny would be catching a flight to London in a few hours. What she couldn't fit into her suitcases, she would leave at Tom's apartment, and he would ship for her. She had called this morning, and they agreed to meet outside the historical museum at noon. It had taken him a few minutes to spot her among the crowd. Perfect weather had sent people outdoors. The broad, red-tiled plaza was enclosed by two museums and the public library, and above them, the cloudless blue sky.

At one of the umbrella tables, ragged men gathered around a chessboard. At another, map dealers unwrapped their bag lunches. Red ribbons fluttered from their name tags. Tom had one like it pinned to his shirt. THOMAS W. FAIRCHILD. THE COMPASS ROSE. MIAMI.

"Are you going to be living with your mom?"

"Maybe. I haven't told her I'm coming." Jenny laughed. "Don't want to give her a chance to say no."

He noticed an empty table near the food kiosk. "Can you stay for a minute? Let me buy you a soda or something."

"I really can't. I have to be at the airport pretty soon."

"This is kind of sudden, isn't it?"

"I'm so tired of Miami, the whole bloody scene."

"Since when?"

"Since I got here! This is one of the most shallow places I've ever been to. Except for you and about two other people I know, nobody cares about anything but how they look, and what they drive, and who they know."

Tom shook his head. "Jen, you don't have to talk to the police. Are you afraid they'll find out your visa has expired?"

"They might. I don't want to be deported. I could never come back."

Jenny had called him the day after she had found Royce Herron's body, wanting advice, maybe thinking that because Tom had his own experiences with the police, he could tell her what to do. Jenny didn't want to ask her attorney, Allison Barlowe. She didn't like her connection to Larry Gerard, who had a Miami police lieutenant on his payroll, or so Jenny alleged. Tom doubted that but believed Gerard had friends in the department. He'd heard rumors about Gerard from people he'd met at a bar or nightclub, like the call girl with a client list that included bankers and politicians, or the Miami events planner who needed some pharmaceutical favors for celebrities passing through. Tom couldn't help it if people told him things. But if the Weasel ever found out who Tom's friends were, he would be overjoyed to run to the judge with a violation report.

What surprised Tom was that Allison had come back, and apparently for good. She used to tell him that even flying to Miami for Christmas was too much. Tom had expected to bump into her at the map fair, but she hadn't shown up either day. On Friday night Rose had seen her at the cocktail party, chatting with a woman from the Library of Congress. Rose had smiled and waved, but Allison hadn't recognized her—or had pretended not to.

"Tom?" Jenny's voice broke into his thoughts. "If anyone asks you where I went, say you don't know. Promise?"

He looked at her. "Why don't you tell me what's really going on?"

After a couple of starts she took a breath, then said, "I'm so totally freaked out by what happened to Royce Herron. I found him, Tom. Lying there. Blood all over his face. You can't imagine."

He put an arm over her shoulders. "Babe, they killed him for his maps. They're not going to come after you." When she didn't answer, he said, "Jen?"

"What if they are after me?"

"Why would they be?"

"I don't know. There's just too much stuff happening. Like my roommate. She's gone. She disappeared about a week ago. She went out—I don't know who with—and never came home. Sometimes she does that, but when I got home Wednesday night, everything was gone from her room. Clothes, papers, address book, everything— but not the stuff in the bathroom, like her toothbrush and a new jar of La Prairie face cream that she bought for a hundred and twenty-five dollars. Carla would have taken it with her. I called her brother in San Diego, and he hasn't heard from her in months. I asked everybody at work, and they don't know. They're like, oh, Carla, well, what do you expect? She probably took off with some guy to Las Vegas."

"Did you call the police?"

She shook her head. "They arrested her twice for prostitution. I really don't think they would care, would they? I have to go."

"Jenny, wait—"

She gave Tom a quick peck on the mouth. "Take care. I'll e-mail you when I get to London." With another glance around the plaza, she hurried across, vanishing under the colonnade near the library.

Like her friend Carla, Jenny Gray had been hired as a hostess and server for a private club, the Blue Orchid, lo- cated in one of the high-rise bank buildings on Brickell Avenue. Larry Gerard had a stake in the club. Jenny's real job was being eye candy for VIP customers. What Gerard didn't know: She was having an affair with his stepfather. That hadn't lasted long. When Barlowe dumped her, Jenny came over to Tom's house one night crying about it. They had slept in the same bed, but she turned away when he kissed her. She never had sex with friends, she said; it always ruined a good relationship. So Tom had lain there in a sweat, listening to her breathe, wishing she hadn't liked him so much.

The name tag on Tom's shirt took him past the line of

people waiting to go into the museum. He nodded at the volunteers selling tickets. In his khaki pants and long-sleeved white shirt with the cuffs rolled, he was just another map dealer.

The museum was barely big enough for all the tables and dividers winding through the lobby and corridors and small exhibition rooms. The dealers stood at their tables, their best maps on display behind them. Collectors lifted maps out of boxes, turned pages in Mylar-protected folders, and stopped to stare at a 1513 Waldseemüller world map priced at three hundred thousand dollars. Cheap. The Library of Congress had paid ten million dollars for the wall-size 1507 version, the first to use the word "America."

The Compass Rose booth was on the second floor. Tom went up the carpeted steps two at a time, the polished brass bannister turning at right angles around an immense glass lens from an old lighthouse. He had promised to watch the table while Rose took the girls to lunch. Her sales had been no more than break-even. Most customers had bought the cheaper items: a Caribbean sea chart that Tom had hand-colored; a U.S. map from 1875; an Esso or Phillips 66 highway map from the fifties. People who had bought nothing took the shop's publicity flyer for the Ortelius map on the reverse side.

Rose had a customer, a bald man with a New York accent and a blue sport coat that rode up on his thick shoulders. Tom saw the dealer ribbon and guessed he was sniffing for bargains in the few hours remaining. Behind the table, the twins sat side by side in folding chairs with the latest Harry Potter novel open on their laps. Tom reached over and ruffled their bangs.

"It's about time," Megan said, closing the book. "We're starving to death."

Jill elbowed her and found their place again. "We have to wait for Mommy."

Rose asked Tom to take down the Crusoe on the display wall, *A Map of the World on wch. is Delineated the Voyages of Robinson Cruso*, a small map about eight-by-eleven inches mounted on mat board. Two circles represented the hemispheres of the world as known in 1711. California was an island with nothing above it but empty space.

The bald man gave it a cursory glance. "How much are you asking?"

"One thousand dollars."

"C'mon. I'll give you seven hundred. You won't do better."

Tom said, "Hold out for a thousand, Rose. I've had two people show interest. One said he'd be back."

With a laugh the dealer said, "You bet. I'll check with you later. If somebody offers you more than seven, grab it."

As he walked away, Rose rolled her eyes and blew out a breath that puffed her cheeks. She had been working flat out for a week with barely any sleep, and it showed. "I refuse to sell it for less than I paid! Here, Tom, hang this back up, will you? Let's go, girls. Lunch. We won't be gone long. I want to take them over to the library after. Do you mind?"

"Not much going on here," Tom agreed.

For the next half hour he watched the crowds slowly moving past the tables. He smiled and answered a few questions and straightened the maps in the boxes. He saw people pause to gaze up at the display wall, where he had painted islands, wooden ships, and sea monsters.

A woman with an expensive silk scarf around her

neck began turning the big pages in the map folder. The lights flashed in her diamond rings. Tom walked over. "Welcome to The Compass Rose. Are you looking for anything in particular?"

"Do you have Georgia? We're from Atlanta. I want something for my husband's office."

He lifted a box to the table. "Let me show you a nice one of the Southeast, printed in 1757 in Paris." Tom showed her a copperplate engraving. "It's a beauty. I can let it go for four hundred."

At the other end of the table a tall man with a gray-flecked beard stood silently watching this. He held a copy of the Compass Rose flyer. A purple ribbon hung from his name tag; the gold letters spelled out DONOR. Tom thought he looked familiar.

The woman said, "It's French. I'd rather have something in English. And I really don't want to pay that much."

Tom showed her a less expensive, four-color map of Georgia a hundred years newer. Rose had penciled the price on the back: $250. "It was printed in Philadelphia. Notice the distance chart there in the corner."

"This is nice," she said. "Do you have anything else?"

He brought out a map of South Carolina and Georgia, which she looked at for a minute or two before deciding she didn't want both states in the same map. The man still waited at the end of the table, and Tom began to grow impatient with his customer's dithering.

"If you want the Georgia map," he said, "I can let you have it for two hundred. You'd be getting a bargain."

When the man turned to flip through the box of European maps, Tom took another look at him. Gray tweed jacket, dark gray slacks. Thin fingers, plain wedding band, a leather strap on his watch. His face was narrow, with a high forehead, a straight nose, and dark, sad eyes with prominent circles underneath. The lights painted shadows on his cheekbone and temple. His cheeks were shaved; the mustache and beard compensated for a thin upper lip and an overbite.

This was Allison Barlowe's father. Tom had last seen him getting out of a limo at the Pierre Hotel in New York City, meeting Allison for high tea, making a detour on his way back from Europe. Tom had taken a taxi with Allison and watched from across Fifth Avenue in a freezing rain. Allison hadn't wanted to go, but Tom had talked her into it. *He's your father. Have some respect.*

The woman said, "Would you take one-fifty?"

Tom focused on her again. "Sorry, I really couldn't do less than two hundred."

"Look here. There are some brown spots on the corner."

"The price takes that into account," he said.

"I don't know. Let's split the difference. One seventy-five."

Without looking around, the man at the other end of the table murmured, "Madam, the map is two hundred dollars. Don't haggle. This isn't a rug bazaar."

She stared at him, then dropped the map on the table. "Then buy it yourself."

With an audible sigh, Tom put it back into the box.

Barlowe opened his wallet. "All right, I will."

"I didn't ask you to pay for it," Tom said.

"I insist. It's my fault you lost the sale." He laid two hundred-dollar bills on the table, and with a shrug, Tom reached for the receipt book.

"The price is two hundred and twelve with the sales tax," Tom said.

More bills were added to the stack. "My name is Stuart Barlowe."

Tom put down the pen to shake the offered hand. "How are you? Tom Fairchild."

"Your grandfather, William Fairchild, was a collector. He and my father were acquainted through maps. I know your sister, Rose. Rather, I know the shop."

Tom put the map of Georgia into a bag. "We do acid-free framing, if you want this framed. We can also color your maps with archival-quality paint."

Leaving the bag on the table, Barlowe held up the publicity flyer. "Tell me about this map. It says here, 'Original Art by Tom Fairchild.' What does that mean?"

"It means the map doesn't exist. I drew it. My apologies to Mr. Ortelius."

"As he died several centuries ago, I doubt he can object." Barlowe studied the flyer. "How did you do this? Freehand? Or did you base it on a photograph?"

"Trade secret," Tom said.

"Remarkable." Barlowe put the flyer into his pocket. Hands behind his back, he strolled down the length of the table, then returned. He smiled at Tom, then retraced his steps to the other end, where he nodded at the Crusoe map that Rose had tried earlier to sell.

"*Robinson Crusoe*," he said. "Daniel Defoe's masterpiece. These maps were included in the first edition of his book, I believe. How much are you asking?"

"Twelve hundred." Tom added, "It's firm at that price."

"No courtesy discounts for a fellow collector who

just overpaid for a mediocre map of Georgia that he didn't need?"

Tom smiled. "I'm already subtracting what you paid for Georgia."

"Are you?" Barlowe gazed at the map on the wall. "I'd like to buy it, but I don't have a check on me."

"We take credit cards."

"I prefer to pay by check. Can you deliver it to my office?"

"You can take it now if you want and pay later. You're good for it."

"No, I'd rather you deliver it. This evening, if possible. You'd be doing me a great favor." From the breast pocket of his tweed coat Barlowe withdrew a thin silver case and took out a business card, which he extended to Tom. "It's just on Brickell, not far. I'll tell the guard in the lobby to let you in."

CHAPTER 7

F ar over the Atlantic, the tops of the clouds had
faded from pink to gray. Tom could see the red tail-
lights on the causeways, the lights in the apartment
buildings at the tip of South Beach, and the dim glow of
a cruise ship on the inky blue horizon. He leaned closer
to the window to block his own reflection and watched
the ship slowly vanish over the curve of the earth. He
wondered where it was headed. He imagined himself at
the wheel of his sailboat, turning around to watch the
skyline of Miami fade into darkness. One of these days
when his sailboat had sails. And the mooring lines to the
Department of Corrections had been cut.

He noticed a movement in the glass. Stuart Barlowe
was coming from his desk with the check he'd just written. He had to walk around a table with an architectural
model of the area just west of downtown on the river, with
three new towers, still at the imaginary stage. A sign announced THE METROPOLIS, and there were some color
brochures lying beside it. Tom hadn't bothered picking
one up. He'd heard about the project from his neighbors.

A few of them, after too many drinks, wanted to bomb the first bulldozer that showed up.

"Are you building this?"

Barlowe smiled modestly. "No, no. However, my company, Pan-Global, is one of the major investors. You can say we have some input." He came to stand beside Tom at the window. "Wonderful view, isn't it? Have you ever been mountain climbing, Tom? The feeling is very much like this." The check appeared, held vertically between Barlowe's fingers. "It's made out to cash. I hope that's all right."

Tom glanced at the figure: $1,200, which failed to include the six percent sales tax. He wavered between not wanting to make a big deal out of it and keeping the transaction on the level. He didn't know whether Stuart Barlowe was dishonest or just cheap. Avoiding the choice, Tom said, "It's seventy-two bucks short, but don't worry about it. The shop can take care of the sales tax." He put the folded check into his shirt pocket and withdrew the bill of sale he had written earlier, which would establish the provenance of the Crusoe map. "I put your map of Georgia in there, too. You left it on my table."

Barlowe returned to his desk and closed the heavy, acid-free folder on the maps.

Tom asked, "Would you like to have the Crusoe map framed?"

"Not really. I'll probably give it to the museum." Smiling down at the folder, Barlowe pushed it aside. "I have to confess, I'm not the map fancier you are."

"That's more my sister than me."

"Rose. She owns the shop, doesn't she? The Compass Rose. A clever name." Barlowe gestured toward the wet bar in the cabinet across the room. "Would you like a drink?"

"No, thanks. I guess I ought to be going."

"Stay for a few minutes. There's something I'd like to talk to you about. Have a seat. Please." Barlowe took one of the armchairs near the window and adjusted the knee of his trousers as he crossed his long legs. "Do you think The Compass Rose would be interested in selling some of my maps for me? I inherited nearly two hundred of them from my father. He died owning over a thousand, most of which went to the Royal Ontario Museum. There are many I don't need, and I think the shop could make a nice profit."

"Absolutely. Rose would be glad to talk to you about it. Do you want her to call you?"

"I'll get in touch as soon as I've had a chance to go through them. Royce Herron was going to help me with that, but . . . Did you know Royce well?"

"Not really. He was a friend of my grandfather's." Tom sat on the edge of his chair and noticed the antique clock on the bookcase. Nearly six thirty. The clock was under a glass dome, and its four gold balls rotated one way, then the other.

Barlowe stroked his neatly trimmed beard. "Too bad you missed the reception on Friday. Quite a tribute to the man. Everyone telling funny stories about him, commiserating over what his death will mean to the cartography program at the historical museum. We were all disappointed, of course, that there was only a blank space on the wall where his exhibit would have been. Royce was working on the maps the night he died."

Tom nodded. The clock made one soft chime.

"I had lent him some of mine. The police say that the

person who broke in stole several maps from his study, but we won't have an exact accounting until Royce's son finishes going through the house."

Muffled tones came from Barlowe's gray tweed jacket. He took out his cell phone and glanced at the screen before returning the phone to his pocket. "My daughter. I'll call her later. Allison. You and she went to high school together, didn't you? Or am I mistaken?"

"No, you're right," Tom said. "Wow, that was a long time ago. The last I heard, she went to college in New York."

"College at Barnard, law school at Columbia. She's been in Boston for several years, and she recently returned home."

"No kidding. That's great." Tom was aware of lying, keeping Allison's secrets when it didn't matter anymore, but there wasn't any reason to spill the truth to her old man. Tom stretched his arms out and glanced at his watch. "Look at the time. I ought to be getting back. I'll tell Rose about the maps. She'll be really excited about it."

Barlowe remained in his chair. "I asked you here because I need your advice, Tom. I think you might be able to help."

"Help with what?"

"A map. May I show you? It's in the conference room."

Tom followed him into a room with a long row of uncurtained windows. Beyond them, the sky had deepened to indigo. Barlowe flipped a switch, and pinpoint halogen lights illuminated a conference table, in the center of which lay a large black portfolio.

"You've heard of Gaetano Corelli."

"Vaguely," Tom said.

"Corelli was a Venetian cartographer and publisher of sea charts. His maps were used by Christopher Columbus, among others. In 1511, Corelli planned to publish a folio-sized, hand-colored atlas of the world. Unfortunately for Corelli, his main competitor, Peter Martyr, had been sending his own people to interview explorers as soon as they docked. This meant Martyr had better maps, and he announced that he too would publish an atlas. As a result, Corelli couldn't sell any of his, and he was stuck with the one proof copy. A few years later he went bankrupt, and his creditors took over his inventory, including the atlas. In the next five centuries, it passed through various hands—a Genovese merchant, a count in Venice, a monastery in Constantinople. I won't bore you with the entire history, but in the 1950s the Corelli atlas became part of the collection of the state museum in Riga, Latvia. When the Soviet Union fell apart in the early 1990s, the atlas disappeared."

During this recitation, Barlowe slid the heavy brass zipper tab around the portfolio. "Among the various regional maps, Corelli included his map of the world. He'd done a fairly good job with the latest discoveries in the Caribbean. Florida wasn't named until two years later by Ponce de León, but the Corelli map clearly showed that it was part of the mainland, not an island. I wanted the map for my collection, and I finally got a lead on a woman in her eighties residing in Albuquerque, New Mexico, whose husband used to own a map shop. After a good deal of haggling, I flew out to take a look. She let me go through some boxes, and there it was. The provenance was a little shaky, but I knew the history. She let me have it for ten thousand dollars, quite a bargain, really. Allison asked me if I would lend it to Royce Herron for his exhibit at the map fair. I said of course."

Reaching inside the portfolio, Barlowe took out a folder about two feet by three. "Royce was holding the map when he died. I persuaded the police to return it to me."

When the folder fell open, Tom saw the continents of the world in a configuration that he didn't recognize. A closer look told him that the reddish-brown shapes were not landmasses. They flowed over the land and extended in blots and spatters across the oceans.

"Jesus. Is that . . . blood?"

"Yes. Notice the bullet holes. Three of them. Here. Here. And here. Royce fell on top of the map and creased it." He pointed to North Africa, where the bloodstains made a mirror image, like a Rorschach test.

Tom exhaled. "If you're asking me whether it can it be restored—"

"It can't. I know that. It's a complete loss."

"Did you get it insured?"

"I don't care about the money. Call me eccentric, but I was particularly fond of this map. When I saw it like this, I wanted to weep." Barlowe sat on the edge of the table, one foot swinging. His shoes would have paid Tom's rent for a month. "Then I had a thought. Why not make a duplicate? A twin. A map exactly like this one. Tell me, Tom. Is there a way—any way at all—that it can be done?"

"How exact do you want it?"

"I want to be able to examine it with a magnifying glass and be convinced it's the original."

"Good luck. You're talking about something that's five hundred years old."

"Go ahead, take a closer look. Pick it up."

Avoiding the bloodstains, Tom tilted the map so that the light fell at an angle. The fold down the middle indicated it had come from an atlas. The paper was excellent, probably a mix of cotton and linen. He could clearly see the impressions made by the wires on which the pulped rags had been left to dry. Corelli or someone in his workshop had first engraved the map in reverse on a copperplate, inked the plate, then pressed it into the paper. The plate had left pressure marks around the edge.

Tom brought the map closer and squinted at the fine black lines, the minuscule letters in the place names, the details of the cartouche. The map's title, *Universalis Cosmographia*, was visible through the smears of blood. Aside from the blood, there were age spots, one missing corner, and a four-inch tear in the fold line.

"I've never done anything like this," Tom said.

"But it could be done, wouldn't you agree?"

"Theoretically, I guess."

"You're an artist, Tom. You have an extraordinary talent. I saw it in the Ortelius map you made for The Compass Rose. This project would be more difficult, I grant you, but surely not impossible."

Tom held the map over his head so the light passed through it, then turned it over. "If I were you, I'd go to a commercial printer for a high-resolution scan, take out the bloodstains with Photoshop, and print it on laid paper with a good rag content. You frame it under nonglare glass, and I guarantee you won't be able to tell the difference."

"Of course I could," Barlowe said. "It would be a digital image! The pixels would show under magnification. No?"

Tom shrugged.

"I want a handmade duplicate," Barlowe said.

"Where are you going to find paper like this? Office Depot?"

"Paper can be found. I've seen blank end pages bound into old manuscripts and atlases. The ink has to be of the period, too. You find an old recipe and make your own." Barlowe was watching Tom avidly for any signs of doubt. "It can be done."

Tom wondered if Barlowe had all his marbles. He put the tip of his finger into one of the bullet holes. Only an expert engraver would have a chance of making a map like this. It wasn't a drawing; it had been printed on a copperplate press. Even with the right paper and ink, it would be next to impossible. But hell, if Barlowe wanted it that badly—

Tom lowered the map to the table. "How much were you thinking to pay?"

"You tell me."

"Assuming I had the right materials? There's a lot of detail work in this map. I'm going to say . . . six thousand dollars, plus expenses."

Barlowe said, "Half to begin and half on delivery."

"That's fine." Tom had to clear his throat to keep from laughing in amazement. "I need to talk to some people. Advice on technique, that sort of thing."

A telephone rang on the narrow table under the window. Barlowe ignored it. "All right. If you have to, go ahead, but tell no one why you need the information or for whom you are working. No one. If I hear so much as a whisper, there is no deal. One other requirement. I need the map as quickly as you can do it. I'd like it within three weeks."

"That's not much time. I have other commitments."

"Can't you put them off?"

"I'm not sure."

"Get sure and let me know tomorrow."

The telephone was still ringing. Barlowe strode over, picked it up, and snapped out, "Yes, what is it?" He listened, and surprise showed on his face. Then he slowly replaced the handset. "That was security in the lobby. My daughter is on her way up."

Sunday night, and they were still playing that insipid music in the elevator. Allison wanted to throw her shoe at the speaker. She had been feeling pretty good today, until her watch had ticked past six o'clock and she still hadn't heard from her father, who had told her—promised her—that they would go out to dinner tonight. Just the two of them. Not Rhonda, and for God's sake not Larry.

Allison had dressed up for the occasion: lipstick, high heels, her trusty Fendi handbag, and a green cashmere jacket with a fox-fur collar that she'd snagged for half price on eBay. She couldn't help liking fur—her Canadian blood, no doubt. She would stop wearing fur when the animal rights activists stopped eating fried chicken.

The polished steel doors threw back an image of a woman frowning, face framed by long brown hair, eyebrows drawn together over the black rectangles of her glasses. Allison took a deep breath to relax. There were things she wanted to discuss with Stuart. A frown would only put him off. She tilted her head, smiled at herself, then said, "How phony is *that*?"

The elevator deposited her into the silence of the thirty-fifth floor. Absolutely no one about. The door to her father's office opened just as she got there. He was talking to someone, a man wearing a white shirt with the cuffs rolled. Nice shoulders. Spiky, dark blond hair. Baby-doll mouth and light green eyes. He turned toward her, and she froze.

Her father said, "There she is. Allison, do you remember Tom Fairchild? He just dropped off a map for me."

"Tom. Right." She kept her right hand curled around the strap of her shoulder bag. "Well. This is a surprise."

"I'll say. Haven't seen you since . . . high school. You're all grown up."

She made a polite smile. "So. You're a map seller now?"

"That and other things." They stared at each other for a few empty seconds before he said, "And you're practicing law in Miami."

"As soon as I take the bar exam." It occurred to Allison just then that he had to know where Jenny Gray had gone to, but engaging Tom Fairchild in conversation was too high a price to pay for finding out.

He shook Stuart's hand. "Mr. Barlowe, I'll be in touch. Allison, it was . . . just great to see you again."

Allison watched him until he went out of sight around the bend in the hall. There was something going on. "He'll be in touch about what?"

"Come in while I turn off the lights. You look very nice."

"Thanks." She wandered after him into his private office. "What map did he drop off?"

"That Hermann Moll on my desk. I bought it at the map fair."

She went over to see. "It's Robinson Crusoe. Why did you buy that?"

"You don't like it?"

"Oh. Oh, my God! You bought it for *me*?"

Her father looked at her, then smiled. "Not if you don't want it."

"I *do*. It's the first thing you've bought for me in a long time. I mean, something personal." She hugged him. "This almost matches my favorite gift of all time. Remember when I was three years old, what you brought me back from Dublin?"

He tilted his head. "Dublin?"

"Here's a hint. It was in a little velvet box."

"A ring?"

"I was only three! You said that this object would always tell me where you were."

"A map? No, maps don't come in boxes. A . . . compass?"

"Wrong again. Come on, you remember."

"I'm sorry, Allison." He smoothed his side-parted hair off his forehead. "My mind is a blank."

"Well, I'm not going to tell you. This is a test. We'll see if you're getting senile."

She held up the map of Crusoe's make-believe voyages and followed the dotted lines from England to the islands in the South Seas. "I really like this. I'll have it framed for my office." She laughed. "It's probably too juvenile, but I don't care."

As her father waited by the door with his finger on the light switch, Allison closed the map into the folder. She hesitated, then turned around.

"Dad? Before we go, I have to get something off my

mind. Larry says he's going to have all the restaurant fa-
cilities in The Metropolis. That's huge. The only way he
could get so lucky is if you backed him. I think it's a mistake."

Stuart looked into the empty corridor and sighed.
"Allison."

She held up her hands. "Okay, maybe I have no right
butting in, but you're my father, and I love you. I don't
like to see you taken advantage of. If anybody says I'm
sniffing around for your money, they're wrong. Totally
wrong. I have enough for myself, and I'm going to be a
success at my career. What I want is . . . I want to help
you. In your business. Or whatever you want me to do.
I'm a good lawyer. I really am. But if you'd rather keep
your family and business separate, I understand."

"No, no. We can find some work for you."

"Not unless you really need me. No charity. I mean it."

"You have a deal."

She returned his smile. "I'll even give you a discount."

"No need for that."

Allison tucked the folder under her arm. "How
much— No, don't tell me. I just hope Tom Fairchild
didn't overcharge you."

As they crossed the reception room, Stuart said,
"Where do you want to go for dinner? I didn't think to
make reservations."

"Oh, it doesn't matter. Sunday night's not too
crowded. You like French. We could go to Les Halles. I
can call on the way. I have the number in my Black-
Berry."

"Perfect." He opened the front door. "After you."

In the hall she kept up with his long strides. "May I

ask you something? What did Tom Fairchild mean, 'I'll be in touch'?"

"Well, I thought he could take a look at the Corelli map and give me an estimate on restoring it."

"Oh, Dad. That map is beyond restoring. Did you tell the man you sold it to what happened?"

"No." Stuart's voice was near the level of a whisper. "If you should happen to see Tom Fairchild again, please do not mention the map. Very important. All right?"

"All right, but . . . why don't you send it to New York? There are scads of restoration experts in the city. They might not be able to put it back exactly the way it was, but at least they'll give you an honest opinion."

"I've already asked Tom to do it." Her father pressed the elevator button. "I'm sure he'll give me his best judgment."

When the doors had opened, and closed, and they were alone in the elevator with the music playing softly in the background, Allison said, "I have some news. Judge Herron's son called me this afternoon. Not only are two of your maps missing, at least a dozen of his maps are gone, all the cash his father kept at home, and some of his mother's jewelry."

"Damned bad luck all around," said Stuart.

Allison went on, "I had a background check done on Tom Fairchild. Jenny Gray—you remember—is a client of mine. She told me that Tom showed up at Judge Herron's house the day of the murder to deliver a map. Tom is a friend of Jenny's. It's possible that Jenny—and I'm sure she didn't realize what she was doing—might have told somebody—like Tom Fairchild—about Judge Herron's maps, and *somebody* broke into his house to steal them."

Stuart's brows lifted. "What are you trying to tell me? That Tom Fairchild is a murderer?"

"What I'm saying is that you shouldn't bet on his being so trustworthy. He has a criminal record. He's on probation for burglary and grand theft."

"I know."

"You *know*?"

"It's irrelevant. I'm sorry you disapprove, but I am in a bit of a bind." Stuart's voice had iced over. "End of discussion."

She faced forward and saw the image of her own astonished face. She closed her eyes. "You know, I think I'll just go home."

"Why?"

"You don't want to have dinner with me. We planned this, and you forgot. You didn't even make reservations."

Stuart was watching the floor numbers counting down on the digital display. "Aren't you a little old to be having temper tantrums?"

The elevator opened at the lobby, an expanse of polished marble, glass walls, and indoor palm trees.

"We'll just do this some other time," she said.

He lifted his hands, giving up. "As you wish."

"Thank you for the map."

"Certainly."

Allison walked ahead of him across the lobby, not looking back, the tap of her heels echoing in the empty lobby. She took the fur collar from around her neck. She was burning. All she wanted was a drink.

Chapter 8

Tom went by The Compass Rose to drop off Stuart Barlowe's check and the keys to the van. Interior stairs led from the workroom to the second-floor apartment. He found his sister at the sink washing the dishes from dinner.

Tom slid the check under a refrigerator magnet. "He stiffed us for the sales tax."

"It doesn't matter." Rose dried her hands on a dish towel. "I can't believe you got that much. We did all right this year. Not great, but okay. Have you eaten? I have some spaghetti left."

"No, I picked up a sub." Popping the top on a soda, Tom walked down the short hall to the living room and saw the twins sitting at the coffee table doing their homework. At their age, he had calluses on his thumbs from playing video games. "Hey, ladies."

"Hi, Tom." They sent him a smile and went back to their books.

The living room had once been the upstairs master bedroom, when his grandparents had been alive. Even then, it hadn't been much of a house, with creaking wood floors and plumbing that groaned when you turned a tap. Rose had started renovations, but that ended when the money ran out.

In the kitchen, he hung his jacket on the back of a chair. Rose said, "Bob Herron was here earlier."

"Who?"

"Royce's son. He brought me a gorgeous Civil War map of Florida. He said Royce would have wanted me to have it." Rose opened a cabinet and put away the plates. "He says that a lot of the maps were stolen. The police are going to make up a list so all the dealers can be on the lookout. The person who broke in got some pieces of his mother's jewelry, too, and the cash Royce kept in the bedroom closet."

Tom said. "Rose, you need to get a dog with big teeth."

"I have an alarm. Royce left his back door unlocked. Poor Royce. At least he didn't suffer. That's what the detective told Bob. The funeral is on Tuesday."

"I hate funerals," Tom said.

"You have to go." Rose shook her head. "Oh, God, I can't think about it." She crossed to the table. "Look what else he brought." She took a framed photograph out of a mailing envelope. "He found it on Royce's desk. See if you recognize anyone."

Tom set down his soda. The black-and-white, eight-by-ten group photo had to be at least forty years old, to judge from the outdated clothing. "Hey, that's Granddad."

"It was taken at a map fair in Toronto he went to with Royce. Look who else is there, if you want a chuckle. There's a list on the back."

Among the men in their dark suits and narrow ties, smiles frozen by the flashbulb, stood a woman and two teenage boys, obviously brothers. They shared the same high forehead and short, straight eyebrows. Tom turned the frame over and read the list. William Fairchild, Royce Herron. Half a dozen VIPs from the Royal Ontario Museum. The premier. Frederick Barlowe. Margaret Barlowe. Sons Nigel and Stuart, but someone had reversed their names. Nigel had a big smile and a cowlick. Stuart looked older, more serious, with hair angling over his forehead and incipient shadows under his eyes.

"It's Stuart Barlowe. What a geek."

"Be nice." Rose returned the frame to the envelope. "I remember this photograph. Royce had so many hanging on his wall. He showed me. 'Look, there's your granddad and me.' I'll save it for the girls."

Tom finished his soda while Rose wiped the counters. She wore her usual attire—shorts and a baggy T-shirt. After Eddie had moved out, she'd put on ten pounds and stopped frosting her hair. When Tom had mentioned it, she'd asked why she should bother.

"Speaking of Barlowe," Tom said, "he asked me if you'd like to sell some of his maps here at the shop. He inherited a bunch from his father, and I guess he wants to clear out his closets."

Rose's ponytail swung as she looked over her shoulder. "He wants *me* to sell his maps?"

"Why not you?"

She snorted. "I never see him in here. I don't even think he likes maps."

"Barlowe? Sure he does."

"You think so? He's not a real collector. He has no

passion for it. There's no theme to his collection. Royce sold him a Tommaso Porcacchi atlas in very fine condition, and he cut all the maps out for Christmas presents." She shrugged. "But if he wants to put some maps in the shop, I'll be happy to earn a commission."

"Rose, do you know anything about Gaetano Corelli? Venetian, late fifteenth century, early sixteenth."

"I've heard of him, sure."

"Say you had a world map by Corelli in decent condition. What would it be worth?"

"Didn't Corelli do sea charts?"

"He did, but he also put together an atlas—his only atlas."

"I seem to remember something about that." Rose joined Tom at the table. "I'd have to look this up, but I think around the nineteen fifties or sixties, the maps in the Corelli atlas were removed from the binding. You see, Stuart Barlowe isn't the only Philistine in the map world. Who owned the atlas, I have no idea, but you'd see the maps listed for sale, and then they just dried up. You can buy scads of Corelli sea charts, but I haven't seen a land map in years. When that happens, it usually means one of two things. Either they have completely fallen out of favor, or somebody cares enough to buy all of them. So to answer your question, I don't know what his world map would cost."

"Take a guess."

"Thirty thousand?"

"Is that all?"

"It's a guess. Why are you asking?"

"Barlowe owns it."

"Does he?"

"He bought it in New Mexico for ten thousand dollars.

The map included Florida and the Caribbean, so he was going to let Royce show it at the map fair. When Royce was shot, he was holding it, and the blood—" Tom hesitated. "Anyway, the map was totaled." As he watched the surprise turn to dismay on his sister's face, Tom said, "Stuart Barlowe told me it was one of his favorite maps. He said he'd pay me six thousand dollars to reproduce it."

"Excuse me?"

"He wants an exact copy. I mean *exact*, right down to the antique paper. Where do I find some? You don't keep any five-hundred-year-old paper around the shop, do you, sis?"

Her mouth hung open for a second before she said, "Stuart Barlowe wants you to forge a map?"

"It isn't a forgery."

"What would you call it, then?"

"Replacement. Barlowe wants me to replace his map."

"What is he going to do with it?"

"I don't know. Keep it in a drawer. Use it for darts practice. I don't care what he does with it."

"That's the problem. Right there."

"What problem?"

"Yours. That you don't care. What if he wants to sell it someday? What happens then? Tom, you can't put a phony map into circulation. What are you thinking?"

"It wouldn't happen. There's no way this map will be on the market. Ever. Barlowe wants perfect, and he can't have perfect. But say I make a good effort. He'd pay me an advance of three grand, nonrefundable. That's half what I owe in restitution. It would keep the Weasel off my back for a year." Tom looked into her eyes, the same green as his own. "What?"

She put her chin on her fist and stared across the kitchen.

"Oh, Jesus." He got up and tossed his soda can into the trash under the sink. "I am not Eddie Ferraro. I am nothing like Eddie." Tom laughed. "If I were, the map would be so convincing I could collect the entire six thousand."

Rose glanced toward the living room and kept her voice low. "Eddie thought he could do things the easy way, too, and he got slammed for it. There is no easy way, Tom. You have to put one foot in front of the other, day after day, no matter what obstacles life throws in your path. If you haven't figured that out yet, then you're going to end up like Eddie. Or worse."

"You mean living in an Italian village, making my own wine?"

"I'm talking about your integrity! You're going to take money from Stuart Barlowe to do a map that you just sat there and told me you couldn't do well enough to be paid the entire amount for."

"You don't even like Stuart Barlowe," Tom said.

"That isn't the point! Would you do that to me? Take money you knew you didn't earn?"

"No, you're my sister."

She said nothing, but her eyes pierced him.

Tom leaned against the counter with his arms crossed. "I need the money, Rose. I'm tired of asking you for help. I'm a graphic artist, but nobody will hire me; not openly. My customers don't tell their clients who's really doing the work. Barlowe saw the Ortelius map I did for the shop, and he was impressed. It was damned good. He wants me to do a map. It's a job. Do I care what he does with it? No. That's his problem. Not mine. His."

She looked at him a while longer, then shrugged. "Fine. If that's your choice."

"You know, Rose, contrary to what you and everybody else seems to think, I am not destined to be a total fuckup."

"I never said that!" She pressed her lips together. "I just— I don't want anything to happen to you."

"What are you really worried about? Me or the reputation of The Compass Rose?"

"For God's sake, stop feeling so sorry for yourself. You have problems. Guess what? So does everyone else. Life isn't a piece of cake for me, either."

Tom blew out a breath, then reached for his jacket. "I should be going. I've got some work to finish tonight."

"Tom?" Rose's voice stopped him at the door. She said, "I could use your help with some framing this week. We sold some maps. We did all right."

"Yes, we did." He smiled back at her. "I'll see you tomorrow."

Feet skimming over the ground, Tom maneuvered his motorcycle up the cracked driveway of his landlord's house. The headlamp swung across a '58 Mercedes diesel sedan, a row of tomato plants in wire cones, and Tom's sailboat, which rested on blocks. He pulled inside the garage, hung his helmet on the handlebars, and retrieved his roast beef sub from the saddlebag. As he pulled down the heavy wood door, he noticed that Fritz had company on the back patio. Smoke from the grill drifted through the strings of small white lights swagged from the eaves, to the oak trees, and back again.

Tom walked over to see who was there. He recognized the gay couple who lived down the street, the trauma nurse from next door, and some folks from Fritz's AA group, the only ones who seemed to be sober. Fritz's girlfriend, Moon, looked up from changing a CD in the player on the back steps, and told Tom to help himself to some hot apple cider. She was a big woman about fifty with frizzy black hair, a long denim skirt, and a hand-knit red sweater too small for her chest.

The CD came on—the warbling lament of Portuguese fado.

Tom asked, "Is Fritz around?"

"He's inside getting the burgers," Moon told him. "Eat with us. There's plenty."

"No, thanks, I'm okay." Tom noticed a woman at the end of the picnic table with her head down on her skinny arms, sobbing. He couldn't tell who it was, with the pale blond hair over her face. One of the neighbors was patting her shoulder and making cooing noises.

"Who's that?" Tom asked quietly.

"Martha. She's smashed."

He nodded. Martha Framm had been a friend of Royce Herron's. Tom didn't know Martha well, but she had said that when his sailboat was ready for launch, she would send her lift truck over. She owned a marina at the end of the street and often showed up at Fritz's with a bottle of red wine to complain bitterly about development along the Miami River. The old bungalows and little Spanish-style apartment buildings were being bought up and demolished. The entire neighborhood had a big bull's-eye on it. Fritz had been offered half a million dollars for his place and had told the developer where to stick it. If he ever changed his mind, Tom would have to move.

The screen door banged shut. Fritz lumbered down

the steps in rubber thong sandals, carrying a tray stacked with hamburger patties. His belly hung over his shorts, and his sweatshirt had a picture of Jesus Christ as a Rastafarian. Fritz himself had no hair at all on his head except for eyebrows like ledges and a white mustache whose tips hung below his double chin.

"Hey, buddy. Got an extra burger if you want one."

"Thanks, but I picked up a sub." Tom followed Fritz to the grill. A concrete block supported the corner where a leg had rusted off, and a flood lamp on a pole made a circle of light. Tom said, "Somebody ought to take Martha home."

"She's better off here. Between Royce Herron and the city commission, she might try to drown herself. Oh, you've been busy all weekend. They voted on Friday to approve The Metropolis. No big surprise." Fritz tossed the patties onto the grill. "Martha thinks the judge was taken out by the same lowlifes who bribed the zoning board."

"Where'd she get that idea? He was shot by map thieves. That's what the police say." Tom shifted to avoid the smoke.

"Who knows? Martha told Moon and me that the former head of zoning quit because he'd been blackmailed. Somebody set him up with a prostitute and took pictures. Even for Miami, that's pushing the envelope, but I could believe it. There's a lot of money involved in this thing. Retail shops, restaurants, bars, offices. Plus four hundred and thirty-four residential units starting at seven hundred thousand dollars per unit. Top floor will set you back three-point-five mil."

"Okay, but what did Royce Herron have to do with it?"

"He opposed it." Fritz poked at the burgers with a long metal spatula. "Martha says Judge Herron was going to put some pressure on one of the major investors. A friend of yours in the map business, or maybe not a friend. Stuart Barlowe." Fritz raised his brows in Tom's direction.

"No, not a friend," Tom said, "but I know him. What do you mean by pressure?"

"That, I'm not too sure about. Martha says the judge wouldn't tell her. Do you have any idea what he meant?"

Tom shook his head.

Adjusting the propane to produce a steady blue flame, Fritz said quietly, "Martha wants me to look into it. She thinks because I've still got friends in the spook business, I know everything. I don't. Yeah, you want to know what color shorts the president of Mexico wears, I could probably find out, but I don't mess in my own sandbox, you know what I'm saying?"

"Sure." Tom didn't really, but Fritz had a habit of speaking as though somebody was listening through the fence. In the nineteen eighties, a skinnier Fritz, who had once flown choppers in Vietnam, had been employed by a small cargo airline in Panama. He had never flat-out said he worked for the CIA in Central America, but he had dropped enough hints. Drinking his nonalcoholic beers, Fritz would sit on a folding chair and talk while Tom worked on his sailboat. The old guy missed his days in the spy trade.

Fritz was saying, "People like Barlowe like to stay off the radar screen. You rarely see his name in the paper, but he's got a stake in The Metropolis, him and people like him. Not Barlowe personally, but a corporation that owns a subsidiary of a company he owns. You know what I mean. People with no connection to the real world in general. They live in their penthouses or behind gates, fat and happy, while ordinary folks work two jobs to feed their kids. We hoped, naïvely, that this time the suck-ups on the commission would do the right thing."

Tom thought about the implications of what Fritz had said. "I can't see Stuart Barlowe ordering a hit on Judge Herron."

"Only if you're as neurotic as Martha." Fritz laughed, and the face of Jesus in dreadlocks moved up and down. "It doesn't work that way. Doesn't have to. Herron was no threat. The Neighborhood Action Committee might win small fights, but not this one. There's just too much money. This country is going through a postliberal, anti-democratic phase. But it won't last. What you do in the meantime is stock up on hurricane supplies, make sure you've got spare ammo and gasoline, and throw a cook-out now and then. Soon as Martha gets a good night's sleep, she'll feel better."

"I guess so. Listen, Fritz, I need a big favor. I have to sign up for AA. Could you ask one of the guys to be my sponsor and get the paperwork to my probation officer? He's being a prick."

"Sure. How about if you paint my back bedroom for me? I've been meaning to get to it."

"No problem. I also need to find an anger management class."

"That guy must be a prick. Yeah, Moon can hook you up. Her boss at the flower shop has a kid who's a clinical psychologist. You going to sit with us awhile?"

"I'd like to, but I've got things to do. Thanks for the help," Tom said.

"Anytime. By the way, that dynamite-looking black

chick came by today and carried some boxes up to your place."

Tom's one-room apartment, built over a single-car garage, was furnished with pieces he had begged off Rose or bought at Goodwill. One corner had been enclosed for a tiny bathroom, and a ready-made countertop marked the kitchen, which had a two-burner stove, a microwave, and a small refrigerator. This being completely illegal, Fritz had installed everything himself. Tom had added security bars to the windows and a triple lock on the door to protect his computer equipment. The telephone company had put in a high-speed DSL line.

Coming inside, Tom saw four banker's boxes stacked beside the dining table, which also served as his worktable. The lids were taped shut, but clothing was visible through the hand-holes. His extra apartment key had been left on the counter. Tom took off his jacket. As he unwrapped his sandwich, he eyed the boxes.

One night when Jenny was here, she had talked about Royce Herron's collection. She had especially liked his little county maps of Great Britain with drawings of local flowers and trees in the margins. He had given her one. He had also opened his late wife's jewelry box and told her to take one of the gold bracelets. Jenny told Tom she had sold it for $200.

Leaving his sandwich on the counter, he walked over, pulled an X-Acto knife out of the coffee mug he kept them in, and slit the clear packing tape on the first box on the stack. He lifted the lid and found clothes, shoes, DVDs, and a Mandarin Hotel wineglass wrapped in a sweater.

It took him ten minutes to look at everything Jenny

had packed. He found nothing more interesting than a book of art photos of men's private parts, a towel lifted from the Delano Hotel, and two books on map collecting she had stolen—maybe—from Royce Herron's house. They had his name in them.

That there were no maps in the boxes didn't prove she hadn't taken any before calling the police. She could have rolled them up and put them in her suitcase. She could have stuffed the cash from Royce's bedroom into her wallet and pawned the jewelry. Tom would have done it that way . . . if he were Jenny. And if he hadn't decided, about five years ago, to go straight. Like Fritz had decided not to drink. One day at a time.

Tom rummaged through the junk drawer in the kitchen and found a roll of packing tape to reseal the boxes. He didn't feel bad about opening them. If she had put the maps inside, and if for some reason the cops had come in with a search warrant, it would have been his neck, not hers.

He carried a can of Red Bull and his sandwich over to the computer desk and sat down. He figured it would take about six hours to finish what he had to do tonight. The screen saver was rotating through a series of *Sports Illustrated* swimsuit photos. He bit into his roast beef sub, leaning over the paper so the crumbs wouldn't fall on the floor. There were roach traps all over the apartment, but massive palmetto bugs with bad attitudes roamed at will.

With a tap on the mouse, the current project came up: revisions to a Web site for a gastroenterology group on Miami Beach. Tom had designed a dozen logos, all rejected. Then one of the doctors had suggested a hot pink stomach and intestines inside a box shaped like a torso. By tomorrow morning, Tom had to make the logo look like art and put it on every page of the Web site, the medical group's letterhead, and its newsletter.

"This sucks."

The cursor moved to an icon on the bottom of the screen. A double-click connected him to KINK-FM, an indie-alternative station in the Netherlands. Tom ran the volume up and went back to the gastroenterologists' page. He stared at the intestinal tract and thought of the Corelli map. The bullet holes and smears of blood.

Stuart Barlowe had said, *You're an artist, Tom. You have an extraordinary talent.*

The ad agency he worked for was one of his best clients. If he was sidetracked for two or three weeks doing a map for Stuart Barlowe, the client would find someone else. He didn't have time to do Barlowe's map, even if he knew where to start.

The music went off and the announcers' voices smoothly dropped English words into the Dutch conversation. Tom had no idea what they were saying. He copied the hot pink guts and put them onto page one of the newsletter, *Horizons in Gastroenterology.* The music resumed—crashing drums and a singer who sounded like he was in outer space. *We'll be touching the stars . . . We'll be kissing the sun. . . .*

A palmetto bug scurried across the keyboard.

Cursing, Tom stood up so fast his chair rolled backward and slammed into his stereo cabinet. The glass door cracked and fell into pieces on the floor. "Goddammit!" The bug dived off the edge of the desk. Tom ran for the kitchen, grabbed a can of Raid, and aimed the oily fumes at the wall, then down to the floor. Coughing, he closed the connection to KINK. The speakers went silent. He threw his sandwich into the trash and took a four-pack of Guinness out of the fridge. He put on his jacket and killed the lights before opening the door.

No one on the patio noticed him going down the stairs, crossing the concrete pad in front of the garage, and using the ladder to climb onto the deck of his sailboat. He went aft and sat in the cockpit to open a beer.

This was—or used to be—a thirty-three-foot, 1974 Morgan Out Island, a good boat in its time. Eddie Ferraro had known the former owner, who had run it aground in the shallows near Elliott Key. The engine was shot, and the sails were rotting, so he let Eddie have it for the price of the tow. Eddie knew a little about boats because he had bummed around as a fisherman in the Keys. Eddie had thought Tom needed something to do besides get drunk, smoke weed, and get thrown out of clubs on South Beach. They had kept the boat at a marina near downtown, stripping out the insides and patching the fiberglass, until the marina went upscale, and the new owners evicted them.

The hull was in good shape now, but the engine still needed repairs. A mechanic over at Martha Framm's marina would come over with his tools. Then there were sails to buy, a main and a jib for starters. Tom had hoped to get the boat in the water by March 1. It wasn't going to happen.

The lights of downtown Miami flickered through the trees. The music in the backyard had gone off. The neighbors were going home.

Tom drained his beer and set it on top of the first two he had finished, making a pyramid. Reaching inside his jacket, he found his cell phone, pushed a button. The light on the screen made him squint. He clicked to his phone book, hit a number. He listened to the noise on the other end, not a ring but a *brrrrrp*.

A groggy male voice mumbled, "*Pronto.*"

"Eddie?"

"*Chi parla?*" the voice demanded.

"It's Tom. Did I wake you?"

"No, I'm always awake at four o'clock in the morning."

"Sorry. I forgot the time difference. You want to go back to bed?"

"Too late now. What's up?"

Tom took his time telling Eddie about Gaetano Corelli's world map. When he finished, he heard clinking noises, running water, and some thuds. "Eddie? You still there?"

"I'm making some chamomile tea. We had a front come through. It's cold enough outside to freeze the balls off a Christmas tree. Let's see now. Stuart Barlowe's map is shot to pieces, and he's willing to pay you six grand to make an exact copy, three thousand down, three on delivery. Correct?"

"Correct."

"Here's what you want to know." A spoon clinked against the cup. "How can I make a good enough copy so he pays me all six thousand dollars, and this doesn't come back later to bite me in the ass? Is that what you're asking me?"

"Maybe."

A laugh came over the line.

"Well?" Tom heard Eddie slurping tea.

After a while, Eddie asked, "Does Barlowe know you've been in jail?"

"He didn't bring it up, but yes, I'm sure he does."

"No offense intended, but don't you wonder why a respectable citizen like Stuart Barlowe would hire somebody with a criminal past? I'll tell you why. He trusts a fellow crook. Writing a check to cash, not adding the sales tax, tells me where he's coming from. I will also tell you why you're going to get screwed if you try this."

When Eddie paused, Tom said, "Okay, why?"

"Because for the risk you're taking, six grand isn't enough. You should've asked for fifty. At least."

"Fifty thousand dollars? Be serious."

"I am. Look. If Barlowe wants *you*, Tom Fairchild, to make a map for him—to *forge* a map—then something smells. He didn't tell you the truth, my young friend, and believe me, this could bite very hard. If somebody finds out the map is forged, they're going to ask Mr. Barlowe about it. Who's he going to blame? And who will they believe?"

"No, wait, I've been thinking about this." Tom pulled himself upright. "Barlowe told me the police gave him his map back. They know it was ruined. I mean, if he tries to pass the copy off as real, they'll know about it."

"You're telling me the police are that competent? Or that in a year or two from now they're going to remember which map? Barlowe will deny everything." As Tom was mulling this over, Eddie asked, "What's he going to do with it?"

"I don't really know." After a moment, Tom added, "He wouldn't sell it. People know the Corelli was shot up."

"Do they?"

Tom thought about that. "Maybe not."

"You want some advice, Tom? Here it is. Don't do it."

"That's basically what Rose said."

"There you go. She knows when something isn't right. You should listen to your sister. How is she? Has she stopped hating my guts yet?"

"She doesn't hate you, Eddie. I think you broke her heart."

A sigh came over the line. "I'd almost rather she hated me."

Tom put his elbows on his knees. "Let's say I'm willing to assume the risk. Would you help me or not?"

"Not."

"Why?"

"I like you, Tom. I don't want to see you take up forgery as a career. It's easy to slide into but hard to get out of. Do you really want to risk your probation? Hell, do you really want to go the way I did? Jump bail, hide out in another country the rest of your life, never see Rose and the kids again? Think about that. The best help I can give you is, *don't do it*. Now let me go back to bed, all right?"

The sun was coming up and Tom was wired on Red Bull and espresso when he finished his work for the medical group. He saved everything to a backup disk, then selected the files to upload to his client. At the same moment he clicked on SEND he heard a loud rapping noise.

It took him a second to realize that it wasn't his computer going crazy; someone was at his door. He walked over and looked through two slats in the miniblinds that covered the window. A narrow African-American face and a pair of rat-gray eyes looked back at him. George Weems. "What the hell?"

Weems called through the glass, "Good morning, Mr. Fairchild. May I come in?"

"Why?"

"I have a right to enter your premises at any time, with or without your consent. Don't make it difficult."

"Jesus." Tom took off the security chain and opened the door.

The Weasel came inside, bringing a blast of chilly morning air with him. He looked around, noticed that Tom was fully dressed, then saw the line of empty Guinness cans on the counter. "Did we have a party last night?"

"I've been up all night working," Tom said. "What can I do for you, Mr. Weems?"

"Just dropped in to verify your address. Check on your living arrangements."

"Well, this is it."

"The apartment you pay eight hundred dollars a month for."

That wasn't a question, so Tom made no reply. He remained by the door, hoping Weems would do what he came to do and leave.

"Your landlord's roommate, Ms. Sandra Wiley, spent ten years in the federal penitentiary in Atlanta. I've been doing some background checking."

"Who? You mean Moon?"

"In the early eighties, she was married to one Pedro Bonifacio Escalona, a member of a drug gang in South Florida. Ms. Wiley was charged with providing material assistance. It's a violation of your probation to consort with a felon."

"I didn't know Moon was in prison," Tom said. "Nobody ever told me that. Why should they? I don't consort with her. She's my landlord's girlfriend, not mine. What am I supposed to do, Mr. Weems?" Tom could hear his voice getting louder. "Did you come to tell me I'm violated? You're going to make sure I go to prison. That's what you want, isn't it?"

"What I want is to see you lead a crime-free life, Mr. Fairchild. That would bring me great happiness, to see you succeed. If I seem strict to you, it's because I'm doing my job. Do you know what my job is? It's not to be a nice guy. It's not to make my probationers like me. My job is to protect the public."

Tom looked away from Weems's small gray eyes and sat at the table to keep from going after him.

Weems walked around the apartment, leaning close to the computer monitor, peering into the refrigerator, opening drawers in Tom's bureau. "No, I'm not going to file a violation. I could, but not this time. You earned a couple of points, Mr. Fairchild, for getting your payment in last week." Weems stopped in front of the pyramid of beer cans. "What about AA? Did you sign up yet?"

"I'm meeting my sponsor this week," Tom said. "And a psychologist for anger management. That, too."

"I hope you're telling me the truth. Are you telling me the truth, Mr. Fairchild?"

"Yes."

The Weasel turned and smiled at him. "Here's an interesting statistic. Seventy-two percent of the most serious criminals, up to and including your serial killers, are of above-average intelligence. Their downfall is, they think they're too smart to get caught when they lie. I'm here to tell you, I know what your tendencies are, and if I think you're crossing the line by so much as an inch, I'll pull you right back."

Waggling his finger, he walked to the door. "Be good. I have my eye on you."

―――――――

With a Magic Marker Tom drew the Weasel's face on the heavy bag that hung from the eaves of the garage: receding hair line, eyes close together, small nose and chin, protruding teeth. He put on his sparring gloves and hit the thing until his arms ached and he dripped with sweat, even though the temperature was still below seventy.

A final side kick rocked the bag on its chain. Collapsing into a plastic lawn chair, Tom ripped the Velcro closures open with his teeth and dropped the gloves on the ground. His cell phone lay on top of his towel. He mopped his face while his thumb hit the redial buttons.

Brrrrp. Brrrrp. Brrrrp.

He got an answering machine telling him to leave a message after the beep—*un messaggio dopo il bip.*

"Eddie, it's me again. I'm taking the job. Fuck it. I don't care what Barlowe does with the map. I could use the money. Call me when you get this. I need you to tell me what to do."

CHAPTER 9

Music filled the room like a throbbing physical presence, Mick Jagger whooping about "Brown Sugar," as Rhonda Barlowe rode the high of her endorphins. For twenty-six minutes she had been pumping the StairMaster, and she felt like she could go for hours. Her Pekingese, Zhou-Zhou, gazed at her from his sheepskin nest by the window.

Rhonda was watching the driveway below, where a movement had caught her eye. A motorcycle sped between the rows of palm trees, trailing a long afternoon shadow. Tom Fairchild was leaving the house.

She expected Stuart to come upstairs soon. He would tell her how a mediocre graphic artist with a criminal record was going to save him from ruination. She expected to be asked her opinion, not that Stuart would listen. He rarely listened to anything she said. Her husband pretended to, then went into his study, made himself a drink, and thumbed the TV remote for hours. He could tell her the recipe for crème caramel or the number of German airplanes shot down by the RAF in 1940. He fell asleep in his clothes; he didn't fall asleep at all; he worked crossword puzzles at dawn; he rarely came to her bedroom anymore.

In the floor-to-ceiling mirrors Rhonda watched the smooth, hard muscles moving in her legs. Trails of sweat glistened on her chest. She wore running shorts and a sports bra, and her hair was pulled up into a turquoise headband. Her new personal trainer had told her she had the body of a thirty-year-old. He guaranteed she'd be in top shape for the cruise around Hawaii next week. She had a suitcase full of swimsuits and matching sarongs. Stuart was looking for excuses not to go; Rhonda almost hoped he found one.

She closed her eyes and sucked in air, timing her steps to the beat of "Gimme Shelter," feeling the burn in her glutes.

The music went off.

Zhou-Zhou lifted his head and let out a sharp yap, then saw who it was. Stuart's reflection in the mirror put down the stereo remote and walked past the row of machines to the windows. A shadow in pleated slacks and a black pullover. He was too thin, Rhonda thought. He was a wraith.

The steps hissed down to eye level. Rhonda patted her face with a towel. "How was your meeting?"

Stuart kept walking to the thermostat, where he repeatedly jabbed a button on the digital display. "I know you're working out, but for the love of God, it's like the Arctic Circle in here."

"I like it. Tell me what Tom Fairchild had to say."

Gazing past her out the windows, Stuart ran his fingers over his beard. The sun had gone down; the sky was fading. "He said that all things being equal, he'd rather not get involved. It's a risk, given his situation with the law, so if I really want the Corelli, I'll have to make it worth his while." Stuart left a pause into which he dropped a faint smile. "Fifty thousand dollars."

Rhonda couldn't prevent a burst of laughter. "That's insane."

"Fifty *plus* his expenses, which he estimates will run another twenty."

"Good lord. What expenses?"

Sitting on a weight bench, Stuart extended his legs. "There are the artist's supplies, of course. A digital camera. Food and lodging. Travel. He says he can't get to Europe by the normal routes because his passport is flagged, so we arranged that he start his journey by taking a private boat to Nassau. From there he will fly to Jamaica, then direct to London."

"Why London?"

"There are some Corelli sea charts in the National Maritime Museum. He wants to take photographs and study the details. I'm to write a letter of introduction to the curators informing them that Tom Fairchild is doing research for the Caribbean collection in the museum here. After London, he will see more Corellis in the Biblioteca Nazionale in Florence, Italy. This will require another letter of introduction." Stuart rolled a fifteen-pound free weight with the toe of his shoe. "He says he has a source for antique paper. Not one piece, several. At least a dozen. Trial and error could burn up several attempts. He wants to finish the job over there. I told him to ship the map to Miami by bonded courier. We wouldn't want him caught with it on the way back."

"What a lovely vacation," Rhonda muttered. "What makes you so sure the map will be any good?"

"All we can do is hope. No, I think it will be very good—if Tom Fairchild wants his final payment."

"The man is a felon. Surely there's someone else who could do it."

"Is there? Give me a name. Please."

"How is he going to simulate a copperplate engraving?"

"He wouldn't say."

"Marvelous. And if he keeps the money and doesn't come back?"

"It's only fifty thousand dollars, Rhonda. He has family here. If he doesn't make his next appointment with his probation officer, the state of Florida will issue an arrest warrant. He was very candid about what he faces: six years in prison. He doesn't want that hanging over him. He'll be back." Stuart rolled the weight in the other direction. "I wouldn't give him all the money at once. It would be doled out, depending on his progress."

"But you won't be there to monitor his progress, will you?" Standing over her husband, she brushed his straight, lank hair off his forehead. "We're leaving for Hawaii on Saturday, darling."

"That's true. I'll think of something." He pressed his fingers against her thigh, testing the muscle. "You're getting very buff, my sweet."

"You don't like it?"

"I do. You're perfect." He stroked her knee, then his mustache was tickling her skin. She hated being kissed on her legs, had told him, and he still did it.

"Stuart, this isn't going to work."

He pulled away. "I could send Allison."

"With Tom Fairchild, you mean?"

"Why not? She knows maps. And she knows

Fairchild. She warned me against him. I don't think he could pull anything over on her. She's too smart for him."

"Yes, why don't you do that?" Rhonda crossed to the watercooler and held her bottle under the spigot. It would be lovely if Allison were gone for a while. Having failed to get a partnership in Boston, she had slunk home to a family she had despised for fifteen years. Dropping in at any hour as if this were her house. Undermining Stuart's relationship with Larry. Rhonda knew what she was after.

She poured some water into Zhou-Zhou's dish. "Allison can't just walk out of her new job. Besides, isn't she studying for the bar exam?"

"Ah. That's right," he said.

"You see how impossible this is."

"Maybe I should go," he said. "You wouldn't miss me, would you, my pet? You have friends on the cruise, and God knows I can't keep up with you on the dance floor." When she didn't reply his eyebrows slanted quizzically. "What's the matter? Not a good idea?"

"Going to London? I think not."

"Rhonda." He looked at her with mild reproach, which she didn't deserve. He said softly, "I don't know where she is. I don't care where she is. You needn't worry."

Rhonda had tried, really tried, to ignore his occasional lapses of fidelity, which she had to admit rarely ever happened anymore, but the last one had sent her into a rage. The girl had been young and black, one of Larry's employees, a whore, not to put too fine a point on it. Stuart had confessed after he'd already called it off; he'd come to Rhonda's room in tears, on his knees with remorse. He didn't think the girl would make trouble; he'd given her some money and told her not to contact him again. Over brunch Sunday Larry mentioned that the girl had quit without a word, gone back to England was his guess. Stuart had folded his newspaper the other way and kept reading.

"If you don't want me to go, I won't," he said.

"Have you heard from her?"

Stuart's smile was brittle. "No, I haven't."

What could she believe anymore? She sat beside him. "What I really want is for you to tell Tom Fairchild you've changed your mind. Let him keep the money you gave him, but just . . . forget it."

"I promised Leo his map," Stuart said.

"He can't have his map; it's done for. Offer to buy him another one, whatever he wants."

"The map is the crowning jewel of Gaetano Corelli's only atlas. Leo's grandfather owned it."

"Listen to me, Stuart. Leo is a reasonable man. Tell him it was accidentally destroyed, and you're sorry, but there's nothing you can do."

Stuart rolled the weight with his foot parallel to the weave in the carpet. "You don't want to be around when he hears that."

"You're not afraid of Leo, surely." Rhonda smiled in disbelief. Last summer they had spent several days at his villa on the Dalmatian coast, their own guest quarters with a maid and a terrace where they were served breakfast overlooking the sea. Leo Zurin played cello. He collected fine art and antiques. But Stuart's grim expression made her ask, "What would he do, have you shot?"

A slight smile tugged at his mouth. "Dismembered, perhaps. No, I'm joking. It would be painful enough if he pulled out of the investment group. Let me handle it. All right?"

Thirty-one years ago, seeing this man for the first time, Rhonda had felt an electric sizzle that had pushed waves of heat through her body. He had been handsome, but it was more than that. He had been quietly powerful in a way that nobody had recognized at the time, eclipsing his brother or even his father, such plodding creatures they'd been. But as the years passed, he'd become more like them—stiff and conservative, afraid of what people might say. He had to know it, and to despise the weakness in himself, because he would do such foolish things to prove otherwise, like sleeping with a girl less than half his age. Or taking credit for a rare map that wasn't his.

"Did Leo know that his map was going to be put in an exhibit?"

Stuart's silence gave her the answer.

"You never told him! You sneak!" Rhonda laughed. "You just had to prove something to Royce Herron, didn't you?"

"I lent him the map because Allison asked me to."

"Bullshit, darling. You could have said no, but you wanted to strut and show off at the map fair. You needed the Corelli, but you didn't dare ask Leo, because he would have said no."

"Correct, my love. I can't put one over on you, can I? I let his map out of my hands knowing he would have me flayed alive if he ever found out."

"He would not. Don't be ridiculous! It would be difficult, I grant you, if Leo refused to invest in The Metropolis out of spite, but the alternative is so much worse. He would tell everyone what you'd done—tried to defraud him with a forgery! We'd be in a fix then, wouldn't we?"

During this, Stuart's face had become red, and now he exploded. "We're already there, idiot woman! I'm nearly broke, and your profligacy doesn't help! That god-damned soiree you threw cost me sixty thousand dollars!" He shot up from the bench and walked away with his head in his hands. "I pay twenty thousand dollars a month in tax on this house. Larry just cost me two million in guarantees for that fucking restaurant. Stop buying me Glenfiddich, Rhonda, I can do with Chivas. We don't need another vacation. I'm bleeding to death!" Stuart's laugh cracked. "And you want me to tell Leo Zurin he can't have his map?"

During this outburst, Zhou-Zhou began to bark and run in circles.

"Shut up!" Stuart yelled.

Rhonda stared up at her husband.

He sat beside her. "Rhonda . . . does it ever cross your mind that we ought to chuck it? This insanity. The parties, the hypocrisy. This life. This fiction we've created—"

"Oh, yes, let's give it all up, why not? Let's buy a little house in the suburbs and shop at the discount malls. We'll go to church on Sundays. An honest, simple life. Do I ever think of it? No, Stuart. I don't."

"I do. Sometimes I do," he said.

She looked at him closely. "Are you taking your pills?"

"Maybe I should take more of them. The entire bottle."

"Stop it!"

"*Je suis désolé.*" He lifted her hand and kissed it. "Forgive me. You know I adore you. Darling, dearest Rhonda. She who has traversed the darkest corners of my soul."

"I'm starting to worry about you."

"Don't. I'm quite all right. Just . . . you know . . . things on my mind."

"Stuart, please don't give Leo a forgery."

"It isn't a forgery. It's a duplicate. Don't argue with me. I've made my decision."

Rhonda saw their reflection, sitting side by side, she in turquoise and yellow workout clothes, Stuart in black and gray. She felt that she was the one who should be wearing black. She exhaled and closed her eyes. "Oh, God. That's it, then."

He put his arm around her. "We'll get through this."

"Do you want Larry to take him to Nassau? Tom Fairchild."

Stuart didn't answer for a while, then said, "You didn't tell Larry about the map, did you?"

"Of course I didn't tell him."

"If he slipped and said something to Marek Vuksinic, we'd have a problem."

"Larry is more intelligent than that, Stuart."

"All right," he said. "Larry can take him. I'll say I'm sending Tom Fairchild to Nassau to meet a collector about some maps. A man I spoke to at the map fair. Will that do?"

Grabbing up beer bottles, a beach towel, somebody's thong panties, and a pack of rolling papers, Laurence Gerard opened a drawer in the entertainment center and dropped everything inside, then slammed it. The big plasma screen showed a golfer teeing off at Pinehurst. Marek had been watching this shit for an hour, making himself at home, chain-smoking Marlboros.

He was already packed, had his bags by the door of

his room. At seven-o-fucking-clock in the morning they would drive up to Orlando. Marek wanted to do Disney World before flying back to Albania or wherever the hell he was going.

Larry was ready for Marek to leave. It wasn't just the smoking; having Marek around was getting on his nerves. Marek took no shit off anyone, which was admirable to an extent, but Larry was starting to feel like he'd walked into a Balkan version of *The Sopranos*.

A knock came at the door, three quick raps. Three more. His mother's pattern.

Marek's head turned toward the sound. Alert as a Rottweiler.

Rhonda had called to let Larry know she was coming. He'd had to stall her to get everyone out of here, put away some things, change his shirt, spray air freshener. He grabbed the remote and turned down the volume on the TV before he went to the door.

He stood back to let her in. "Hello, Mother."

After lifting her cheek to be kissed, she walked past him in her fringed, silver leather jacket and tight jeans. When she spotted Marek, an eyebrow lifted. Marek stared back at her, cigarette smoke curling from the fingers of one hand, arms spread across the back of the sofa.

"Why, it's Mr. Vuksinic. You're still in Miami, then."

"Hallo, Missus Barlowe." His mouth was hidden behind the mustache. "I love Miami."

"I wish we could chat, but I need to talk to Larry. Would you excuse us?"

"It's okay. I'll go outside." Marek went out on the terrace and leaned against the railing, the breeze whipping his pink-and-green Tommy Bahama shirt. It had to be below sixty degrees out there. Larry's blood had thinned, living in the tropics. If he ever moved back north, he would freeze to death.

His mother was heading toward the kitchen, and Larry followed. He had wiped down the black granite countertops, pitched the liquor bottles into the trash, and dimmed the halogen lights. His mother sat on one of the stools and crossed her legs. She wore high-heeled cowboy boots with silver toe caps.

"I thought your guest would have left by now."

"He was supposed to." Larry gestured toward the espresso machine. "Can I make you a cappuccino? Get you a glass of wine? Anything?"

"No, thanks."

"Well. What's up?"

She placed her bag on the counter. "Could you take a day or two off this week?"

"I don't think so," Larry said. "Marek wants to see Disney World before he heads home. I'm babysitting. I mean, unless I have a reason not to."

"Stuart needs someone taken to Nassau by boat. You'll be reimbursed for the fuel and docking charge, naturally."

"Who's the passenger?"

"His name is Tom Fairchild. You might know him. He was in Allison's class in high school. He sells maps now."

"Fairchild." Larry smiled. "I remember him."

Larry had lost a brand-new Mustang GT to Tom Fairchild on a two-lane road in the western part of the county, weekend entertainment if you had some money and didn't mind risking the title to your car. Give the referee an extra ignition key and the papers, line up, and hit the gas. Allison had gotten him into this. *Your Mustang isn't as fast as Tom's Camaro.* Tom had jumped the signal. Larry had objected and ended up with a broken tooth and a cracked rib. He had thought seriously about having Tom turned into fish chum, but he'd cooled off. And then Tom Fairchild had moved to New York, failed out of college, and accumulated a string of felony arrests. Funny, a guy like that ending up as a map geek.

"Why am I taking him to Nassau?"

His mother looked toward the sliding doors that led to the terrace. Nothing out there but the lights of a building farther up South Beach. "The fact is, you aren't." Her sea-blue eyes, outlined in black, shifted to him. "You're going to help me save Stuart from a very bad decision."

After she left, Marek came back in with his cigarette. The place was stinking of smoke. Larry didn't know if he could get the smell out of the carpet and leather furniture. He lifted a sofa cushion and found the pills he'd stuffed under there earlier. After what his mother had told him, he needed one. Maybe two.

Marek exhaled smoke. "That stuff messes your head."

"You'd prefer to get lung cancer." Larry followed the pill with a swallow of pomegranate juice. He set the glass on the side table. "Listen, Marek. There's been a slight change of plans. Stuart is sending me over to Nassau tomorrow on business. Unfortunately, I can't get out of it. Joe can go up to Disney with you instead, all right? He loves Disney. He'll take you to Universal Studios as well."

Marek's eyes stayed on Larry. Not blinking. Cigarette smoke drifting toward the recessed lights in the ceiling.

Larry said, "I'll call Joe right now, tell him to be over in the morning."

"Oscar Contreras is in Paradise Island. Are you going to see him?"

Oh, fuck, Larry thought. He had forgotten that Contreras would be doing some gambling before heading back to Peru. "No. No, it has nothing to do with Oscar. This is something else. It's . . . okay, Stuart wants me to take a guy over there to look at some maps. He's a map dealer. The problem is, he doesn't have a valid passport, so he'd have trouble getting back into the U.S."

"Who is he?"

"Name's Tom Fairchild. He's a friend of my sister."

Marek let some more seconds go by. "You're going in the boat?"

"Right. The boat."

"I'll go with you."

Larry wished he had taken the other pill. "What about Disney? You can't miss Disney World."

"That's okay." The cigarette found its way to the slit under the mustache, paused there. "I'm not in a hurry. I'd like to see the Bahamas."

At home, Allison's favorite place to work was on the floor of the living room, her back against the sofa, papers spread out around her, notebook computer on one side, and a can of mixed nuts on the other. She would wear something comfortable, like thick socks, an oversize T-shirt, and pajama bottoms. Her fluffy black cat, Othello, curled up behind her, licking his paws and shedding on the cushions. Othello had been small enough to fit in a shoe when Allison had found him under a bush outside her apartment in Boston.

She had bought her place in Coconut Grove because it was near her new office, but she'd fallen in love with the view. From the tenth floor she could see a canopy of banyan trees, a marina full of boats, and a spectacular sunrise. The building had a social room, where men her age sat around playing Texas Hold 'em and watching ESPN. There was a gym where she could work out. Could, but hadn't. Every night was taken up with studying for the bar exam.

For furniture, the apartment had the usual sofa-armchair-and-loveseat with end table and lamp. That and a big flat-screen TV for watching the classic movies and foreign films she didn't have time for. She hadn't yet found a carpenter to do built-in shelves, so her books and DVDs were all over the place. She had loads of decorating ideas. Every trip to the grocery store produced another copy of *Real Simple* or *Metropolitan Home*. The stack was up to her knees, and she intended, when she found a spare weekend, to go through them all and cut out photos and articles she liked and file them in indexed folders. Until her apartment looked like a home, she didn't feel like entertaining. But the truth was, she hadn't made many friends. The only date she'd had was dinner with a man she'd met in line at a Barnes & Noble. It was the Italian cookbook that grabbed her attention. In a booth at Bacio, she told him about her undergrad year in Rome, he confessed he was married, and she walked out halfway through her chicken arrabbiata. So far the men in Miami had been a big disappointment.

Allison reached into the can of mixed nuts, fishing for a cashew. She was still buzzing on the Cuban coffee she'd had at eight o'clock, just enough to keep alert until midnight, when she would go to bed with her notes on Florida criminal procedure.

The telephone rang, and she moved Othello aside to

get to the handset that lay on the sofa. The doorman said her father was downstairs. "My father?" Allison shifted a notebook off her lap. "Yes, of course, tell him to come up."

When Stuart came in, he seemed not to notice the piles of papers and books, nor did he comment on what she was wearing—a Columbia Law sweatshirt over SpongeBob SquarePants pajama bottoms. Arms crossed, Allison let him kiss her cheek. If he had come to demand an apology, he wasn't going to get it.

He laid his suede jacket across the arm of the sofa and stared down at it. "First, I want to say that I'm sorry for last night. You were right. I forgot to make dinner reservations. I had a lot on my mind, but that's no excuse, is it?"

This caught her off guard. "I'm sorry, too, Dad. I shouldn't have blown up. I can get way too sensitive." She rushed to clear a stack of study guides off the end of the sofa. "Excuse the mess. Do you want to sit down?"

But her father wandered across the room, hands behind his back, to look at the unframed map of Robinson Crusoe's voyages that Allison had fixed to the wall with push-pins. He said, "Last night I told you I'd asked Tom Fairchild to restore the Corelli map. That wasn't the truth. He's going to make me a duplicate, for which I will pay fifty thousand dollars, plus his expenses."

Before she could recover from her shock, he said, "I came to ask for your help, Allison."

CHAPTER 10

Early the next afternoon Tom went by The Compass Rose, which was closed for the day due to Royce Herron's funeral. His sister had just come home, and Tom found her in the upstairs apartment in a dark blue dress, their mother's pearl necklace, and a pair of sandals—black, to suit the occasion. He apologized for not going with her; he'd spent the morning rearranging his work schedule and he still had to pack, then get to Stuart Barlowe's house on La Gorce Island by five o'clock. He would be in the Bahamas before midnight. By Thursday morning he would be in London.

Rose busied herself making a pot of tea as Tom explained everything. When she brought the cups to the table, she saw the fat envelope he'd put there. "What is this?"

"Twenty-five hundred dollars. It's for you and the girls."

"I don't want it," she said.

"Come on, Sis. Don't be like that. Take it off of what I owe you."

"You don't owe me anything, Tom."

He pushed the money toward the salt and pepper shakers. "It can sit there. I'm not taking it back."

"I'll keep it for you," she said. "If you need it . . . I could wire it or something." She looked at the envelope as if it contained a dead mouse. "You shouldn't travel with a lot of cash. Don't forget your hat and gloves—it's cold in London. And buy a calling card because I want you to let me know you're all right."

"My cell phone is set up for international calls. You can use my local number." Tom reached for his tea, not wanting any, but making the gesture. "I'll call you as soon as I get to London. I'll be there for a couple of days, then head on down to Florence."

She twisted her necklace. "Firenze," she murmured. "*Che bella città*. I don't suppose you'll have time to see the Uffizi Gallery . . . or the statue of David."

"Probably not. I'll be working."

"You should buy an Italian phrase book, Tom. Don't assume everyone speaks English."

"All right."

"And promise me you won't stay in hotels near the train stations. I've heard they're very dangerous."

"Okay, Rose. Listen, if George Weems calls from the probation office looking for me—I don't know why he would, but he might—tell him I went to Key West for a few days and forgot my cell phone. If by some chance you can't get hold of me—" Tom hesitated before reaching into a thigh pocket of his cargo pants for a folded piece of paper. "This is Eddie's number in Manarola. He'll know where I am."

Rose diverted her gaze toward the ceiling as Tom slid

the paper across the table. She said, "Are you going to stay with Eddie?"

"Maybe. It depends."

"On what?"

"On what we decide to do, I guess."

Rose's green eyes pinned him. "You've been in touch with him ever since he left, haven't you?"

"I like Eddie. He's a good man. He made some mistakes in his past that caught up to him. He didn't want to jump bail, but it was either that or spend twenty years in a federal prison."

"So Eddie Ferraro is going to help you forge a map. Well, who better?"

"It's my decision, Rose. I don't want this life anymore. It's got to change. I don't care what it costs." Tom stood up and pushed his chair in. "I'd better be going."

He was heading for the stairs when Rose called across the kitchen, "Tom! Wait." She ran to the refrigerator and moved a magnet off a snapshot of Megan and Jill, herself behind them. She smoothed a rumpled corner. "Take this with you."

Tom smiled at her. "I'm coming back, Rose. Honest."

"You'd better."

"Want me to leave the picture with Eddie?"

"God, no." She laughed. "If you do, cut me out first. I look so goofy."

"You are goofy."

She threw her arms around his neck. "Call me the minute you get there."

Stuart Barlowe had paid Tom ten thousand in cash, five toward his fee, five for expenses. And he had added a couple of conditions to their deal. No more expense money unless Tom turned in receipts. And second, he had to show his work in progress to collect more of his fee. Show it to whom? The last time they'd talked, that detail hadn't been worked out. Tom didn't see how it could be done, so he was prepared to ignore that part of the deal. He wasn't without bargaining power. Barlowe might have the money, but without Tom, he wasn't going to get his map.

Turning his motorcycle through the chain-link gate of the Miami River Boatworks, Tom drove to the high-lift storage shed in back. Engine idling, he asked the Cuban guy who ran the forklift if Mrs. Framm was around. "*No, señor, está en casa.*"

She was at home. Tom went three blocks up the street and around a corner, stopping at a two-story frame house with white columns, built in the early 1900s, one of the few that had survived in this neighborhood. He could hardly see it behind the tangle of pine trees and native palms. Leaving his bike inside the fence, he went up the steps and rang the bell.

Martha Framm peered through the lace before unlocking the door. She wore a black pantsuit that made her look like a sharp-angled stick figure. Strands of bleached blond hair fell across her leathery face. "Whoo-hoo. Tom Fairchild. You're just in time, cutie-pie. I made a pitcher of frozen mango margaritas."

"Sounds great, Mrs. Framm, but I've got to be someplace." He dug into his pants pocket for an envelope. "I brought you a thousand dollars for the engine repair. If it's more, let me know."

"What engine?" She sipped from the pale orange slush in her martini glass.

"My sailboat. You were going to send Raul over to work on it at Fritz's house."

"Right, right. Senior moment." She laughed.

Tom said, "I'm leaving this afternoon to go out of town for a couple of weeks, and I didn't want you to think I'd forgotten. I'm sorry about Judge Herron. My sister went to the funeral, but I couldn't get away. We sent some flowers."

"Royce. My old friend. What a special person he was."

"Yes, ma'am, he was."

"Those fuckers." She leaned her head on the door frame.

"Yes, ma'am." Tom stood there with the cash in his hand, wondering if she was going to remember where she got it. "If you don't mind, could I get a receipt?"

The heavy living room curtains were closed, but Tom could make out the kind of stuff that his grandmother used to keep around: house plants on mahogany tables, porcelain knickknacks on shelves, and family photos on the mantel. Gold-framed paintings of the Everglades took up the space on the walls. Tom nearly tripped over a cardboard box.

"Watch your step," Martha said. "I need to throw that shit out." She opened a set of double doors to a converted sunporch, where light streamed through the glass jalousies onto a massive oak desk. She found some plain notepaper in a drawer and asked if that was all right. Tom said it was. She wrote his receipt, and a heavy gold charm bracelet jangled on her thin, sun-mottled wrist. "Don't you worry. We'll have that baby purring."

"I appreciate it," Tom said. "I'm hoping to get her in the water at the end of the month."

"You have your sails already?"

"I called the sailmaker this morning." As he took the receipt he noticed another open box by the desk, antidevelopment pamphlets spilling onto the terrazzo floor. SAVE OUR HERITAGE. STOP THE GREED. "Were these for the rally last weekend?"

Martha snorted. "Didn't do any good because the whores at city hall had already been bought off. This time next year, there could be fifty-story concrete towers on the river. I'm going to chain my naked body to the goddamn bulldozers. Scary idea, huh?"

On the way out, Tom paused at the front door. "Mrs. Framm? Could I ask you about something you told Fritz? You said Judge Herron might've been killed because he opposed The Metropolis. What did you mean by that? The police think it was map thieves."

"It wasn't map thieves! It was bribery. Payola. Royce knew the truth, and they had to silence him." Lines fanned out from her mouth as Martha tightly pursed her lips. "I talked to the detectives on the case, and they think I'm a crazy old broad. I am not crazy."

"No, ma'am. How does Stuart Barlowe fit into this?"

"He does financing, you know. Very high-level. He puts deals together. So he's got this consortium of foreign investors funneling lots of money into The Metropolis. Colombian drug lords. The Russian Mafia. Wise guys from New Jersey. God knows. Oh, I hear things. Royce was pretty tight with Stuart Barlowe, and I think he found out too much. The night he died, I phoned him up. I wanted him to speak at the rally. Well, he wouldn't do that, but he told me he'd already taken care of the problem. It sounded to me like Royce was doing some major arm-twisting."

Tom waited for her to expand on that. "How did he take care of the problem?"

"He wouldn't say."

"You think he had some dirt on Stuart Barlowe?"

"Of course! It's obvious. I told the police everything! I said look, you gotta follow this up. Did they? Hah! They waltzed me right out the door. They didn't want to hear it." She studied her glass, which was empty except for an orange puddle at the bottom. "Where'd my drink go?"

At his apartment, Tom's backpack lay open on his bed. He wedged a thirty-inch map tube inside, tucked his leather jacket around it, and closed the heavy zipper. He double-checked his pockets to make sure his passport and cash were still there. The place was neat, the garbage was out by the curb, and his computer had been backed up. Fritz would take him over to the beach.

With his backpack slung over one shoulder, Tom turned out the lights and locked the door. At the bottom of the stairs he detoured to take a final look at his sailboat, making sure the tarp was bungeed down tight. Winter was dry season, but the hatch covers leaked, and he didn't want to come home to a coat of mildew below deck. He slid his hand along the sloop's curving white hull. She had a name already: *Sun Dancer.* Not Tom's choice, but it was bad luck to rename a boat. Tom didn't need any more bad luck; he'd had enough of it.

Moon, her big arms covered with flour, stood at the kitchen table punching bread dough into submission. She told Tom he'd find Fritz in the living room. The early edition of the news was on, and Fritz sat in his lounge chair with a plate of leftover pizza on his stomach, getting a jump on dinner. Tomato sauce flecked the drooping white handles of his mustache. He looked around. "Hey, bud. Ready to roll when you are."

Tom pulled a chair over and took out his wallet. "Here's eight hundred dollars for my rent, two hundred for the guy with AA, and two hundred for the anger management class. If they could get the forms signed and sent over to my PO's office this week, that would be great. Any problems, call my cell phone. You've got the number."

As a commercial for a car dealership ended, Fritz held up a hand. "Shhh. I was waiting for this. It's a repeat of the lead story at noon. They found a woman dead in the Glades this morning. I think we might know her."

A pretty announcer with glossy lips said that hunters had been shocked to discover the badly decomposed body of a female in a wooded area off U.S. 41, five miles west of Krome Avenue. The screen switched to video of police vehicles alongside a dirt road. A yellow body bag, a gurney being pushed through the weeds. Then Tom was staring at a face on a California driver's license. A locket on the woman's bracelet had led to the identification of Carla Kelly, twenty-six, a resident of the Raymore Apartments on Miami Beach . . . *undetermined cause of death . . . police investigation under way.*

"Hey, Tom, isn't that the same girl who used to come to the AA meetings over at the Unity Church? She wasn't there more than a couple of times, but I remember her."

"You're right. That's her. I dropped out before she did."

"She was taken out for a reason." Fritz gave a knowing nod. "A casualty behind the lines."

"Excuse me a minute, Fritz. I need to make a phone call."

Tom went out on the front porch, sat on the top step, and punched in the number for Jenny Gray's mother in London. It would be going on ten o'clock at night, he calculated, so they ought to be home. But all he got was a robot voice with a British accent telling him the party was unavailable. He hit the disconnect button.

He sat for a minute watching the sparse traffic on the street, people starting to come home from work. A kid on a bike. A pickup truck rattling with yard tools and the illegal Nicaraguans who lived down the block. Good thing Jenny hadn't been home. He couldn't have told her about Carla. Not yet. She would be spooked, and he needed her. They had arranged to meet outside the Oxford Circus tube station, two o'clock on Thursday, London time. She would be his guide to a city he knew nothing about. He needed to check into a cheap hotel, to locate the National Maritime Museum, to find computer equipment, a camera shop. He would pay for her time, whatever she thought it was worth.

Head in his hands, he stared down at the cracked porch steps between his sneakers. Jenny had been right about Carla. She'd been murdered. And now Jenny's quick departure made more sense. Maybe. The girls had something in common: They'd both worked for Larry Gerard. But having a boss who asked you to put out for customers wasn't exactly a life-threatening situation. In Miami, it was almost normal.

No, she hadn't left because of Carla. She hadn't known for sure that Carla was dead. More likely, she had left because of Judge Herron's murder. On the plaza, Tom had heard the fear in her voice. She'd been scared.

Tom didn't buy Martha Framm's idea that Herron
had been killed by a hit man from some criminal gang
who wanted to protect their investment in The Metropolis. That was way over the top. The judge might have
known about Barlowe's affair with Jenny Gray. She
might have told him about it. She had told Tom. She'd
found a plain envelope in her mailbox with five thousand
dollars in crisp hundreds and a typed note on plain paper:
Immigration will be called if you contact me again. As
dirt went, it wasn't enough to kill a man for, even if Stuart Barlowe had been capable, which Tom thought very
unlikely. Royce Herron was dead, but this fact didn't
make Tom so nervous he could turn down fifty thousand
dollars. Not when he had a better answer: A map thief
had pulled the trigger.

The screen door squeaked on its hinges. Fritz said,
"We'd better scoot, kiddo, or you'll be late."

Tom went in to say good-bye to Moon and get his
things. When he came out to the driveway, Fritz already
had the old Mercedes going, engine clattering, diesel
smoke drifting from the tailpipe. Tom got in and had to
slam the door twice, rattling the chrome frame around
the window. Fritz shifted into reverse just as a horn and
the screech of tires sounded behind them. Tom looked
around to see a black BMW sports car blocking the
driveway.

The driver's door opened. A woman got out. Sunglasses, long brown hair, low-rider jeans, a little red
sweater. She stood with her feet planted slightly apart.
Chunky black shoes.

"Who is that?" Fritz asked.

"Trouble," Tom said. "Hang on. I'll be back." He got

out and left the door open. "Allison, what are you doing?"

"I'm taking you over to my father's house."

"No, you aren't."

"Yes, I am. Get in the car. I'm in a hurry."

They stared at each other for a moment before he finally said, "Jesus."

He went back to retrieve his bag. Fritz was staring into his rearview mirror. "Nice ragtop. Who's the chick?"

"Somebody I used to know. She wants to play chauffeur. Thanks for everything, man."

Allison told Tom the trunk was full already, and he'd have to hold his backpack on his lap. He fell into the low leather seat and wedged the backpack between his knees. She told him to put on his seat belt. When she took off, Tom's head hit the headrest. "Do you think we could get there alive?" he asked.

Her body moved like part of the machine: downshift, brake, turn, shift, accelerate. Her chin was raised slightly, exposing a long white throat. She'd lost her tan, living in the north. Her hair was glossy and thick, the color of polished walnut. She wore gold hoop earrings, a thin chain with one diamond, and a stainless steel watch with numbers big enough to read across a room. No lipstick. He noticed a smile line at the corner of her mouth. She was his age, a couple of weeks older. But she looked good. She'd put on a few pounds where it counted. Last time they'd been this close physically, she had slugged him.

The sunglasses turned toward him a fraction, then she put her eyes back on the road. He wondered what was going on. He braced himself as the car blew through a light turning red at Southwest Eighth, went left, then right, spiraling up the ramp onto the interstate. Downtown Miami whizzed by the window, the mirrored spires and the construction cranes building more mirrored spires. In the distance, Biscayne Bay glimmered in the late-afternoon sunlight. Beyond that, Miami Beach.

Allison zigzagged between a semi and a massive SUV. Tom closed his eyes. A memory jumped into his head: Midnight, a long straight road in New Jersey. Allison's slender hands on the wheel of his stealth car, a Camaro SS that on a bad day could hit 60 miles per hour in 5.9 seconds. Allison doing cartwheels down the center line after edging out the girl in a tricked-out Nissan who had called her a skinny-ass city bitch. Won the Nissan but wouldn't take the key. Didn't want it. Just wanted to show her. Then on the way back to Manhattan, telling Tom to pull off the road; showing her gratitude—showing him until a cop came by shining a light in the window. In those days Allison had lived in an apartment on the Upper West Side, Tom in a walk-up on Garden Street, Jersey City.

"Soon as I drop you off," Allison said over the hum of the engine, "I have a plane to catch. I'm going to New York tonight, then on to London. I'll be there tomorrow. You'll get there a day later, Thursday, about nine o'clock in the morning, flying into Gatwick. I'll meet you outside customs."

"Why would you imagine," Tom said, "that I'm going to London?"

She smiled. "I know about the map, Tom."

"What map?"

"*Universalis Cosmographia,* Gaetano Corelli. Where is it, in your backpack? A map tube would fit in there, I think."

"Excuse me?"

"You're making my father a duplicate, and he wants me to supervise your progress. Right, go ahead and groan. I'm not thrilled about it, either. I had to take a leave of absence at work, and I should be studying for the bar exam, but he asked me to do this for him. I can study in England as well as here. It might actually be less distracting."

Her mouth quirked into an apologetic smile. She checked the rearview, then crossed two lanes to get onto I-195, heading east toward the beach. "We're just going to have to get along, Tom. I'm sorry about this, but I couldn't tell him no, could I?"

The highway arched over a boat channel, then came down onto a long causeway lined with palm trees and oleander, which Tom had heard was poisonous. Roast your hot dog on one of the sticks and you die.

Allison said, "There's no one else he could have asked to do this for him. I know the Renaissance period fairly well. I have four Mercator maps, two Gastaldis, and a Hondius. It's a small one, but I like it."

"Great." Watching the foliage whip past the side window, Tom said, "You mind telling me how you plan to work this?"

"We can fine-tune it later, when we meet in London, but basically, I'll check on the map and pay according to how well you're doing, and if it's on schedule. My father gave me your cell phone number. I'll give you mine so you can call if you don't see me right away at the airport. I've made hotel reservations already in central London. You're at the Bayswater Court. Your room has a single bed and a desk. I hope that's all right. There's no room service, but there's a coffee shop downstairs."

"Where are you staying?"

"Nearby. Claridge's."

"I'll bet they have room service."

"If you want to stay at Claridge's, Tom, I'll be happy to deduct it from your fee." She glanced at him, then took the exit at Alton Road and circled north. Tom stared through the windshield.

Allison said, "Larry is taking you to Nassau in his boat. Did my father tell you?"

"*Larry?* Wonderful." Tom laughed. "Want to know the last thing Larry ever said to me? 'I'm going to get you, shithead. You're going to pay.' That was for breaking his tooth."

"He got it capped. Don't worry about Larry. He's over it. I want you to promise me something, Tom, and this is important. Larry thinks you're going to be in the Bahamas for a few days to look at some maps for my father. He doesn't know about the rest of it. The Corelli. The fact that you're flying to Europe in the morning. You mustn't tell him."

"Really? Is this supposed to be a secret?"

"I mean it, Tom."

"He might ask why you didn't just drop me off at MIA."

"Larry's aware of your travel situation, being on probation and so forth."

"Yeah, I'm a convicted burglar. Is Larry going to believe that your father would let *me* buy maps for him?"

"Why not? You're in the business. You're going because Rose can't leave the shop."

"O-kay."

"Larry doesn't know I'm going with you. Neither does my stepmother, Rhonda. It's between you, me, and my dad. All right?"

"Fine."

Slowing at the entrance to La Gorce Island, Allison lowered her window and flashed a smile at the security guard. He waved at her and raised the striped barrier. She followed a curve, made a turn, and pulled off the street into a grassy area beside a high hedge. Tom recalled that the Barlowe house was around the corner.

"I'll let you out here, okay? Tell Larry your friend dropped you off. But don't get out yet. I need to ask you something." He could see himself doubled in her dark glasses. She turned on the seat, and the little red sweater fell open; a thin white top underneath. No bra. Tom shifted his eyes to the leather-wrapped steering wheel. Her hand on the gearshift. Pink nail polish. Sunlight flickered through the palm fronds.

Allison's voice was softer now. "Tom? I've been trying to get in touch with Jenny Gray. She's a friend of yours, isn't she? Do you know how I can reach her?"

"Why are you looking for Jenny?"

A little sigh. "Well, there's this case I'm handling for her. I really can't get into it. Attorney-client. You know. But I do need to tie up some loose ends, or she might not ever be permitted back into the U.S."

"She left the States?"

"I'm sure of it." Allison took off the glasses. Big brown eyes. Innocent little me. "I went by her apartment yesterday, and a neighbor told me he'd seen a pile of her stuff in the trash, and the next day she gave him the food out of her fridge and took a taxi for the airport. She's definitely gone."

"I didn't know that," he said.

"Well, I thought since you're going to London, you

might have made plans to see her. You don't have her phone number? She didn't give you her address?"

"No, she never said. That's too bad. Gee, if I'd known she'd be in London, I'd have asked. We could hook up."

The smile stayed in place. "Are you lying to me?"

"No."

"You know what? I think you are. I also think you might be lying to my father. I don't believe anybody can make an exact copy of the Corelli, but I'll give you the benefit of the doubt. You'd better not disappoint him. I know a fake when I see it."

Tom smiled back. "What are you going to do, Allison? Make me file reports? Look over my shoulder? Knock on my door checking up on me? Nuh-uh. You want to go to Europe, hey, have a good time. But please stay out of my way. I'll show you the map when I'm finished with it."

He reached for the door handle, but she hit the child-proof lock. "As hard as it might be for you, Tom, you have to follow the rules. Otherwise, as far as I'm concerned, the deal is off."

He looked around at her. "Are you running the show now?"

"Yes, I am."

"Okay. Here are the rules. I do my job, and you leave me alone. When I see you at the airport, you give me another five thousand in cash. I want fifteen a week after that, and the balance of twenty-five on delivery, if your father is satisfied with the map. Expenses are separate, payable on demand. That's the deal. Thanks for the hotel, but I'll find my own. Unlock the door."

She took a breath through her teeth. "If you dare try

to scam my father, I'll have you arrested for fraud and grand theft."

He got out with his backpack, then leaned down to say, "See you in London. Enjoy your flight."

The tires on the roadster left long black curves on the street.

CHAPTER 11

Larry Gerard used the guest cottage on his mother's and Stuart's property as a storeroom for his boat. Beach towels, lantern batteries and propane, plastic cups, liquor, a crank radio. He would throw it all into a cart and push it along the brick path that went past the tennis court to the seawall.

Today he jogged to the boat. He had to get under way by five o'clock to reach Bimini before dark. The harbor was tricky at night, and Larry wanted to top off the tanks. On his first trip to Nassau, running at fifty knots, he had bypassed Bimini and wound up drifting for three hours before Sea Tow showed up with some fuel and a credit card receipt for a thousand dollars.

Huffing from exertion, Larry stopped the cart on the dock. Marek Vuksinic lounged in the captain's seat with his foot on the helm, enjoying the breeze. Larry's mother hadn't been happy about his showing up, but Larry had asked her what the hell he could do about it. With The Metropolis funding still at the handshake stage, was Larry supposed to tell Marek he couldn't go?

Rhonda put up with Marek because she thought he'd come over to look at plans for the penthouse. That was all she knew. Larry wished he knew less. He would jerk awake in the middle of the night, sweating through his sheets, hearing the dull crunch of a woman's neck being broken, and Marek turning his own head just enough to keep his cigarette out of the way.

Larry held out an armful of seat cushions. "Hey. Marek. Take these, will you?"

"Sure, sure." He set his beer bottle in the holder on the captain's bench. When they were finished attaching the cushions and stowing everything else below deck, Larry came topside. His watch showed 4:52 PM. He looked at the house. Nobody on the terrace, nobody walking across the lawn.

In the stern Marek stretched out and turned his face toward the sun, which was sinking fast. The buildings downtown, five miles to the southwest, stood out starkly against the clear sky. There would be no moon tonight, nothing but channel markers to guide a boat through the narrow, rocky entrance to Bimini harbor.

Going below again, Larry took a beer from the small refrigerator under the sink, opened it, and washed down two OxyContins. He lifted his billed cap and blotted his forehead with a napkin. Standing in the galley, he could look up the steps and see legs in a pair of dark green Tommy Bahama pants. Brown leather sandals and socks. One hairy forearm reaching down, a hand grabbing the pack of Marlboros and a plastic lighter off the deck.

Just past noon Joe had called to ask if Larry had heard the news. Carla's body had been found. Joe had wanted to know what they were going to do now, what if this, what if that. Larry had told him not to worry; they had left nothing out there in the Glades, nobody could reliably put them with Carla that night. Larry talked it over with Marek, who said the same thing. Even so, Larry was about to jump out of his skin.

Marek's presence complicated the job Larry had to do for his mother: Get the Corelli from Tom Fairchild. Use persuasion if possible, force if necessary. Don't do anything permanent, Rhonda had said. Just take the map. She would deal with Stuart.

With Marek Vuksinic on board, she'd thought it would be better to discreetly take the map out of the tube and drop it over the side after dark. With luck, Fairchild wouldn't know it was missing until he got to London. Then it would be too late. Larry drank his beer and thought of ways that that could be accomplished. It would be easier if Fairchild went over too, but that would be difficult to explain.

He heard Marek calling him. "Larry?"

"Is he here?" Larry went up the steps.

"No. I have to tell you something." Marek lay with his ankles crossed, his head resting on a bent arm. "I killed Joe today. I'm sorry."

"You . . . what?" Larry hadn't heard him right; he couldn't have.

"I had to do it. Joe was too scared. A guy like that makes problems. Not for me—I won't be here, but for you, yes. So today when you went to get food for the boat, I walked to his apartment. I used a knife. I left some of your pills and cocaine for the police to find. Don't worry. No one saw me. No fingerprints. And you have good alibi from Epicure Market. Yes?"

Slowly, carefully, Larry lowered himself into the captain's bench, grasping for something to hold on to.

Words came softly from under Marek's mustache, which shifted as he smiled. "Don't be afraid. You're my friend. Your parents are friends of Leo." Marek took a puff on his cigarette. The wind took the smoke. "This is why I am bringing all my suitcases, my new clothes and everything, on the boat. I'm leaving America." He put his fist to his heart. "You are excellent host. Thank you. I had super wonderful time in Miami."

Tom followed Rhonda Barlowe and her apricot Pekingese down a wide, terra-cotta hallway that extended off the living room. Her loose, white silk pants moved around her legs as she walked. She was tall and athletic, with a sway to her hips. He couldn't see a panty line.

Tom said, "I'm supposed to be on the boat by five o'clock."

"Don't worry about it. Larry won't mind waiting a few minutes."

The Peke's fur hung nearly to the floor, and its tail waved like the feathered crest on a helmet. It broke into a run every few steps to keep up with its owner. Finally they arrived at a large, wainscoted room, where the low sun came through wooden louvers and painted stripes on the red walls. A switch was pressed, and small spotlights in the ceiling shone on framed antique maps. The dog jumped onto an armchair, where it sat snorting softly through its flat nose. A long table had been placed in the center of the room, and one wall was taken up with shallow cabinets, not metal ones like Rose had at the shop, but polished oak.

"This is Stuart's map room," said his wife.

"I see that." Tom slid his backpack off his shoulders and pivoted for a look around. He came to a conclusion:

Rose had been right. Some fine examples of cartography, but Barlowe didn't know squat about organizing a collection. A woodcut map of India hung next to a baroque map of Holland, which followed a sea chart of the South Pacific.

"Tom?" Mrs. Barlowe's golden blond hair swooped off her forehead and curled to her shoulders. Her lips were full, her skin slightly shiny. A white V-neck sweater revealed a braided gold necklace and a lot of cleavage. "This isn't going to be easy for me to talk about." She touched his arm. "You don't mind if I speak frankly, do you, Tom?"

"No, ma'am."

"Oh!" She rolled her eyes and smiled. Her forehead seemed unnaturally smooth. "Please call me Rhonda."

Tom nodded.

"I'm worried about my husband. This is strictly between us, okay? He's not well. I'll go ahead and tell you—he's been under the care of a doctor."

"He's not—"

"No, no, no. He's perfectly *fine*, physically, but he has become . . . I hate to say *obsessed*, but what other word is there? It's this map. The Corelli. Yes, I know all about it, Tom. What he wants you to do. Where he's sending you. How much he said he'd pay for a copy. Old paper, old ink. You have to admit, it's bizarre."

Her eyes were the same shade of blue that Tom used for hand-coloring sea charts, and outlined in black, like India ink. She came nearer, lowering her voice to the level appropriate for a hospital corridor. "Stuart has been so distraught about Royce Herron. They'd been friends for many years. Stuart loaned Royce some maps to put in an exhibit at the map fair. Thieves broke in, and Royce was holding the Corelli map when they shot him. I think that Stuart subconsciously feels a certain amount of guilt. He can't bring the man back to life, but he can restore the map. That's only my theory, but if you knew Stuart as I do, I think you'd agree."

With no idea where this was headed, Tom said, "Why are you telling me this?"

"I'm asking you not to go through with it."

"You mean, forget about the map?"

"Stuart has already paid you ten thousand dollars. Let's see what else we can do." She squeezed his arm, then crossed the room to a writing desk a couple of hundred years old. From the chair the dog watched her with its glossy black, protuberant eyes. She produced a key from her pocket, inserted it into a lock, and opened a drawer. Tom saw stacks of hundreds. She set them in a neat row on the desk.

Tom said, "What are you doing, Mrs. Barlowe?"

"I'm giving you another ten thousand dollars."

With a laugh, he said, "Why?"

"You're going to leave the Corelli map with me and walk away a happy man. Did you bring it? Is it in your backpack?"

"Mr. Barlowe doesn't know what you're doing, does he?"

"I'll take the blame. He won't be angry at you." She bent one of the banded stacks and let it ruffle past her thumb. "Easiest money you ever made."

"That's a tempting offer," Tom admitted.

"Tax free."

"Uh-huh. I don't know. He really wants the map."

"Are you demanding the entire amount? I won't pay it."

"No, I wasn't suggesting that," Tom said.

Above the desk hung an early-seventeenth-century map of Northern Europe in a gold frame. Acanthus leaves, fruit, birds, cherubs, and small animals filled the borders. It must have cost a master engraver months of work with a magnifying glass, etching every hair-thin line onto a polished copperplate—backward.

"Take the money, Tom. You won't get a penny more even if you do finish the map."

"Why won't I?"

Her laugh carried a breath of impatience. "You're a graphic artist, and I'm sure you're very good at what you do. I saw the little map you made for your sister's shop, but Tom, a folio-size Renaissance map isn't that easy. Do you really believe that you can make a duplicate so convincing that no one, not even an expert, could tell the difference?"

It was a fancy way of insulting his talent, but Tom had asked himself the same question. He replied, "I guess we'll find out."

"Oh, please. Be honest with yourself. Stuart wants a perfect copy. Perfect. Indistinguishable from the original. That's what he told you. Isn't it?"

"You know . . . this is kind of shabby."

She stiffened. "Meaning what?"

"To go behind a man's back. I have a problem with that."

"Are you moralizing to me, Tom? I'm not the one with the criminal record."

He stared at her.

She grabbed the money in both hands and shoved it into his chest. "Don't be a fool. Take it."

He pushed past her, picked up his backpack, and swung it over his shoulder. The little dog in the chair threw back its head and barked.

Rhonda Barlowe crossed the room. "Where are you going?"

"Nassau."

She sent him a chilly smile. "Bon voyage."

CHAPTER 12

Even sitting motionless at the seawall, the boat was fast. Forty feet of gleaming white muscle with a long nose, a swept-back windshield, and a forward-thrusting radar arch. As he came closer, Tom heard the grumble of diesel engines and saw two men on board preparing to cast off. This told him that somebody had called from the house to say the passenger was on his way. The dark-haired man in the stern held on to a piling to keep the boat from drifting; a man on the foredeck loosened the bowline, a pudgy man in khaki pants and a blue knit shirt, a billed cap pulled low over his sunglasses. Tom hadn't seen him in fifteen years: Laurence Gerard.

Tom stood on the dock with his hands around the straps of his backpack. "Larry. Sorry I'm late, man. I got into a conversation with your mother."

Tossing the line to the seawall, Larry told Tom to get in. Tom went aft and stepped onto the swim platform, then up to a walk-through that took him to the cockpit. The other man was squinting into the sun, but his dark eyes followed Tom as he boarded. Aside from a loud shirt and green pants, the man wore socks with his sandals. That and the wiry salt-and-pepper mustache said he was European, possibly Greek.

Tom gave him a nod. "How's it going?"

No reply.

Larry swung around the radar arch, jumped down to the cockpit, and went to the captain's seat at the helm. Standing at the wheel he toggled the bow thruster, which swung the front of the boat away from the dock. With a push on the throttles, La Gorce Island quickly fell behind them. Water splashed on the hull as the boat zipped along at about twice the legal no-wake speed.

"Tom, this is Marek," Larry said cheerfully. "He's from Croatia, over here on business. I thought he'd like to come along for the ride."

With another nod to Larry's unlikely companion, Tom shrugged out of his backpack.

"There's beer in the cooler there. Liquor's in the galley. We've got meat, cheese, bread, shrimp. What else? Tortellini salad, which I made myself this morning. We'll make a stop in Bimini for fuel, but we're not getting off until we reach Nassau. Go ahead and put your bag below."

Narrow steps descended to the cabin. Tom looked behind a curtain and saw a sleeping compartment with a double bed, satin-covered pillows, and a flat-screen TV bolted to the polished teak bulkhead. Opposite the compact stove and refrigerator, he opened a narrow door and found a compartment with a pump-toilet, a sink, and a handheld shower spray. He carried his backpack to the V-shape of cushioned seating in the bow. A box of groceries, a small leather duffel, and three big black suitcases were already stacked there. Each of the suitcases was bound with a buckled strap and a lock. No name tags, but Tom didn't think they were Larry's. A lot of luggage for a one-day trip.

By the time he came topside the boat had exited the passage between North Bay Village and Golden Isles. The route would take them up the bay to the channel under Haulover Bridge, then into the Atlantic. With a Guinness from the cooler, Tom sat on the captain's bench beside Larry rather than in the back with his friend, who so far hadn't opened his mouth. Sunlight winked off the windows of the waterfront houses on Miami Beach. A fairly stiff wind came from the east. The temperature was around seventy-two, not a cloud to be seen.

The weather in Easthampton had been like this the last summer with Allison. She had taken him with her for a weekend to the home of another girl from Barnard and introduced him as a friend from Miami. They put him in an attic room usually occupied by one of the younger brothers, who had already left to do his fall semester in Barcelona.

There were ten young people in the house that weekend. The girl's grandfather took them all on his sixty-year-old teak sailing yacht up Long Island Sound. Tom had caught on fast to the balance between the sails and the wind, and the old man had left him at the wheel for most of the trip. That night they wore sweaters for a cookout on the beach. Everyone got drunk. Allison's friends talked about a bar on the Vineyard, who couldn't get into Brown, and wasn't that party last weekend just gross? Tom rolled joints and kept the fire going, his little contribution to the party. Walking back over the dunes with some firewood, he overheard Allison telling another girl that he was hot, but they weren't, like, *serious* or anything. Tom tossed the firewood, went back to the house, packed up, and hitchhiked to the train station. Allison caught up with him as the last train to Grand Central that night was pulling out. She'd left her suitcase behind. She sat beside him; he moved to another seat; she followed. Finally he put his arm around her, and she cried and said she loved him and please, Tom, please forgive me.

"So what's up?" Larry asked, as though they'd last seen each other a week ago.

"Not much."

Larry talked about his new boat. The GPS and satellite dish. Larry's Rolex, which the boat dealer had thrown in to sweeten the offer. Larry's restaurant, which would be called The Mariner's Club. Somebody had suggested Chez Gerard, but Larry wanted an unpretentious ambience.

As they glided north, Tom zoned out and replayed the scene with Larry's mother. He had just walked away from a sure $10,000 in cash. He had turned down Rhonda Barlowe's offer not because she'd been wrong but because she'd been a bitch. If she had stuck to her story about wanting to help her husband get past his grief, Tom might have taken the ten grand. Or not. Tom didn't like being lied to. Stuart Barlowe wasn't torn up over Judge Herron's death. This left Tom wondering what Rhonda was really after, and if it mattered. He thought about what to say to Stuart Barlowe. Decided it could wait till he reached Nassau. Or better still, until he got to London and collected more of his fee from Allison.

Turning to see how far they'd come, Tom saw the

man in the back watching him. The wind lifted his hair, showing the gray at his temples and a groove over his ear, like a bullet had creased his skull. His small, dark eyes shifted away as he cupped his hands and lit a cigarette.

Larry stood up. "Tom, can you take the wheel for a minute? I need to use the head. Keep it between the channel markers. Red triangles on your left." He paused at the cooler and opened a bottle of Heineken on the way down the steps.

The man—Marek—came forward to sit with Tom on the bench. For something to say, Tom asked him, "Your first time in Miami?"

"Yes, but I want to come back. I love the weather. Also the nightclubs."

"You're from Croatia. What city?"

"Dubrovnik. It's on the coast, near to Italy. Many islands. I have a boat, not so big as this one. I love to go fishing."

"There was a war over there," Tom remembered.

"Always a war." Laughing, Marek aimed his thick forefinger at Tom's head like a pistol. "We are fighting five hundred years to get Muslims out of our country. For this, America and the United Nations tore us into little countries, and now you are killing Muslims. A funny world, isn't it?"

"Hilarious." Tom said, "You were in the army?"

"Yugoslav army. It's kaput. Finished."

"What do you do now? In Dubrovnik."

Marek paused, his cigarette at his mouth. "I sell equipment and parts for heavy trucks, for construction. And you're a map dealer."

Tom hesitated, then said, "That's right. I buy and sell antique maps." He guided the cruiser around a two-masted sailboat named *Odd-e-Sea*. The names people come up with.

The wind swirled cigarette ash over the top of the windshield. Marek said, "You're going to Nassau for map business?"

Tom looked around. The man had eyes the color of used crankcase oil. "That's right. For Larry's stepfather, Stuart Barlowe. He's a collector."

"To buy maps?"

"Maybe."

"Will you see Oscar?"

"Oscar?"

Marek waited for some other answer.

Tom said, "I don't know any Oscars."

"How much is he paying you?"

Tom said, "Excuse me?"

"How much? You are working for Oscar or for Larry?"

"What are you talking about?"

This might have produced a smile. Tom couldn't see past the mustache. Marek had turned on the seat to look directly at Tom, and his arm lay across the back. He came closer. "I was in prison, too. In Bosnia. Only for a year and six months, then they let me out. They didn't have evidence."

"Who told you I was in prison?" Tom demanded.

"I know a lot about you," Marek said.

This conversation had taken a turn toward the weird. Tom leaned past him to yell down the steps. "Larry! We're getting close to the Haulover Bridge. Your turn."

When Larry came topside, he wore a Windbreaker. Tom moved to the cockpit. Marek did the same, taking the corner seat in the cockpit. Noticing the whitecaps ahead, Tom sat as far forward as he could get. The ride would be rougher in the back. Tom decided to let Marek find out for himself.

Haulover Park had a marina on the bay side, a beach on the other. In the old days, before a deep channel had been dredged, the narrow piece of land was a place where a small boat could be hauled over to the ocean. Larry fell in line with another boat under the bridge, but about a hundred yards clear of land, he turned around and yelled, "Hang on, crew!"

He shoved the throttles forward, and the big engines roared in response. The bow shot up, left the water completely, then slammed down and leveled into a plane at fifty-plus miles an hour. Tom grabbed the handhold on the back of the captain's bench. He figured two minutes of this rock and roll before Larry was forced to cut the speed.

Larry's hat flew off, and his bottle fell out of the holder and spun beer across the deck. Tom's feet left the floor each time the boat dropped from crest to trough. *Thud thud thud.* Marek slid off the bench, crawled to the walk-through in the transom, and heaved. Tom hit Larry on the shoulder and pointed. Larry saw the mess and threw the engines into reverse.

The boat came to a stop, wallowing drunkenly in the waves. Marek staggered below.

Larry threw his empty bottle overboard and hosed off the deck, cursing. He kicked the hose back into its cabinet. Looking at his watch, he said, "Goddammit!" He ran a hand over his head. "Did you see my hat?"

"Yeah, it went overboard about a mile back."

"Shit!" Larry got back in his seat and found a speed where the boat rocked but didn't fly off the waves.

After a while Tom said, "You think he's okay?"

"I hope he flushes himself down the goddamn crapper." Larry folded his sunglasses into a case and pitched them into a compartment under the wheel. The light was fading. "Give me another beer, would you?"

Holding on to the helm, Tom made his way to the cooler and grabbed two of them. He returned to his seat beside Larry, whose thinning brown hair swirled in the wind. Faint stars appeared in the sky, and stripes of purple lay over the horizon. A sailboat a couple of miles distant vanished behind a container ship heading south.

"Your friend is a strange dude," Tom said.

"Yeah."

"What's he doing in Miami?"

Larry swallowed some beer. "He's looking at real estate. He's interested in buying a couple of units at The Metropolis."

"The truck parts business must be pretty good." When Larry only looked at him, Tom added, "He said he sold truck parts in Croatia."

"He's into a lot of things." Larry jerked his chin toward the cabin access. "Go tell him there's some Dramamine in the first aid kit. Look in the nightstand next to the bed."

Tom went down the steps and saw Marek in the bow with his back turned. He had changed his clothes. Red flowers now, and black pants. Tom was about to speak to him when he noticed his backpack on the table. Marek was sliding the zipper down one side.

"What are you doing?"

Bracing himself against the jerky movement of the boat, Marek turned and looked at Tom without embarrassment. His head nearly reached the cabin roof.

"I said, what are you doing? Why were you opening my bag?" Tom grabbed it off the table and staggered with the weight as the deck tilted.

Marek shrugged. "I am curious about you."

"Keep your hands off." Leaning against the sink, Tom rode the movement of the boat. "Who are you? Why are you on this boat?"

"I want to know why you're going to Nassau."

"I told you. Stuart Barlowe is sending me. What is your problem?"

Marek braced himself on the arm of the seat. In the weak light through the porthole, his skin looked gray. His forehead shone with sweat. He was close to needing another trip to the head. "Tell me the name of the man you will see. The man with the maps."

"I'm not telling you a damned thing." The boat moved, and Marek took another step, possibly to catch his balance, but Tom dropped his backpack and went into a half crouch.

"Tough guy." Marek laughed, a flash of small teeth with gaps between. Then his face went white, and he grimaced.

Tom laughed. "You going to be sick again? Larry won't like it if you puke on the carpet."

The man staggered to the head. Tom heard him dry-heaving in there. Then some coughs. Water ran. Tom zipped his backpack closed and shoved it under the table. Marek reappeared. He stood in the narrow doorway mopping his face with a towel, which he threw back inside. His teeth showed under his mustache. "We'll talk some more in Nassau."

"Go take a walk off the back of the boat," Tom said.

With a malevolent grin over his shoulder, Marek went up the steps.

Tom leaned against the table and took some deep breaths, trying to figure this out. Insanity seemed like a reasonable explanation. The guy was a lunatic. Then he dropped to one knee, pulled the backpack from under the table, and unzipped the main compartment. He felt inside. The map tube was still there. He took one end off and saw the spiral of antique ivory-colored paper.

Tom didn't know what Marek had been looking for, but one theory made sense. Rhonda Barlowe wanted the Corelli map, and she had sent this thug along to make sure she got it. Or it could have been Larry's idea. He couldn't steal the map on his own; he needed help. This made sense except for one thing: the strange questions Marek had asked him. *Will you see Oscar? How much are they paying you?*

The pitch of the engines increased. Everything in the cabin bounced as the boat crashed against the sea: the table vibrated; dishes clattered; anchor chain clanked in the hold. They would arrive in Bimini soon, refuel, and go on to Nassau. One hundred and twenty-five miles of open water. And then what? Without the map, Tom had nothing.

It wouldn't be a bad idea, he thought, to hide it himself. Whichever one came below the next time might think the other had taken it. At least it would slow them down. He glanced around the cabin. He lifted one of the bench seats and found a storage space with rope and rain gear inside. Closed it. He opened other cabinets and drawers, then noticed the sleeping compartment. He scrambled across the slick satin comforter and drove the map tube between the bulkhead and the mattress.

When he went topside, both men looked at him. Marek sat on the side bench with his arms spread over the back of it and a cigarette protruding from his mustache. The wind lifted the hem of his red flowered shirt, revealing a barrel torso with a mat of black hair.

Larry gave his empty beer bottle to Tom and asked for a replacement.

Tom pitched the bottle into the trash and opened the cooler.

A second later he was going backward, his feet dragging across the deck. A thick arm was around his neck, the elbow at his larynx, the bicep and forearm squeezing his throat, cutting off the blood to his head. He dug his fingers into the arm. He'd been grabbed like this before, by a Latin Kings gang member in the Dade County jail. In seconds he would pass out.

He thrashed his legs and heard Larry shouting.

Then he was conscious of being underwater. A fist held the back of his pullover, and as the boat moved up and down, the waves swirled over his head. He lay on the walk-through to the swim platform. The boat dipped again, and he held his breath for the next wave. He came up coughing.

Then somebody grabbed his legs and pulled. His chin hit the step, and his teeth came together on the side of his tongue. His shirt scraped up his abdomen. He was dumped on the floor of the cockpit. He rolled over and spat out seawater and blood.

Larry was screaming, "What the fuck? What the fuck was that?"

Marek flicked water off his hands. His cigarette still hung from his mouth, still lit. "He needed a walk off the back of the boat. Some fresh air."

Tom sprang to his feet and came for him. In two seconds, he was on the deck again, and a fist was poised to break his cheekbone. Then Marek smiled and patted his shoulder. "A joke. It's only a joke. Look, my knees are wet!"

When Tom got up again, Larry held on to his arm. His eyes were wild. "Don't do it, man. Let it go. He'll kill you. Just leave it. Tom, leave it!"

Tom went below and stripped off his clothes, transferring everything from the pockets of his wet cargo pants to dry ones: passport, wallet, address book, cash. Drops of water leaked out of his cell phone. He pushed buttons, but the screen stayed dark. He thought of throwing Marek's suitcases overboard, then thought better of it.

The sun was no more than a vague wash of orange in the west when the low spot of land called Bimini emerged from the sea, first the channel markers, then pinpoints of light onshore. On a map, the island looked like an empty triangle: one island at the bottom, another on the west, and low-lying marshland making up the rest of it. Most of the people lived on the western strip called North Bimini.

Tom had been here a couple of times with Eddie to fish. They had stayed at one of the cheap hotels in Alice Town and drank at a bar that Ernest Hemingway had gone to. The island had been a drug runner's rendezvous in the 1980s, Eddie had told him, but the DEA put a stop to that. As the lights drew closer, Tom remembered the layout of North Bimini: There were marinas and bars on the east side, facing the harbor and shops on King Street, the only main road. The police station in a one-story pink building. Cinder-block houses with tin roofs, chickens in the yards. Everything within walking distance.

As they approached the narrow channel between the islands, Larry cut the speed and told Tom to take the spotlight forward and look for rocks. Following the beam of light, the boat went straight, then took a hard turn to port, coming up the east side of the island. Past the entrance, Tom clicked off the spotlight and sat cross-legged on the bow. They passed the Blue Marlin Hotel, then a couple of waterfront bars with loud music, then the Sea Crest Motel, where Tom and Eddie had stayed.

Larry finally pulled up next to a run-down dock about half a mile north of the port of entry, avoiding customs inspectors, Tom assumed. An old Bahamian in an unbuttoned shirt and rubber thong sandals got up from a folding chair at the fuel pumps. Cutting the engines, Larry shot a dark look at Marek and said they were lucky to have made it. Another ten minutes, the pumps would have been closed. Tom went forward and tossed the old man a line, which he looped over a piling. Larry did the same at the stern.

Marek stepped off and said he would be back; he wanted to get some chips. Light came through the screened windows of the marina store; a woman laughed; someone spoke with a heavy island accent. Larry opened the fuel access hatch in the stern so the attendant could get at it with the hose. Numbers spun on the old-fashioned pump, and a bell rang for every gallon.

Standing on the side of the boat, Tom took a look around. A floodlight under a metal shade lit the cockpit, but a shadow fell across the foredeck, cast by a head-high stack of lobster traps on the dock. A wooden lobster boat was tied just ahead of Larry's cruiser. Beyond that some dinghies lay quietly in the unmoving water. Then the rocky shore, a wooden shed, some coconut palms and scrubby pine trees, and a gravel parking lot that fronted King Street, which, if Tom remembered correctly, led south to Alice Town.

"Larry, you mind if I have some of your tortellini salad?"

"Help yourself," Larry said from the dock. "Make me a plate while you're at it. Try the shrimp, too. I used jerk seasoning."

Tom went below. He looked up at the ventilation hatches. Two small hatches forward, two bigger ones in the galley. He put his hands on the hatch above his head and estimated twelve inches wide, thirty inches long. The cover was down, held in place by two metal rods with black handles that tightened against the frame. Tom went over to his backpack, removed most of his underwear and a fleece pullover, and shoved them out of sight under the table. He retrieved the map tube from behind the mattress in the sleeping compartment, put it into the half-empty bag, zipped it up, and tightened the straps as far as they would go.

He remembered the rope he'd seen under one of the forward seats. In a drawer near the sink he found a chef's knife and cut off about six feet of it, which he tied to the top handle of his backpack. Then he got on top of the counter with the knife, crouching to slice the hatch screen close to the metal frame. He unscrewed the hatch locks, pushed, and slowly raised the cover. The angle wasn't right, but he could get his arms, then his shoulders, through. Hands on the deck, he pushed up and saw Larry watching the pump dial spin. Marek stood in the stern opening a bag of Cheez Curls.

Having lost his footing on the sink, Tom had to swing over and feel for it before dropping to the cabin floor. With the rope between his teeth, he climbed back on the sink and went up again, this time bringing his legs out as well. Through the windshield he saw Marek turn and walk toward the cooler. Tom flattened himself on the deck, a darker shape in the shadows.

He heard the clanking of glass, then a lid closing. The nozzle being hung back on the pump. The old Bahamian said, "One hundred twenty-eight dollars."

In a minute or two they would cast off. Lying on his stomach, Tom pulled the rope hand over hand up the hatch. The backpack swung free, came closer . . . then caught. He pulled harder. A strap had snagged on one of the hatch locks. He cursed for not having pushed the bag through first. He reached an arm through and felt for the strap. The boat dipped slightly as Larry stepped onto it.

Tom lowered the backpack and tried again to pull it through. He felt the vibrations of the engines, heard the splash of water at the stern. Larry said, "Marek. Go untie the stern line, then get the one at the bow."

"Where is Tom?"

"He's down below getting something to eat."

Tom had the top of the backpack out. He pulled and jerked but it remained stuck. He saw the problem. The hatch was narrower at one end. The bag wouldn't fit through unless he took more out, and there was no time. Tom's mind raced over a list of things in it that couldn't be replaced. Gripping the top handle, he opened the zipper far enough to take out the map tube. He let go, and the bag fell away.

Staying low, Tom scooted to the railing and stepped onto the dock. He went behind the lobster traps, got his bearings, and ran.

CHAPTER 13

At Claridge's, a man in a greatcoat and top hat opened the taxi door as Allison paid the driver. She had just come from Victoria Station after a half-hour train ride from Gatwick Airport, preceded by a fruitless hour waiting outside customs in the faint hope that Tom Fairchild might, after all, have been on the 8:55 AM flight from Kingston, Jamaica. Allison hadn't expected him to show up, but Stuart had asked her to go and make sure.

Tom had called Stuart from Jamaica at two o'clock yesterday morning. Allison had only heard it second-hand, from Stuart, but he'd said Tom had asked him what in hell was going on; that somebody had tried to kill him; that he was stuck in Jamaica, and what was Stuart going to do about it? At first Stuart had thought Tom was drunk. It had taken a half hour of apologies and begging before Tom had said he might consider finishing the map. Or he might not.

And now? Gone. Tom Fairchild had vanished. He had taken the Corelli map and disappeared with it. Allison's mood was as gray as the weather, not only for wasting three hours when she could have been snuggling under a down-filled duvet, but more for the distress she'd heard in her father's voice, and for having trusted Tom Fairchild when she'd known better.

As she stepped from the taxi, a gust of wind flipped back the fur-trimmed edge of her coat and threatened to dislodge her red beret. Holding it on, she looked up at the five-story brick facade of the hotel, with its white marble columns, colorful flags, and filigreed iron portico. The doorman touched the brim of his hat, and Allison found herself smiling as she hurried to the entrance.

She was staying at Claridge's because her family had always stayed at Claridge's. Her grandparents had honeymooned here. Her father stayed here when he came to London on business. Once, when she was ten, and Rhonda had wanted her out of the way for a week, Allison had come, too. She had tagged along to a bank or a government office, so glad to be with him that she hadn't thought for a moment of being bored.

But this trip to London would be cut short. It would be best, she had decided, to go straight back to Miami. The concierge could arrange a flight. Othello wouldn't know what to think, seeing her back so soon. Allison had left him with Fernanda at Stuart's house, told him to stay inside the fence, leave the birds alone, and she'd be back in two weeks. Now the poor cat would be stuck in the condo again, gazing through the tenth-floor window.

Gloves in hand, Allison pushed through the revolving doors to the lobby. An immense Art Deco chandelier gleamed on the checkerboard marble floor, and a fireplace burned cheerfully opposite the wide, curving staircase. People came and went, putting on coats and hats as they walked toward the street. Allison went straight on toward an arch that led to the elevators.

She became aware of a movement, someone getting up from an armchair near the fireplace, walking quickly in her direction. Her eyes went to the blue logo on the front of his sweatshirt: Toronto Maple Leafs. His hair was sticking up, and he needed a shave. His cargo pants were grimy, and a knit cap hung out of one pocket.

"Tom!"

"Good thing you showed up when you did," he said. "The management was about to throw me out of here."

"How did I miss you at Gatwick? I was right outside customs. Didn't you see me?"

"I wasn't at Gatwick. I got in at Heathrow about the same time on a flight from Canada."

"I don't understand," Allison said. "Why did you take another flight? You could have flown straight here from Jamaica."

"It's been an interesting trip," Tom said. "Nice coat. Leave it on. We're going to a bank."

"A bank?"

"That was the deal, remember? Upon arrival in London, I get another five grand, plus expenses. Does your father still want the map?"

"Of course he does. You could have called," she said. "Why didn't you? We've been trying to reach you ever since yesterday. My father is frantic."

"My cell phone was full of seawater," Tom said. With a hand on her elbow, he turned her toward the entrance. "I'll tell you about it later. Right now, I need some money, and I need to get some sleep."

She pulled backward. "What have you done with the map? Where is it?"

"Don't worry, it's safe." His hand tightened on her arm. "Let's go."

"Not until you tell me what's going on."

One of the hotel staff was watching them intently. Tom said, "You want answers? I want to be paid what's due. Or I can leave right now, and you can tell Stuart he's not getting his map back."

Allison made a face of utter disgust. "I knew this was a mistake."

On the street, a misting, icy rain shone on the pavement. Allison took a small umbrella from her tote and hit the button to pop it open. Tom pulled his blue knit cap from his pocket. A Maple Leafs logo was on the front of that, too. Hands in his pockets, he hunched his shoulders against the cold.

"Where's your coat?" she asked.

He laughed, and the vapor puffed out of his mouth.

She shook her head at the doorman who gestured toward the boxy, black taxi at the curb. "My father wants the map, so I'll pay you the five thousand—as long as you can convince me I should. There's a tea shop on the next corner. We can talk there."

"The tea is on you," Tom said. "I'm running short of cash."

They were shown to a small, wooden table by the lace-curtained window. Allison ordered a pot of Earl Grey and tea biscuits. It was early for lunch, but Tom wanted a roast beef sandwich, which he ate greedily as he told her why he had gotten off the boat in Bimini.

Allison's tea went cold in her cup as she listened. She interrupted to say, "It's hard to believe you were in *danger*. I mean, he wasn't really trying to drown you."

"Well, Allison, I guess you just had to be there," Tom said.

"And you're sure he was trying to steal the map?"

"I couldn't take the chance. Who is that guy, anyway? He told me he sells truck parts in Dubrovnik, then Larry told me he was looking to buy apartments in The Metropolis."

"Marek's last name is . . . I can't remember, but Larry told me he's a friend of one of his customers at the restaurant. I've met him. I can't say I liked him, but I don't think he's a psycho."

Tom used a toothpick to pick up the last bits of meat. "Marek was in the Yugoslav army shooting at Muslims. He spent eighteen months in prison. Might have been for using civilians for target practice."

Filling their cups with more tea, Allison said, "This is so different from what Larry told my father."

"I'll bet it is."

"Larry thinks you stole the map, and you were going to hold it for ransom or something."

"You told me he didn't know about the map."

"Well, he does," she said. "Rhonda probably told him."

In the gray light that came through the small panes of glass, Tom's eyes were so green. Looking at him across the table, Allison could see the changes that twelve years had made. His blond-stubbled cheeks were leaner. The lines at the corners had become permanent, and the crease to the left of his mouth had deepened. Allison remembered that his smiles began on the left. His lips were fuller than a man deserved.

He raised his brows. "What?"

"You have some mayo on your chin," she lied. "Right there."

He swiped it with his thumb, then picked up his napkin. "Does the name 'Oscar' mean anything to you? Did Larry ever mention anyone named Oscar? Maybe in connection with The Metropolis?"

"No. Why?"

"Marek asked me if I was going to see Oscar in Nassau. He asked if I was working for him or for Larry. What does that mean?"

"I have no idea." She watched Tom drink from the little porcelain cup. His knuckles were scraped.

When she lifted her eyes, they met his. The left side of Tom's mouth curved up. He said, "I like the red beret. It's cute with the glasses."

"Oh. Thanks."

"You're looking good," he said.

She shrugged.

"I mean it. You are."

Breaking eye contact, Allison chose one of the tea biscuits on the plate. "What will you do after the bank?"

"Buy some thermal underwear. Catch up on my sleep."

"You have a reservation at the Bayswater. I didn't cancel it."

"No, thanks. After what I went through, I want a place where they bring me breakfast in bed."

"Where will you stay?"

"I don't know yet," he said.

"Are you going to tell me?"

"Soon as I buy a cell phone."

"When are we going to Italy?" she asked.

"Probably Monday. I'm not sure."

"What city? I can book the flights for us."

"I'll let you know, Allison. I'm still working all that out, okay?"

She put her hands on her hips and mocked his baritone voice. " 'Don't worry, Allison, I've got it all under control.' "

He gave her a sharp look. "Exactly right—starting at the bank."

"You're not getting cash. My father made arrangements for a Barclays bank card. All I have to do is transfer the money to your account."

"Five thousand plus expenses," Tom said.

"Yes, plus expenses."

He scooted back from the table far enough to reach into his thigh pocket for a small notebook. He flipped to a page with a perfectly straight column of numbers in fine-point black ink. Beside each number he had written a few words. He explained the entries:

$100 to a bartender in Alice Town, who had pointed out a fisherman who wouldn't ask questions; $200 to the fisherman to take him across the harbor to South Bimini. $1,500 to the retired Chalk's Airline pilot who borrowed a friend's single-engine Cessna to fly Tom to Nassau. $3,000 for a private charter flight from Nassau to Jamaica, just in time to catch an 8:10 AM Wednesday flight to Toronto, $950. Hat and sweatshirt at the Toronto airport, $75. Flight to London, $625. The other $150 covered food, the Heathrow Express to Paddington Station, and the taxi fare to Claridge's.

"It comes to six thousand, six hundred dollars," Tom said.

"Why should my father pay for all that?" Allison objected. "Bribes? Private charter flights? A hat?"

Tom flipped the notebook closed. "Yeah, maybe I should've stayed on the boat and let that Croatian gorilla take the map. Maybe I should've come back to Miami with it and dropped it off at your dad's house."

Allison lifted her eyes and let out a breath.

He said, "I also need eight thousand for some things I need to buy in London."

"Eight thousand dollars? What things?"

"Computer equipment and a high-resolution digital camera. He knows about it."

She stared at him. "On top of the expenses you just showed me? Plus the additional five thousand toward your fee."

"Correct. A total of nineteen-six."

"I'll have to talk to my father."

"You do that, but when we leave here, we're going to the bank. I want the five thousand plus my expenses. Otherwise, he can find some other sucker to do it."

She refilled her teacup, added some milk, dropped in a sugar cube, stirred it, then set the little spoon on the saucer and crossed her arms. "I'll give you the five and I'll reimburse your expenses getting to London, but you get nothing for the computer and camera until you show me your receipts."

"Whoa. What a hard-ass. Did you take that course in law school?"

She looked at him without comment.

"Allison?" Tom leaned across the small table. "How did your father persuade you to commit a crime?"

"What are you talking about?"

"You're helping me commit forgery. Did you ever consider that?"

"I am not helping you do anything. I'm helping my father."

"To forge a map."

"It's not a forgery." Even as she spoke the words, they sounded false. But only technically false. Stuart wasn't buying a forgery. He was buying a *replacement* because he had to; there was no choice.

Tom interrupted her thoughts. "You know what I don't get? Your father told me he paid ten thousand dollars for the Corelli map. But he's willing to pay me fifty—plus expenses. Why?"

Allison took a sip of tea before she said, "Money isn't that important to him. He wants the map, and he can afford it. Collectors are like that. You should know."

"I didn't think your father was really that much into maps."

"You're so wrong. He started collecting when he was a child."

"I heard he tore the pages out of a seventeenth-century Tommaso Porcacchi atlas and gave them away as Christmas presents."

She felt an angry flush creep up her neck. They had fought about the Porcacchi, but that wasn't any of Tom's business. She said, "What right do *you* have to criticize anybody?"

"Oh, man." Tom hung an arm over the back of his chair and laughed. "Yeah, you got an A in that course, didn't you? Are you done with the tea?" He put on his ugly Maple Leafs cap.

"Almost." She lifted her teacup. "One other condition. I want Jenny Gray's address. Don't tell me you don't know."

"Maybe I do, but you're not getting it. By the way, Allison, I don't believe your story about needing to find her for some immigration case."

"Okay, here's the truth. I'd like to know what happened to the maps stolen from Judge Herron's house, his and some of my father's. I just want to find out, that's all."

Tom said, "The police say map thieves took them."

"The police aren't sure. They also think that Jenny could have tipped someone off."

"Someone like who? Me?"

After a long moment, Allison shook her head. "I considered it, but . . . no. Unless your time in prison changed you. They say it can."

"I've never been in prison, Allison. Jail, yes."

"What's the difference?"

"Jail is for misdemeanors. Prison is for serious crimes. Do I look like a career criminal to you?"

"Well . . . you do look a little scruffy." She smiled. "Must be the hat. Want me to take you shopping?"

"Are you buying?"

"No. We'll go to Marks and Spencer."

He stood up and pushed in his chair. "I should have flown first-class. I could've used those little toiletry bags they hand out. It was a pain sitting up in coach for sixteen hours. Have you ever flown coach, Allison? Ever?"

They went to the Barclays Bank on Regent Street. Allison asked to see the manager. She mentioned her father's name, and they were taken into a private office paneled in mahogany. Stuart had chosen Barclays because he knew someone in upper management. With a couple of phone calls, Tom Fairchild's account was quickly approved.

While Tom showed his passport and filled out the forms—using Allison's hotel as his London address—she studied him from the other end of the desk. A few days ago she had wondered if he'd been involved in Royce Herron's murder, and if his detour by London was to pick up his share of the loot from Jenny Gray. Allison had tried out that theory, but it didn't ring true . . . unless he had changed more than he was admitting.

Tom Fairchild might not be capable of murder, but fraud? Theft? Absolutely. Aside from going over her outlines for the bar exam, Allison had one goal: to make sure the map was done correctly and delivered to her father on time.

Coming out of the bank, she had to grab Tom's arm to keep him from walking into the path of a double-decker red bus that swept toward them from the right in a rush of mist and engine noise.

Tom laughed. "I love those buses!"

Allison said, "Let's go find you a coat." She lifted her closed umbrella to signal a taxi, and a moment later one stopped at the curb. Tom opened the door and let her get in, then told the driver to take the lady to Claridge's.

"Wait!" Allison said. "Where are you going?"

"I'm a big boy. I won't get lost."

"But I need to know where you are."

"I'll call you," he said, backing away.

As the taxi took off, she fumbled for the door handle. "Stop!"

"Make up your mind, young lady. Claridge's or not?"

Allison scrambled around on her knees and looked through the back window as Tom in his sweatshirt and blue knit cap vanished into the crowds on Regent Street.

CHAPTER 14

His wife's bedroom smelled of her clothes, perfume, the roses on her dresser, and, more faintly, of dog. Stuart stood in the doorway of the hall that connected his suite to hers. The dim light leaking through the curtains revealed to him the chaise longue with heavy tassels on the arms, a four-poster bed piled with pillows, and a leopard-print satin robe that had slid to the carpet.

When he approached, a shape suddenly leaped from the folds of the comforter, yapping and snarling. Stuart ignored it.

Rhonda mumbled, "Fernanda? Just leave the coffee on the table."

He said, "Rise and shine."

She lifted her eyeshade. "Zhou-Zhou, no barky! It's just Daddy." Rolling over, she squinted at the clock. "Oh, Christ, Stuart, it's six forty-five. Why did you wake me up?"

He turned on a lamp. The dog sniffed the hems of his suit pants as if it had never seen him before. Stuart picked it up and tossed it onto the bed, where it tunneled under the pillows. He swung around a poster and tickled the bare foot that hung out of the covers. Rhonda pulled her leg in.

He said, "News flash. Allison just called from London. Tom Fairchild has arrived."

Rhonda sat up and threw her eyeshade to the nightstand. "What does he want?"

"To finish the map—as we agreed. I always thought we could count on him."

"Don't gloat, Stuart." She scooped her hair off her face. "Showing up is one thing. Forging a map is something else."

A low growl came from the bedcovers. Stuart wondered if dogs ever became trapped under so many layers and suffocated themselves. He said, "Rhonda, I would like to know two things. First, what was Marek Vuksinic doing on that boat? And second, why was he looking through Fairchild's bag?"

"How should I know? What did Allison say?"

As he paced from the end of the bed to the window, to the chaise, and retraced his steps, Stuart told her. But he didn't mention the amount of money Fairchild had demanded this morning, or that Fairchild would probably get more, and more.

"Where is Marek Vuksinic now?" he asked, flipping the curtain aside to look out the window. Another day blue enough to tear out your soul.

"Larry says he flew home."

"Home?"

"That's all he told me, Stuart."

He said, "I used to trust Larry. I'm never sure anymore what's up with him. Something's going on,

Rhonda. I am swimming in the ocean at night, hearing splashes that are not my own."

With a roll of her eyes, she said, "You aren't happy, are you, unless you have something to agonize about. I imagine that Marek is giving his report to Leo. Telling him you were charming, the project is under way, and Leo can have the penthouse. I don't *know*."

"What did Larry tell Marek about the map?"

"Nothing! Larry knows the consequences. My God, Stuart, coming in here at the crack of dawn to harass me like this!" She stood on her knees, and her full breasts wobbled under the thin silk negligee. "Why don't you go ahead and confess everything to Leo? Everything! Or just shoot yourself and get it over with!"

"That would simplify things for you, wouldn't it, my love? Good-bye, Stuart. Hello, life insurance."

"For God's sake."

In no better mood than his wife, Stuart snapped his fingers and said, "I almost forgot. Allison believes that Fairchild has Jenny Gray on his London agenda."

"What for?"

"Who knows? Could be . . . anything. Should I go find out?"

Rhonda lay back against the pillows, and her lovely golden hair fanned out around her face. "If I see you with that slut again, I will kill both of you."

He laughed. "I believe you would." As he stared across the room at her, his desire withered, and anger and grief rolled over him in equal measure. He had wanted her from the first moment, and she had used it—used *him*. He had always known this and did not care, cared only that she would stop using him. But Stuart had come to see, lately or years ago, that she had never loved him.

He let the curtain fall shut. "Tell you what. Go to Hawaii without me. I've got a pile of work to finish here. I'm sure you'll enjoy it better on your own. I'd only hold you back."

"If you're going to be petulant, I'd rather be by myself," she said.

He patted her foot through the covers as he walked by. "Go fuck your tour director."

The dog hurled itself after him. Strange reaction, to bark when someone was leaving, but the dog had the intelligence of a radish. Stuart thought that if its teeth tore his trousers, he would be justified in bringing his foot down on its neck. As if reading his thoughts, the dog turned away and jumped back on the bed.

Stuart closed the door.

Curving down the stairs to the first floor, he hummed a tune that matched the electrical buzzing in his brain. As though long-dead circuits had come on, he saw that he'd let Larry go too far. Stuart liked the mathematics of international markets; it was the brass-knuckled swagger of the street he couldn't stand. So he'd let Larry do it. The problem with Larry, though, was that his ambition exceeded his intelligence. Larry could pick out a good wine. He could throw a good party. People liked Larry. Too often, the wrong people. Larry had brought Oscar Contreras into the tidy group of investors in The Metropolis. Contreras, a swarthy Peruvian partial to Italian suits and too much jewelry, who was—or pretended to be—the right hand of the next president of Peru. Oh, delusions!

But if they could hold it all together . . . if Leo Zurin put in his share of the cash. If the bank could see an account balance of fifty million dollars by the end of the month. If Tom Fairchild could turn back the clock on that map. Then Stuart could sell his interest in this godfor-saken development . . . and retire to Provence, to Fiji, to Tierra del Fuego. If Rhonda wanted to go with him, she could. If not, he would find a mistress. Several of them. Warm and brown-skinned—

Suddenly his stomach roiled.

Why was Tom Fairchild seeing Jenny Gray? What was he after? How much had she told him?

There was hardly any traffic on the causeway to Mi-ami, and no one in the Pan-Global reception room when he unlocked the door. He went immediately to his office and turned on his computer. The link for British Airways was on his desktop.

Six days a week at exactly 8:00 AM, Fernanda would bring a tray to Mrs. Barlowe's room with coffee, rolls, and juice, or tea and dry toast if the Barlowes had gone out to dinner the night before. She would bring folded copies of *The Miami Herald* and *Investor's Business Daily*. She would open the curtains slowly, allowing Mrs. Barlowe's eyes time to adjust. She would start Mrs. Bar-lowe's bath, lay out a fresh towel, then take Zhou-Zhou downstairs for breakfast and a walk.

This morning, as Fernanda balanced the tray on her hip to reach the doorknob, she heard Mrs. Barlowe shout-ing. Not at her husband—he had left an hour ago. The words were muffled, but Fernanda could make out some of them.

. . . right now . . . I am losing my mind . . . have to do something before it's too late . . . he's already at the of-fice. . . .

Uncertain what to do, Fernanda knocked lightly and went in. She was surprised to find the sliding door to the terrace wide open and Mrs. Barlowe fully dressed. The big suitcase she had packed for their cruise was lying on the luggage rack, and Mrs. Barlowe was taking things out of it. Phone to her ear, she walked to the closet with an armful of swimsuits and returned with two sweaters and a fur coat.

She saw Fernanda and said into the phone, "Wait. Hold on." She motioned toward the dresser. "Just leave it there. I'll pour the coffee."

"Mrs. Barlowe, is everything all right?"

"Yes, fine. Just leave it, I said."

Fernanda noticed the dog on the end of the bed at the same moment that Zhou-Zhou leaped off, barking at something that had just brushed past Fernanda's leg. In another instant Zhou-Zhou was across the room, then behind the chaise, and on the bed again, and off, and Mrs. Barlowe was screaming, "What is that? A cat! How did it get in here?"

"*Ay, Dios mío.*" Fernanda hurriedly set down the tray as a large black cat streaked into the closet. Zhou-Zhou stood at the closet door barking so hard his topknot trembled. "Mrs. Barlowe, I am sorry, that's Othello, Miss Allison's cat."

"What's it doing in *my house*?"

"She's in London, and she didn't have anywhere—"

"Get it out or I'll call the Humane Society!"

With the cat draped over her arm, Fernanda slid through the bedroom door. It slammed shut behind her. She hurried down the stairs. "Bad cat. Bad! How did you sneak out?"

Fernanda wondered if she would be fired. She herself had thought many times of quitting. She would have done it long ago, except that the pay wasn't too bad, and the things that Mrs. Barlowe threw away had sent two of Fernanda's nieces through dental hygiene school. Fernanda would take Mrs. Barlowe's old clothing and lamps and pillows and dishes out of the trash and give them to her sister to sell at the flea market.

Fernanda still had hope that one day she would be working for Allison, and that Allison would have a good husband and a baby or two. But the girl was not beautiful in the way that men liked, and she had a brain, which was another drawback. Fernanda had lit candles and prayed, but Allison would be thirty-three her next birthday. She would be like Fernanda, a woman alone with a cat.

Larry came from inside the house, and the movement of walking made him queasy. He'd been out until four o'clock this morning. His mother sat at the far end of the screened enclosure in a wide pink hat with a glass of orange juice—more likely a mimosa—and the business section. Her sandal dangled from her foot. A waterfall splashed over coral rocks, and the glitter on the pool was like a knife between his eyes. He hoped she'd make it fast, whatever she had to say to him.

He stood over her chair. She folded the newspaper, set it aside. They looked at each other through their sunglasses. Her lipstick was the same hot pink as the hat.

"Good morning, Mother. You look well."

"Shall I ask Fernanda to make you some breakfast?"

"I'm not hungry."

"Thank you for coming so quickly." She held out a hand. "I'm sorry if I was bitchy over the phone. I've been so worried. You know that better than anyone. Stuart is eating antidepressants like peanuts. I don't know where his mind is anymore. Sit down."

He pulled out a chair. "It's probably not as bad as you think."

"Oh, Larry." She made a soundless laugh and shook her head. "It's bad. We're balanced so precariously right now. It all depends on that damned map. Have you ever heard of anything so insane? Stuart wants to go ahead with it! I tried talking to him, but he still thinks he can fool Leo Zurin."

Larry shifted to get the sunlight out of his eyes. "It could work. Zurin hasn't seen the original. If Stuart gives him the copy, how would he know the difference?"

"Oh, please. An obvious forgery? Think about it. Think what would happen." She leaned forward, and he felt the pressure of her gaze like heat off the sun. "I like this house. I like our life. I like what we've built over the years. I like being able to see you succeed, but we're this close to losing everything." She held up her thumb and forefinger and looked at him through the gap.

Shit, Larry thought. He would be spending the afternoon on a 747. "You want me to find Tom Fairchild."

"Mmm-hmm."

"How am I supposed to do that?"

"Allison is at Claridge's. He'll show up, or she'll meet him somewhere. You'll have to hurry, because they'll be leaving for Italy soon. You don't have to do it yourself, but it has to be done. I want the Corelli to disappear, too. It can't be found, not by Stuart, not by Leo Zurin. Not by anyone. Ever."

"What do you want done with Fairchild?"

She returned to her newspaper. "I'll leave that up to you."

CHAPTER 15

Past the tree line, the small figure was a moving dot on a field of white, cutting back and forth, tracing long curves as he came down the mountain, hitting a mogul, airborne for a second, cutting around an outcrop of granite, then settling down in a tuck, ski poles straight out behind him, coming very fast now, a blur through the trees, hurtling toward the stone wall, toward the gate, going through, then across the yard, between the trunks of two pine trees, and at the last moment turning his skis and coming to a dead stop beside the terrace in a shower of snow.

Leo pushed his goggles to his forehead and grinned. When he had caught his breath he said, "A good run, eh, Marek?"

"You frightened me. I was afraid you would miss the gate."

"So was I! Welcome back. How did you find the women in Miami?"

"They are all bones, and those that are not, have bottoms like horses."

Laughing at that, Leo clicked out of his skis, gave them to Marek to carry, and thudded up the steps in his boots. Marek pinched the burning end off his cigarette and flicked the ashes into the snow. The rest he returned to his pack.

Leo said, "I hope you're hungry. Luigi is making veal chops tonight."

"In that case, I'll stay for dinner," Marek said. It was a pleasure to speak Italian again, the language that he and Leo Zurin had in common. Marek had picked it up as a boy working in resorts in Italy. He could speak some Russian, but he wasn't fluent, and Leo knew very little Croatian, though he owned a house on an island within sight of Dubrovnik.

Marek propped the skis on the rack while Leo sat to take off his boots. His leather clogs waited for him under the bench.

The cold had reddened Leo's large, pointed nose. Thick brows angled up over his dark eyes, and deep folds went from his nostrils to the corners of his thin lips. In order not to show the sparse gray hair on his head, he shaved it all off. He was on the short side of average, and tears would often spill down his cheeks when he played his cello. And yet he'd never had any trouble attracting women. A puzzle.

The tops of the mountains reflected the setting sun, and the shadows were turning purple. At dusk, the lasers around the perimeter would go on, and the dogs would be let out to roam inside the wall. The windows were made of bulletproof glass. This house was a fortress, yet Leo would go skiing alone, not a pistol with him, not even an emergency locator.

By now he had pulled off gloves, hat, jacket, and

scarf, and when his houseboy came out onto the terrace, Zurin laid them all across his outstretched arms. The boy, a Kazakh with a flat face and Asian eyes, looked over the top of the pile and, speaking in Russian, said: "Excuse me, Leo Mikhailevich. There is a telephone call from the United States. He says his name is Stuart Barlowe."

Leo looked at Marek as if for an explanation. Marek responded with a slight shrug. They went inside to the main room, where a fire warmed the rough stone walls. Leo picked up the telephone.

"Stuart? Hello! I've just come off the mountain. You're lucky to catch me. How's the weather in Miami?"

To Marek's ear, Leo's English was flawless, but he couldn't be sure, since his was so bad. He went over to the fireplace and put on another log. The room had thick rugs on the wood plank floors, a U-shape of sofas facing the fire, and a high, beamed ceiling. Windows on the west side overlooked the Valle di Champorcher and the small town of the same name, whose steeply pitched roofs were now covered in white. The area was too remote to attract many tourists—the same reason Leo Zurin had bought the chalet.

To get to the top of the mountain, Leo would traverse for half a mile, then go down one of the ski runs to the bottom and get on the chair lift. It would take him to the top, where he would go through some woods, come out in the open, and slalom down to his house.

He was talking to Barlowe about a map—an antique Italian map of the world that he had wanted for a long time. A copy of it, made from a photograph Barlowe had sent, occupied a heavy gold frame by the fireplace. Marek had often seen Leo gazing at the copy as if it were the Virgin Mother. Marek suspected that Stuart Barlowe had delayed sending the original until he had Leo's money. So far, Leo had been patient.

"No, no, don't trouble yourself, Stuart. Really, it isn't necessary. . . . Well, then, if you're sure you want to." He stood with one hand on his hip, leaning back slightly to stretch his muscles. "That's wonderful. Excellent. Ciao."

He set down the phone and clapped his hands together.

"The Corelli?" Marek asked.

"Yes, the Corelli. Barlowe will deliver it himself, but first he's taking it to a restoration expert in London. He wants to see if they can erase a few water spots and fix a tear in the fold. He won't tell me more. He wants to surprise me. Do you know how long I've waited for that map?"

Marek had heard the story, but he said, "A very long time."

"A lifetime. Four lifetimes." Leo walked over to the replica and ran his fingers across the gold frame. "It will be the last piece in the atlas that the Communists stole from my grandfather before they put him against the wall. He used to hold me on his lap and show me the places I would go someday. Yes, Marek. I remember quite well. He had been given the atlas on his twenty-first birthday by my great-grandfather, who purchased it in Odessa. Before Odessa, the atlas had seen Constantinople, and before that, Milan and Venice."

The Kazakh returned with a bottle of red wine, two glasses, and some cheese and bread. He filled the glasses as Leo stretched out with his feet toward the fire.

"The general who ordered my grandfather's execution lost it in a game of Three Aces, and it wound up in the museum in Riga for fifty years before the regime fell apart and someone lifted it off the shelf. Imagine the pittance the thief must have got for it. If I knew who cut it to pieces, I would do the same to him. But sit down, Marek. I want to hear about The Metropolis. How is the view from the penthouse in Tower One?"

Marek smiled. "You will have a fabulous apartment. I brought the plans with me, and some photographs of the site."

"What will I see from the fiftieth floor?"

"The city, the river, Miami Beach, the Atlantic. Your terrace goes around three sides."

After giving them each a glass of wine, the Kazakh bowed and quietly left the room.

Leo said, "Two years till it's built, do you think?"

"Barlowe says it could be sooner, as early as eighteen months. They have obtained the last of the approvals. Larry Gerard kept telling me it wasn't easy."

"I believe that. American bureaucrats are expensive." Leo tore off some bread and laid some cheese across it. "I've promised Pan-Global enough money to buy my penthouse five times over. Barlowe says the developer demands the money by the end of the month. Should I go ahead with it, Marek?"

"If you believe Barlowe," Marek said.

"And you don't?"

"He's hiding something. I don't know what it is, but I sense it."

"We all have secrets. As long as he doesn't pick too much from my pocket—and he delivers my map—Stuart and I have no quarrel. Now, this other matter . . . how did Contreras impress you? You know I don't like doing business with strangers."

"He is a peasant but very shrewd. I think you can trust

him, although, as I told you last week, he's on the Americans' radar screen."

"What about that girl they were questioning? Did they get anything from her?"

"No. I made sure of it. She had a roommate who also knew Contreras, but the roommate had connections to a judge. Larry thought there would be problems if anything happened to her. The judge is now dead, and the girl is in London." Marek hesitated, then said, "One thing bothers me. She's a friend, perhaps a lover, of Tom Fairchild."

"Fairchild. An odd name."

Marek said, "I don't believe that he was going to Nassau to look at maps. His sister owns a map shop, but that could be a cover. He has a criminal past. He avoided my questions. He's strong and quick. I think he's had martial arts training."

"What are you telling me? That Fairchild is an American agent? What does that make Stuart Barlowe? No, Marek. Not Barlowe. I know him too well. It's not in him."

"You are probably right." Marek nodded. "Do you think Barlowe could have been used?"

"Possible, but why do you suspect Fairchild?"

"He had something in his bag. Long, but not too heavy. When he saw me opening the zipper, he almost attacked me. I would have found out what it was before we reached Nassau, but he left the boat. Whatever it was, he took it with him. I was thinking of a high-powered folding graphite rifle."

"Not yet. Those rifles are still in development. No one has them, not even the Israelis, who are making them." Leo held up a hand. "Fairchild wasn't going after

Oscar Contreras. Our contact in Peru told me that Contreras returned two days ago."

"Then I can't explain it." Marek refilled Leo's glass, then his own. "Fairchild is not in Miami. This much I do know."

Through the closed door came a muffled ringing, and a few moments later the Kazakh reappeared. "Another phone call for you, Leo Mikhailevich. A woman, Rhonda Barlowe."

"Really? I just spoke to her husband." With a quizzical lift of his brows in Marek's direction, he put down his wine and leaned over to pick up the extension. The door closed quietly.

"Rhonda? Is it really you? My goodness, what a surprise. *Come stai, cara?* You are well? . . . Yes, I just arrived in Italy three days ago. The skiing is fantastic. I've been out all afternoon, and now I'm by the fire warming my toes and having a glass of excellent Barolo. But do tell me why you called. I'm all curiosity." He frowned. "Oh? . . . But why not tell me now? . . . Yes, if you wish, but to go to so much trouble . . . All right, then. Have a safe journey. *Buon viaggio*, Rhonda."

He disconnected and tapped the phone on his small, cleft chin. "*Che strano.*"

"How is it strange, Leo?"

"She's coming to Italy. Her husband thinks she's on a cruise around Hawaii, but she's arriving in Milan on Saturday. She wants to speak to me face-to-face, but she can't discuss it over the phone. A mystery, eh, Marek?"

"They are not trustworthy people, the Barlowes."

"Oh, I know. Very few of us are, but once you accept that, you'll find *la comédie humaine* quite entertaining." He got up to put another log on the fire. He gave it a jab with the poker, and sparks shot up and reflected in his black eyes. He leaned his crossed arms on his knee, staring into the flames. Shadows extended upward from his eyebrows. "I'd like to know more about this man who disappeared from the boat. Tom Fairchild. Quite a trick, to vanish so completely."

"Not completely," Marek said.

Leo glanced around. "Oh?"

Marek smiled. "We found a shipping receipt in his backpack. An address in London."

CHAPTER 16

Tom Fairchild sat on a stool at the Genius Bar in the Apple computer store on Regent Street waiting for the clerk to put his computer together. Since meeting Jenny Gray at two o'clock, Tom had purchased a cell phone, a digital camera with a macro lens, some clothes, a new backpack, and a suitcase on wheels. He had also paid Jenny two hundred pounds to be his tour guide.

At the moment, she was playing with an iPod Nano, dancing to whatever tune was coming through the earphones. The white cords bounced on her orange sweater, her curly hair swung around her face, and her belly showed when she raised her arms. She was drawing a small crowd of appreciative male customers who had come here expecting to find USB hubs and hard drives.

Jenny had asked Tom outright, then teased him and cajoled, to tell her what he was doing in London and how he had lost his backpack. He had finally said, straight-faced, that he was on a mission for the CIA, and he couldn't talk about it. She had laughed, then said, "Really, Tom, why are you here?" He had said, "If you knew, I'd have to kill you."

He was entering names and numbers into his cell phone. The pages of his address book had gotten wet when the Balkan thug had put him underwater. Tom had to peel them apart, but the writing was legible. Several times since seeing his backpack drop to the cabin floor, he had mentally searched inside it for anything that might give a clue to his whereabouts. He didn't think he'd left anything, but jet lag was making him loopy. He kept hitting the wrong buttons on the phone.

After he'd entered Eddie Ferraro's number in Italy, he tried it out, but voice mail picked up. "Hey, this is Tom. I have arrived. I'm at a computer store in London right now, getting the stuff we talked about. . . . I'll call you tomorrow." He left his new number and cut the call short; it would be hard to squeeze the past thirty-six hours into a message.

Next he dialed Rose, who told him she'd just come back from taking the kids to school. She said his proba-tion officer was looking for him. Tom said, "What the frick does he want?" Rose didn't know. As instructed, she'd said that Tom was fishing in the Keys, and he'd left his cell phone at home, but something told her that Weems was suspicious. She said Tom ought to call him back right away.

"I can't," Tom said. "I need a phone with a local Mi-ami number. I'll have to think of something." After he'd hung up, the solution came to him: Allison Barlowe. He would use her phone to call the Weasel—if he could get it away from her long enough. Tom's finger hesitated over the speed-dial for Allison. He decided it could wait. He didn't want her to think she had a leash around his neck.

But soon he would be forced to call Allison: He was running out of cash already. The bill for the computer and various accessories had come to £3,488. He had stuffed the receipt into his wallet with the others. The bank card had dwindled to a few hundred pounds, and he still had to pay Eddie half of what he'd collected in fees.

The clerk came back wheeling a cart full of boxes. He was in his early twenties, red hair, wearing the store uniform of black shirt and black pants. He lifted the laptop off the cart, plugged it in, and turned it on. Two of the young guys who'd been drooling over Jenny came to stare at the equipment. The clerk turned the laptop so Tom could see the screen with the computer specs on it.

"Okay, you've got your one-point-eight-gigahertz, fifteen-point-four-inch MacBook Pro with two gigs of RAM and a one-hundred-gig hard drive, complete with SuperDrive, a 256-megabyte graphics card, a five-megapixel camera with videoconferencing. This box here is your Bluetooth Wacom tablet. This is your firewire connector. Here's your Adobe Creative Suite Two. Plus one compact laser printer. And for storage, one sixty-gig video iPod—in black."

One of the young guys murmured, "Sixty-gig."

The clerk ran down the list, then smiled at Tom. "Right. That's it, then."

Tom motioned for Jenny to come over, and she helped him take everything out of the packaging and fit it into a padded messenger bag. Tom put on his jacket, shouldered the backpack, and hung the messenger bag crossways over his chest. They pushed through the glass door to Regent Street. Pedestrians dodged around them, and Tom kept a tight grip on the strap. Six-story buildings of gray stone, columns, and arches extended in both directions. The rain had stopped, but there was no break in the sky. Mist from the churning traffic hung over the pavement.

Jenny wrapped her scarf around her neck and put on a fuzzy black hat. "What next?"

Tom said he needed to find a hotel.

"They're awfully expensive round here. Just stay at my house. It's only fifteen minutes on the tube. I'll make supper." When Tom asked what her mother might think of a stranger staying over, she took his arm and turned him toward Oxford Street. "She won't care. She's working the night shift at a veterans' home, so you might not even see her." Jenny told Tom she didn't like living in Brixton—hated it—but it was temporary, till she found the right job. She wanted to live in Chelsea. That was her plan.

As they curved around Oxford Circus toward the underground station, Tom noticed the reflection of a man in the glass front of a shoe store. He wouldn't have paid attention, but he'd seen the same guy outside the camera shop. Black overcoat and dark hair. Looked Italian or even Middle Eastern. Tom turned around and scanned the faces on the crowded sidewalk. The man wasn't there.

"What's the matter?"

"Nothing. I'm hallucinating."

Tom followed Jenny to the platform for the Victoria Line. He wanted to lean his head back and close his eyes as the car swayed around curves, but he kept his arms crossed over his messenger bag. When the doors opened at the Brixton station, they had to trudge up a broken escalator, finally coming out to the street under a modern glass wall with an immense red-and-blue Underground sign. The street itself quickly deteriorated to redbrick buildings, small shops with steel security screens, and graffiti on the walls. They walked south through the major intersection at Coldharbour Lane. A block on, Jenny stopped at an Indian take-away.

Night had fallen in Brixton. They walked to Abingdon Road, a narrow street of attached, two-story houses with meager gardens in front and small cars at the curb, all of them pointed in the wrong direction, Tom noticed. As they reached Jenny's house, the front door opened, and a stout, middle-aged blond woman in a brown coat came down the steps. Her expression turned as chilly as the weather.

"Hello, Mum. This is Tom. He's a friend of mine visiting from Miami."

Without a word Jenny's mother continued toward the street. Jenny unlocked the door. "The old cow. She hates me. I gave her some money, so she can't say anything, can she? God, I will be so happy when I can afford my own flat."

It was a dark little house, done in a color scheme ranging from brown to gray. Jenny told Tom to take his things upstairs to the back bedroom while she put dinner on the table. Her room was hardly bigger than a closet and littered with her clothing and shoes. Tom groaned when he saw only one single-sized bed. He set the backpack out of the way, put the messenger bag and jacket on top of it, and went to find the bathroom. As he stood at the toilet, the mirror reflected ladies' stockings and cotton panties, large size, on the shower rod. Washing up, he looked at his face, the puffy eyes and two-day beard. "Yeah, Tom, why *are* you here?"

In a shop window on Regent Street his eyes had briefly met those of the man who'd been following him.

Or maybe not following him. Tom didn't know if he was jet-lagged or just paranoid.

His unease had started before Larry's friend Marek had thrown him to the deck of the boat, and even before Rhonda Barlowe offered him ten thousand dollars not to do the map. He'd started getting nervous the moment Stuart Barlowe said he would pay fifty thousand in cash for a fake Corelli. Supposedly Barlowe wanted it for himself, but Tom had never really believed that. Tom believed there were reasons that Barlowe hadn't told him about. He believed that Barlowe would screw him over if he got the chance. Barlowe had cut pages from a rare atlas. He had cheated Rose out of seventy-two bucks in sales tax when he'd known that The Compass Rose was barely holding on. What would Barlowe do once he had his hands on the map? Would he pay what was owed? Or would he tell Tom to sue him for it? If the Weasel found out, Tom would be wearing a shirt with a number across the front.

Tom needed some leverage. The map wasn't enough.

He came downstairs as Jenny was spooning curried chicken and lentils onto their plates. The kitchen was as cramped as the rest of the house, made even more so by the canned goods and boxes stacked on every available surface, as though somebody were expecting a food shortage. A framed linen tea towel, a 1998 calendar in memory of Princess Diana, hung over the gas range.

There was a thump against the wall, then shouts in a language Tom didn't recognize.

Jenny said, "It's just the Moroccans next door. They're always fighting, those people." She brought glasses of dark beer to the table. "One of them will wind up dead someday."

"Is this neighborhood safe? I don't want my stuff ripped off."

"It's fine—if you like common and boring. We don't have a lot of burglaries." She swung around to sit on Tom's thigh. She kissed him full on the mouth and held his face in her hands. "It's you! I thought I'd never see you again."

"I should've brought some sunshine."

"You should have! You're in London for only three days? That's not fair."

"I'll have to get a hotel tomorrow," he said.

"Why? There's room here."

"I need to get the computer running, check it out. You know."

"And then where will you go, after you leave London?"

He saw no reason not to tell her. "Florence, Italy. I'm meeting a friend, a guy I used to know in Miami."

She looked at him sideways, bit her lip to hold back a smile, then said, "Have you been bad? Where did you get all that money for a fancy computer and the camera and all?"

Jenny thought he'd stolen the money. It was not an unreasonable guess, Tom had to admit. "Somebody's paying me to do a job for him."

"A job?" She draped her arms over his shoulders.

"I can't really talk about it," Tom said.

"I could help. I could go with you. You don't know your way around Europe. I do. I speak a little Italian. I could be a big help."

Tom felt the pressure of her hip on his groin. His fatigue was giving way to something else. Even with the heat rising up his body he was able to see the benefits of taking Jenny with him that had nothing to do with sex. "I'll think about it."

"Will you? Really?"

"Yeah. I will."

"Super."

She kissed him again and started to get up. Tom held on to her. "Jenny, did you take some maps and jewelry out of Royce Herron's house before you called the police?" She looked away, and he said, "I don't care if you did, and I didn't come to London to track them down. I'm trying to figure out a few things, that's all."

Sweeping back her hair, she said, "Yes, I did. I'm not sorry, especially not sorry that some of them belonged to Stuart Barlowe. I pawned the jewelry in Miami. It wasn't worth much. And when I got here, I took the maps to a dealer in Kensington. I got two thousand pounds for the lot. I know they were worth more, but I couldn't guarantee the provenance, so I had to let them go. I gave my mother most of it. Spent some on a coat. It's all gone now."

"Okay," Tom said.

She went to her chair. "Eat before your food gets cold."

"I do need your help, Jen. I need to ask you about Stuart Barlowe."

She made a face. "Can't we just enjoy supper?"

"A couple of questions," Tom said. "I can't explain why right now, but . . . did you ever meet Martha Framm? An older woman, one of Royce Herron's friends."

Digging into her curry, Jenny said yes, she'd met her.

"Mrs. Framm called Judge Herron the night he died. They talked about The Metropolis. She wanted him to go to a public rally against it. He wouldn't do that, but he told her he had another way to put pressure on Stuart Barlowe. She asked what he meant, and he wouldn't tell her. Do you know? Did he talk to you about it?"

Ripping a piece of naan bread down the middle, Jenny said, "I've no idea."

"Maybe it was about you," Tom said.

"Me?"

"You and Barlowe. Did Royce Herron know about that?"

"Not really. We never talked about it, not like, oh, this is what I did with Stuart Barlowe, but he knew. Royce was a smart man, very smart. *But.* He would never have used me like that. He was a gentleman," she said firmly.

The neighbors were screaming at each other again. Jenny turned her head, listening. A few seconds later, a door slammed.

"What was it, then?" Tom gazed across the room, toward the peeling wood cabinets over the sink. He drank more of his beer. "I think about Barlowe's connection to Larry Gerard, that whole crowd, and The Metropolis, and the way they finessed the zoning."

Jenny seemed to be deciding what to say, or whether to speak at all. "A few weeks ago, around the new year, I think, I overheard a conversation Royce had with Stuart. Royce was in his study, and the phone rang. He put it on mute and told me to go make him a drink and wait in the kitchen. He shut the door, but I was curious, so I stood there. I couldn't hear very well, but Royce sounded angry. He wasn't the kind of person who would normally raise his voice, so I stayed and listened some more to see what would happen. Stuart had just ended our relationship . . . well, I was afraid Royce would get on him for it, but they were talking about The Metropolis. Royce said it was too much, far too big, and Stuart had to do something about it or else. That's what he said: 'or else.' And he said, 'I know about you. I could make your life very unpleasant,' or something like that. He said . . . oh, God, what did he say? 'I know the truth, so don't think you can get away with it any longer. I know who you are.' I don't remember the exact words, Tom. I ran to the kitchen to pick up the extension, but I was too afraid they'd hear me. I made Royce his drink and acted like I'd been there all along."

"And you didn't ask him what he'd meant?"

"God, no. He'd have known I was eavesdropping, wouldn't he? Around that same time I was waiting for Stuart to send me some money like he'd promised, but it didn't come, and it didn't come, so I called him, and he said he wasn't going to pay me a dime, and if I called again he would report me to immigration. So I wrote him a letter and sent it to his office marked 'personal.' 'Dear Stuart, you lied, you broke your promise, and so on, but I know the truth about you. I know what you did. I want the money you promised, or I will reveal everything to the media.' I wrote about twenty drafts of that letter."

Tom said, "He gave you the money."

"Five thousand dollars," Jenny said.

"But you never knew what the truth was?"

"No! It was all air! I made it up. And then Royce Herron was killed, and . . . oh, my God. I thought it could've been because of this, and maybe I'd be next. I couldn't get out of Miami fast enough." Jenny laughed. "And I still don't know what they were talking about! I should've asked for a lot more."

When she stopped laughing and reached for her beer,

Tom said, "Does Stuart Barlowe know where you are?"

"He knows my mum lives in Brixton, but I'm not worried. First of all, I'm so far away, and second, who would believe me?" She gestured with her fork. "You don't like curry? You're not eating."

"No, I do, I was just ... Jenny, if you took the maps ... The police are saying map thieves killed Royce Herron. I thought so, too. Now I don't know."

"I didn't take *all* the maps," she said. "If you're asking my opinion, I'd look at Larry Gerard. Did you know, Tom, that he's going to have this huge enormous restaurant at the top of The Metropolis? He wants to call it Chez Gerard. I mean, *yuk*. So if the building were like a normal size, *only* twenty stories, he'd be so disappointed."

"You think Larry killed Judge Herron?"

"He could have! Larry is a shit of the first order. He's more into The Metropolis than Stuart is. I mean, okay, it's mostly Stuart's money, but Larry's the one everybody talks to. The investors, and the interior designers, and the salespeople ... they all kiss his bum. He gets off on it."

Tom tried the curry, which was so hot it made his eyes water. He took a swallow of beer. "Got another question for you. Do you know of a friend, or acquaintance, of Larry's named Oscar? I don't have the last name."

"Yes. Why are you asking about him?"

"I'm not sure yet. So who's Oscar?"

"Oscar Contreras. He's from Peru. I think he's in the drug business, and I don't mean a pharmacy. You get a feeling for people like that. The way he dresses, the way he acts."

"What's his story?"

"He's like an aide or PR person to some politician or somebody running for president in Peru. He was telling me about parties at the presidential palace, and how he's going to be very important, blah blah blah. He was investing with Stuart, or with Stuart's company. I don't know how that works. I think Larry brought him into it."

"How did you meet Oscar?"

She snorted. "Larry asked me to go out with him. We went to dinner with some people, then to Larry's club on Brickell. Larry had a limo for Oscar with some champagne in a bucket, and we drank that and did some coke. Then we went to Oscar's hotel, a bunch of us. He had this suite, and we partied till, like, four o'clock, and then Oscar's friends left and . . . you fill in the blanks."

"You were his gift for investing in The Metropolis."

She made a wry smile. "I guess so. Look, Tom. I didn't take money for it. It just happened."

"I know that. Where's Oscar now? In Nassau? I heard he might be over in Nassau."

"Maybe. I don't know. I don't care where Oscar is . . . but he told me he liked to go over to Paradise Island and gamble. He wanted me to go, too, but my visa had expired, and it would've been hard for me to get back to Miami."

"Did you ever meet a guy from Croatia named Marek?"

"Oh, him. He's scary. He was there at Oscar's that night. Is he from Croatia? He offered to pay me five hundred dollars if I'd do him, but I said I was with Oscar, so bugger off. He didn't like that, but Oscar came over and got him off me."

"What's his last name?"

"I totally don't remember."

"What kind of business is Marek in? I heard he sells truck parts in Dubrovnik."

She laughed. "What? Well, maybe, but I'm pretty sure he's another of the investors. I heard him and Larry talking about The Metropolis, and buying the penthouse, so he probably has scads of money."

This didn't fit, Tom thought. It didn't fit with a former soldier in the Yugoslav army, a man with a missing thumbnail and wicked judo moves. And why had Marek wanted to know if Tom was going to see Oscar? As if Tom had been running a side game with Oscar Contreras on Paradise Island. The facts and suppositions and guesses were a pile of loose bricks in Tom's head. He couldn't lift them. He couldn't think anymore. His eyes were burning; he wanted to sleep.

"Carla was there that night, too," Jenny said.

Tom looked up. "Carla."

"I'll tell you what a piece of shit he is. He paid her to go out with his customers. *Paid* her. He set her up with this guy in the city government who had something to do with The Metropolis. They took pictures. Then, what do you know? He votes for the project. That's what Larry did." Jenny stacked their plates. "I would have left Miami sooner or later."

Tom dug into his pocket and unfolded some crumpled bills. They added up to £230. When Jenny came back from the sink, he pressed the money into her hand, squeezing her fingers around it when she pulled away. "Take this. Seriously. I'll be getting some more soon. It's between friends, okay? I don't expect you to do anything. If you get lucky someday, you can pay me back."

She kissed his forehead. "I'll say it's part of my salary, if I go with you to Italy."

He stood up and put his arms around her. "Jenny? I have to tell you something. It's about Carla."

Tom could have slept on concrete, but he spooned next to Jenny on her narrow bed, and during the night he heard her crying. For her friend. For having to live in this house with a mother who didn't want her there. For having been used.

When Tom drifted back to sleep, he dreamed of a girl in a red beret.

CHAPTER 17

The overcast was giving way to patches of pale blue when room service arrived. A woman in a black skirt and tuxedo shirt wheeled the cart in and set it up by the window. She lifted the silver lid from the quiche and the tea cozy from the pot.

Allison said, "I think it's stopped raining." She signed the receipt.

"Yes, Miss. It's a fine day for a walk."

Still in her pajamas at half past eleven, Allison had been looking down at the bare branches and gray street four stories below, the people on the sidewalks, and the red double-decker buses that occasionally passed the hotel. She'd thought of leaving her notes for a while and finding a used bookshop. She wanted something smooth and warm that would fit in her pocket. A small book bound in green leather, with gilded pages. The Romantic poets, to put her in the mood for Italy. Byron. Keats? No, Elizabeth Barrett Browning. *"How do I love thee? Let me count the ways . . ."*

During Allison's college year in Rome, a tour had

been organized to Florence. Allison had seen the house where Elizabeth Barrett Browning had lived with her husband Robert after they had eloped from England. She'd been an invalid spinster—

Allison's cell phone rang as she was biting into a croissant. She hurried to pick it up and saw her father's mobile number on caller ID. "Hello, Dad."

"Am I catching you at the hotel? Or are you out?"

"No, I'm here. I'm studying this morning. It's all I do, study for the bar. Are you on your way to Hawaii?"

"I've decided to let Rhonda go on her own. The idea of another cruise didn't thrill me. Have you spoken again with Mr. Fairchild?"

"Not yet, no."

"You haven't seen him? Hasn't he called you?"

"He will, I'm sure of it."

"Where is he staying?"

"I don't know. He said he would find a hotel and get back in touch."

"I see. You don't know where he's staying. What was the name of that girl he knows in London, the one who used to work for Larry . . ."

"Jenny Gray."

"You said he would probably look her up?"

"It's just a guess." Feeling unjustly put under interrogation, Allison said, "I don't know where she is either. He has her address, but he isn't sharing it."

She heard Stuart let out a breath of exasperation. "What are we to do, then? I envision Tom Fairchild going on his merry way, doing as he pleases, where he pleases, on his own timetable. Do you completely appreciate the dire situation I'm facing?"

"Yes, I do. If Mr. Zurin doesn't get his map, you and Rhonda will be living in a cardboard box—"

"Don't be flippant. The point is, Allison, you haven't any idea where Fairchild is. But I understand. You're a young woman alone in London. Tom Fairchild is attractive, in a rough way. He thinks he can walk all over you."

"That is so not true!" she protested. "All I am to Tom Fairchild is a bank. He knows that he won't get anything more out of me unless he tells me exactly where he is and what he's doing—"

"Where is my map? What progress is being made?"

"When he calls me, I'll find out," she said.

"No, you will tell him to call me immediately. I'll deal with this."

Allison laughed.

"You think it's funny?"

"I think it's hopeless. Lots of luck. What do you want me to do, go home?"

"No, don't go anywhere until he turns up. If he calls you, let me know about it. Use my mobile number, will you? I'm traveling."

She heard the sound of a disconnect. She held the phone out and smiled at it. "And how are *you*, sweetheart? . . . Oh, just great, Dad, thanks. I'm having a wonderful time in London."

Her quiche had gone cold. She nibbled a piece of crust and stared through the window at the clouds. "I should go home. Let him deal with it." When Stuart had come to her apartment asking for her help, he had described horrible financial consequences if his Russian investor didn't get the map promised to him. Allison had reluctantly said yes; her father needed her. It would be nice, she thought, if he showed appreciation for her moral sacrifice.

She flopped down on the small sofa with her cell phone and hit the number for her father's housekeeper. She put her bare feet on the windowsill and traced a circle on the glass with her toe.

"Fernanda, hi. It's Allison. I didn't wake you, did I? How's Othello? Is he being a good boy? Does he miss me?"

Fernanda told her that she'd had to keep Othello locked up in her room—a little problem with Rhonda's wretched mutt. "Yesterday he got loose, and he went into Mrs. Barlowe's room, and Zhou-Zhou chased him. So I can't let him out. I thought maybe to put Zhou-Zhou in the garage, but he would bark and bark. Do you know when Mrs. Barlowe might be back?"

"I think her cruise lasts for ten days."

"Well . . . I don't think she went on the cruise." Fernanda told Allison that she'd seen Rhonda taking her beachwear out of her suitcase and putting her winter things inside it. Fernanda stopped, as though caught between the demands of loyalty to her employer and the guilty pleasure of gossip. She gave in, speaking in a whisper even though, except for a dog and a cat, she was the only one at home.

"I asked Mrs. Barlowe where she was going, and she told me Hawaii, but why was she packing sweaters? I checked her closet, you know, straightening her room, and her white fox fur coat is gone and her snow boots."

"Maybe she went skiing," Allison said. "They have friends in Aspen."

"Yes, maybe she is there."

"Did you tell my father?"

"He left yesterday, and I don't want to bother him."

"Where is he?"

"He said New York, some business to do."

That was weird, she thought as she ended the call. Rhonda wasn't on the cruise either. So where was she? Allison decided not to call Stuart about it. She didn't want to get Fernanda in trouble. And she didn't see what difference it made where the witch was—Hawaii or a ski lodge.

She dropped the lid over her breakfast and went to her laptop on the desk. She had just sat down when her cell phone rang. With a sigh she walked over to the sofa and picked it up. A London exchange.

"Hello?"

"Hey. It's me. I'm downstairs. Can I come up?"

The knock sounded just as she was tossing her pajamas into the closet. She smoothed the comforter over the pillows, shook her hair back, and opened the door. She had put on wool slacks, a turtleneck top, and her shoes.

Tom Fairchild came in, took off a camera bag, then a navy blue jacket. He removed a wool newsboy's cap and straightened the front of his hair with his fingers. He had found time to go shopping. He had shaved. Allison gestured toward the sofa and told him to have a seat. She sat in her desk chair and crossed her legs.

"What? You're not happy to see me?"

"After waiting twenty-four hours? Where have you been?"

"I should've brought flowers," he said.

"Tom. Let's not."

He leaned back and put a foot on his knee. New hiking boots. He took up too much space on the striped satin sofa with its delicate legs. He reached into a pocket of his cargo pants. "I did bring you something—the receipts that you asked for."

"How much?"

He handed them over. "Four thousand, seven hundred and eighty-eight pounds, and change. Most of it's for a camera and computer equipment. I paid for the clothes myself. Like the jacket? North Face. Got it on sale, a hundred pounds. The problem is, I've only got about four hundred pounds left on my bank card. I need more traveling money if I'm going to get to Italy."

"How much?"

"Five hundred pounds should do it. Then I'll give you those receipts, too."

"My father called," she said. "He wants a progress report on the map. How's it going?"

"The map's going great. I'm a busy bee." Tom reached for the croissant on the serving cart. It had one bite missing. "Are you going to finish this? I had some pretty bad Indian food last night and not much of a breakfast."

"Tom, could we discuss the map? It's extremely important to my father. It's what he's paying you for. Would you please tell me exactly what you've done, and if you're on schedule to finish it?"

He chewed the croissant. "Well . . . I'm on my way to the Maritime Museum in Greenwich to take some photos of the Corelli sea charts. They have two pretty good ones, and I want to compare the ink and the paper to the world map. Your father wrote me a letter of introduction. I called the curator, and he'll show me around. That reminds me. I have a phone."

She wrote down the number when he read it off his

screen. "When will you actually start on the map?" she asked.

"I have started on the map."

"Where? Are you working in your hotel room? But you don't have the antique paper yet, do you?"

"No, I'll pick that up in Italy." Tom lifted the lid on her plate. "You don't want the strawberries?"

"Take them."

He popped one into his mouth, and chewed as he said, "Allison, I told you. I don't talk about my work. How I do it, that's my business. I told Mr. Barlowe he could have the map within two weeks, and unless something happens—like another incident with your step-brother's psycho friend—I'll have it on time."

"We need to know where you are. Don't think you can disappear and call me from God-knows-where in Italy asking for more money."

"Florence. When I'm ready to leave, I'll tell you. Probably tomorrow, so don't get too comfortable here at Claridge's. I'll take care of the travel arrangements myself because, frankly, I get nervous thinking that certain people might know where I am. No offense, but that's how it is." He held up her telephone. "May I use this? I need to call Miami. I'll just leave a message. The guy I'm calling is never in the office before eight o'clock."

With a sigh, Allison said, "Sure. Go ahead."

Walking away a few paces, he put a finger to his lips for her to be quiet. He listened for a second, then wordlessly mouthed *damn*, before he said, "Mr. Weems! Hi! This is Tom. Tom Fairchild. You left a message with my sister for me to call. I'm out of town right now, fishing. In fact, I'm on a boat just south of Grassy Key. This is my friend's cell phone, and the battery's getting low, so I can't talk long. What's up? . . . Sure I did. Yeah, I signed up for that class. I think it starts in a week or two. . . . Well, I don't have his phone number with me, but as soon as I get home. . . . Uh-oh, you're breaking up." Tom crinkled one of the receipts, held the phone at a distance, and hit the disconnect button.

Allison stared at him. "Who was that?"

"My probation officer. Rose said he was looking for me."

"Oh, great. Now he has my phone number. Damn it, Tom."

"You've got caller ID. Don't pick up." Tom ate another of the strawberries.

"My God! After I hear you flat-out lie to your probation officer, you expect me to believe anything you say?"

He came back and sat on the end of the sofa nearer the desk. He looked at her awhile, his brows lifting to make lines across his forehead. His eyes were wide and green as a meadow. "If I tell you something is the truth, it is. I might not tell you everything, because I can't, but I won't lie to you."

"How do I know that? I've given you almost twelve thousand dollars already, and I don't see anything for it."

"Look at the receipts. That's what I've spent preparing to do the map, and that's what I'm asking for. That's the deal. In all my life, Allison, I've never cheated you. Never. And you know that."

"I could laugh. I could just roll on the floor—"

"Never. In all the time you've known me, have I ever promised you, Allison Barlowe, you personally, anything that I didn't deliver? Have I?"

"I don't know who you are. We haven't seen each other in . . ."

"Twelve years. A long time, but we're the same people. Just the same. At least I am. I have never broken a promise to you, and you know it. We split up for reasons that had nothing to do with whether you could trust my word. And I'm making this promise to you now. I will finish the map. It will be good enough. It will be done on time."

She tossed her hair back from her face. "You should tell that to my father. He wants you to call him."

"I get it. He's taking control of this, isn't he?"

A call to Stuart's cell phone produced nothing. Allison left a message. "Dad, it's me. I'm with Tom. We're just discussing the map. It seems to be proceeding as scheduled. I've reviewed his receipts, and I'm going to reimburse him. Call me when you get this." She put down the phone, praying she hadn't screwed up past any hope of redemption.

"Okay, then," Tom said. "Grab your coat. Let's take a taxi to the bank. I need to get over to the museum pretty soon."

"No, I can do it online." She went to her laptop. Tom stood behind her. She swung around. "Do you mind?" She found her father's account with Barclays, tapped in the PIN, then went to the page for transfers. She pushed her glasses a little farther up the bridge of her nose. "How much was that?"

"Five thousand, two-eighty-eight. That includes five hundred advance on my expenses. All right?"

"Fine."

"And that's pounds."

"Right. Pounds." After typing in the amount she hesitated before pressing MAKE TRANSFER. She let out a breath. "Done. Do you want to go into your account and make sure?"

"No, that's okay." He picked up his camera and the jacket, then turned around to look at her again. "I don't know why my life went the way it did. You know, the bad choices. Mistakes I made. Long sad story, I guess, but I've moved on. Maybe you believe that, maybe you don't, but I am not going to screw this up. It could be the last, best chance I ever get."

On the way out, he picked up her red beret from the dresser. He twirled it, then sent it sailing across the room like a Frisbee. She caught it.

"You've got lipstick on your front tooth," he said.

She waited at the window and presently saw a man in a navy blue jacket and hat moving quickly toward the intersection with Davies Street. He turned the corner and was gone. Soon Stuart would call back. She felt that Tom would follow through, but could she convince Stuart of that? She'd have to explain too much to him. Too much of the past, and how she knew Tom Fairchild's intentions better than she could admit.

The receipts were stacked on her desk. She couldn't remember a receipt for his hotel. Then she thought: Of course there's no receipt; he hadn't checked out yet, had he? But what hotel? Allison had asked him. Hadn't she? How had he slid past that question?

Glancing at the number he'd given her, she called his cell phone, walking back to the window as she listened to the British *brrrrp brrrrp brrrrp*.

No answer. Not even a message machine. She imagined him taking the phone out of his pocket, looking at the screen—

"Dammit." Then she laughed. "Jenny Gray. You're staying with her, aren't you?"

Allison looked at her watch, then scrolled through her phone book for a number in Miami. After several rings she heard a woman's voice. *This is the law office of Marks and Connor. If you are calling outside regular business hours, please leave your name and number—*

"Hello, this is Allison calling from London. This message is for Miriam. I need a huge favor. Could you pull somebody's file for me?"

At Marks and Connor, all clients filled out an initial intake sheet. The basic information included permanent address and next of kin. Allison could not be absolutely sure, but she believed that Jenny had used her mother's address in London. Allison even remembered the name: Evelyn Gray. Surely Mrs. Gray would know where her daughter was.

Brixton lay on the south side of the Thames, a multicultural, working-class area of Victorian redbrick, ugly blocks of apartments, and tiny shops tucked under the arches of an old railroad line. Money from the Olympics had spilled over to nudge the business district toward recovery. The taxi driver smiled at her in his mirror. "The yuppies will move in soon, see if they don't."

Allison looked out the window at a sidewalk flea market, chip shops, and people bundled in dark clothing. Graffiti on the side of a building suggested what the prime minister could do to himself.

Clouds obscured the low winter sun, making the day

seem later than three o'clock. Ms. Connor's secretary had called back with the information Allison had wanted, but Allison had heard nothing from her father. She'd been relieved, because any discussion would almost surely have led to an argument. When she had something to tell him, she would try again to reach him.

The taxi stopped in front of a small row house with a muddy garden that in summer would probably look just as neglected. Allison checked her notes to make sure she had the right address, then paid the driver. A metal gate swung open to a short walkway, and four steps took her to a small porch set into an alcove, from which Allison glanced back at the quiet street. At the end of the block two boys kicked a soccer ball. No one else was around.

The door had a long, oval window with etched glass reinforced with flat security bars. Through the floral design on the door, Allison could just make out a hall with stairs to the second floor. The curtains in the narrow window to her right were slightly open, and she could see through them into a drab and dark front room. The lamps were off. Allison had not thought what to do if Mrs. Gray was not at home.

She heard footsteps, or more accurately, felt the slight shudder through the boards of the porch floor. Someone was rushing down the stairs. A man. She couldn't make out his features, but he wore a dark coat. He got to the bottom and froze.

Allison took a step back, embarrassed to have been caught peering into the house this way. The glass vibrated as he came quickly toward her. The door opened, and a hand reached out and pulled her inside.

She was looking up into Tom Fairchild's face. He was breathing in great gasps.

"Tom? I didn't know you'd be here. I had this address—"

Not releasing his grip on her wrist, he stuck his head out far enough to glance up and down the street, then shut the door. He pushed her against the wall and spoke through his teeth. "Bad timing. Who knows where you are?"

"Nobody! I got this address from my office. Jenny gave it to me. Her mother lives here. Doesn't she?"

"Yes." He pressed the heel of his hand to his forehead. "Okay. Let me think."

He was wearing his coat. She saw the strap of a messenger bag over his chest. "You were leaving," she said. "Where? Italy?"

"Allison, I want you to listen to me. Don't move. Just stay there and listen."

She pushed, and in her struggle got around him far enough to see a wide opening framed in dark wood that led to the room she had observed from the porch. Dim light through the lace curtains fell on a woman lying on the floor. Her arms were out, and her legs were twisted, almost as though she were running. Her blond-streaked hair flowed out behind her.

Allison's cry of surprise and horror was cut short when Tom's hand went across her mouth. "She's dead. I came back to get my things, and I found her like that."

Muffled screams caught in her throat. She went for his eyes, his ears, and her gloved hands slid off his head.

"Goddammit, Allison, I didn't kill her! I'll knock you unconscious if you don't stop that!" He thumped her against the wall to make his point. "Shut up and listen! I got here ten minutes ago. I was going to pick up my things and go to a hotel. She gave me a key last night. I came in and found her dead. I had no reason to kill her!"

Allison stared at him. He tentatively removed his hand. Tears welled in her eyes. "Don't hurt me. Please, Tom."

"Look at me," he said. "Look at my face. My clothes. Do you see any scratches? Any blood?"

She shook her head and ventured another glance toward the living room. "Jenny. Oh. Oh, my God."

"We've got to get out of here. *Now*."

"You have to call the police."

"What can I tell them? I don't know who did this. I haven't got one freaking idea who did this. If they find us here, what will they think?"

"Tell them what happened. Tell them you found her—"

"That's really going to fly, isn't it? How did you get here?"

"A taxi."

"Did you take it from Claridge's?"

"No, I—I—"

"Come on, babe, *think*."

"From a bookshop on Oxford Street. I didn't buy anything. I took a walk—"

"Okay. No one saw me come in. I've cleared out my stuff and wiped my prints off anything I touched."

"We can't leave her lying there!" Allison cried out.

A metallic clank came from outside. Tom looked toward the door. The thin areas of clear glass allowed them to see a heavy figure in brown coming up the walk from the gate.

"It's Jenny's mother," Tom whispered. "Let's go."

"We can't do this!"

Tom jerked Allison closer. "They'll take us both into

custody and they'll have the map. How will your father get it back this time?" His eyes were fierce, and a drop of spittle hit her cheek.

Allison looked back and forth from the woman approaching the house to the body of Jenny Gray, sprawled on the floor. Her mother set a sack on the porch and reached into her handbag. There was the jangle of keys.

"Okay."

Tom picked up a backpack by the stairs, and Allison ran after him around a turn, then into a kitchen, holding her purse tightly against her side.

Tom jerked his head toward the door and mouthed, *Open it.*

Slowed by her gloves, she fumbled with the lock, the knob, and finally got it open.

Tom hissed, "Go out first. Close it behind me. Quietly!"

The untended backyard gave onto an alley, then brick buildings whose windows were grimed with dirt. They looked both ways, then ran for the gate. Tom held his backpack in his arms. Allison's hat fell off, and she scrambled to pick it up as she heard the first screams from the house.

CHAPTER 18

When the Eurostar went into the tunnel at 180 miles per hour, Tom's ears popped from the increase in air pressure. He looked into the black windows and imagined the weight of millions of tons of cold seawater. In twenty minutes they would emerge near Calais on the northern coast of France. Allison had given him no arguments about leaving London. They had flagged down a taxi to Victoria Station, had taken another to Claridge's. Allison had brought what would fit into one suitcase, left the other in the luggage room, and paid her bill.

Now they were hurtling toward Paris. It would be dark when they got there. They would find a hotel and go on to Italy in the morning. The bright interior of the car was reflected back to him, gray seats and yellow trim. He could see Allison's profile as she bent her head over her notebook. Her tears of panic and confusion were gone. Tom had asked if she wanted to go back to Miami. She'd said no, not until the map was finished. She had promised her father.

As Tom gazed into the window, the dim outline of another face seemed to float just beyond the glass. Caramel skin and a wild mop of streaked curls. Jenny. He blinked to rid himself of the image and turned quickly toward the front of the car.

"Tom? Are you okay?"

"Sure, why?"

Allison was looking at him intently. "You're so pale."

"It's warm in here." Tom pulled his sweater over his head and stuck it into the seat pocket. He waited until someone had walked past their row, then said quietly, "I want to explain something to you. Why I was at Jenny's. Yesterday I had some things to pick up, so she took me around London. I stayed with her last night because I was running out of money and dead on my feet. It's her mother's place, but Mrs. Gray was gone when I left this morning. She saw me yesterday, but not for more than two seconds. Jenny gave me a key so I could come back and pick up my stuff. When I came in . . . I found her. There was nothing I could do."

"I know that." Closing her notebook, Allison whispered, "How did she . . . Was she shot?"

"No. She was strangled. I don't know what they used, or he used. I saw marks on her neck. If I could find the guy who did this, I think I would probably kill him."

They faced each other, their shoulders pressing into the seats. Allison said, "I still can't believe it. Oh, God, poor thing. She hadn't been back in London long enough to make enemies. Did somebody break in? Did you see anything like that? I didn't notice any broken glass."

"There wasn't any," Tom said. "The door was unlocked, so maybe she let the guy in, I don't know. Shit. If I'd been there— She wanted to come with me. I said no."

Allison's brows came together. "Stop it. Do you remotely, for an instant, imagine that it's *your* fault?"

He shook his head. "By the way. I didn't sleep with her—in case you were wondering."

"No." Allison amended, "If you did, it's nobody's business."

The light played on Allison's glasses, hiding her eyes, and Tom shifted closer to see her. "I never slept with Jenny. We were friends. She was trying to survive, like most of us. She was over here trying to make a new start."

Cool, slim fingers lightly touched his hand. "I'm sorry, Tom."

"For what?"

"Sorry that you lost a friend."

Allison leaned over so that her forehead rested on his shoulder. He could smell the scent in her hair, which cascaded down his chest. He was afraid to move; she might remember what he was to her: nothing. Running hand in hand from a murder scene had made her forget.

"And I'm sorry that I misjudged her," Allison said. "I thought Jenny might have stolen some of my father's maps from Royce Herron's house. That's why I wanted to find her, to ask her, and maybe get them back. It seems so inconsequential now."

"She did steal them."

Allison lifted her head.

"Jenny took some maps and a couple of pieces of jewelry that she pawned in Miami. She sold the maps to a dealer in London. Didn't get much for them. He probably guessed they were hot."

"Somebody needs to tell the Miami police about that. Map thieves didn't murder Royce Herron. They'll never find his killer going down that blind alley." Allison sat up in her seat. "Tom . . . do you think, maybe, that Jenny's death is related to his?"

Not something Tom wanted to get into. He said, "I don't see how. Listen, we need to decide what we're going to do when we get to Paris. You want to go on to Florence tonight? Otherwise, we'll lose half a day."

"You don't want to talk about Jenny. It's okay."

Tom nodded slowly. The truth was, he didn't want to talk about Jenny because he was beginning to get an idea of who had killed her, and he couldn't share that with Allison. Not yet.

"Hey, Betty Boop. I want you to promise me something."

Her mouth opened a little, then she laughed. "Well, what dusty file drawer did you pull *that* out of?"

"Promise me you'll never mention I was over here— not to anybody. If it ever got back to my probation officer that I was out of the country, I'd be circling the drain."

"They could send you to prison for something so minor? No way."

"To serve the remainder of my sentence. Six years, two months and change. It was a felony conviction, about ninety-five percent bogus. I'll tell you about it sometime. I'm taking a big risk, but if I can get back to Miami within a couple of weeks, I should be okay. The Weasel wants me to report to him every month or whenever he feels like yanking my chain."

"Who's the Weasel?" She leaned closer to listen.

"George Weems, my PO." Tom pulled a pen from his pocket and drew a caricature in the margin of Allison's notebook—the narrow face and rodentlike nose. "If he doesn't like my job, or my friends, or where I live, technically, I could be violated for that."

She smiled—her first in hours—at the face. Tom drew an X through it. "So you and I need to forget what we saw, at least for now. When we get back, you should also forget you know me. It could get complicated for you."

"How?"

"Being with me. The Florida Bar wouldn't like it. Applicants have to be squeaky-clean. That's what I've heard. After you're sworn in, you can go wild."

"You want to see if we can get to Italy tonight? Why not?"

Allison pushed her tray table up and began putting her notebooks and study guides into her tote bag. "They have wireless Internet on the Eurostar. I can use my laptop to find a flight to Florence. We get into the Gare du Nord about seven. We'll transfer to an RER train for Charles de Gaulle or Orly Airport, depending on where the next flight leaves from, and . . . *siamo in Firenze alle dieci*. We're in Florence by ten o'clock."

"You are too much," Tom said.

"I should arrange a rental car and a hotel, too." She smiled. "No more Claridge's. I'll get two rooms at a reasonably priced hotel . . . near the Arno River? I'd love to show you . . . well, if we have time. I know you have to work. Tom, would you please tell me what you're going to do? There's no reason to keep me totally in the dark."

"Okay. You're right. I'm hooking up with a friend of mine who used to live in Miami, Eddie Ferraro. He's worked in print shops all his life, and he came over here about four years ago. He lives up the coast, but we'll meet in Florence. I'm paying him half what I earn. Don't worry, the map isn't going to be a digital image. We're just taking some shortcuts on the computer. I'll explain it all later. This morning I went by a print shop in London and got a high-res scan of the map, and after we talked, I took some closeup images of the Corelli sea charts in the Maritime Museum. This gives me a better idea of Corelli's techniques as a printer. I'll take some more photos at the national library in Florence."

"The Biblioteca Nazionale," Allison said. "I can show you where it is."

"I can find it." He held up a hand. "Don't worry, I'll keep in touch. Eddie and I will work on the map, I'll take it to Miami, and voilà. You owe me twenty-five grand. Plus expenses."

"If the map is acceptable to my father."

"It will be," Tom said.

Allison tilted her head. "Eddie Ferraro. Isn't he the same man your sister Rose used to date? I think I've heard of him."

"You've heard the gossip. They were living together. Rose would have married him, but Eddie got arrested on a federal counterfeiting warrant and jumped bail. He was already out of that life, and he'd never been a major player, but the government wanted twenty years. You're consorting with some bad people, Allison. That's what happens when you decide to go into forgery. Now you tell me something. Why does Stuart want this map? He told me it was for himself, but I don't buy that."

"Sorry. I'll have to claim attorney-client privilege."

"After I spilled my story?"

"No," she repeated.

The words were forming in Tom's mouth, telling Allison about Rhonda's offer of ten thousand dollars, but he set his teeth together. Allison didn't need to know. She would go straight to Stuart with it and possibly stir up a

fight. Would the deal be canceled? Could be, and Tom
wanted to ride this pony as far as it would take him before that happened. Basically, Rhonda had said her husband was crazy. Tom didn't believe that, but he added it
to the other bits of information about Stuart Barlowe. He
wanted the truth. He wanted to know what Royce Herron
had known. Tom didn't want to hear Barlowe telling him,
*Sure, I'll help you get back into the U.S., but give me the
map first, and we'll have to renegotiate the price.*

He leaned into the aisle. A sign over the door announced that food could be found four cars ahead of
them. "Are you hungry?"

"I hate train food," Allison said. "Let's just eat in
Paris. I know this little café near Notre Dame that's not
touristy at all. It's ten minutes on the Metro. We have
time."

"Let me just see what they've got," he said, pushing
out of his seat. "You want some coffee or anything? Stay
here, okay?" He shot a quick glance at the suitcases in
the rack over their heads. She nodded and told him to
bring her some juice.

At the end of the car Tom pressed a black square, and
the glass door smoothly slid away. He waited in the compartment between the cars for a group of German
teenagers to come through. Then bright lights rushed at
high speed past the windows. The train had come out of
the tunnel. Tom went over and looked through the small
window to his right. A pale rim of fading gray separated
the sky and the dark landscape of France. A line of posts
blurred by the window; the lights of a house in the distance flickered and vanished.

Staring out the small window, his thoughts turned
again to Jenny Gray and Royce Herron. But there weren't

just two deaths, there were three. Jenny's friend Carla was also dead. They had all had one thing in common: Larry Gerard. The girls had both worked for Larry. They'd been involved in his dirty tricks to win approval for those gargantuan towers on the river—which Judge Herron had opposed.

Removing Carla from the picture, Tom could draw a line to Stuart Barlowe. Barlowe was threatened by whatever secret Herron had discovered, and Jenny had pretended to know about. But in London, Jenny wouldn't have been a threat.

Tom returned to his first theory: The Metropolis. Jenny had known about the bribery and blackmail. Stuart Barlowe wasn't really the kind of guy who could lift a phone and hire a hit man in London. Larry, on the other hand . . . Larry knew people who would choke a girl's life out of her. Tom had been on the boat with one of them.

A woman came through the compartment with a bottle of wine and some cups, reminding Tom where he had intended to go. He pushed the button to open the door and was about to step into the next car when he noticed a man coming out of the washroom at the other end. Dark slacks and sweater, dark hair. The man sat down in a row facing the rear of the train, and his face was quickly hidden behind the seat of the passenger in front of him.

Backing up, Tom leaned against a luggage rack crammed with suitcases. It had only been a glimpse. Two seconds at the most, but he knew he'd seen this man before. Muscular build, mid- to late thirties. Arching eyebrows, a narrow nose, a widow's peak on his forehead. The same face he had seen in the shopwindow in London.

Tom hit the door. It hissed opened and slid back. When he got to the end of the car he stood next to the man's seat until, with a quizzical expression, the man looked up at him. Tom leaned a hand on his seat back. "Excuse me. Do I know you?"

That produced an equally quizzical little smile and an accent Tom couldn't place. "I'm sorry. I . . . don't speak English."

"Didn't I see you on Regent Street in London yesterday afternoon?"

"Sorry." The man shrugged, kept smiling. The other man in the row glanced up at Tom without interest, then went back to his *Times* newspaper.

Tom stood up. "My mistake."

He made his way back through the train, having lost any sense of which car was his, until he saw Allison and stood beside her. She'd been watching through the window.

"You didn't get anything?"

"The line was too long." He glanced in the other direction, toward the washroom at the rear of their car. "I'll be right back."

He went in and closed the narrow door. The light came on, shining on stainless steel. The *tick-tick-tick-tick-tick* of the wheels came through from below. Tom turned on his cell phone and waited while it went through its routine of finding a tower.

No mistake. That had been the same guy. Tom had seen him three times. Twice, he could have said it was a coincidence, but not three. Like three murders. Too many for a coincidence.

He thumbed through his address book. Put the phone to his ear. A few seconds later, a voice said, "*Pronto.*"

"Eddie, it's Tom."

"Where are you?"

"We just got into France on the Eurostar. I think we have a problem."

CHAPTER 19

Having visited Paris more than a few times, Allison knew how to navigate the Metro system. When she and Tom rushed off the Eurostar with five or six hundred other passengers at the Gare du Nord, she followed the signs for the RER line heading for Charles de Gaulle Airport. Tom pulled her red beret off her head and told her to stash it in her pocket; it was too obvious in the sea of dark clothing. The wheels of her suitcase clicked on the tile floor. Birds swooped in and out of the steel roof supports and fluttered at the high, arched windows.

They took an escalator down. Tom turned and looked up at the faces of the people behind them. Allison said, "You're making me really paranoid." She might not have believed Tom's improbable story—a man following him in London, then showing up on the train—except for what she herself had seen: Jenny Gray lying dead, strangled. Tom couldn't say the man in the black coat had killed her, but he didn't want to take chances.

On the advice of his friend Eddie Ferraro, they had

changed their itinerary. Do not fly to Florence, Eddie had said; take the train to Milan, then another to Genoa, heading south along the Ligurian coast. Eddie lived in a small town where he knew everyone, and this time of year, a stranger would be as obvious as a flamingo.

At the RER entrance, Allison swiped her credit card for tickets that would get them to Charles de Gaulle. The train was crammed with people heading to the suburbs in the north of the city, more workers than tourists, many North Africans, and at least one woman in a full-length black chador. At the next stop they waited till the doors were about to close, then rushed off the train, crossed the platform, and took the next train going back the way they had come.

Tom sat facing inward, leaning against his backpack, cradling his messenger bag. Allison pointed up and told him that if they were walking, they would see the two square towers of Notre Dame cathedral. They could cross the Seine to the Left Bank and walk along the riverbank and browse the little bookshops.

Tom said, "You were going to take me to dinner."

Allison smiled. "Next time."

Ten minutes later, at the stop for the Gare de Lyon, they took a short Metro line to the departure point for the night train to Milan.

They were in the fourth car behind the engine. A uniformed attendant led them along the corridor, windows on one side, faux wood paneling and doors on the other. Before reaching Paris, Allison had phoned ahead to purchase a first-class sleeping compartment with two berths. The attendant helped put away the bags, showed them the tiny bathroom, and requested that they not use the shower until the train was moving. He handed Allison a menu and wine list. They could eat in the dining car or here in their compartment.

"*Ici, s'il vous plaît*," said Allison. She asked if he would bring some water and a bottle of white wine immediately.

"Make that two beers for me," Tom said. He was looking out the window at the people on the platform pulling their suitcases to other cars in the long train. "And tell him we don't want to be disturbed."

She did so in her elementary French, followed by a five-euro note. "*Bien sûr, ma'am'selle*." He nodded and closed the door on his way out.

Wearily, Allison took off her jacket and hung it in the closet; she'd left her long coat in London. They would arrive at Milano Centrale, the main station in Milan, at 6:40 AM, then take the 7:10 to Genoa, arriving in La Spezia three hours later. Eddie Ferraro would drive them to an area called Cinque Terre—five little villages along the coast. Allison had heard of them but had never been there.

Tom lowered the curtain in the window until the magnet clicked at the bottom, then turned on a light over the seats. He inspected the couch that would be made into one narrow berth, the curve above it that would pull down for the other. In the small compartment, on a train that was about to take them somewhere neither had been, there was an intimacy that Allison had not considered when she had bought the tickets. When Tom turned to speak to her, the same thought must have crossed his mind, too.

"Well. This is cozy." A smile slowly appeared.

Allison gave him a warning look. She opened her tote bag, found her electrical adapter and phone charger, and plugged in her cell phone. "I have to call my father. He must be wondering where I am. Don't worry, I know what not to say."

"Tell him we're waiting to board a flight to Florence."

"Why?"

Tom lifted the phone out of her hand. "Listen to me, Allison. No one knows where we are, especially not Larry and his gangster friend." Tom held the phone over his head when Allison reached for it. "Your father tells his wife, his wife tells Larry . . ."

"Larry couldn't care less about the map."

"I said no."

"Okay, then. We're on our way to Florence."

As she dialed her father's mobile number, a knock came at the door. The drinks had arrived. Tom took the tray and paid the attendant while Allison waited for Stuart to pick up. When he did, she told him everything was on schedule. They would be catching a train soon to Florence—

Tom mouthed *airport,* lifted his hands in a gesture of frustration, and Allison grimaced and mouthed *sorry!* She told Stuart she wasn't sure where they'd be staying . . . and yes, Tom had already started working on the map.

"Dad, where is Rhonda? . . . Well, I called Fernanda this morning, and she said that Rhonda took all the cruise wear out of her suitcase and packed her fur coat and some sweaters, so I thought you might know. . . ."

There was a long silence on the other end, followed by Stuart saying that Rhonda had an independent streak, didn't she? He asked to speak to Tom Fairchild.

Putting down his glass of beer, Tom took the phone. His end of the conversation was in monosyllables. Then a laugh. "I'm sorry, but that's not how I do things. We agreed that I would make your map for you, and you would pay me. That doesn't include the right to observe the process. . . . When I'm finished, you can see it." He hit the disconnect button.

"What was that about?"

"If he calls back, don't answer it." Tom returned to his beer. "Your father wants to watch. Nobody watches."

"Did he say he was coming to Italy?"

"No, but it wouldn't surprise me if he shows up. Where is Mrs. Barlowe, if she's not in Hawaii?"

Allison shrugged. "She didn't want to go on the cruise. Neither did my father, apparently."

Tom chugged his beer, then opened the next one and sprawled in the seat by the window to sip it. This was his habit, Allison remembered. First beer to give him a buzz, and the second to enjoy. She sat in the other seat to drink her wine. The liquid jostled slightly in her glass. Tom raised the curtain far enough to confirm that the train was in motion.

"Hell of a way to see Paris," he said.

About ten PM the train attendant, now in a white jacket, collected the trays from dinner. He came back a few minutes later, opened the beds, and took the pillows from a drawer underneath. Did they need more water? Was there anything else he could do for them? Tom growled that he could leave them alone. Allison said, "*Non, tout est bien, merci beaucoup.*" She gave the man another five euros. He touched his cap. "*Bonne nuit, ma'am'selle, m'sieur.*"

When he was gone, Allison frowned at Tom. "You can be so rude."

He held up his hands. "Sorry. Why don't you get ready

for bed, or whatever you want to do. I'm going to take a walk."

"Where are you going?"

"Nowhere. I'm going to let Eddie know we made it. I'll be back. Lock the door behind me. If anybody knocks, ask who it is."

Allison understood. "You're going looking for someone, aren't you? What will you do if you find him? Beat him up?"

"Not me, I'm a peaceable guy." Tom stepped into the corridor, then smiled through the crack in the door. "I'll just shove him off the train."

An hour had passed before she heard his *rat-tat-tat*. She got up from the seat by the window, where she had sat in the darkness with her arms around her knees to watch the flat landscape of central France roll by. Preceded by a mournful, faraway whistle, the train had passed a dozen small stations without slowing.

She turned on a light and asked who was there. "Gaetano Corelli," came the reply. She unlocked the door.

Coming inside, Tom took a long look at what she was wearing: a Boston Red Sox T-shirt and plaid flannel pajama bottoms. "Wow, that's hot."

"Shut up," she said. "Did you see any mysterious men in black coats?"

"Nope." He sat down and untied his hiking boots. "I did the whole train and hung out in the bar for a while. What've you been doing, studying?"

"Not really. I can't concentrate. I keep thinking about Jenny Gray. That was terrible, what happened to her." Allison folded her glasses into their case.

Tom nodded.

"It's so ironic," she said, "so bizarre, even, that Jenny knew Royce Herron—she was working on his maps—and he was shot to death, and now she's dead, too. And you think that man did it. But why? And why would he be after *you*? All this on top of what happened on Larry's boat with Marek Vuksinic. It's all connected, isn't it?" When Tom's only reply was a shrug, she said, "Uh-huh. Sure. You don't know anything about it."

"I *don't* know," he insisted. "Let's get some sleep." Tom took off his pullover. His T-shirt came up too, and he tugged it back down to his waist. His chest was not nearly as scrawny as it had been twelve years ago. Muscles moved over his rib cage.

Averting her eyes, Allison closed her outline of tort law and clipped her pen to the notebook.

"Hey, what's this?" Tom had picked up the miniature globe that sat on the table. It was only two inches high from its top to its little brass stand. The oceans were enameled blue, the continents ivory, and a thin line of gold marked the equator. Without her glasses, Allison could see a fuzzy image of Tom spinning the globe on its tilted axis. "You used to keep this on your windowsill in your dorm room."

A picture flashed into her head: fat snowflakes falling silently in the pale gray morning, and Tom sleeping beside her, his arm around her waist.

"I always take it with me on trips," she said. "My father bought it for me in Dublin when I was a little girl, not even three years old. He was traveling a lot in those days for my grandfather's company in Toronto."

"And he said the globe would tell you where he was."

Allison smiled. "You remember that?"

"I remember a lot of things." Tom held the little globe

under the light and examined the continents. "You used to hate your old man. Is that why you came back to Miami? To see if you could make up with him?"

"That's part of it. I never felt like I belonged in the North. I guess the older you get, the more family means to you—even if it's only one person. We're getting along fine now."

"That's good." Tom set the globe beside its box, which held a negative shape of faded red velvet that the globe would fit into. "So . . . is Larry pretty much running your dad's business?"

"No. Where did you get that idea?"

"Larry was saying some things on the boat."

"He likes to talk," Allison said.

"What about The Metropolis? Larry's in charge of that, isn't he?"

"He thinks he is. I'm not sure how much responsibility Stuart has given him." She let her head fall against the seat. "It was my own choice to stay out of my father's life. I was just this prickly bundle of resentment. I hated all of them, especially Rhonda. She and I will never be close, not that I give a damn. What did my father see in her?"

"Big boobs?"

Allison made a face. "Oh, please. They aren't even real."

His grin fading, Tom said, "What do you know about the investors in The Metropolis? Like, who they are, what they do—"

"Nothing. Why are you so interested?"

"Just trying to fit some pieces together, that's all. Here's something Jenny told me. The zoning approvals were up in the air. There was a man in the zoning department who had to sign off on it, and he wouldn't. Larry Gerard set him up with a prostitute. Her name was Carla Kelly. A friend of Jenny's. They took pictures to black-mail him into going the right way on the zoning."

"What a lie. That . . . that's not remotely true!"

"I'm not accusing Stuart—not unless he knows about it," Tom added.

"Totally did not happen. If it did happen, which I highly doubt, Larry went behind his back."

"But you don't put it past Larry. Do you?"

Allison felt sick. She wanted to call her father, to warn him. "What are you trying to tell me? That Larry was involved in Jenny Gray's murder? Is that where this is going?"

"Well, yours truly is going to take a shower." Tom went over to his backpack and dug around for some clean underwear. "Did you leave me any hot water?"

"Not a drop."

"That figures."

While he was in the bathroom, she tucked herself into the lower bunk. He came out dressed in T-shirt and shorts, smelling of soap, with his hair sticking straight up in front. He unplugged his cell phone from the charger and tossed it to the bunk, then turned off the lights. Allison looked up at his silhouette. She held the top edge of the blanket at her chin.

The way up was to step on a low table, then grasp a handhold on the wall. From the dim light through the window, Allison saw muscled legs and a tattoo just above his ankle, a Celtic design that hadn't been there before. He thumped around for a minute getting comfortable, and when he was quiet, she said, "Is your nose right next to the ceiling?"

"I've got about eighteen inches. Want to see?"

"No."

"Whatever happened to Betty Boop?"

"She grew up. Go to sleep, Tom."

The whistle sounded again and lights moved across the compartment, swinging from back to front. Then the train went around a curve, and Allison could feel her body shifting.

Tom whispered, "Allison. You awake?"

Her eyes fluttered open. "Yes."

"I want to explain some things to you. What happened after I came back to Miami. Why I went to jail."

"You don't have to."

"Yeah, I do. You know the trouble I got into as a kid, starting after my father passed away. Shoplifting, smoking pot, truancy—enough of that, you get tagged as a juvenile offender, and that's how the police and the judge and even your friends see you, and you start thinking of yourself in those terms. I was a bad guy and proud of it.

"We first went out when we were sixteen, after that Green Day concert, remember? How did I get so lucky? That's what I thought at the time. You were beautiful—you still are—and smart, and I wanted to be on your level. You were a little wild, too, admit it, but you turned things around for me. I graduated and put a portfolio together and got accepted to SVA. My family was behind me, and I did all right in the grades department. But you had your rich friends, and I couldn't keep up. Then my mother got sick, and the money ran out. I felt like I'd been robbed of everything. Then she died."

The rush of the wheels on the tracks changed pitch as the train went into a tunnel, then out again.

Tom's voice seemed nearer, as though he had moved

closer to the edge of his bunk. "That was probably the worst time of my life. I was drinking a lot. Two DUIs. Got into some fights. No reason, just generally pissed off at the world. I was in jail four or five times, a couple of days here, two weeks there. I jumped the fence at a rock concert, and a cop grabbed me, and I pushed him. That's battery on a police officer, a felony. It would have plea-bargained down, but I had an attitude and a list of priors. They gave me a month. I finished that, then got stopped in a car with a friend of mine who had half an ounce of cocaine in his pocket. A surprise to me, but since I was already such a badass, they charged me along with him. The court threw that one out, but another felony arrest went on my record.

"I was doing some pickup construction work and helping Rose at the shop when I met Eddie Ferraro. He moved in with Rose, and he kept me going straight and threatened to beat my ass if I didn't. Then he got arrested on that counterfeiting case and jumped bail. By then I'd started my design business, and I was sharing an apartment with a guy I'd met in rehab. I thought he was taking care of the rent, but he didn't, and the landlord changed the locks. All my computer equipment and my stereo and CDs were in there. I didn't have the money, so I went in through a window. The landlord showed up and we got into a fight. Somebody called the cops, and I was arrested for burglary, assault, battery, and grand theft. The landlord claimed five thousand dollars in damages. I didn't do any damage besides the window, but that's what he stuck me with. I was looking at a possible ten years in prison. Rose mortgaged the shop to pay for a good lawyer. He persuaded the judge to give me a three-sixty-four—that's a year in jail, minus a day—plus eight years probation. I've done two years. I have six to go. I still owe four thousand dollars in restitution."

When Tom's silence stretched out, Allison understood that he was waiting for her to say something. "I can't begin to imagine how hard it was for you. I'm so sorry."

"For what? I survived."

"I know, but . . ."

"It'll be okay when the map is finished." Tom laughed. "My European vacation."

From the corridor a bell softly chimed, and a voice announced in French, then in English, that in fifteen minutes they would reach Lyon.

"Tom?" She reached up and felt for his hand. "I'm glad you told me."

Silence. Then he took a couple of breaths. Blankets shifted. More silence. Then, "Allison?"

"What?"

"I'll never get to sleep." He jumped down to the floor, leaned under the upper bunk, and kissed her. His skin was smooth from a shave, and his mouth was warm. She tasted mint toothpaste.

He stood up. "I hope you don't ask me to apologize."

"It's okay. I'll forgive you this time."

"Sleep tight, Betty Boop." He put another kiss on the end of her nose.

When he had climbed into his bunk again, she said softly, "Boop-boop-a-doop."

Twelve years ago, he had rented a room in an old house in New Jersey, a converted attic with a view of lower Manhattan. His drawings of the skyline were pinned up all over the place. The last time they had spoken, Allison had gone over there to have it out with him. He had embarrassed her at a party. Was that it? She had danced with someone else, and he had gotten drunk. Or had it been the time he had gone two days without calling her? Or their arguments about whether to spend Sunday renting a motorcycle or lying in bed. Whatever it was, she came to his place to collect whatever she'd left there. She yelled at him. He yelled back at her and called her a bitch. She slapped him and ran out. Now, after all this time, she couldn't remember, not at all, what they had been fighting about.

Slowly she came out of sleep, aware of a telephone ringing. It took her a while to figure out where she was. She heard Tom shifting in the upper berth, then a thud as he stepped to the floor. A light went on. Hiding her head under the blanket, she went back to sleep.

Then Tom was telling her to wake up. He was fully dressed, pulling on her arms. "Allison, get up. Come on. We have to go."

"Not yet," she mumbled.

"Wake up, sunshine. We're getting off in Torino."

"Where?"

"Turin. We'll be there pretty soon. I let you sleep as long as I could. We're all packed."

"Turin?" She grabbed for the covers and moaned, "It's Milan, not Turin!"

"Allison, listen. When I took that walk earlier, I saw someone—not the man who was following me in London, but the guy sitting next to him on the Eurostar. I called Eddie, and he said to get off in Torino."

"Are you insane? It's just some guy going in the same direction we are!"

"No, it's more than that. It's the way he acted. How he avoided me. We're getting off. Eddie is already on his way." Tom shoved her into a sitting position and lay her clothes in her lap. "Come on, Allison. Move it."

She felt her way to the bathroom, and when she came out again dressed and awake, Tom was in his coat and cap, and the bags were stacked by the door. As she crammed her sleep shirt inside her suitcase, an announcement came over the speakers in the corridor: *Arriviamo in Torino, stazione Porta Susa. Ripartiremo alle cinque e quarantacinque.*

"They said the train is leaving at five forty-five."

"That's ten minutes." Tom put his backpack over his shoulders, then the bag with his computer. The platform was empty except for a worker pushing a wide broom and a man in a trainman's tunic making sure the doors were closed. When he came toward their car, Tom said, "Let's go."

They rushed down the corridor, and Tom pushed through the door. The man on the platform erupted in a stream of heated Italian, but Tom jumped down and turned to take Allison's hand. She swung her suitcase. Tom caught the handle, and she leaped after it.

The man slammed the door just as the air brakes hissed and the deep thrum of the engine grew louder. The train began to move.

Allison noticed Tom staring at the train. When she turned, she saw what he did: a blond-haired man running along the corridor, hurrying for the door.

"Oh, my God, is that him?"

Tom gave the man the finger, pivoting as the train pulled out of the station and the man hit the window with his fist.

"Tom, let's go!"

They ran. The station walls had been refaced in squares of white marble, and fluorescent lights shone on scuffed concrete floors. The wheels on Allison's bag clattered down a flight of stairs that led to a wide corridor hung with posters and train schedules. No one else was about.

Tom looked both ways. "Eddie said he'd be here. Maybe he's outside."

Allison pointed to the door marked USCITA, and they went through to a sidewalk beneath a wide overhang. A light snow was falling. Across a wide intersection, they saw a four-story building, a colonnade of arches, and wires suspended over the streetcar tracks in the cobblestones.

"Where the hell is he?" Tom's breath hung in the still air.

Headlights swerved from the street. A small brown sedan stopped in front of them, and the driver's door opened. A man got out and came around, his boots leaving dark prints in the thin layer of snow.

Eddie Ferraro was a little taller than Tom, wiry, with short gray hair and a face that was all angles and lines. The men embraced quickly before Eddie turned his smile toward Allison.

"Ready? We've got a long drive ahead of us."

CHAPTER 20

A stone fireplace, a glass of red wine. The village of Champorcher in the valley, framed in the windows like a postcard. A church tower, roofs covered with snow. And a cello to accompany the sunset.

Leo was playing Prokofiev. Rhonda felt the fire of the music as she felt the wine and the heat of the flames snapping on the hearth. Leo played with his entire body, elbows angled up, his smooth bald head jerking to the movement of the bow, left hand arching over the strings. She had picked out her clothing with care: a white sweater with rhinestones spangling the low neckline, slim white pants, her white fox-fur coat and hat. When she'd arrived, Leo had kissed her cheeks and said she looked like a snow queen.

She expected to be asked to stay the night. Leo wouldn't want her driving through the mountains after dark. The heavy snows of the past week had left patches of ice on the road, and the weather forecast called for more of the same tonight. Rhonda sipped her wine and examined the pros and cons of spending the night at Leo

Zurin's chalet. Her suitcase was at the hotel in Milan, but she had put a tote bag in the trunk of her rented car. She had thought of calling Stuart and telling him she wasn't coming back to Miami at all.

The cello moaned as the bow attacked the strings. It was difficult music to follow. Rhonda wished he'd chosen something by Bach, not this wild Slavic sawing. The last rays of the sun reached into the timbered room. A patch of light moved by millimeters across the gold frame that held the photo of the Corelli replica.

Leo had been stunned when she'd told him the original had been stolen. She said she had flown six thousand miles to throw herself on his mercy. It was her fault; she'd been the one to suggest that Tom Fairchild deliver the map. He had disappeared with it in Bimini. Stuart was in absolute anguish. Of course they would replace it with another rare map. The price didn't matter.

After an excruciating minute of silence, in which Leo seemed to balance between tears and rage, he had smiled at her and picked up his cello.

Problem solved, or nearly. It only remained to tell Stuart, which could wait until she returned to Miami. *We're safe now. I've fixed everything.*

Rhonda had met Leo Zurin six years ago on a cruise from Barcelona to Istanbul. He had lost thousands at roulette and laughed about it; he had danced like a Cossack in the ballroom while everyone clapped in time; and he had taken her with animal ferocity against the railing while Stuart sat in the bar having another nightcap.

She sipped her wine and relaxed into the corner of the sofa. The disk of the sun had diminished to a slender orange curve between two white peaks. Then it winked out, just as Leo ended the solo with a last, scraping stroke of his bow. Rhonda put down her wineglass and applauded.

"Bravo! Marvelous, Leo. You play with such *passion*. I would love an encore. Could you?"

Leo gasped. "*Stelle!* Look, the sun is down. I've played too long. You will have trouble driving if you don't leave right away."

"But . . . I don't have to return to Milan tonight," she said.

"Oh, forgive me, *carissima,* I have plans." He set his cello in its stand and rushed to the sofa, where she had thrown her coat. "You must go immediately. The roads through the mountains are treacherous after dark."

She held out her arms for the coat and pulled her hair over the collar, smiling to mask her disappointment. She rested a hand on Leo's chest. "Shall I tell Stuart that you quite, quite forgive him?"

"Ah, well. If the map has been *stolen*, what can I do? And you have no information on where this fellow might be? This Tom . . ."

"Tom Fairchild. I'm so sorry, Leo. Stuart has hired some detectives to track him down, and if we hear anything at all, we'll let you know." She put on her hat, checked it in the mirror in the foyer, and collected her clutch purse.

At the door she said, "Do some thinking about what we can get for you. This may be for the best. You'll have a lovely map, something truly spectacular and rare. I know how much you wanted the Corelli, but there are so many maps of better quality."

Leo walked with her onto the terrace. She skidded in her high-heeled boots, and he caught her elbow in a grip painfully tight. "Be careful, my lovely."

The wind ruffled the white fox fur against her cheeks. "Thank you for being so kind, Leo. It's such a relief not to worry. I'll tell Stuart to call you in the next few days, and you can discuss business." She laughed gaily. "I leave that up to you men. But you must let me take you to dinner. I'll be in Italy at least through the week. I'd love to do some skiing."

"Yes, let's do that. I'll call you. Now you must go. Drive carefully."

"I will." She touched her lips to his. "*Grazie mille, caro amico*."

He threw kisses from the terrace as she crossed the snowy driveway to her car. "*Addio*, Rhonda."

"Ciao! Call me!"

From a window in the kitchen Marek watched this display. He had arrived from London half an hour ago and had come through a side door, not wanting to see him. Signora Barlowe got into her rented Audi, waved, and drove through the gate. Her car vanished into the pine woods that surrounded the house. Leo had sent her away just as snow was falling, with a snowstorm moving in. Marek wondered what she had done to make Leo so angry.

He extinguished his cigarette in the sink, earning some curses from Luigi. He walked outside and around to the terrace. Leo saw him. "You're back. Did you hear my conversation with that woman?"

"No, Leo."

"You should have. You would have had a good laugh. My map has been stolen, so she says, by the same man you are looking for, Tom Fairchild." Leo made his hands into fists and screamed in Russian, "*Yobtvuyu mat!*" His voice echoed from the mountain, and veins stood out on his temples.

Marek said, "Her husband told you he was taking the map to a restorer in London."

"Yes!" Leo beamed.

"Doesn't she know?"

"I think not. Which of them is lying? It will be great fun to hear Barlowe's explanation. I'll call him after dinner. Does he have the map, or was it stolen by Tom Fairchild? What about Fairchild? Did you find him?"

"He left London. He was staying with the British girl, Jenny Gray. She's dead. A knotted scarf, they think. A tidy job." Marek smoothed his mustache to hide his smile. "No, Leo. Someone else got to her first. I gave her mother some money to talk to me. She said an American, blond, about thirty, by the name of Tom stayed with her daughter two nights ago. Her daughter told her that this Tom was going to take her to Italy. That is all the mother knows. Scotland Yard has no leads."

"Did Fairchild kill her?"

"Probably yes."

"So he's coming to Italy. Ah. Maybe he's planning to sell me my map. Or shoot me."

When they had settled next to the fire, Marek told him what he had learned from his contacts in Miami. Tom Fairchild had a record of violent crimes. He lived in the same house with, or rented an apartment from, a man named Fritz Klein, who had been, until the mid-1980s, a civilian pilot flying between Miami and Central America, possibly paid by the CIA. Klein's wife, or the woman in the house, whose name was Sandra Wiley, was the widow of Pedro Bonifacio Escalona, a Peruvian cocaine trafficker last residing in Miami. Sandra Wiley herself had served ten years. Her late husband's cousin was a leftist candidate for the presidency of Peru, whose chief of staff was—

"Let me." Leo held up a hand. "Oscar Contreras."

"Everything is connected," Marek said.

Leo pondered for several minutes. "These facts don't prove anything. Fairchild could be an American agent. Or he's working for Contreras. Or he's a map thief."

"When I find him, we'll see."

After more than an hour creeping down the mountain in the snow, Rhonda's arms ached from clutching the wheel. The moment she turned onto the autostrada to Milan, the tension lifted, and her hands began shaking so badly she had to pull over for ten minutes to recover. She took out her cell phone and entered Larry's number, as she had done a dozen times since arriving in Italy at noon. She wanted to hear him say it was over; that the map was a pile of ashes, and Tom Fairchild was at the bottom of the Thames.

After a few rings, the service cut off. It was these damned mountains. She checked the rearview for lights, put the Audi back into gear, and continued toward her hotel. The four-star Hotel Colosseo, a kilometer from Malpensa Airport, had been designed to resemble the Colosseum in Rome, but the windows were sound-proof, and the rooms a soothing, minimalist beige. She and Stuart always stayed there when flying in and out of Milan.

A valet took her keys. Rhonda put her Louis Vuitton tote over her shoulder. Her heels clicked across the lobby, then slowed as she saw her husband sitting in a boxy chrome-and-brown chair on the other side. His overcoat lay across his suitcase. He was holding a short glass with ice in it.

He smiled and lifted a hand in greeting. Taking a breath, Rhonda went over to find out how this had happened.

"There she is," said Stuart, putting a kiss on her cheek. "You weren't on the cruise, so I asked myself, 'Where would she go?' "

Rhonda maintained her smile. "Did you just fly in from Miami?"

"No, no, from London. I was trying to find Tom Fairchild—just missed him. Allison called me last night en route to Firenze. She and Fairchild are traveling by train. And she informed me that *you* had skipped out on the cruise to Hawaii."

"She loves to play tattletale," Rhonda said.

"Lay off her," Stuart said. "I'm glad she told me, because I would hate, hate, hate to think that my dear wife had come to Italy *behind my back* to make my life difficult. I've been here for three hours. Waiting for you. Hoping you would return my calls."

"My cell phone isn't working."

"Of course. Shall we go up?"

In the elevator she smelled alcohol on his breath. The mirrored doors flashed their images back to her: blond woman, white fur; a tall, thin bearded man in a black cashmere sweater, dark circles under his eyes.

The doors opened. Rhonda walked ahead and slid her card key into the slot. She tossed her coat and hat onto the bed. The smooth brown duvet matched the plain curtain on a rod at the silent window. Like the lobby, the room was designed for business, all squares and no froufrou.

Stuart set his suitcase against the wall and hung up his coat in the closet. "What are you up to, my sweet? Please don't tell me you were planning to see Leo Zurin."

"I've just come from seeing him. That's where I've been, Stuart. With Leo, solving our problem."

Stuart turned slowly, staring at her. He wet his lips and put a hand flat on his stomach. "Oh, Rhonda. What did you say to him?"

"I did what you didn't have the guts to do. I told him he couldn't have the map. I created a story, the only story that had a chance of working. You paid Tom Fairchild to deliver the Corelli. He's an expert with maps. He owns a shop, so you trusted him. You put him on Larry's boat because of some problems with his passport, and he vanished with the map at the first chance. You were devastated. He betrayed you—"

Laughing, Stuart combed his hair off his forehead.

"I had to! There is no way that Tom Fairchild can forge a Renaissance map. I'll tell you the kind of artist he is—a con artist, and Leo would see it immediately."

"Oh . . . Rhonda."

"I told Leo you were desperately sorry. I begged him to forgive you. I even said it was my fault. I took the blame. I was the one who'd suggested that you hire Tom Fairchild. I told him we'd buy him any other map he wanted. It doesn't matter how much it costs. We can sell some of the paintings. My jewelry. Leo didn't say anything about pulling out of The Metropolis. It's all right now. We're fine."

"We . . . are not . . . *fine!*" Stuart's palm swept toward her, and a fire exploded behind her eyes. Rhonda sat heavily on the ottoman.

He stood over her. His voice cracked. "Two days

ago . . . I told Leo that I was delivering the Corelli to London myself . . . to have it restored. I promised Leo . . . two weeks, maybe less. You see, Rhonda, I was trying to buy enough time for Fairchild to make the duplicate. We didn't have a problem until *you created one!*"

Through her dizziness, her thoughts went back to the house in Champorcher, and Leo smiling, showing his small white teeth. She moaned. "Why didn't you tell me? If you had told me, do you think I would have gone to him?"

"We're dead. It's over." Stuart sank onto the end of the bed.

"Don't say that! We can fix it. We can think of a way." Rhonda stood up, steadying herself on the ottoman. "You have to call him. Tell him . . . Leo, the map was already gone when I spoke to you before. Tell him that. You knew Tom Fairchild had it, and you wanted time to get it back."

"It's too late," Stuart said.

She took his shoulders. "Do you want to see everything we've built swept away? That's what will happen if Leo pulls out of The Metropolis. I won't let you roll over and give up! I won't allow it! Stuart, look at me. This will work. Look at me. You have to call him. Apologize for not being truthful. You'll find the map. You're sure of it. Tell him Tom Fairchild is on his way to Italy. He's run away with your daughter, and you can track him that way—"

"No, I can't bring Allison into it," Stuart said.

"How else can you find Tom Fairchild? Tell him Allison doesn't know. Tell him anything. Fairchild contacted you. He thought you wanted him to deliver the map. He has it, and you'll get it from him. Tell him I was wrong, the map wasn't stolen at all. Tell him your wife was mistaken. Stuart, it will work. It will."

The vaguest of smiles lifted the corners of Stuart's mouth. "In for a dime, in for a dollar."

Rhonda wrapped her arms around his head and stroked his hair. "Yes, darling. It's going to be all right."

"Fairchild has to finish the map," he said.

"He will. I'm sure he will."

Stuart pulled away and rubbed his hands down his face. "You and I will stay in Italy until this thing is resolved. Call your friends and make whatever excuses you like."

"Yes, Stuart. That's what we'll do. Are you hungry? Shall I order some dinner to the room?"

"Please."

"What are you in the mood for?"

"I don't know. . . . Fish. Veal."

"Osso bucco, then. And some wine."

"I might take a shower."

"Why don't you?"

Stuart went into the bathroom. Rhonda heard the rattle of a pill bottle. The rush of water into a glass. When he did speak to Leo, his voice would not betray him. Stuart had always possessed an ability to show perfect confidence, an odd gift for a man who had been crumbling for thirty years. Rhonda had only recently begun to see this. It was worse than she'd feared. Stuart was very close to a breakdown. Rhonda wasn't sure what could be done about it.

Flinging back the curtain, she looked past the tarp-covered swimming pool, over the opposite wall of the hotel, to the lights of some low industrial buildings, and the airport. A jet was just taking off. If it were day, the white peaks of the Alps would be visible.

As she went to pick up the room service menu, she noticed her purse in the chair, and her cell phone halfway out of it. She tilted her head to see the screen. It was working. The icon for messages was flashing.

She would have to call Larry. She would go down to the gift shop or her car to get something she'd forgotten, and she would call him. Larry had his own interests, but they were linked as tightly with hers as two sides of a coin. She would tell him what had happened, because he should know, but it wouldn't change anything. They would have to continue as planned. Really, there was no choice.

CHAPTER 21

Eddie Ferraro lived in a narrow, four-story yellow building among a jumble of pastel blocks pressed tightly together on a promontory that overlooked the Ligurian Sea. His great-uncle made wine in the basement, and at street level, a cousin owned a bakery. Eddie's apartment took up the third level, and wooden stairs led to his workshop, where he printed and framed hand-colored sketches of the five villages of the Cinque Terre. In winter, when the tourists were gone and most of the shops were closed, Eddie helped patch the roof, paint the wooden shutters, or clean out the vineyards that terraced the brown, winter-dead hills. He would sit in a bar and watch the little fishing boats go in and out of a harbor so small they had to haul the boats up with winches and swing them out of the way.

Eddie had never seen Italy or spoken the language until he jumped bail on a counterfeiting charge and arrived in Manarola with $822 to his name. He confessed there wasn't much to do in this town; he was glad for the distraction of helping Tom Fairchild duplicate an old map with three bullet holes it in, and splatters of blood across five continents.

While Tom loaded software onto his new notebook computer and brought up the scan of the 1511 *Universalis Cosmographia*, Eddie unrolled the real thing on the other end of the long wooden table. He weighted the corners with bags of lead shot and leaned over the map with a magnifying glass. Four years of walking up and down hills had made him thinner, and his hair had gone gray at the sides. He wore a green sweater with a hole in one elbow and jeans so old the hems had frayed. Tom thought that if Rose were here, she would reach for her sewing basket.

"This is doable." Eddie moved the glass across the map. "Clear, strong lines. Not a lot of cross-hatching and shading. I'm talking about the printing. The rest of it . . . that's your department. You're the artist, not me."

On the drive from Torino, Tom had filled Eddie in on the map's history, from its publication in an atlas in Venice, which then passed through the hands of merchants and minor royalty in Genoa, Milan, and Constantinople, then to a Socialist-era museum in Latvia, the last place the atlas had been seen. The thief broke the binding and sold off the maps. The world map eventually ended up in an attic in Albuquerque, New Mexico, where Stuart Barlowe had found it.

At dawn, Allison noticed Eddie's head drooping and volunteered to drive. While Eddie slept in the backseat, she told Tom that there were no police cars patrolling Italian highways. The speed limit was left to the common sense of the drivers. She floored it. They stopped only once, at an Esso *autogrill* to fill up the tank of the elderly Lancia, sixty euros, and to buy cappuccinos and croissants. Arriving in Manarola, they parked at the bottom of a hill and dragged the suitcases another hundred yards up the steep, cobbled streets past people going in the other direction. It was Sunday morning, and bells were ringing in the twelfth-century Chiesa di San Lorenzo. Eddie gave his room to Allison, put Tom on the sofa, and stretched out on a cot in his workshop.

Now the sun slanted through the windows, warm enough to imitate spring. There was no snow on the ground, and the clouds had blown out to sea. Allison had left an hour ago for a walk, accompanied by one of the kids in the family, to make sure she found her way back through the maze of streets. Tom, stuck behind his computer, had asked Allison to take some photos. It could be the only chance he got to see past the walls of Eddie's workshop.

"Let me show you the kind of plates we're using." Eddie crossed the room to some shelves and came back with a flat piece of steel about eight inches by ten. The surface was covered with a thin layer of opaque polymer.

"This one's a throwaway," he said. "Here, you can hold it. I've done etchings—plenty of them—and the beauty of this is, no toxic chemicals. Basically, we're going to print your digital image of the map onto a transparency, lay it over a plate, and expose it to UV rays for five or ten minutes. I'm building a UV light box, but heck, you could even set it out in the sun. The polymer hardens where the light hits it. The rest you can wash away in tap water. Presto. You put the plate into a press, ink it, add the paper, and you've got what it took Gaetano Corelli weeks to do. He'd wet his pants if he could do a copperplate engraving that fast."

"Fantastic," Tom said, turning the plate over in his hands.

"I had to special-order the big ones from a wholesaler in Berlin, cost me a hundred euros each, plus shipping. I bought six, which gives us a few to mess up. They're going to a print shop in Firenze, arrival on Wednesday. We'll run over there and pick them up. It's a couple of hours by car. The same printer can work with a CD and give us a transparency. We can either come back here and prepare the plates, or take all our equipment to Firenze. I'd rather do it here, then go back for the printing."

"Fine with me. What about the ink? Where will you get that?"

"On the balcony. Take a look."

Tom got up and opened the door. An old wooden table was out there, and on it, a dozen or more oil lamps. Eddie had rigged up a box frame with a piece of thick glass inside, which he had suspended about a foot over the lamps. Soot blackened the glass chimneys and the glass over them. "Might as well fire 'em up." Eddie struck some kitchen matches and adjusted the wicks until the smoke rolled around inside the frame and drifted over the metal railing of the balcony.

"You see why I don't do this indoors. My neighbors think I'm *pazzo*." Eddie made a circle next to his head. "Loony tunes." He left the door open a crack to keep an eye on things.

Tom was skeptical. "Is that going to work?"

"Heck, yes. In the old days you might make it with burnt bones or grape vines, but lampblack's just as good. It's a damn good thing this isn't a manuscript map, because you'd have to make ink out of gall nuts and gum arabic and whatever, and it would take weeks. Engraver's ink is a piece of cake."

He showed Tom a jar half full of black powder. "I've been scraping soot off that glass for three days. By the end of the week, we'll have more than enough. I'll mix this with some ready-made burnt-plate oil. That's mostly boiled linseed oil. I could make it myself, but I don't want to blow the roof off my house. The ready-made will work. There's not going to be anything in this ink, or in the paper, that wasn't around five hundred years ago. So unless Stuart Barlowe runs the map through a spectrograph, and maybe not even then, there is no way he's going to tell."

At the table Eddie touched the map with the backs of his thick, callused fingers as gently as touching a woman's cheek. "We've got eleven sheets of paper coming from an antique dealer in Milan. You wouldn't trust him with your house keys, but he knows paper. He won't tell me where he found it, except that it's blank end pages, Italian in origin, from atlases or folio-size manuscripts dating from the early sixteenth century. The color varies. We'll have to match the original as best we can. We have to check the absorption rate, too. Ink can spread more on one piece of paper than another. I'm going to have to clip a corner off this map so I can test it. Is that okay with you?"

"Do what you have to. How much was the paper?"

"Three hundred euros a sheet."

"Jesus."

"This guy is reliable," Eddie said. "If he says sixteenth century, you're not getting a blank sheet out of a Currier and Ives book. I have a buddy in Firenze who can put us into a shop with a press from the late seventeen hundreds. The technology didn't change from the time of Corelli. The press is one of those kinds with two big rollers." Eddie tugged at the spokes of an imaginary wheel. "Hard as hell to pull and slow as the devil, but it leaves a plate impression on the paper that you just can't fake. It's going to be beautiful."

"How much do I owe you so far?"

"I've paid out about four thousand euros, with another thousand to come. This is busting my savings account, so I need the money back pretty quick."

"No problem. I can probably do a wire transfer online. You want to write down what I owe you? I've been paid ten thousand dollars in fees so far. Half of that's yours, but I had to spend it getting here."

"We'll settle up later on the fees." Eddie gave Tom a firm pat on his shoulder. "Show me that fancy computer of yours. Can you imagine going back a hundred years with that and a color laser printer? You could have turned out greenbacks like confetti. No, no, I'm out of that life, Tommy. I'm just saying, it would have been quite something to see."

Tom had already opened the file in Illustrator. The scan was so large he could only pull up a fraction of it on his computer's seventeen-inch screen. "What you're seeing is just one piece of the map," he said. "It's a lumbering giant. It takes ten minutes to open the whole file, so I cut it into a grid. It's all mathematics, so I can put it back together later. Looks like we're on the coast of North Africa." Tom pointed at the screen. "See that dark brown in the upper right? That's dried blood. You can just make out what's underneath. Watch. I'm going to put a transparent layer over the bitmap and trace the line."

Using a tool in his program, Tom zoomed in on the square until the fibers in the paper were visible, and a shadowy image of coastline appeared under the bloodstain. Using the pen on his wireless tablet, he drew a smiley face on the map.

"Should I leave it there? Maybe not." Tom made the face disappear, then drew an S-curve. "Is that too thin? I can make it fatter. Or thinner. You see? The bullet holes will be easy to fix, but I'll have to fill in the empty spaces with something. Luckily they missed the cartouche. Under the bloodstains there are some places I can't make out. That's why I ought to look at the Corelli maps in the National Library—to see what place names he used in other maps and use them for this one. It's not going to be difficult, but it is time-consuming. It's a bitch, if you want to know the truth."

Eddie leaned against the table with his arms crossed. "Do you think you're being paid enough?"

"Fifty grand is a lot of money. Or twenty-five, because I owe you half."

"Think about it, Tom. This map seems to drag a lot of bad luck around with it. A man was shot to death holding it. Your friend Jenny was working for him. You've got some guys on your tail and you don't have a clue why. Who are they? Are they the ones who murdered Jenny Gray? Did Larry Gerard send them? I'm not sure you're getting paid enough for the risk you're taking. As for me, heck, I'm ecstatic with twenty-five. You didn't have to pay me anything. I told you, I'll do it for the pleasure of seeing you again after four years, my friend."

"We're splitting the fee," Tom said firmly. "Okay, sure, I'm a little jumpy because of what's going on, but I can't see how Stuart Barlowe is involved. I made a deal with him, and I'll stand by it unless something changes."

"All right. It's your decision, and I'm with you. Here's some two-bit advice. Keep looking around for that dirt on Barlowe. If things work out like you expect, you won't need to use it, but if he leaves you hanging, you'll have a way out."

A woman's voice called up from the street. "Hello–o-o-o."

Eddie went to the window. "Guess who?" He pushed the window open on its hinges and waved. Tom leaned out beside him. Allison was down there with a little boy about eight years old. They would have to climb the steep steps in the alley to come around to Eddie's street.

Her red beret was a dot of color on the gray stones. She pointed to the balcony. "I thought it was a fire. I see now. It's lamps! What are you doing?"

Tom called down, "Eddie is *pazzo*! He's crazy. Come up."

She took a bottle from a brown bag and showed them. "Limoncello! Lemon liqueur. The lady in the gelato shop makes it. It's delicious." Motioning to the boy to follow, she walked out of sight, clomping up the hill in her heavy shoes.

"She's a funny girl," Eddie noted. "What's going on with you two?"

"Nothing." Tom amended, "Nothing yet."

"Don't miss your chances when they come along."

"Are you talking about Allison? Or Rose?"

Eddie closed the window against the cold air. "How's she doing, really?"

"She doesn't have anyone in her life, if that's your question. Why don't you call her?"

He shook his head. "What good would it do? I'd start

wishing for things that aren't going to happen. I can't go back to Miami, and she can't come here."

"She could visit, if you wanted her to."

"I don't want her to. It's too far and too expensive, and she ought to spend the money on the girls."

Tom went over to his messenger bag, where he had stashed his address book. "I forgot to give you something. Rose wanted me to bring it to you. The water got to the edges, but I dried it out."

He gave Eddie the photograph that had been stuck to the refrigerator in Rose's kitchen. Rose and Megan and Jill with their arms around each other. Eddie looked at it for a while and straightened a bent corner. "It's fine. They look very happy. Thanks."

Tom heard a door close in the apartment below. Allison's voice came up the stairs. "I'm back. Do you guys want to try the limoncello?"

Eddie was lost in the photograph.

Tom leaned over the railing. "Yes! I'll be right there." He turned on his cell phone and set it on the table within Eddie's reach.

"I just dialed Rose's number. It's ringing."

Eddie looked startled. "Don't do that. Come on. She's probably in bed asleep."

"It's not even nine o'clock in Miami."

"What would I say to her?"

"Pick it up, you coward."

Eddie reached out, took it, then, with a glance at Tom, turned away for some privacy. As Tom went down the steps, he heard him say. "Rose? . . . Yeah, it's me. How're you doing?"

It took a day to reconstruct the areas destroyed by the bullet holes and obscured by blood. Working on such small pieces of the map, Tom had to glance at the original every so often to remember where he was. Eddie had pinned it to a board, which sat on an easel next to the table. The next day Tom started tracing the existing lines in the map. It was tedious work, recreating every line in the map, every letter and number, every dot that marked a town, every coastline and river. He had to make them all a minuscule fraction thinner than the originals, to allow for the bleed—the fact that the ink, under pressure, would expand farther than the etched grooves in the plate. If the engraving were made from only the scanned map, the lines would come out a hairsbreadth too wide in the print. It was worth fifty thousand dollars, plus expenses, to give Barlowe what he wanted: perfection.

Barlowe had been calling; Tom had let Allison deal with him. Barlowe had told her he'd flown to Milan and he would like very much to know where they were. Good old Allison had repeated what Tom had told her to say: *Dad, I'm sorry, Tom doesn't want to be disturbed.*

With his headphones on, Tom listened to music he had downloaded to his iPod using Eddie's Internet connection. At sixty gigs, the iPod would store not only the map files but a staggering amount of music as well.

In a detached mental zone produced by the music and the boredom of tracing one line after another, Tom had been thinking about Stuart Barlowe, wondering what Royce Herron had known—the dirt, the scoop, the inside information. All Tom had to go on were a few words Jenny had overheard: *I know about you. . . . I know the truth. . . . You can't hide it any longer.*

The judge hadn't been on the inside of Barlowe's corporation, so he wouldn't have been aware of any financial crimes. He'd known about Jenny's affair with Barlowe, but he wouldn't have talked about it. Royce Herron had been born in another time, and men in those days had a sense of honor.

Tom's pen came to a stop on the sketch tablet as he stared past the screen. Barlowe's secret didn't have to be something recent; it could have happened in the past. Royce Herron had known Stuart Barlowe for many years. He and Barlowe's father had attended a Toronto map conference together in the late 1960s.

Allison had talked about her family, mostly complaints, when she and Tom were dating. She had never known her mother, who died soon after Allison was born. Her father remarried a divorcée with a son when Allison was still very small. Stuart Barlowe inherited a Canadian company worth multimillions from his father. There had been two brothers, Stuart and Nigel. Tom remembered the name from the back of the old photograph that Judge Herron's son had found in his father's study and had given to Rose.

The music in Tom's ears suddenly stopped when the headphones were lifted off his head. Allison had come upstairs. She swung her hair out of the way and put one of the headphones to her ear. "Nice saxophone. Who is it?"

"Sonny Rollins. I snagged it off the playlist of a buddy of mine in Miami."

Allison moved to the music as she looked over Tom's shoulder at the screen. The islands of Japan reflected in her glasses. "My father called again. I told him you're working very hard, and the map is coming out great. But he wants to see you."

"No," said Tom. "I can't take the time. If I'm not back in Miami soon, the Weasel will have my ass in jail."

She put the headphones down, and her face grew serious. "You have to, Tom. I told him we'd be in Florence tomorrow, and he wants to talk to you. No, really, you have to. I'm supposed to pay you another fifteen thousand dollars on your fee on Thursday, and he refuses to authorize it unless he's satisfied how things stand with the map."

Tom had been working without a break, because nothing would get done the day they went to Florence. He would take photographs of the Corelli maps in the library while Eddie picked up the plates and the antique paper. After that, they had to go over to the print shop and do a couple of test runs on the old press. Wasting an hour or two with Stuart Barlowe was not in the cards.

"Allison, I've explained to you how I'm doing the map. You've come up here and you've seen the process. I told you to describe it to him, and I assume you did."

"Don't take that tone with me," she said.

"Okay. The point is, he can talk to *you*. I mean, that's why he made you come along, to report back to him. Isn't it?"

"Yes, but he has this idea that—" She laughed. "Well, that we're hiding out somewhere and having way too much fun, and nothing is really getting done."

Leaning back in his chair, Tom smiled. "What kind of fun?"

"I told him this is a business arrangement," she said. "We're in different hotels, I'm studying for the bar, and you work day and night on the map."

"Different hotels?" Tom drew in a breath. "Allison, you lied to your father."

"It's not a lie. We *are* in different rooms."

"You should call him back and tell him the truth. I sit up here all day and think about you."

"You do not."

"Yes, I do."

A single loud chortle escaped her mouth. Over her jeans she'd put on one of Eddie's sweaters. It hung below her neat little butt, and the sleeves were rolled up her slender white wrists. Tom reached for his drawing pad and flipped to a page, then set it on the table.

Her eyes cut over to see it. "What's this? Oh, my God. That's *me*."

The pencil sketch showed a girl walking up the hill, a wide smile, a beret, the clunky black shoes, and the glasses. He brushed at some of the pencil marks. "It could be better."

"It's perfect! The houses and the balconies. The church steeple. The hills with the vineyards. Can you see all that from up here?" She ran to the window and pushed open the green shutters. The sun hit the painted yellow stucco, and a small cloud moved across the upper left corner of the bright blue rectangle of light. Allison's hair swung and gleamed as she looked out. "It's just what you have in the drawing. Oh, Tom, you really have to get out of this room."

"I will. We're driving to Florence tomorrow."

"No, before we leave, you have to *see* this place. Walk on the stones, and look at the statue of the Virgin Mary in this little tiny niche in the wall, right down there. In the basement they have the most *immense* wine jugs in baskets that take two men to lift. You have to see the harbor. Marcello showed me a path that leads along the bottom of the cliff, and the waves just *boil* up, and sometimes without warning it sprays through this little hole, and I had to jump back, and Marcello laughed at me. I think he took me there on purpose! But I bought him some gelato anyway."

This, Tom thought. This was why he had fallen in love with her in the first place, and now, unknown to him, without warning, it had happened again.

"All right. I'll meet your father. I don't have a lot of time, though."

"I came up to ask you something else. Eddie and a bunch of the family are walking to Riomaggiore to see the sun set and have a drink. It's only a mile, and they say the view is spectacular. They're leaving in a little while, and Eddie said for me to make you come with us. Your body is going to fuse to the chair. Turn off the computer. Please?"

"Okay, okay. Give me ten minutes. I need to back up my work."

Allison said sternly, "Ten minutes. That's all you get."

"Fine. I'll be right down."

He watched her swing around the railing at the top of the stairs and sink out of view. She didn't look back at him, and he knew she was pretending not to care if he was looking after her or not. The thumps of her footsteps faded.

After Tom had backed up his work to the iPod and uploaded the changes to a server somewhere in Finland or the planet Jupiter—who knew?—he clicked the icon for his e-mail account. He typed:

Hi, Rose. Working hard, call you soon. Do me a favor ASAP? Scan that old photo of Granddad

and Royce Herron at the map conference in
Toronto and e-mail it to me. Also the back. 300
dpi if possible. Thanks mucho. Say hi to Megan
and Jill.

Love, Tom.

Riomaggiore was the most southerly village of the
Cinque Terre, a little bigger than Manarola. To get there,
they followed Eddie and his great-uncle's family. The old
man's cane didn't slow them down, and the wife was
bundled into scarves and boots. A male cousin smoked a
pipe and talked to Tom mostly in gestures. The little kid,
Marcello, ran in zigzags with his arms out, pretending to
be an airplane. His mother chatted with Allison in Italian.
They went uphill on Via Discovolo to the platform level
of the narrow-gauge railway that connected the five
towns. The path went into a long tunnel that over the
years had been filled with paintings of flowers and views
from the cliffs, and the names of lovers, and signatures
of tourists and the dates.

Eddie turned around and said to Tom, "Do you know
what they call the path to Riomaggiore?"

"No. What?"

"*La Via dell'Amore.*" He winked at Allison. "You
want to translate for him?"

"I can figure it out," Tom said.

Marcello giggled and skipped ahead.

Past the train station, they took the walkway that
curved around the cliffs. A sturdy metal railing separated
pedestrians from the two-hundred-foot drop to the sea.
The waves surged up, turned to foam, and fell back. A
ferryboat left a trail of white on the inky blue water, cutting across a swath of orange painted by the setting sun.

A mile away, Riomaggiore was turning pink, and flashes of reflected light winked from the windows.

The images would fade. In a month or a year they would be gone. Tom knew this, but still he grabbed each detail and tried to press them into his memory. He had left his drawing pad on the table, not expecting to see much more than water and rocks.

As they rounded another corner, the cold wind fluttered scarves and lifted the old woman's hem. Her husband cackled and kissed her cheek. Tom pulled his cap down over his ears. He noticed a tumbledown stone arch that had once been part of a cottage overlooking the sea. Allison aimed her pocket camera at it, then Eddie told her and Tom to sit on a stone bench so he could take their picture.

"Sit closer. Tom, put your arm around her. Like that."

Allison wanted to get a picture of Eddie's family with Riomaggiore in the background and waved for them to stand right there against the railing and smile.

When the family had gone out of sight around the next bend in the path, Tom pulled her closer by the front of her jacket. Momentarily off balance, she had righted herself by the time he kissed her. Her lips were cool from the wind, warm inside. Tom put his arms around her and didn't let go until he was out of breath.

Laughing, Allison buried her face in his neck. "I've been wanting you to do that again."

"How was it?"

She took off her glasses and lifted her face. The sun turned her eyes to the color of cinnamon. "One more time. I'm not sure yet."

The next one lasted longer. She held him tightly and whispered, "Whatever happened to us, Tom?"

"We were kids. I didn't know anything."

"I didn't, either. I'm sorry for . . . oh, God. Everything."

"It doesn't matter now," he said.

"We were *such* babies. I know I was. We had no idea about life, did we? And it wasn't easy, you know, me living so far uptown, and you in New Jersey, and then your mother got sick. You know that guy I went out with, the one you almost beat up? Randall. I never went out with him again. He was such a poser, and you never were that, Tom. I didn't think about it then. You were always true."

"Allison, be quiet. Please."

She held his face and kissed each corner of his mouth, then full on his lips. "I forgot how delicious you are. Do you think Eddie would mind if . . . if we slept in the same room?"

Tom laughed. "He's been asking me why we aren't." He slid his arms down her back and pressed against her. "Do you want to keep walking? Or what?"

A smile lit her face as she glanced up the path. "I suppose we'll see Riomaggiore someday."

"Count on it." He held out his hand, and they turned back the way they had come.

CHAPTER 22

The Biblioteca Nazionale Centrale di Firenze, which had begun as the personal library of a duke in the seventeenth century, had morphed into the largest library in Italy, with millions of books, hundreds of thousands of old manuscripts, and most of the papers of the astronomer Galileo. They also possessed a good number of rare maps, and among these were two by the Venetian cartographer and map publisher, Gaetano Corelli.

Tom hoped another five centuries didn't elapse before he got to see them. He and Allison had been passed from one person to the next for almost an hour. They had come in through the main entrance under two square Tuscan towers, into a lobby with a high glass ceiling and several balconies looking down on a floor of gray and pink marble. The letter of introduction on Miami Historical Museum letterhead, signed by Stuart Barlowe of the Board of Directors, had to be translated and pondered at every office, but they had gradually worked their way farther into the buildings, which spread over several acres, until finally they arrived at an unadorned waiting room in the map department, where they sat on a bench and listened to muffled conversations and the occasional ring of a telephone.

Allison said, "If it gets any later, I should call my father."

Tom looked at his watch. "We'll give them ten minutes before I go pound on the door and ask what's the problem."

They had arrived in Florence just before noon. Eddie had to pick up the supplies for the map and bribe the printer, so he had dropped Tom and Allison off to rent a scooter in Oltrarno, south of the river. They would all stay at a hotel tonight and leave early for Manarola. They would return to Florence when the new engraving plate was ready for the printing press.

In an hour from now, more or less, Stuart Barlowe and his wife expected to talk to Tom about his progress on the map. They had flown in yesterday from Milan. It was funny, Rhonda's coming along, after she'd tried to bribe Tom *not* to do the map. He hadn't decided yet whether to tell Stuart about it. He hadn't said anything to Allison. No point stirring up more trouble between her and her stepmother.

That family had its secrets. Royce Herron had discovered something, and Tom had been looking for a chance to find out more from Allison. He couldn't have talked to her on the drive from Manarola with Eddie in the car. Last night in bed, making love to her, the subject hadn't entered Tom's mind. Allison wasn't at arm's length to him anymore, and he couldn't just tell her that her father might have committed a crime so dark that Royce Herron could have used it to shut down a billion-dollar real estate development.

Tom put his camera bag aside and took Allison's hand, lightly rubbing his thumb across her knuckles. "How long has your dad been married to Rhonda?"

With only mild surprise at the question, Allison replied, "Let's see . . . almost thirty years. My mother died when I was a baby."

"I know. Of what?"

"A heart attack. It was a rare condition that had never been diagnosed. She was shopping in a department store in Toronto, and she just fell over and was dead in minutes. Twenty-three years old. Her name was Marian. I have no memory of her, but my father loved her very much. Then he goes and marries someone with no motherly instincts whatsoever. Go figure."

"Your dad had a younger brother. Nigel, right? What happened to him?"

"No, he was actually a year older. He died in a car accident in the Alps."

"Too bad. How did it happen?"

"My father and Rhonda had rented a house near Chamonix, on the French side, in ski season. Nigel had some business to do in Geneva, so he decided to surprise them. He drove to Chamonix, but on the way, he went off the road in a snowstorm. They didn't know he was coming, so by the time anyone missed him, snow had covered the car, and it took weeks until someone saw it. My father had to identify the body. It must have been horrible for him, to lose my mother, and then his only brother. He never went back to Toronto. Rhonda came to get me and brought me to Miami, and we've been there ever since."

Tom nodded. "Must've been rough on your dad. Was your grandfather, Frederick, already gone by then?"

"Yes, I think so. That's right, he was. I was so small I don't remember much from those days. Stuart doesn't like to talk about it."

"Nigel never married? No kids?"

"None. There's only me. I have some distant cousins in Edmonton, but I don't even know their names anymore. Why are you asking me about that?"

Tom was saved from having to invent a reply when a door opened and a small, mild-looking man came out with the letter of introduction in his hands. First Tom noticed thick glasses and a beard, then a smile.

"*Buon giorno, io sono* Guido Grenni." He glanced at the letter as if to confirm he had the right people. "Mr. . . . eh . . . Fairchild?"

They stood up. Allison said, "*Buon giorno, signore.*" She introduced herself as Stuart Barlowe's daughter, then apparently said her friend didn't speak the language. "*Parla inglese?*" she asked.

"Forgive me, yes," the man said. "I speak English, but not well. I regret that you wait so long. You are here from America to see the maps of Gaetano Corelli. Come with me."

They went down a hall, around several corners, and into an elevator. As they descended, Guido Grenni politely asked about their interest in the early-sixteenth-century Venetian mapmaker. Tom replied that he worked in a map shop, and Corelli was one of his favorite cartographers.

Grenni smiled uncertainly, as if this might have been a joke. When Allison mentioned the Miami International Map Fair, he brightened. "*Sicuro!* I know the fair in Miami. I hope someday I will go."

Eventually he led them to a metal door, slid his key card through a magnet, and took them inside to the reception desk. He and the woman behind it traded some Italian back and forth, and he left the letter with her. "Signora Santini will help you find what you need. She speaks perfect English, not so like me. A pleasure to meet you. *Benvenuti a Firenze.*" He smiled again and went out.

As the woman came from behind her desk, Allison said, "We're very grateful to you."

"My pleasure. *Dottor* Grenni said to assist you in any way possible."

"Is he someone important here?" Tom asked.

The woman gave him a long look. "*Dottor* Guido Grenni is the curator of maps at the Biblioteca Nazionale Centrale. He may look like an ordinary clerk to you, but no one knows more than he about Renaissance cartography. Libraries all over the world call him for opinions, even your Library of Congress."

"Oh," Tom said.

Amused by his embarrassment, she said, "Follow me, please." She led them through a door into a large room full of shoulder-high cabinets. After passing a dozen of the cabinets she took a right and ran her finger down a column of flat metal drawers. "Corelli. Corelli. *Ecco.*" She removed two folders, which she placed on the nearest table. "You may take photographs, but no flash, and if you don't mind, I will stay here with you. It's our policy."

"Not a problem. We appreciate your time." Tom unzipped his camera bag and got to work. After hours of staring at Corelli's world map, he recognized the man's style. The first folder held a regional map of Sicily, of no use to him. Tom focused his lens on the other one, the

ports of the Mediterranean. The blood on the world map
had spilled across North Africa, and what Tom saw here
would fill in the blanks. He took high-resolution images
with the regular lens, then attached the macro for ex-
treme close-ups.

When he had finished, Allison motioned to him from
a framed map on an easel. "Tom, look!"

Signora Santini smiled. "You know this map? Beautiful, no?"

"It's a Henry Martell. I've seen it in books." Allison
leaned closer to read the description. "*Henricus Martellus.
Planisfero tolemaico.* Fourteen-ninety. I'm getting chills."

The hand-colored double page had come from an atlas. The known continents of the world—which in 1490
did not include the Americas—had been projected into
the shape of a bean, a long curve at the bottom, a shorter
one on top. There were animals, plants, ships, leaping
fish. Ten heads with full cheeks and waving brown hair
blew winds from a pale blue sky toward ivory landmasses
and deep-blue ocean. As in all maps of the era, the language was Latin. Tom thought of how much he would
charge to duplicate this one. Half a million wouldn't be
enough. He wondered again why Stuart Barlowe was so
keen on Gaetano Corelli.

"We have so many wonderful things at the Biblioteca
Nazionale. Would you like a tour? I can arrange it. As
special guests of *Dottor* Grenni—"

Allison groaned and sadly shook her head. "We'd
love to, but we have to meet someone. You don't know
how much we'd love to."

Tom had parked the rented scooter along the curb a block
away. Coming out the main entrance, he paused behind a

column and held on to Allison's arm to keep her from going down the steps. He looked at the people walking through the piazza and at the cars parked on either side. A hundred yards directly ahead, traffic moved along a street fronting the Arno River, which flowed lazily west. Tuscan yellow or beige stucco buildings under red tile roofs faced the river on the other side. Their windows were closed against the chilly weather, and Tom saw no one on the roof terraces or balconies.

Allison said, "Tom, we're in the middle of a city. If those men on the train did follow us—and I doubt it—they won't do anything here."

"You're right. Let's go."

It took a minute to find the right scooter in a long line of them. They all leaned the same way, and their windshields were turned at the same angle. Tom straddled the scooter, walked it out to the narrow street, and Allison got on. He waited for a car about the size of his shoe to clatter past on the cobblestones. Allison had insisted on helmets; the drivers, she said, were suicidal.

With Allison calling out directions, Tom crossed the river to avoid the congestion and one-way streets in the historical center. From the road on the south bank, he could see the Ponte Vecchio with its collection of little shops. Stone arches reflected in the lazy green water. Allison tapped on his shoulder and pointed out the Uffizi museum and the terra-cotta dome of Santa Maria del Fiore, *Il Duomo*. She put her chin on his shoulder. "Tomorrow! You have to come with me. I'll show you Firenze!"

They crossed the river again on the Amerigo Vespucci Bridge and took a right to the Hotel Cellini, five stories of marble with a rooftop terrace overlooking the city. The doorman waved Tom toward the next street, where he parked in another long line of scooters.

Taking off his helmet, he heard his cell phone ringing in his thigh pocket. He reached in and looked at the screen. "It's Rose."

"Answer it," Allison said. "We can be a few minutes late."

"Hey, Rose. What's up?"

Bad news. The Weasel was asking questions again. Why hadn't Tom started his anger management classes? Why had his landlord, Fritz Klein, made excuses for his not being home? Mr. Weems had told Rose he'd tried to reach her brother through the cell phone Tom had last used, and he had heard a woman's voice telling him she would be out of town for a couple of weeks, leave a message. Where was Tom Fairchild?

Rose said, "Tom, you need to get back here soon. I'm very nervous about this."

"Oh, great. What did you tell him?"

"That you and he were just missing each other, I guess."

"Okay. Stall him as long as you can. I'll be back in Miami in about ten days, if nothing gets screwed up here."

When he ended the call, Allison said, "Your probation officer."

"Damn it."

"Use my cell phone to call him," she said.

"He smells something fishy with that number. I'll have to come up with another idea."

"My father has a Miami number. Use his cell phone."

"Uh-huh, sure. Come on, let's get this over with." He took the messenger bag from Allison, who had worn it on her back. Tom had brought his notebook computer, some color screen shots of the map, and a sample engraving plate.

She put her arms around his waist and looked at him earnestly. "I won't let anything happen to you, Tom. I'll lie for you. I'll tell the Weasel you were with me. If he does file a probation violation, we'll fight it. I don't care how much it costs. No, listen to me. I don't want you going to prison for six years. Not for six days. In fact, when we get back to Miami, I'm going to ask one of the lawyers at my firm to take your case."

Tom reluctantly said if she wanted to, he wouldn't object, even as he knew that the Weasel would make it his goal in life to see Tom Fairchild behind bars.

The Barlowes didn't have a room; they had a suite whose decorator had been told to go crazy. The twenty-foot ceilings had been painted with alternating fleur-de-lis squares of Florentine orange and blue that matched the pattern in the heavy curtains, which were held open with braided silk ropes with gold tassels. There were enough carved and gilded mirrors, reproduction tapestries, Venetian crystal chandeliers, wall sconces, potted plants, and rose-and-ivory silk upholsteries to induce nausea. Sliding doors opened onto a bedroom with more of the same stuff, including a king-size bed under a brocade canopy.

Allison and her father took the sofa. Tom sat on the blue velvet cushion of a medieval folding chair and unloaded his bag onto a thick piece of beveled glass that rested on ornate gold legs. He turned on the computer and brought up the file. Mrs. Barlowe sat across from him rotating the toe of her pink suede pump and sipping a glass of red wine. Tom guessed she had chosen the hotel.

She had met them warmly at the door, but the looks she was giving Tom across the table said that if he mentioned her attempted bribe, she wouldn't know anything about it. She was the kind of woman you wouldn't care to be alone with on a sixth-floor balcony.

Room service had brought in a tray of cheese and fruit, but Tom was too keyed up to want any. After explaining how the map would be made, he walked over to the window to wait for Barlowe's reaction. He could see the Arno and the purple-blue hills in the distance, and slender cypress trees, and others that formed a perfect semicircle of branches. He brought his gaze downriver, passed a crenellated tower or two, then the Ponte Vecchio, and a half mile beyond that, somewhere in the jumble of streets, was the print shop where Eddie was at this moment slipping five hundred euros to one of the pressmen.

"I'm not sure about this." Barlowe stared at the computer screen. "I don't know how it can work." His voice sounded strained, and he looked like he hadn't slept in days.

"Mr. Barlowe, the map is going to be perfect," Tom said. "That's what you wanted, and that's what I'm giving you."

"But it's on a *computer*. I told you, I wanted a duplicate original."

Allison broke in. "Dad, he explained it. He's making a new engraving plate."

"These prints don't show me the texture of the paper, do they? Where is the original? You should have brought it so we can compare the two."

"I don't have it with me," Tom said.

"I *see* that. Can you bring it?"

"No, I can't. It's not in Florence."

Rhonda said quietly, "I think what he means, Stuart, is that he's keeping the original until he collects fifteen thousand dollars tomorrow. If you can't make a comparison, you can't refuse to pay him."

Allison said, "Rhonda, please let my father decide."

"Look, darling. Your father and I are in this together. I'm not sure where *your* loyalty lies."

As Allison started to reply, Barlowe said sharply, "Rhonda. Please."

"All right, but I *don't* want you taken advantage of—not by anyone."

"I appreciate that. Now let me talk to Mr. Fairchild." He raked his hair off his forehead. "Tom, how soon can you have the map finished?"

"When we originally talked, you said you wanted it within three weeks. That's eleven days from now. That's what I'm projecting."

"I need it sooner than that. Can you get it to me within a week?"

Tom exchanged a look with Allison. "No. I can't do it that fast."

"If you're doing the engraving plate from a scan, I don't see why it takes so long."

"I can't do it from the scan. I've explained about the ink bleed. If you want a halfway job, I can give it to you, but you wanted it done right."

"I want it done *quickly.*"

Allison said, "Tom has been working as fast as he can according to the terms you agreed on."

"Isn't she the lawyer, though?" Rhonda refilled her

glass. "Sounds like she's negotiating for Mr. Fairchild."

"I am *trying* to ensure that this project is *done*," Allison retorted, "and that the quality is up to my father's demands."

"Are you and Mr. Fairchild lovers?"

Allison colored. "Oh! How dare you say that to me?"

"I don't *care* from a moral standpoint," Rhonda said, "but a man with a criminal past . . . A person has to wonder what's going *on*."

Tom said, "Excuse me? It's none of your business what Allison does. She's not a child."

"He defends you. How telling."

Barlowe murmured, "Rhonda, please."

Allison stood over her stepmother with her hands in fists. "You've always hated me, haven't you?"

"No, I just don't *trust* you. You've done everything possible to come between me and Stuart. You failed to make partner at the law firm in Boston, and here you are, wanting to be a daughter. How sweet, after all these years. Excuse me for thinking you're after something else."

"Rhonda, shut the hell up! Stop it! Both of you, stop it!" Barlowe's voice cracked. When the room was quiet, he looked at Tom. "Talk to me, Mr. Fairchild. Can you possibly get the map done faster? Possibly?" The lines in his cheeks deepened with a smile that resembled a grimace. "If I increased your fee, could you get it done a week from today? How much do you require?"

"Who's it for, Mr. Barlowe? Why do you want it so fast? If I'm going to bust my ass for a piece of paper, I'd like to know why."

"Ten thousand? An increase of twenty percent seems fair."

Exhaling heavily, Tom turned around and pressed a hand to his forehead. "That wasn't the deal."

"Twenty. No, let's say an extra fifty. A total of one hundred thousand dollars."

Rhonda Barlowe's wineglass stopped on its way to her lips. "Stuart." She stared at her husband as if he had lost his mind. "My God, Stuart."

"Change of terms," Barlowe announced. "I'll give you one hundred thousand dollars for that map. Allison, you are authorized to transfer fifteen thousand tomorrow *and* the balance of fifty thousand to Mr. Fairchild a week from today, when the job is finished."

Allison was shaking her head slowly, wanting an answer from Tom. He said, "I'll try."

"You'll do more than try. Let me ask you again. Can you get the map to me within a week?"

Allison clung to his back, and even with the noise of the scooter and the traffic, Tom thought he heard her crying. He pulled off the road and went into a grove of cypress trees in a little park.

They were tears of anger. When Tom tried to put his arms around her, Allison ran into the park, picked up a rock, and flung it into the trees. Then another one, and one more. "I hate her. I hate both of them. That miserable bitch has changed him into someone I don't even know. I must be crazy thinking we could ever have a relationship."

She threw more rocks until she was spent. Tom went over and put his chin on top of her head. "Feel better now?"

"Tom, you shouldn't have said you'd do the map in a week. What if you can't?"

"A week is possible. I can do it. I'm nearly finished,

and the rest depends on Eddie." He gave her a squeeze. "It means more time at my computer, less with you."

"Why did you avoid telling them the truth? We *are* sleeping together." She turned to face him. "I'm not ashamed of it."

"You used to be," Tom said and immediately added, "Sorry. I guess things are different now."

"I hope they are." Her deep brown eyes fixed on his. "What am I doing here? My father is dealing directly with you. I'm useless. I might as well go home."

"Come on, Allison—"

Twelve years ago, Tom might have said sure, go home, then. Be that way. But now he could see what she really wanted to know. He tilted his head, came close to her lips, and said, "No. You're staying. Don't make me get out the handcuffs."

She laughed and let him kiss her.

"Let's get going," he said.

"Tom, wait. You should know the truth. The map isn't for my father. It's for one of the investors in The Metropolis. His name is Leo Zurin. He's a Russian map collector. Mr. Zurin has been trying for years to reconstruct Gaetano Corelli's only atlas, which had been in his family for a long time. It was seized by the Communists and put in a museum in Latvia. Somebody stole it and cut the maps out. Mr. Zurin found them all except the world map. My father found that one and promised to give it to him, sort of a thank-you for investing, and if Mr. Zurin doesn't get it, he'll throw a hissy fit and withhold his money. It's a lot—five million dollars. My father needs it to prove to the bank that he has the financial strength to be a partner in the development. It's complicated."

"No, I'm following you," Tom said. "Stuart couldn't

give Mr. Zurin the real map, so he wanted me to make a duplicate."

"He came to my apartment begging me to help him. He's never done that before! How could I say no? He could be wiped out from this, Tom. I didn't like the idea of a forgery, but I thought . . . on balance, that it was worth it. Maybe it is. When Mr. Zurin has his map, and Stuart can stop taking pills for his nerves, maybe he'll be himself again."

Tom hesitated, then said, "The funny thing is—and don't bring it up with your dad because it would just start a fight—Rhonda offered me ten grand not to make the map. I'm serious. Before I got on Larry's boat she took me in the map room and showed me the cash. I said forget it, I had a deal with Mr. Barlowe."

"Oh, my God. Why did she do *that*?"

"She said your dad was obsessed with guilt because Royce Herron was shot holding the map, and she wanted him to get over it. Looks like she changed her mind."

"Rhonda is the crazy one. You should have said something back there!"

"No! Jesus, no. Look, everything's fine. I get another fifteen thousand today, I do the map, I collect another fifty in a week. I go home, pay my restitution, and tell the Weasel to kiss my ass. Do not rock the boat. Please."

Allison didn't like that; he could tell. He hooked an arm around her neck and pulled her close. "I want you in the picture too, babe. If I don't get this map done, what have I got? Just a rap sheet and a broken down sailboat that's never going to see the water. You deserve better."

"Oh, thank you for telling me how shallow I am."

"All your friends would say, 'What are you going out with him for?' "

"I don't care what people say about me."

"Yeah, you do. You should. You try not to, but you have to live in the world. I've learned that much." He gave her a helmet. "I'll get the map done on time, and it's going to be good. It's going to be perfect. When I put my hand out for that last fifty thousand dollars, I don't want to hear anybody bitching and moaning about it. I'm not talking about you. I mean your dad and that . . . person he's married to."

Allison snapped her helmet under her chin, and a sudden smile curved her lips. "Did you hear him scream at her?"

"Maybe she's on her way out." Tom sat on the scooter and started the engine.

"I can only hope," Allison said.

They went back to the hotel. Eddie had chosen the Hotel Brianza in the San Niccolò district across the river. Their rooms were on the third floor, accessible by a creaking elevator hardly bigger than a phone booth. The minuscule bathrooms had been added a century ago, and the gas heat came from a register in the floor. But they had a view. They opened the old wooden shutters, uncorked a bottle of wine, and watched the hills change from green to blue to purple as the sun went down. Then Tom turned on his computer, and Allison leaned against the pillows on the double bed to study. She was keeping her feet warm with two pairs of socks.

At 6:30 PM Eddie called from the print shop. They were ready to do some tests on the antique printing press and needed to look at the original map. Eddie said to bring Allison, too, if she wanted to come.

Tom said to hold on, he would ask.

"Right now? I thought we were going to go eat."

"Eddie," Tom said into the phone, "how long will this take? Allison's hungry."

An hour, Eddie told him, and Allison agreed she could wait that long, and no, she didn't want to go to the print shop, thanks all the same.

Tom put on his jacket and hung the map tube across his back. He kissed Allison and went out the door. In a hurry, he took the stairs, which turned around the metal-mesh cage of the elevator. A couple of French tourists stood at the reception desk, checking in. Tom walked through the small lobby and went around to the alley at the side of the building. There was a bar next door, and the patrons had locked their scooters to a long iron railing in the wall. Tom had left his among them.

Eddie had told him to turn east on the road along the river. Pass two bridges, then take the third street to the right after the Piazza Ravenna. Turn left at Ristorante La Flamma, then look for a sign, LUCCHESE E FIGLI. That would be the print shop.

As Tom was unlocking the scooter he heard footsteps and glanced up. A man had come into the alley, a stocky figure about Tom's height, a silhouette in the light from the street. Tom thought he had probably parked in the alley, too, but the man slowed his steps and walked past the other scooters. Tom pulled the steel locking cable out of the wheel.

"Hey, Tom."

He whirled around.

"Take it easy," the voice said. "It's only me." The man stepped out into the light, and Tom could see his face.

Larry Gerard.

CHAPTER 23

L arry stood a couple of yards away, his smile showing in the dim light of a metal-shaded bulb at the other end of the alley. His hands were in the pockets of his brown zip-front jacket. Vines grew in front of the light, and their shadows moved across his face.

"What are you doing here?" Tom demanded.

"I need to talk to you. I followed you and Allison from the Cellini, but I didn't want to come up to your room with her there. Can I buy you a drink?"

Tom looped the cable and lock around his hand. "No, you can't buy me a drink. Just say what you have to and leave."

"You're still mad about what happened on the boat, aren't you? My apologies, though I swear to you, I did not know Marek would flip out like that. Did not know."

"Where is Marek?"

"I left him in Nassau, and he flew home—back to Dubrovnik, I expect. You've got a map tube. What's in it? The Corelli or the copy?"

"Why don't you shove off?" Tom said.

Larry rested his left hand on the scooter windshield; tapped the top of it with his open palm. "Okay, what I wanted to say. Stuart just upped your fee for the Corelli to a hundred grand. Don't hold your breath waiting for it. The map isn't for Stuart. It's for a friend of his, a map collector who is more than familiar with Corelli. There's a high probability that he's going to see yours for the forgery it is, and if that happens . . . we're you and me both up the creek. This man, Stuart's friend, has promised to put a ton of money into The Metropolis, but if he thinks he's been cheated with a phony map, he'll back out. This is why my mother offered you ten thousand dollars to walk away. That wasn't enough, obviously. So let's talk about a figure we can agree on."

This story had enough truth to sound at least partly plausible, but it was too late. Tom had already looked into Jenny Gray's dead eyes, and he could connect Larry to two other killings. No proof, but plenty of motive.

"What do you say, Tom?" Larry was still smiling. "I'm offering you a one-time-only deal. We're in this together, man."

"Who is this person? The investor?"

"That doesn't matter. This deal is between you and me. I'll have you back here in half an hour. Allison won't even miss you. My car's down the block."

"What's his name? Leo Zurin?"

The smile faded slightly, and Larry took a second to say, "I don't know where you got that from."

"Jenny Gray. She told me some things."

"Yeah?"

"She's dead." Tom waited for a reaction. "Not a surprise, Larry?"

"I am surprised. What happened to her?"

"She was strangled last Friday in her mother's house."

"That's too bad." Larry looked at him, then said, "Did you do it?"

"When was the last time you were in London?"

"Hey, it wasn't me. I'm sorry about Jenny, but I wasn't in London, and I have no idea who killed her."

"Lucky for you she's not around anymore," Tom said. "She can't talk about the public officials you blackmailed or bribed to get The Metropolis approved."

"That is such bullshit," Larry said. "She told you that? Did she also tell you she was a prostitute? The manager at my club caught her making offers to the customers."

Tom thought of the bruises on Jenny's neck and felt his fist tightening on the cable. "Jenny's friend Carla knew about you, too, and she's dead. What about Royce Herron? He knew what you were doing. Did he threaten to go to the media?"

"Come on, Tom. We've got things to talk about. I'm going to offer you more money than you've ever imagined having."

Keeping his voice steady, Tom said, "No deal. Turn around and get your ass out of here before I kick it down the street."

"Oh, man." Larry laughed and tapped on the windshield again. "Tom." Then his face tightened. He took his right hand out of his coat pocket, and a gun came with it.

Startled, Tom ducked to one side, and his arm hit the handlebar of the scooter. The windshield pivoted, and Larry glanced toward it. Tom crouched, leaped forward, and plowed into Larry's stomach. The gun clattered to the stones. Larry collided with the vine-covered wall, and the air left his lungs in a loud grunt. Leaves spiraled down.

The map tube swung wildly as Tom sent kicks into Larry's side, his upper leg. Larry went down and curled into a ball with his arms over his head. Straddling him, Tom grabbed the front of Larry's jacket, picked him up, and slammed him into the ground. "What did you do to Jenny, you son of a bitch? And Royce Herron. What did you do?"

"I didn't— Let me go. Stop!"

The cable was still tight around his fist. Tom raised his arm and brought the rubber-wrapped steel down on Larry's face, then did it again. His arm was raised a third time but he saw the blood gushing from Larry's mouth. Breathing hard, Tom stood up. "Go on. Get out of here before I kill you."

Larry crawled away on all fours, then staggered to his feet. Tom started after him to be sure he kept going. Larry ran faster and went around the corner. Tom opened his fingers, and the end of the cable curled heavily to the ground. "Oh, Jesus." He took some deep breaths and backed up into the alley, thinking he would have to call Eddie and go upstairs to tell Allison to get her things together. They would have to leave, find a new hotel, or drive back to Manarola tonight.

He was turning, going to get his helmet and take the scooter key out of the ignition, when he saw the men walking toward him. He stopped dead. There were two of them. The man to the right had a short blond cut. The man on the left wore a black coat. He held Larry's gun loosely by one finger through the trigger guard. "Good job. I gotta say, I'm impressed."

The widow's peak and arching brows belonged to the

man Tom had seen on the Eurostar, but this time, the accent was American. "Who are you?"

"You're coming with us."

Before Tom could run, someone grabbed him from behind and twisted his arm up and bent his hand toward his arm with a practiced, almost delicate touch. Tom went to one knee, then flat on the ground.

The man in the black coat told his blond friend to get the car, then came forward to speak to Tom, who was nearly gagging from the pain. He bent down, and a pair of dark eyes looked into Tom's. "Do you have any weapons?"

"No," he gasped.

Hands went around his ankles, up his legs, under his coat. Someone slid the strap of the map tube over Tom's head. Then his arm was jerked down, and he felt plastic go around his wrists. A car came alongside. The man opened the back door, and Tom was hauled to his feet. A hand went on top of his head, and he was shoved inside.

The blond man drove, and the other two pinned him between them. The car went out of the alley and made a quick right. A tire caught the curb and squealed. Lights swept over the interior.

Tom smiled, then laughed.

The dark-haired man glanced at him. "What's funny?"

"I don't know your names, but I know who you are."

"Who are we?"

"Miami cops. You forgot to read me my rights."

"This isn't Miami."

CHAPTER 24

Tom was wrong; they weren't Miami cops. Trapped in the backseat of a car traveling at high speed away from the city, he had reached for any explanation that made sense, even that the Weasel had sent them. But when they arrived at a small house on an unpaved road about fifteen miles out of Florence, and put him in a kitchen chair, still cuffed, Tom found out who they were.

The man in the black coat took it off and tossed it over a broken-down table. He pushed up the sleeves of his gray turtleneck sweater like a man about to get his hands dirty. Taking the map tube from his blond friend, he shook it and asked Tom, "What's in here?"

"An old map."

Tom watched him remove the plastic cap and turn the opening toward the weak fluorescent tube in the ceiling. He unrolled the Mylar-covered map and lay it on the table. The others turned their heads toward it. From where he sat, Tom couldn't see the map, but he saw their reactions. Then all three looked at him.

"Is this blood?"

"What do you think?" Tom said.

The dark-haired man dragged a chair over and sat facing Tom. "My name is Manny Suarez. I'm with the Bureau of Alcohol, Tobacco and Firearms."

"Bullshit. ATF doesn't operate overseas. Who sent you to grab me?"

"Shut up and listen. I'm going to ask you some questions, and if you want to get out of here any time in the next century, you'll answer them truthfully."

Suarez said he was a special case agent for the ATF based in Washington, D.C. He introduced his two friends, the blond and a shorter man with black hair, as Ricker and Ianucci. Through an uncurtained window in the front room Tom could see a fourth man standing on the porch watching the road. They were dressed in the casual dark clothing of Italian workers on their day off and wouldn't draw a second glance.

Tom said, "What agency are they from, CIA?"

Suarez nudged Tom's shoulder. "Pay attention. Why were you beating on Laurence Gerard?"

"How do you know who he was?"

"Answer the question."

"Because he tried to kill me. He had a gun. What would you have done?"

"Why was he trying to kill you?"

"When do we get to the part where you tell me what you want?"

"Let's start over. What are you doing in Italy?"

"No, you tell me why you grabbed me off the street. This isn't Baghdad, last time I checked. Do the Italian police know what you're doing in their country?"

"We'd rather they didn't," Suarez said. "To avoid

that, we could drop you down that well out the back door and walk away. We could say you're wanted by Scotland Yard for the murder of a young woman in London. Lose the attitude and talk to me."

Tom glanced at the other two, then back at Suarez. "I was sent here to make a copy of that map. It's five hundred years old. It belongs to Stuart Barlowe. He's a map collector in Miami. He loaned the map for an exhibition at the museum. An ex-judge named Royce Herron had the map at his house when somebody broke in and shot him. That's his blood. Stuart Barlowe sent me to Italy to make a duplicate."

Ricker smiled. "You're here to forge a five-hundred-year-old map. Oh, that's cute. Sell it to Toys 'Я' Us. The real story is, you're working for Oscar Contreras."

Trying to process this, Tom stared into the man's pale, square face. "What planet are you from?"

Ricker shoved him, and the chair went over. With his hands cuffed behind him, Tom's shoulder hit the floor first. Ricker leaned over him. "Try again, asshole. What are you doing in Italy?"

"Learning to make pasta."

The men pulled Tom back into the chair.

Suarez dragged another chair over and sat facing him. "You asked what we want. Here it is. We want information about an illegal shipment of weapons going out of the port of Genoa within a week to ten days. We think you know something about it. Interesting story about the map, but it's bogus. It's a cover."

"I have no idea what you're talking about."

"Here's what we know about you, Mr. Fairchild. You have no real job. You pick up work as a self-employed computer technician and would-be graphic artist. You rent an apartment from a woman whose late husband was a member of a drug cartel. You're a college dropout, a three-time-loser convicted felon currently on probation. Answer the questions, or we can and will put you on a U.S. military transport back to the States tonight, and I guarantee you, smart-ass, you will be in prison for a long, *long* time."

Tom's nerves were making the muscles twitch in his chest. He concentrated on keeping his breathing steady.

"You slipped out of the U.S. a week ago on Laurence Gerard's boat. You were traveling with a Croatian by the name of Marek Vuksinic. He works for Leo Zurin, a Russian arms merchant living near Dubrovnik, Croatia. Mr. Zurin is presently at his chalet here in Italy."

Arms merchant? Tom opened his mouth but said nothing.

Suarez went on, "Laurence Gerard is the person who brought Zurin and Contreras together. He's also Stuart Barlowe's stepson. We're unclear on Mr. Barlowe's involvement in the deal, but we think you can help us with that."

A laugh escaped Tom's lips. Ricker and his pal Ianucci looked like they wanted an excuse to pound him between the grooves in the old plank floor. "I swear to you, I don't know anything about it. I've met Marek Vuksinic, but I just came over here to make a map, a duplicate for that one. It's for Stuart Barlowe. Royce Herron borrowed it, and somebody shot him. Look, it's got bullet holes—"

Suarez lifted a hand, a signal for Tom to stop talking. "Keeping track of Mr. Vuksinic, we ran into you. We know that you and he boarded Larry Gerard's boat behind Stuart Barlowe's house on La Gorce Island, Miami Beach. We tracked the boat from Miami to Nassau, where both you and Vuksinic got off. Oscar Contreras was also in Nassau. We lost you, but we put a trace on your passport and found you again in London last Thursday. We were watching Claridge's and saw you arrive to meet Stuart Barlowe's daughter, Allison. After that, you and she went to a Barclays bank—"

"Yeah, she was paying me to work on the map! That's why she's here."

"Did I say you could talk? The next day on Regent Street you bought a high-end digital camera and a laptop computer. You spent the night with a young lady by the name of Jenny Gray, who used to work in Miami for Mr. Gerard. On Friday afternoon we followed you back to Ms. Gray's house in Brixton. Ms. Barlowe arrived a few minutes later, followed by Ms. Gray's mother, who reported to police that her daughter had been murdered. She said that Jenny had told her that the young man who had spent the night was going to take her to Florence, Italy. You and Ms. Barlowe slipped out of sight, but she used her MasterCard for the Eurostar. As it stands now, Scotland Yard doesn't know who you are, but that could change."

Tom had thought of coming completely clean— telling them who the map was really for—but that would mean kissing the fifty thousand dollars good-bye. He would spill only as much of the truth as he had to.

"I didn't murder Jenny Gray." Tom started to stand up, but Ricker moved a step closer. "Allison had nothing to do with it, either. Her father sent her here to supervise the map! She came to Jenny's house looking for me, and we found Jenny dead. If you want to know who killed Jenny, go ask Larry Gerard. Ask him about Judge Herron and Carla Kelly."

Suarez stared at him a second, then said, "Go on."

"I think Larry or someone he hired shot Herron and hit the map by accident. Jenny and Carla were working for Larry. They all knew he was paying bribes on a real estate project in Miami—The Metropolis. Stuart Barlowe has a major stake in it, but there's no way he's involved in selling weapons. Larry, yes. I would believe that. You just told me he's the one who put Oscar Contreras together with what's-his-name—Leo Zurin."

"We'll get there," Suarez said, "but right now, let me finish." He leaned back in his chair with his hands loosely clasped in his lap. He had a nice manicure, but a scar went across his knuckles.

"We've been tracking Ms. Barlowe's credit card purchases, so we were able to follow you to Italy. You disappeared in Turin, but she used her card to reserve two rooms at the Hotel Brianza in Florence. We also know that Stuart Barlowe is in Florence with his wife. We tracked Mr. Gerard arriving in London on Friday, Milan on Sunday, and here last night. Seems like all the participants in this transaction are converging."

"Jesus. Don't you listen? I'm making a duplicate map for Stuart Barlowe. I don't know these other guys."

"Never heard of them."

"No."

"We arrived at the hotel to have a talk with you when we saw you come out and get into a scrap with Laurence Gerard." Suarez's curved brows lifted. "And that brings me back to my first question. What was going on between you and him?"

"Larry doesn't want me sleeping with Allison."

"This is a reason to kill you?" Suarez smiled. "We don't have a lot of time, Mr. Fairchild. We need some information, and you're the logical person to ask because, frankly, we have your dick in a wringer. We'd rather not bring Allison into this, but Scotland Yard would really like to know who that woman was, the one who got out of the taxi just before Jenny's mother arrived and found her daughter dead. Think about it."

Tom did. Then said, "How about taking off the cuffs?"

"Sure."

The short guy, Ianucci, went into his pocket for a cutter and walked around Tom's chair. The plastic let go. Tom flexed his fingers and rotated his bruised shoulder. "Larry doesn't want me to do the map."

"We're back to the map?"

"Stuart Barlowe promised it to Leo Zurin. And you're telling me he's an arms dealer. Jesus." Tom had to get his thoughts together. "Zurin agreed to put a lot of money into The Metropolis. He collects Corelli maps, and Stuart promised him that one, but it was destroyed before he could give it to him, so he hired me. Larry thinks that if Zurin finds out it's a forgery, he'll back out of his investment, and The Metropolis would be dead in the water. I guess you'd say Larry and Stuart have a difference of opinion on how good a job I can do."

Ricker and Ianucci exchanged a glance, but Suarez's dark eyes were still fixed on Tom, who said, "I thought Larry was going to kill me tonight. Then you guys showed up. He's the one you should be tracking, not me. I need to call Allison. If I'm not back, she'll call the police."

"Later," Suarez said. "You'll be here awhile. You mentioned a woman, Carla Kelly. Go back to that. You said Larry Gerard killed her."

"I'm only guessing," Tom said. "He used her to blackmail somebody on the Miami zoning board. Carla knew what was going on. Jenny Gray told me about it. She was a friend of Carla's."

"Did Ms. Gray say anything about a connection between Carla and Oscar Contreras?"

"Carla had sex with Oscar. Larry arranged that, too."

"Did you know Carla?"

"I never met her."

"Do you know Oscar Contreras?"

"You asked me that."

"I'm asking again."

"The answer is the same—no. I never met him. The first time I heard his name was on Larry's boat, and then it was only 'Oscar.' Marek Vuksinic asked me if I was going to Nassau to see Oscar. He wanted to know if I was working for Oscar or for Larry."

"And you said?"

"That I didn't know what he was talking about. A little later I went down to the cabin and caught him looking in my backpack. I told him to keep his hands off. When we went back on deck, he flipped me upside down off the transom and put my head underwater. You're wrong, I didn't get off the boat in Nassau with Marek. I got off in Bimini because I didn't know what he would do next. He told me he used to be in the Yugoslav army, and now he sells parts for trucks and heavy equipment in Dubrovnik. Does he?"

Suarez smiled. "No."

"He said he'd been in jail in Bosnia. Do you know what for?"

"Participation in the murder of seventeen unarmed men, and burying their bodies in a mass grave. That was the accusation. The war crimes tribunal couldn't prove it."

Tom had to take a slow breath.

"Why did you go to London?"

"Jenny lived there and knew her way around. I had to see some Corelli maps at the Maritime Museum, and I needed to buy a camera and computer to work on the map for Stuart Barlowe. I stayed at Jenny's house on Thursday night. I asked her who Oscar Contreras was. She said he was in the cocaine business, or used to be. I think that's how Larry Gerard knows him. Larry doesn't deal, but he knows people who are connected to it." Tom paused to get the events in the right order. "Friday afternoon I went back to her place to pick up my stuff. I found her dead. Like I said, Allison was looking for me. She got there a few minutes later. I saw Jenny's mother coming and told Allison we had to get out. We couldn't let the police find us there."

The room was silent for a time.

Ricker spoke: "You know, this idiot may really be as ignorant as he claims."

Rising to his feet, Suarez walked over to the map and smoothed it flat. "How old did you say this is?"

"Five hundred years. It's by Gaetano Corelli. *Universalis Cosmographia,* fifteen-eleven. It came out of an atlas. Be careful with it."

Suarez held it up and looked at the light through the bullet holes.

"I'll tell you about Mr. Zurin. Leo Mikhailevich Zurin is the only son of a major in the Soviet army. His mother was a violinist in the Moscow Symphony. In 1953, his grandfather was executed by Stalin for treason. Zurin's father was demoted and exiled to a post in Kazakhstan, where Zurin worked in the oil industry. Eventually he went back to Moscow, and they sent him to southern Asia and the Middle East, where his job was obtaining weapons for Soviet-sponsored insurgents. After the Soviet Union fell apart, Zurin made a fortune buying up parts of the previously state-owned oil business. He bought a villa on an island off the coast of Croatia, where he keeps his yacht. He has an apartment in Paris and a house in the Italian Alps. That's where he is now. As soon as The Metropolis is built, he'll have a place in Miami."

Rolling up the map, Suarez slid it back into the tube. "Zurin has a lot of interests. Skiing. Music. Fine art. Yachting. And now we find out he likes maps." Suarez came back to Tom's chair and stood looking down at him. "Where is the duplicate?"

"I'm still working on it. It's on my computer."

"How are you doing it? Photoshop?"

"Not exactly. Similar." Barely in time, he held back Eddie Ferraro's name. "I'm making a new engraving plate. Then I'll print the map on antique paper and put in some age spots and a tear along the fold line."

"You think it will fool Leo Zurin?"

"I don't know. I hope so."

Ricker said, "How much is Barlowe paying you for this?"

"Enough to make it worth doing."

"How much?"

"I'll net about a hundred thousand—if I finish on

time and Leo Zurin believes it. Barlowe wants it a week from now."

The men looked at each other.

Ianucci shrugged. "That works."

"You give it to Barlowe," Suarez said, "and Barlowe delivers it to Zurin, and Zurin approves or he doesn't. Is that the plan?"

"That's right."

Suarez crossed his arms and thought for a minute, then sat down again. "Pay attention. Contreras is buying about two million dollars' worth of small arms, machine guns, RPGs, antitank weapons, ammunition, and other assorted hardware from Leo Zurin. The weapons are currently en route from one of the former Soviet republics, scheduled to arrive in Genoa in a week, give or take. Unfortunately, we don't know where they are or what route they're taking. When the weapons arrive in Genoa, they'll be shipped to a location in North Africa, then flown to South America, where they will be used in destabilizing a country that until recently has been on our side."

"Peru," Tom said.

"Correct. The arms trade is not illegal. Selling or importing arms without the proper licenses is. Contreras's boss is a former drug trafficker who gave up the cocaine trade to go into politics. He wants to be president and work for the rights of the poor and oppressed and stand up to Uncle Sam. That's all well and good, but he's still a narco-thug. If he loses the election, his supporters—well armed, thanks to Contreras—will contest the results. You see how it goes. Now we come to the part where we tell you what we want. We want to know the name of the ship and the day it's leaving Genoa."

"I don't know that," Tom said. "How would I know something like that?"

"You're going to find out for us. I thought, until we talked, that you might be here on Oscar Contreras's behalf, and that you'd have that information. It's possible you're lying, but I don't think so. Stuart Barlowe is here to see Leo Zurin; that seems fairly certain. Maybe he's here about the weapons deal, maybe he isn't, but he has to give Zurin the map. That makes things easier. Zurin sticks close to his house in Champorcher when a deal is in the works, so I don't see him coming here to Florence. It's more likely that Mr. Barlowe will deliver the map there. Champorcher is in the Alps about an hour north of Milan. You go with him. We want you to leave a couple of listening devices in Zurin's house."

Tom looked from one of them to the other, too stunned to reply.

Ianucci said, "They're amazingly small nowadays. No one will notice. We'll meet you again and show you how they work."

"I can't go with Stuart Barlowe. I can't just invite myself along. He wouldn't let me."

Ricker put a hand on the back of Tom's chair. "Ask his daughter to fix it up. She's your girlfriend. Right? You shared a sleeper on the overnight train to Italy."

"Don't ask me to get her involved. I won't do it. Plant the bug yourself. You guys are experts at it."

"We can't get inside," Ricker said. "You can."

"Leo Zurin is an arms dealer. If Marek Vuksinic sees me again, you think he won't ask what I'm doing there? You think I'll be alive a week from now?"

"You'll be with Stuart Barlowe," Suarez said. "You have to go because Zurin has to approve the map. You simply tell Barlowe to introduce you as his map expert. If we thought there was any serious risk, we wouldn't ask you to help us."

"Bullshit. You people are such liars. You're *worse* than cops. Go ahead, send me back. I've got six years to serve. That's better than a bullet in the back of the head."

"Then let me put it this way." Suarez came in closer, elbows on knees. "Eddie Ferraro. Is he a friend of yours?"

Tom looked at him.

"Eddie Ferraro," Suarez repeated. "He checked into the Hotel Brianza with you and Ms. Barlowe. I think you're basically a good guy. Despite your record, I don't think you're the kind of man who would sell out a friend. Eddie has twenty years to serve, and I would be just as happy to put him on the same flight back to the U.S. that you're going to be on. It's up to you."

CHAPTER 25

They would keep Larry overnight in a semiprivate room at Santa Maria Nuova. They had wanted to patch him up and send him out the door. Nobody could speak English, or else they were being typically Italian. Your son isn't so bad—*non è molto grave.* But Rhonda had demanded that he be taken care of properly. She would pay whatever was required. Finally they gave in. Tomorrow. *Domani, signora.* Come for him tomorrow.

As soon as Larry was wheeled into his room, which he shared with a withered old man who smelled like death, the nurse allowed Rhonda *cinque minuti,* five minutes, no more. They had shot Larry so full of painkillers and sedatives he would be out for hours.

Stuart waited just inside the door with his coat over his arm, as if a black eye and a broken nose were catching. Leaning over her son, Rhonda touched her lips to his bruised forehead and swollen cheek. She carefully straightened his hair—getting bald already; how he hated it.

"We should go," Stuart said quietly.

"Not yet. A little longer."

Larry had called as she was dressing for dinner, and she'd had to scream at him to make him slow down, tell her what had happened, where he was. Stuart came out of the shower, but by then Rhonda was reaching for her coat and her purse. She took a taxi to pick Larry up, and she used her scarf to staunch the bleeding. *Talk to me*, she had told him. *What the hell happened? How could you fuck it up so completely?*

The taxi driver had known the nearest *pronto soccorso*—emergency facility. Rhonda stayed with him as long as she could. *Say nothing. Nothing. I'll deal with this.*

But it was her fault, not Larry's. She had failed. Failed utterly, without recourse. The forged Corelli would be made—no doubt about that now. Leo Zurin would tell everyone that Stuart had tried to cheat him, and the edifice of their lives would collapse into a charred heap of rubble.

She felt Stuart looking at her. As soon as they left, he would start asking questions. She could hear them already, buzzing around in his mind. What would she say? *I asked Larry to kill Tom Fairchild for me. What do you think of that, Stuart?*

Her fault. She should never have sent Larry to do it himself. He wasn't brilliant. He wasn't strong or vicious. This hadn't been like the situation with Royce Herron. That had been easy. Rhonda had told Larry to find someone, and he had persuaded Marek Vuksinic to do it. Quick, professional. No charge. Thank you very much.

The nurse came back. "*Mi dispiace, ma adesso dovete—*"

"Yes, we're leaving," Rhonda said. "*Grazie.*"

"*Grazie,*" said Stuart. "Thank you."

Rhonda picked up her white fur coat from the chair. Stuart wouldn't touch it, would he? Larry's blood was on the sleeve. Stuart had seen it and said she could probably leave it with the concierge, who would know a good dry cleaner.

They followed the corridor toward the exit, accompanied by the tap of their shoes and low voices from the nurses' station. Stuart took her elbow. "Are you all right?"

"I'll be better in the morning when we pick him up."

"He'll need a dentist," Stuart said. "He should go back to Miami immediately."

"That's probably best. Tomorrow I'll see how he feels." A nurse walked by, then an orderly with a cart. Rhonda said quietly, "I'm sorry to have left you at the hotel, rushing out that way, but I couldn't wait. I had to go to him."

"A mother's instinct," he murmured. The lights in the ceiling slowly moved over his face, deepening the shadows under his eyes. "What is he doing in Italy?"

Rhonda leaned on his arm. "I should have talked to you first. Larry has been so pressured lately—you have, too—the developer, the designers, the bank, picking at him like crows. He wanted to talk to you about The Metropolis, away from all of them, so I said yes, come over. We'll surprise Stuart."

"Yes, well, you've certainly done that. Have we had dinner? I can't remember."

"I don't think so." Rhonda sighed. "You're so good to wait with me. Larry will appreciate it."

"We'll order room service. I think we have a few things to discuss."

Taking his arm, she said, "Larry arrived this afternoon. He wanted to talk to Tom about what had happened on the boat—what Marek had done. He wanted to apologize—"

"Not here, Rhonda. Other people—"

"They aren't listening. They don't hear us." She put her head on Stuart's shoulder as they walked. "I told Larry where they were staying, and he asked Tom to have a drink with him. They met outside Tom's hotel. They argued. Tom attacked Larry. He hit him in the face with a motorcycle lock."

"Good God."

"Tom Fairchild is a violent man. Larry could have died. Thank God he was able to get away. He called me." Rhonda turned away from the corridor and reached into her bag for a tissue. A sign on the wall informed the staff that the morning rosary had been changed to 8 AM. "When I answered the phone I didn't know who it was at first. Just this voice crying, 'Mama, Mama—'"

Standing behind her, Stuart put his hands on her shoulders. "Larry will be all right. The doctor said no permanent damage. One of the staff asked me if we wanted to report it to the police. I said no. I don't think we should involve them at this point. Do you?"

Years ago there would have been anger, outrage . . . something. Rhonda took his arm again, and they walked toward the lobby. A group of old women in dark clothing sat on a sofa waiting like a chorus of mourners.

Rhonda held her tissue in her fist. "No. We'll let it go. If Tom is in jail, he can't finish the map, can he?"

"Calm down, Rhonda. I'll have a talk with him."

"Expect to be lied to. He'll probably blame Larry. God knows what he'll say to you. He's a sociopath."

"Leave it alone, Rhonda." Stuart's voice had some bite. "Can we please get out of this place?" His lips barely moved. "You should think about accompanying Larry back to Miami. He might need you."

The women's eyes followed them as they crossed the lobby. Through the glass front of the lobby, over the buildings across the small piazza, rose the terra-cotta dome of the cathedral of Santa Maria del Fiore, lady of the flowers. Rhonda slowed her steps. She didn't want to be outside on the sidewalk alone with him. Not yet. He wouldn't lose his temper with people looking on.

She stopped and waited until he turned to her. "Stuart, I have to tell you something—a confession? I was so afraid that if Leo Zurin knew the map was a forgery, he would make things so much worse for us than if we just admitted it had been destroyed."

"You've made your position on that very clear. Is there more?"

"Yes. Whatever I've done, I did for us, and if I was wrong . . . I'm sorry, and I hope you can forgive me. Before Tom Fairchild left Miami, I asked him not to do the map. I offered him money not to do it, and today I asked Larry to go around to his hotel and offer him whatever it took. That may be why Tom attacked him. I feel so guilty, so sorry for everything."

Stuart's face sagged with disbelief. "You did that? Why? To deliberately sabotage me—to lie to me—"

"I was trying to help you—to save what we've built together. Because I love you. Because I was foolish and afraid." She pressed her lips to his cheek, his neck, and slid her arms under his coat, holding him tightly. "Please forgive me. I was so wrong, and I know that. I've told you everything. Don't make me leave you. I would die without you. Let's not talk anymore tonight. Take me back to the hotel. Please. I want to be with you. Tomorrow I'll come back for Larry, and I'll send him home, but don't make me go, too. I need you. I've always needed you. I want to go to our room and go to sleep with your arms around me and forget everything except what we are to each other. Say you love me." A small laugh escaped her. "Say it before I want to kill myself. You do love me. Don't you?"

"God help me, yes. You drive me to insanity, Rhonda. I've wished you dead, and you've wished the same for me. Don't deny it." His breath was in her ear. "It's what we have in common."

"We'll be home soon." She felt his beard under her lips. "We'll be home in a few days. Tom Fairchild will finish the map. We'll give it to Leo, and we'll go home."

CHAPTER 26

When Oscar Contreras pushed off on his return lap of the pool, he saw the downstairs maid coming out of the house through one of the stone arches of the portico. She carried a telephone, and Contreras assumed the call was of some importance, since any employee who disturbed him during his morning swim without a good reason would be fired.

As he stroked through the water, he could see her brown feet and splayed toes in their leather sandals keeping up with him. He finished his lap of the pool and stood up. "*¿Quién es?*"

"*Perdóneme, señor. Es el señor Zurin de Italia.*"

He told her yes, yes, he would take it, go get him his towel. He waded up the steps, water running down his chest, over his belly. Mopping his face, he walked quickly across the hot deck to the umbrella table, where she had put the phone. "Leo, is that you?"

"Ciao, Oscar," came the voice on the other end. "I hope I didn't wake you." Leo must have heard the sounds of the pool. He was being sarcastic, a trait of the Europeans.

"I swim one hundred laps every morning for my health." Oscar put on his sunglasses.

"How *macho*." Leo Zurin said, "You must come to Italy and do some skiing. It's exhilarating, but one must be careful not to slide off the trail into a crevasse. Forgive me for getting immediately to the point, but where is my money?"

Contreras said, "Where are my goods? Excuse me to get to the point, too, but you haven't sent me that information."

Zurin replied, "This is because my company hasn't received the third payment, which is due before the goods are shipped. Those are our terms."

"How do I know all my items will be in the container?"

There was a pause before Leo Zurin said, "Are you questioning my integrity?"

"No, this is business. I don't know you. You don't know me. I put the order with your company on word of mouth. Next time, when we establish more of a track record, then we don't have to go through this shit."

"There will be no next time, Señor Contreras. Do you want your items or don't you?"

The maid set a glass of orange juice on the table. Contreras drank some of it and chewed the ice. "I tell you what, Leo. Don't play games. I can buy the goods somewhere else. I'm not in a hurry. Okay, this is what we're going to do. I'll send you a wire transfer when everything's in order. I know somebody over in Italy right now, in fact. When I have the word that the goods are checked off a list, and so forth, then I'll tell him to release the money. This is a person we both know, Larry Gerard from Miami. He's an excellent personal friend of mine. I'll ask him for this favor. When I say release the money, then you can have it. Not before. Okay, the second thing."

With the phone under his ear, Contreras toweled under his arms and between his legs before sitting in a cushioned patio chair. "Your prices are high as hell. What if I pay the costs of shipping directly? My company saves money, and you don't have to worry about getting the stuff all the way over here. Sound good to you?"

The answer came back quicker than Contreras had expected. "Excellent idea," Leo Zurin said. "I'll have a representative from my company contact you again soon."

The line went dead. Contreras motioned to the maid, who stood silently in the shade of the portico. "I'm ready for my breakfast."

Leo Zurin slid his mobile phone back into the pocket of his ski jacket, which hung over the adjacent chair. His mouth was a tight, thin line. In the space of sixty seconds, Marek had watched him go from annoyance to rage.

"Trouble from the Peruvian?"

"Son of a pig. As soon as the products are loaded, they're his. After this, I won't sell him a slingshot, and I'll make sure no one else does, either. This is the last time I do business with a South American. They're corrupt and backward. This is why they keep having revolutions."

Marek and Leo were sharing raclette for lunch outside

a restaurant on the little piazza in Champorcher. The table gave a good view of the mountains, and Marek could smoke. The sun shone on Leo's bald head and reflected in his dark glasses. Leo picked up the long, flat knife and scraped melting cheese onto his bread. "Here's another surprise. Contreras is going to ask Larry Gerard to be his eyes and ears before he pays me. Ha. I thought that would make you sit up."

"It's my fault," Marek said. "I let Gerard put Contreras in touch with you."

"Don't worry about it." Leo followed the cheese with a sip of wine. "From time to time we all draw a bad card. Can you be in Genoa on Tuesday? The shipment arrives that afternoon or evening. As soon as the parts are loaded into the container, they belong to Contreras. I don't get all the money I wanted, but on the other hand, I don't have to guarantee delivery in Peru. Where exactly is Peru?"

"South of Colombia," Marek said. "So. It looks like Tom Fairchild doesn't work for Contreras after all."

"No, he doesn't," Leo agreed. "I finally heard from my friend at the International Map Society yesterday. Fairchild's sister owns a map shop in Miami. He works there. His specialty is cleaning, coloring, and framing old maps."

With his fork Marek dragged one of the thumb-sized potatoes through the bubbling cheese. He turned the wedge to put the cooler side toward the coils of the heater. Leo was waiting for him to say something.

"Yes, he works in a map shop. We knew that. But I still smell a dead fish."

"Some things are exactly as they appear," Leo said. "Those mountains. This bread. The sun on our faces. And sometimes—not often, but occasionally—people do tell the truth."

Not twenty-four hours after Rhonda Barlowe had showed up at Leo's house claiming the Corelli map had been stolen, her husband called Leo to say she'd made a mistake. Barlowe said Tom Fairchild had gone to London to talk to experts about fixing the stains in the map, but Rhonda didn't know, so she thought the map had been stolen. Tom Fairchild went on to Italy to buy the special solvents and glue. The cleaning would be finished before the weekend, and Stuart Barlowe would personally deliver the map to Champorcher.

This made no sense to Marek, but Leo wanted to believe it.

Leo's black eyes looked at him over the top of his sunglasses. "You think Barlowe is lying."

Marek imagined Stuart Barlowe's face under the raclette heater. What lies would he tell then? "Why doesn't he know where Fairchild is?"

"They stay in contact by telephone," Leo said. "Fairchild insists on being left alone to do his work."

"If he cleans old maps, why did he strangle the British girl?"

"Maybe he wanted sex and she refused. I don't care. He can do what he likes except ruin the Corelli, and if that should happen, I will tear off his arms and feed them to Stuart Barlowe. What in the name of Christ's grandmother is taking so long?"

Marek took a cigarette from his pack and lit it. "Will Larry Gerard be in Genoa?"

"If Contreras sends him. Why?"

"He's a big problem. He talks too much."

"We need him to approve the shipment."

"Yes, but after that?" Marek let out a cloud of smoke.

"Do what you want. You don't need to ask my permission," Leo said. "As long as I have my map, I wouldn't be sorry if an avalanche took the lot of them."

Chapter 27

Under an old umbrella with a broken rib, Allison hurried back to Eddie Ferraro's house with a bag that his elderly aunt Lucia had filled with food—rosemary chicken and some Ligurian pasta and green beans. Allison went around puddles and stepped over small rivers that gurgled down the cobblestones from higher streets. The rain was melting the dusting of snow that a cold front had left two days ago. It was late on a Sunday afternoon, and the weather had sent everyone inside. Tomorrow the children would line up for the school bus and the shops would be open. Crates of vegetables and fruit would be put out on the sidewalks—if the rain stopped.

The plan was to leave for Florence in the morning and print the map tomorrow night, but that depended on whether Eddie could make a usable engraving plate. Of the six blank plates shipped from Germany last week, he had already ruined three under the ultraviolet tubes in his light box. Unable to stand the suspense of waiting for another one to be thrown across the room, Allison had volunteered to fetch dinner. They had all been so busy with the map that the food had run out. Eddie had called Aunt Lucia to see if she had any leftovers.

Turning the corner at the tobacconist's, Allison went up the steep incline of Via Rossa. The wooden doors, which by optical illusion seemed to slant uphill, faced each other across narrow sidewalks and a street of flat, gray stones incised to keep pedestrians and pushcarts from slipping.

Unless something unexpected occurred, the map would be finished a day ahead of schedule. Eddie had built his light box and mixed the ink and showed Allison how to make ink daubers for the engraving plate. Drinking pots of espresso, Tom stayed glued to his computer. At dawn this morning Allison had awakened to find a note on his side of the bed. He and Eddie had taken off for Florence with the digital image on a DVD. Six hours later, they returned with a transparency of the map and two backups, and they started on the engraving plates.

Allison had wanted to go with them, but Tom had left her sleeping. It wasn't that he was being nice. He was avoiding her. He didn't want any of her questions about what had happened last Wednesday night. She and Eddie had been sick with anxiety, arguing whether to wait for a phone call or to contact the police. Then Tom had come back and said he'd fought with Larry. That, Allison could believe. It was the rest of it she found incredible. After Larry had left, Tom had been taken by kidnappers who thought he had money and they could get a ransom. After finally convincing them he was only a student, Tom had been released.

Of course it was BS, but Tom had said to leave him alone, he had to work, and why didn't she go study? Allison was sick of studying. In two weeks she would be in Miami taking the bar exam. She would either pass it or not. It seemed to have about as much relevance to her life as the tide tables in Fiji.

She reached Eddie's building and looked up at the tightly closed shutters of the workshop three floors above her. Whatever lies Tom had told her, Eddie had gotten something else. More than once she had walked into the room and they had stopped talking, then one or the other would come out with some inanity, like was there any beer left? Or was it still raining out there?

The stone staircase at the side of the building led to a small porch, where Allison set down the bag and closed the umbrella. She had her hand on the doorknob when she heard someone inside shouting. Slowly she opened the door.

It was Tom, and the anger in his voice surprised her. She didn't hear anyone else and gradually realized that he was on the telephone. Not having seen Eddie on the street, she wondered if he was upstairs, too. She quietly closed the door and carried the bag to the small kitchen, taking care that her shoes didn't squeak on the tile floor. Still in her hat and coat, she went to the stairs and looked up.

He was saying something about being left twisting in the wind.

"You could go back to Miami and say too bad, so sad, and leave me here. What would I do, sue you? . . . The map *is* what you want, but the way things are, I can't be sure you're going to agree with that. . . . It's not for you, it's for Leo Zurin. Let him decide."

Realizing that Tom was talking to her father, Allison

went up another step. The wood creaked, and she stopped.

"Explain it to Zurin however you want, that's up to you, but when you take him the map, I'm going along. That's the deal. . . . Sure, you can get back to me, but make it quick. If we don't have an agreement, there will be no map. . . . You know how to reach me."

There was a short silence, then Eddie Ferraro said, "Do you think he'll go along with it?"

"I don't know. Maybe."

"You'd better think about putting a squeeze on him, Tommy. You might need some ammo if he tries to come back at you."

"Let's wait and see what happens. I'll tell Suarez it's a go and keep my fingers crossed."

"I think those guys are the ones you have to worry about more than Barlowe."

"No shit. What's an ATF agent doing in Italy, is what I want to know." Then Tom laughed. "Hey, Eddie, you need a roommate? I might be staying in Manarola if this doesn't work out. Jesus, I'm tired. Is that plate dry yet?"

"Come have a look."

By now Allison had reached the top of the stairs. Carbon dust from the ink-making had grimed the floor, and shipping boxes had been tossed into a corner. Beer bottles and espresso cups littered the shelves. The two men leaned over the workbench, and the pool of light caught the gray in Eddie's hair, and the movement of Tom's magnifying glass over the engraving plate.

"Dinner's downstairs," she said.

They looked around at her from the worktable, then quickly at each other. Allison took off her jacket and her beret and laid them on the stair railing. She crossed the room and saw an engraving plate about three feet by two. Eddie had washed away the parts of the plate not hardened by the UV light. The polymer surface gleamed, revealing a tracery of fine lines, Corelli's *Universalis Cosmographia* in reverse.

"I guess we finally have one that works."

No one could pretend she hadn't overheard their conversation.

"Fourth time's a charm," Eddie said. "Tom did a brilliant job, but we still have to print the map, so we'll make one more tonight just in case."

Allison shifted her eyes to Tom. "Why don't we take a walk?"

Eddie said, "Allison, we didn't want to keep you in the dark. That's a fact." When Allison only looked at him, he sighed. "You two stay here. I think I'll go pick up a bottle of wine. Give me a buzz on my cell phone when dinner's ready."

He went downstairs. The door closed. Allison said, "You were yelling at my father. Why?"

Tom's hair was standing up in front as though he'd been running his fingers through it. "I didn't tell you everything."

"What a shock."

"I couldn't, Allison. There's a lot I still can't tell you, and I wish you would trust me on that. We'll be home in a week. As soon as we're out of here, I'll explain everything, but not now."

"Oh, I thought you were staying in Manarola with Eddie."

"I was just talking."

"Stop lying to me, Tom. You said you never lied to me, but that's what you've been doing."

"Look. I told your father I want to go with him when he gives the map to Leo Zurin. I have to. What if he says Zurin doesn't like the map? Or if he decides not to pay me? What recourse would I have? I don't want to be left hanging."

"Do you want me to walk out that door right now? I can, Tom. I can go right back to Florence and ask my father."

"All right. I'll tell you." But he hesitated.

"Stop trying to invent something!" Allison said, "Just tell me the truth. Is it that hard? You can start by telling me where you went Wednesday night. Did you talk to my father about Larry? Did you have it out with him?"

"No, he called me the next day. I haven't seen your father. Come here. Sit down." Tom put her on the end of Eddie's cot, and he sat beside her. He took her hand. "Some of this Stuart can't know about. I'm serious, babe."

She slowly said, "All right."

"I didn't go anywhere—not voluntarily. Do you remember the men following us on the train? They were outside the hotel. They'd been tracking your credit card, so they knew where I was. They were going to come inside, but I came out, and they saw me and Larry get into it. After Larry split, they grabbed me and threw me in their car."

Allison stared at him. "Please tell me that's a lie."

"You want to hear this or not?"

"Yes. Go on."

The pale light leaking through the shutters gradually

faded and went out entirely before Tom had finished talking. Allison understood, at the end of it, that two of the investors in her father's real estate project were involved in an illegal arms deal that certain agents of the United States government wanted to prevent, and that to do so, they expected Tom Fairchild to plant listening devices in Leo Zurin's house in the mountains near Champorcher.

"Just two or three of them," he said. "This morning, when Eddie and I went to Florence, they showed me one. It's very small. It has a sticky side. I could put it under a table or on a wall. When we go back to Florence again, I'll meet Suarez one more time."

"Oh, my God." Allison leaned her forehead into her hands.

"Nothing's going to happen," Tom said. "Leo Zurin will be in a good mood. He's getting his map. He won't be looking for microphones. That's the last thing he'd expect, somebody bugging his house."

"What if Marek Vuksinic is there? What then?"

"What if he is?" Tom shrugged. "He'll mind his manners in front of Stuart."

"Are you really that sure?"

"Yes. Don't worry, Allison."

She searched his face. Long hours at the computer had left their mark, but she couldn't see any sign of uneasiness. "Does Agent Suarez believe my father is involved in any way?"

Tom hesitated, then said, "I don't know what they believe."

"It's Larry," she said. "He's behind it. He's using Stuart. He always has. He's a surrogate for Rhonda, you know that. Her little hand puppet."

"You really think she sent him after me, don't you?"

"Of course she did. It wasn't my father. It's Rhonda who's been trying to stop you. First bribery, then Larry with a gun. I think she meant for him to kill you."

"I don't know about that. What if he was trying to scare me off? I beat the shit out of him for nothing."

"What were you supposed to do, wait until he pulled the trigger?"

"Wow. Tough, aren't you?"

"Please let me tell Stuart. All he's getting is lies."

"Don't," Tom said. "I want to finish the map and get paid. After that, all hell can break loose between those two. But leave it alone for now."

"What a *bitch*."

"I mean it, Allison." Tom held up a finger, warning her.

"Okay. I won't say anything." She scooted around and sat Indian fashion on the cot. "May I be your attorney for a minute? When you see Suarez again, ask him to fix things with your probation officer. That's the least he can do."

"I did ask him. He said no. They're the federal government, and Weems works for the state."

"That doesn't matter. The feds can crush the state if they want to. They can. They could say, 'Tom Fairchild is ours, and if you touch him, we'll charge *you* with a federal crime.'"

"Thanks for the legal opinion, babe, but Suarez won't go for it. You see, he can't let it be known that he's operating out of his jurisdiction, can he, or his agency would get fried in the media. All he promises is a free pass through Homeland Security, and I hope he doesn't screw that up." Tom pulled Allison within reach and kissed the top of her head. "It's not just me on the line, it's Eddie.

They threatened to send him back to the U.S. to stand trial on that old counterfeiting charge. He could go to prison for twenty years. I didn't tell Eddie. I mean, why worry him, right?"

Allison pulled away to look at him directly. "You're doing this for Eddie? No, it's okay, I just meant . . . my God, that's so . . . noble."

"Noble? Not really. It's my ass on the line, too."

"What did Eddie mean about needing ammunition against my father?"

"Excuse me?"

"You and Eddie were talking, and he said you might have to put a squeeze on Stuart, and you said— You said you'd wait and see how it goes first. What did you mean?"

Tom was shaking his head, looking blank. "I guess it meant . . . we would have to persuade Stuart to let me go with him to deliver the map. Sorry, Allison, I'm so tired right now I can't think straight. All I want to do is get the map done, get the hell out of Italy, and forget this ever happened."

After a second, Allison nodded. She laid her palm against Tom's and flattened them together. Her fingers were shorter and more slender. "We're both starting over, in a way. I don't know what's going to happen with you and me, but . . . we'll just see. I've thought about my career, too. I'm just not as frantic about it anymore. And Stuart . . . well, I'm still trying to figure him out, but it's changing. Most of my life, I've never cared if we ever spoke to each other, and even now, I don't know what he really thinks of me, but I do love him. I can't help it. He's my father."

"Be careful, babe. People can disappoint you."

"Why do you say that?"

"Just that . . . sometimes they aren't what you want them to be."

Allison said, "How did Suarez get the okay to work in Italy?"

"What?"

"He's an ATF agent. He's looking into an illegal arms deal, but the weapons aren't going into the U.S. The ATF is a domestic agency, like the FBI. And who are his friends working for?"

"I asked him. He told me to shut up." Tom looked at his watch. "Four thirty. What time is that in Miami?"

"Ten thirty in the morning."

He rolled off the cot and went to his cell phone, which he'd left plugged into its adapter on the workbench.

"What are you doing?"

"I've got this friend . . . my landlord, Fritz. He's retired from working for a private air-cargo business in Panama. Unless he's totally full of crap, that's not all he was doing. He was CIA. He says he's still in touch with his pals. I'm going to give him an assignment: Who is Manny Suarez?"

CHAPTER 28

The shipment arrived just before nightfall on Tuesday at a warehouse near the port of Genoa. The Ukrainians who had accompanied the boxes across six international borders got back into their trucks and left. Men from the warehouse pried open the lids and laid the contents on a tarp on the concrete floor. The man working for Oscar Contreras checked the contents against a list. After each box was nailed shut again, it was loaded onto a cart by a dark-skinned Algerian and a Sicilian who was missing one eye. They took the box outside to a steel shipping container. This had been going on for hours.

The boxes had been logged in as used German auto parts destined for Caracas, Venezuela. In their container, the boxes would be loaded into the ship *Ulysse*, gross tonnage 17,500, sailing under a Tunisian flag. The ship would go through the Straits of Gilbraltar to a port in Western Sahara. The container would be unloaded, put on a flight to Venezuela, and taken overland to Peru. Marek Vuksinic had worked out the details of the itinerary, but after the door of the container was sealed, the boxes were no longer his problem.

When Contreras's agent was satisfied that everything on the list had been accounted for, Larry Gerard would call a certain banker to confirm the transaction and tell him to release the money to an account identified only by a number. On the day the ship was loaded, Contreras's man would return and accompany the container to the dock.

Larry Gerard sat watching this from a chair he had rolled out from the office. He carefully put a glass to his lips. Ever since he had arrived, he had been drinking the shipper's Scotch whisky. A heavy white bandage went across his nose, and one eye looked like a plum with a red slit in it. What Tom Fairchild had done to Larry made Marek think that Fairchild was more than a clerk whose sister owned a map shop.

There were only a few boxes left. Larry set the bottle of Scotch on the floor and motioned for Marek to come over. "Want to talk to you." His mouth barely moved. His lips were swollen, and two of his teeth had been knocked out.

They went through a side door and into the yard, which was taken up with the dark shapes of stacked shipping containers and a few stunted trees. Larry stopped walking just beyond reach of a floodlight on the corner of the building.

"Want you to do something. I'll . . . pay you for it. First, I gotta tell you about the Corelli. The ma-map for Leo Zurin." Larry was having problems with his Ps and Bs.

Marek smoked his cigarette and waited.

"It's a forgery. A fake. Zurin isn't going to get the real thing. It's ruined."

"I don't understand."

"The map is a du-duplicate of the original. It's a scam. Don't you know what you did? When you shot Judge Herron, you shot right through the Corelli. Three . . . bullets. Blood all over."

"No."

"Yes!" Some air came through Larry's nose, a laugh, which turned into a wince. "It's funny in a way . . . when you think about it. If I were you, I wouldn't tell Zurin."

Smoke drifted past Marek's head. "So you are telling me . . . I destroyed the map? And Stuart Barlowe will give Leo a fake map?"

"Yes. Exactly. He's . . . paying Tom Fairchild a hundred thousand dollars. Believe that?"

This news was so staggering that Marek couldn't think how to react. "Where is Tom Fairchild?"

"Right now he's in Florence. He's going to . . . print the map tonight. Could be done already."

"Where?"

"That I don't know, but he'll take it to Stuart. They're staying at the Cellini. Then Stuart will take the map to Leo."

"Is it a good forgery?"

Larry shrugged. "I haven't seen it yet, but Leo isn't stupid." Larry came closer and put a hand on Marek's shoulder. "Don't worry. I won't tell him what you did. Okay? But you have to help me convince him to stay with The Metro-Metropolis. He has a damn good . . . apartment. I can make sure he gets more of the . . . profit. There are ways to do it. I have a creative accountant." Larry's swollen lips stretched into a smile. "But I can't do anything with Stuart there. Do you know what I'm saying?"

Marek watched the dim light shift on Larry Gerard's ruined face. "No. What are you saying?"

"Stuart needs to go. Shit, Marek. He's a dead man already. When Leo finds out the map is a f-forgery, he'll go nuts." With his good eye, Larry looked past Marek toward the door to the warehouse before he spoke again. "Stuart's been losing it for a long time. He's on medication. I'm the one making decisions on the . . . project. He's deep in debt, but he has a lot of life insurance. I want you to take out Allison, too. How you do it is your decision. Tell me how much you want."

Tapping some ashes to the side, Marek said, "Why your sister?"

"My stepsister. Why? Aside from . . . being a cunt?" Larry laughed. "If she's alive, she gets half his life insurance and a lot of . . . other property."

"You don't care if people in your family die?"

"They aren't my family. They're nothing to me." Larry's tongue slid over his broken teeth. "How much do you want?"

"For two people?"

"Yeah. What do you get for this kind of job?"

"What about Tom Fairchild?"

"Sure. Him, too. What he did to me, he deserves it. Okay. Three. How much?"

"We'll talk about it later." Marek motioned with his head toward the door of the warehouse. "Let's go inside. It's cold tonight. We'll have a drink and wait until the boxes are in the container, then we'll talk."

At 2:35 AM the container was sealed with a steel cable and a plate with the name of a shipping agent that existed only on paper. The warehouse workers left right away, but Marek told the Algerian and the Sicilian to stay until all the business had been settled. They went into a back room with their hashish pipe.

Marek went outside to light a cigarette while Oscar Contreras's man made a call to Peru. After that, Larry Gerard would speak to the banker.

Walking down the slope behind the warehouse, Marek could see the old section of Genoa. The hill was high enough to give him a clear view of the port, which was lit as brightly as an American shopping mall. Loading cranes pierced the black sky, and two dozen or more freighters were tied to docks. Cruise ships waited for their morning embarkation.

He gazed through the chain-link fence. A long breakwater separated the omega-shaped harbor from the Ligurian Sea. Marek had learned from the Italians in the warehouse that Christopher Columbus had sailed from this port in the days of its glory. A hundred and fifty years before that, the Black Death had arrived on the backs of rats from Odessa running down the hawsers to the dock.

Holding the cigarette between his teeth, Marek went into the breast pocket of his coat for his Walther P99 and its noise suppressor. He screwed the suppressor to the end of the barrel. The dull black finish reflected no light. After routinely checking the magazine, Marek returned the gun to his coat.

He watched the distant blinking lights of a jet cross the sky and disappear behind a mountain. He could never allow Leo to know that the Corelli was a fake. How would he explain that his bullets had destroyed it?

Marek had shot the old map collector, Herron, because Larry had said it was necessary. Larry had told him the old man had to die because he knew about the bribery and prostitution, and if he told the police, this might have prevented The Metropolis from being built at all. Marek had done it for Leo Zurin, but he had accidentally destroyed the thing that Leo wanted most.

Marek wondered if the forgery was any good. He wondered if he could give the duplicate to Leo and say nothing. If only the fake existed, then in its own way, it was real.

He heard footsteps behind him. In the dim light from the city, the fence made a pattern of squares on Larry's face and his zipper jacket.

"You made the phone call?" Marek asked.

"Uh-huh."

"The bank will transfer the cash?"

"I said yes." Larry noticed the harbor. "Check out those yachts down there. That's what I want. I'm going to sail the world on a . . . big-ass boat, eighty feet, with an all-female crew." The red in his left eye was the only color in his face. The bruises were dark gray. "Did you decide on a p-price?"

"Larry, you think I'm a hit man?"

"You took care of Judge Herron."

"Not for you. For Leo."

"Okay. You did it to save Leo's investment. That's why . . . you have to convince him to stick with it."

"And you won't tell him what I did to his map."

"Course not. Our secret."

Marek took the pistol from his coat and shot Larry Gerard twice in the chest, then once through the forehead. Larry fell into the weeds, twitched for a few seconds, and lay still.

Marek walked back up the hill and told the others to

get a tarp. They rolled the body into it and carried it around to the front of the building. They dropped it on the ground in front of the shipping container.

"Open the door."

The Algerian used a heavy set of bolt cutters that sliced easily through the cable. The door swung open, and they wedged the wrapped body between two of the wooden boxes and laid another on top of it.

Marek crushed out his cigarette and flicked it inside. "You wanted to go on a big boat. Have a nice trip."

He motioned for the men to close the door and reseal the container.

CHAPTER 29

The sign by the door read LUCCHESE E FIGLI, STAMPATORI, DAL 1826. Lucchese and Sons had been in the printing business for almost two centuries. The front rooms had been updated—probably just after World War II—and the original printing press had been shoved into a long, narrow storeroom with an arched, brick ceiling. The heavy, wooden timbers of the press supported a table and four long, metal spokes connected to a central gear that would turn two rollers. The rollers would press the engraving plate and paper together with such force that as they went through, the paper would suck the ink from the fine lines in the etching.

Tom unloaded a box on the workbench while Eddie Ferraro pulled the dustcover off the press and plugged in some lights so they could see what they were doing. Eddie put on a blue printer's apron and gave Allison another. She gathered her hair into a clip at the nape of her neck and announced she was ready for orders.

Tom had to keep his hands clean, so Eddie put him to work laying out sheets of modern laid paper on blotters and sponging water onto both sides. These would be test sheets. Eddie explained that unless the fibers were pliable, they couldn't be pressed into the grooves in the plate. When the sheets were evenly damp, Tom put them in a neat stack next to the printer.

Eddie slid the eleven sheets of antique paper out of the box they had come in. "Now wet these—and remember, they're fragile."

He let Allison help him daub ink onto the plate and wipe it off until the polymer surface shone. Their hands became as oily and black as the ink. Eddie worked on the plate for nearly an hour before he announced it was ready. After cleaning his hands, he lay a test sheet on top of the plate and placed these between several blankets of thick wool felt. He pressed the stack against the age-blackened metal rollers.

"Here goes."

They watched as Eddie walked around to the side of the machine, reached up, grabbed a spoke handle, and pulled. His face reddened with effort as the rollers began to turn. The old wood creaked. He shoved on a bottom spoke with one foot, and the felt blankets, plate, and paper slowly disappeared under the top roller and reappeared on the other side. Catching his breath, Eddie lifted the blankets. Holding the damp proof sheet by one edge, he carefully pulled it off the plate.

Tom leaned closer. This was not antique paper, and this would not be the map, but all the same, he felt a thrill run along his spine. He was looking at the *Universalis Cosmographia*—minus the bullet holes and blood.

"What do you think?" Eddie asked.

"Wow." Tom had to laugh in amazement.

Allison peered through her glasses. "Is it all right?"

"Nearly." He glanced up at Eddie. "Let's try again. We've got a little too much ink on this one."

They repeated the process until finally the proofs were coming out of the press the way Tom wanted.

"Okay, let's boogie," he said.

Eddie positioned the plate on the first sheet of damp, five-hundred-year-old paper and placed the felt over it. He crossed himself before taking hold of the spokes that turned the gears. The muscles in his forearms stood out, and the rollers turned. When the plate came through the other side, Eddie was breathing hard. He removed the felt, exposing the paper, which lay facedown. Holding two corners, he slowly lifted it away.

"Come on, baby. Come on. Be good to Daddy."

Spinning around, Allison clapped her hands. "It's gorgeous!"

"Nobody get too excited yet," Tom said. "Let me look at it." He carried the map closer to the light and flipped down the lenses of his magnifying headset. "Sorry, guys. We've got some blank spots on the top edge of the border."

They started over. It was nearly 3 AM before Tom saw one that he liked. At the workbench, he told Allison to turn on the hair dryer. When the ink was dry enough not to smudge, Tom moistened a thin camel-hair brush with watery brown paint for the age spots. They would be paler than those on the original; Stuart had told Leo Zurin that the map had been cleaned. Chemical testing might pick up modern ingredients in the paint, but that could be attributed to the restoration process.

For the most part, the age spots were at the margins. The original map was in good condition, except for the rip in the fold, which Tom would re-create in the duplicate. Inside the border of alternating black and white, Corelli had drawn the continents where they should be, although many parts of the world he had guessed at or left blank. Europe was more accurate than the New World or Asia. Florida was a short little nub, and the Atlantic coast of what would someday be Canada swept toward northern Europe. The original had a few broken lines and letters, and Tom had duplicated these errors in the plate.

Hair-thin lines extended from compass roses situated in the Atlantic and Indian oceans. The place names began with simple capital letters, not the swooping flourishes of later maps. Tom was thankful that Corelli hadn't lived in the seventeenth century, when every square inch of a map might be decorated.

As he rinsed out his brush, he saw Allison's hands on the edge of the workbench. She had managed to scrub off most of the ink. Tom swiveled his head to look at her from under his magnifiers. "You can take a nap if you want."

"God, I can't, I'm too excited." She looked back and forth from the original map to the copy. "I got used to all those red splotches," she said. "This one seems so empty."

He told her to give it a few passes with the hair dryer on the low setting. As she did so, he glanced over at her cell phone, which lay on the workbench. She had left it there in case her father called. He wouldn't, not in the middle of the night, but Tom had begun to worry that Stuart would say no.

At ten o'clock this morning Tom had to be in the Piazza di Santa Maria Novella, a plaza south of a church near the train station. Manny Suarez would give him the listening devices that Tom would place in Leo Zurin's house in Champorcher—assuming that Stuart let him go along to deliver the map.

Tom was reasonably sure that Suarez and his goons hadn't followed him to the print shop. Small, iron-barred windows looked out on a courtyard invisible from the street. The narrow entrance had been built for horses and carriages. Eddie had parked his car in the courtyard after taking such a complicated route through the city that only a helicopter with a spotlight could have followed them.

"Eddie? Is it possible to have one more? If I mess up our only copy, we're screwed."

"Oh, Jeez."

"Sorry."

"I thought you had the copy you wanted. I didn't clean all the ink off the plate. If it's dried already, there's no way . . ." Eddie held up his hands. "All right. Let's do it." He returned to the printing press, and Allison opened another jar of ink.

At the workbench Tom added a light touch of mildew-colored gray to the map, then blotted most of it off as though it had been recently cleaned. While the map dried, and to rest his back for a while, he wandered over to watch the progress on the second copy.

The engraving plate vanished as Eddie gently lay another sheet of antique paper on top of it. Ink had worked into the deep creases on his large, callused hands, but a little ink on the edges of the paper wouldn't matter. They would be trimmed to the size of the map.

Tom looked at his watch. "It's ten after four. What day is this?"

"Tuesday, I think." Eddie placed the felt blankets

over the paper. "What are you going to do when you get back home, Tommy?"

"Finish my sailboat. I paid somebody to work on the engine while I was gone. Soon as I buy some sails, I'll take her out for a test run."

Allison asked, "Do I get to go?"

"I'm expecting you to crack the champagne over the bow."

"Deal."

"I've got to see that." Eddie wiped his hands on his ink-stained apron, then reached up to grab a spoke. "You send me some photos, will you?"

"We'll sail to Italy and pick you up," Tom said. He sent a smile across the table, but Eddie was concentrating on his work. The old wood creaked, and the gears groaned dangerously. Tom expected them to give way any second.

Eddie grunted and ground his teeth together. "Holy Mary, mother of God, I hope this is the last one." When it was done, he passed a towel across his forehead.

Allison leaned against the table and said, "Eddie, what are you going to do when this is over?"

"Me? Well . . ." Inch by inch, he lifted the paper from the plate. "I'll have the money to bring Rose and the kids for a visit." He shot a quick glance Tom's way. "I should've stayed in touch with her. I did a lot of things wrong, that's for damn sure. But we'll see each other again."

"Do you think she would move here?"

"Oh, no, don't think so. The girls. You know, they're happy where they are. But they could all come over for a few weeks in the summer. They could stay at my place. I think that would be fun, don't you?"

"They'd love it. You can show Rose the *Via Dell'-Amore*."

To Tom's surprise, Eddie blushed. "Might do that. It's going to be hard to see her go back, though. Real hard." Then he laughed. "Listen to me. I haven't even asked her to come over yet." He held the print so Tom could see it. "Okay?"

Tom examined the second copy and said it would do, but the first was better. He would finish that one, then start on a backup if they had time. He told Eddie to put his feet up for a while, which Eddie did with a groan of exhaustion. Tom said, "You, too, Allison. Take a nap. There's nothing you can do now except wait."

"You sure?"

He gave her a kiss. "Get some sleep."

After washing her hands again, she folded her apron, lay on a rolled carpet in the corner, and closed her eyes. The only light in the room came from the lamps aimed at the original Corelli and its duplicate in progress. Tom's espresso had gone cold, but he reached for the cup.

The age spots had dried quickly, a scattering of pale freckles on the old paper. Tom trimmed the map to size with an X-Acto knife and a straightedge, then lightly curled the edges and rubbed them gently on the dirty workbench, leaving smudges that resembled the oil from fingers turning the pages of the atlas. When the edges looked like those of the original, he folded the map in the middle, turned it the other way, then back again.

In his pocket, his cell phone vibrated. He had put it on mute to not wake the others. Before answering, he looked at the numbers on the screen.

"Hello," he said quietly. "Fritz?"

"No names. Did I wake you?"

"Not at all. I'm working. What's up?"

"That question you had. I just got the info for you. It wasn't easy, but the person you inquired about? He is with the organization he referred to. He put in for vacation."

Fritz was talking about Manny Suarez. Tom said, "Run that by me again?"

"The man is off his turf. Essentially, he's freelancing. The guys with him? They're legal. They're with the outfit I used to have contacts with. I think they're sort of doing a favor."

"You mean they're CIA?"

"Watch it," Fritz said. "Is this line secure?"

"Sorry. So what's the deal?"

"The deal is, your man is Peruvian. Born in Miami, but you know, they stay close to the folks back home. His only brother was a police officer down there working an antidrug detail. Word is, the brother couldn't be bought. He had a wife and kids. The bad guys took him out. Same outfit as the person who is now purchasing things from the Russian. Do you follow?"

"I follow."

"That's as much as I could get. You need anything else?"

"It's more than I expected. Thanks."

"Take care of yourself over there, kid. I'm signing off now."

Tom disconnected and looked around at Allison curled up on the old rug. Eddie sat in his chair with his head against the wall, snoring. Tom decided to let them sleep awhile longer. He went back to work on the map.

He had made a fold mark down the middle, where the map would have been folded into an atlas. He scraped the fibers of the paper on the reverse side of the fold until they began to let go, then carefully opened a tear in the paper exactly as long as the tear in the original. With his paints he created a thin, narrow strip of discoloration along the entire fold line, as if the map had been glued to a thicker piece of paper, called a tongue, bound into an atlas. A bookbinder would have used glue made from animal hide or wheat. Not having any animal-hide glue, Tom had made some from wheat paste. He brushed on a thin, broken layer of that and sprinkled on a pinch of dust from inside a drawer in the workbench.

When the glue was dry, Tom turned the map facedown. To simulate a recent restoration, he brushed polyvinyl acetate glue onto a thin strip of paper four inches long, and affixed that to the tear.

The security light winked out in the courtyard, leaving the gray light of morning to filter through the grime on the window.

Over the noise of the hair dryer aimed at the repair, Tom thought he heard something else and glanced at Allison's telephone. He clicked the switch off. Chimes signaled a call coming through. Quickly, Tom dropped the dryer and grabbed the cell phone. He fumbled for the right button. "Hello!"

But it wasn't Stuart Barlowe. Tom spun around on the chair and mouthed a silent curse.

Allison scrambled up. "Tom? What is it?"

Signaling her to be quiet, he pressed another button, and a thin voice with a vaguely Southern accent came out of the speaker. ". . . chasing you for over a week now, Mr. Fairchild. Your sister says you're visiting friends, but I suspect she's giving me a story. I'm going to ask you straight out, and if you lie to me, I'll get you for perjury. Where are you?"

"At this moment?"

"That's the moment I'm referring to, Mr. Fairchild. Right now. As we speak. Where . . . are . . . you?"

Eddie had come over to listen, and he and Allison stared at the cell phone.

Tom was holding it a foot from his mouth. "I'm with a friend. We were in the Keys fishing, and she was followed down there by her ex-boyfriend. He beat her up. She had to go to the emergency room. I've been taking care of her. We're still in the Keys—at a safe house. I can't divulge the location, not even to you, Mr. Weems, because this phone is probably being tapped."

"Oh, my God," Allison whispered, exchanging a glance with Eddie.

A laugh came through the speaker. "That's good. I haven't heard that one before. Uh-huh. You tell the lady you're with, whomever she may be, to get herself another nurse. Listen well, Mr. Fairchild. If you are not in my office before five o'clock this afternoon—today, not tomorrow or next week—I *will* file a violation of probation on you, and I *will* have a warrant issued for your arrest. Do you hear me loud and clear?"

"Yes, sir, Mr. Weems. Loud and clear." Tom disconnected, then looked at his watch again. "Jesus! It's one o'clock in the morning in Miami. Know what he said when I answered? 'Gotcha!' "

"What are you going to do?" Allison asked.

"Shoot myself?"

Eddie said, "Can this guy be bribed?"

"No way. The Weasel would pay *me* to have this happen. He's loving it. I've never heard him so happy." Tom slowly took off his lenses and rubbed his forehead. "Suicide is an option, definitely."

"Tom, shut up, please," Allison said. "We'll figure something out."

Eddie said, "The map is done. I'll take you to the airport right now, and you get on a flight out of here. Allison and I will take the map to her father. Suarez and his buddies can go screw themselves."

Allison calculated on her fingers. "You can make it. With the time difference you have twenty-two hours."

He stared from one of them to the other. "Even if I did have time, which I don't, how am I going to get past Homeland Security? They've got my passport flagged."

Eddie said, "Come on, Tommy. They'll delay you a bit, but they won't refuse entry. You haven't done anything. Your probation officer can't hang you for being a few hours late."

Tom shook his head.

Allison spoke. "He won't leave, Eddie. He's going to Leo Zurin's house if it kills him, because the government said they would bring *you* back to the United States for prosecution, too."

"What'd you tell him that for?" Tom demanded.

"It's true, isn't it?"

"Oh, Jeez." Eddie leaned against the workbench. "You didn't have to do this for me, Tom. They won't go to the trouble of extraditing me from Italy."

"I was thinking more like kidnapped," Tom said.

"No, no, no. That's how they talk. They mess with your mind and get you running scared." Eddie put an arm across his shoulders.

"Are you positive about that?"

"Well . . . reasonably positive." The smile had left Eddie's face.

Tom said, "It's not just for you, okay? I've busted my

ass for this fucking map, and I'm not giving up now. If I
violate my probation, so be it."

"Don't say that!" Allison shook him. "I will not let
you go to prison. Either of you. It won't happen, I swear
to God. My father has friends. He knows people in Washington."

"Look, would you both calm down?" Tom held up his
hands. "Everything's okay. It's going to be fine." He
walked over to the other end of the workbench, where he
had left the extra copy of the map. He ripped it down the
middle.

"What are you doing?" Allison cried.

"There's no time to do a backup. We'll go with the
one I just finished. It's good enough. No, screw that. It's
perfect." Tom placed the original Corelli and its newer
twin between sheets of Mylar and rolled them to fit the
map tube. "We need to clean this place up and get out of
here. But first— Allison, I want you to get on your phone.
Call that hotel out on the autostrada and cancel our reservation."

"Why?"

"Because we're going to stay close to Santa Maria
Novella—as close as we can get."

CHAPTER 30

The Hotel Mercurio, five stories of Tuscan gold stucco and brown shutters, was directly on the Piazza di Santa Maria Novella. Allison phoned ahead and reserved two rooms, immediate occupancy. It was just before nine o'clock in the morning when they arrived at the front entrance. After Tom and Allison quickly unloaded the car, Eddie went in search of a place to park it out of sight.

After the porter had left with his tip, Tom went to the window and pulled aside the sheer white curtain. Allison stood beside him and looked out.

The hotel was on an oval of winter-brown grass circled by a sidewalk and a narrow street. To their right, at the north end, the gothic facade of a church dominated the piazza. White marble inlaid with black created intricate patterns of rectangles and arches under a triangular pediment and an immense round window that on a sunnier day might have glowed with color. At ground level a set of massive wooden doors had weathered to gray. A stone path led to a thirty-foot white marble obelisk and

some park benches. An old woman in a long brown
sweater walked through with her little white terrier on a
leash. The distance was close enough that Allison could
make out the flowers on the lady's skirt.

She swept her gaze round the piazza, from the church
to the buildings on the opposite end. Clouds over the sun
had dulled the colors. "I don't see anybody in a black
coat."

"It's too early. We still have an hour." Tom cranked
the window open. As the wooden frame swung out, cold
air came in. The lady had stopped to chat with a friend.
The dog put its paws on her knee, and she picked it up.
Tom aimed his camera, clicked the shutter, and checked
the screen.

"Watch this." As Tom pressed a button, the tiny
tableau enlarged until the woman's face took up half the
screen. "I can enlarge it on the computer even more. I
turned the date stamp on, and the battery is charged. I'm
not sure if Suarez will give me the stuff right there or if
he'll want to go somewhere else. If he does, just keep the
shutter going until we walk out of sight. But if he walks
away, and I'm still there, keep the camera on me." Tom
held up the strap so she could put it around her neck.
"You try it. Take your glasses off and adjust the
viewfinder. Got it?"

Allison put her glasses into her pocket. "What if he
sees me?"

"He won't. Step back a little. Right there. Can you locate the benches? I'll be on the one facing the hotel.
When I get back to the room, I'll take some close-ups of
the electronics."

Allison pressed the shutter. "When are you going to
tell Agent Suarez you've done this?"

"I haven't decided. Probably after I go to Champorcher."

She focused on a man riding a bicycle. He went in front of the church and continued around the oval, weaving in and out of the sparse traffic. "Why do you have to go at all? Just show Suarez the photographs. That ought to be enough."

"Enough?"

Allison lowered the camera. "To get you back into the U.S. To make him ask the state attorney to drop your probation violation."

"I want more," Tom said. "I want to be off probation. I want the Weasel out of my life. I want my record cleared."

"That's asking a lot, Tom."

"You said the feds could crush the state prosecutors."

"Within limits, but this?"

"Why not? I'll have photographs of an employee of a domestic agency working a case on foreign soil. If they don't want to see them all over the Internet, they'd better help me out."

"I don't think it's going to be that easy," Allison said.

"He pushed me, and I'm pushing back." Tom stared down at the piazza. His green eyes narrowed. He seemed suddenly older, as though the events of the past two weeks had been working on the inside, and now had come to the surface. A muscle tightened in his jaw, and his words came out hard. "Oscar Contreras is responsible for murdering Suarez's brother. Suarez wants to stop the weapons shipment from getting to Contreras. Fine. I'll drop the damned bugs at Zurin's house. But Suarez has to do something for me. The photos are to make sure he does. Are they enough? We shall see."

Allison gave him back the camera. "You need to call my father and tell him the map is done."

"I will, soon as I take care of Suarez." Tom smiled, triumphant. "It came out good, didn't it?"

"Yes," she said. "It's very good."

"It's perfect."

Allison was aware that somewhere in the past week, she had slid across the line to Tom's side. The moral boundaries had shifted. She didn't care about passing a forgery off to an arms dealer. But that wasn't the only consideration. She had taken on this job for her father.

She hesitated. "I can't say if it's perfect. That's not up to me, is it?"

"No, it's up to the Russian." Tom set the camera on a table next to the window and cranked the window shut. "I have to get my computer set up." He crossed to get his messenger bag from the stack of luggage they had left near the door. He opened it on the bed and took out his laptop computer, which he carried to the table.

"Allison, there's something else I need you to do for me. Persuade your father to take me with him. I have to get into Leo Zurin's house. You know that. Our last conversation on the phone, he said he'd think about it. What he's thinking about is a way to say no."

She should not have felt so pulled, but she did. "Are you certain it's not dangerous? Please be honest. Leo Zurin buys and sells machine guns and grenades."

"He's a businessman."

"Right. And what's Marek Vuksinic? His sales rep?"

Tom laughed.

"It is *so* not funny," she said.

"I'm sorry, babe. If he searches my pockets, what are they going to do? Shoot me? No, no, no. They'd kick my ass out the door. And Leo Zurin would tell your dad he'd rather not invest in Miami real estate."

Allison muttered, "You're delusional."

"Well, would you please give me an alternative? Look. I promise you, I won't do this unless it looks safe. Suarez told me that if it doesn't feel right, don't take any chances. All right? Okay?"

"I want to go with you."

"No, and don't ask me again."

"A simple no would be nice."

"No." He kissed her. "Sorry."

After a second, she nodded. "Do you want me to call my father now?"

"Let's wait till after I get Suarez taken care of. One thing at a time." Tom sat down and turned on his computer. "Could you ask the desk where the nearest Internet kiosk is? I need to get the photos off the camera and onto my Web site. *No parlo italiano*."

"*Non parlo*." Allison knelt on the floor to unzip her suitcase. Unpacking would occupy her mind.

"Babe, find me the one-gig flash card, will you? I've only got the five-twelve in the camera, and I want to be sure you don't run out of space. It's in the bottom of the messenger bag."

Sitting on the side of the bed, Allison pulled out several sheets of paper, most of them color screen shots of the map, so when she saw a large black-and-white image of faces looking back at her, she put her glasses on. It was a copy of a photograph. The men were in suits and ties and the one woman in the photo wore a sleeveless sheath dress—clothing several decades out of date.

Allison was about to set it aside when she saw her grandfather, Frederick Barlowe. She held the copy with both hands as she recognized more faces. Her grandmother Margaret. A much younger Royce Herron. And two young men—boys, really. The slightly shorter one was her father, with his long narrow face, as now, but without the wrinkles and shadows and the beard she was used to. His brother, Nigel, had been caught in the middle of a laugh. His eyes—dark, like Stuart's—looked back at her with open amusement. She couldn't remember if she had ever seen Nigel. Surely she must have, but she'd been a baby when he died. The copy was stapled to another sheet, which was a handwritten list of the people in the photograph.

"Tom? Where did you get this?"

Tom glanced up from his notebook computer. She turned the copy so he could see it. He said, "That's a photograph taken in Toronto at a map fair in the late sixties."

"Why do you have it?"

A couple of seconds passed before he said, "Rose e-mailed it to me. Royce Herron's son gave her the original. I thought it was interesting, both our grandfathers in the same photograph."

"Are they?"

"The man with the short gray hair. That's my grandfather, William Fairchild."

Allison looked at the second page again. "Right." Puzzled, she said, "Were you going to show it to me?"

"Yeah, I forgot it was in there. Did you find the flash card?"

She lifted her eyes and met Tom's. "What is it you aren't telling me? I'm picking up something strange here. The other day at the library, you were asking me questions about my family. How did my mother die?

What happened to my uncle Nigel? Now you have this photograph. Why?"

Tom walked over and took it from her and looked at it. "You've never seen this before?"

"No."

"You probably didn't notice. It used to hang on the wall in Judge Herron's study. After he was killed, his son found it on the desk and gave it to Rose. I saw it at her house. We were in Manarola, and I remembered it and asked her to send it to me." Tom sat on the bed beside Allison. He said, "The truth is, I was trying to find out as much as I could about your father in case he tried to back out of paying me."

"What's this photograph got to do with it?"

"It's nothing. Come on. Eddie's on his way up, and I've got to get ready to meet Suarez."

Furiously, Allison jerked the photograph out of his hand. "I don't know what's going on here, but you're sneaking around trying to get evidence against him, like you did against Manny Suarez. What are you thinking? That my father is part of the deal with Contreras? Or he sent Larry to kill you? What?"

"We are not going to talk about it now. Give me the photograph, Allison."

"No."

"Fine, then." Tom got up and walked away from her, then came back. "You used to hate him, and now you've gone so far the other way you can't see anything but this fantasy you've created. You and your dad had a misunderstanding, and if you could just get past it, things would really be great again, like when you were three years old. He isn't what you think, Allison. The only thing he cares about is his money. Why is he paying me a hundred thousand dollars to forge a map? Because he's desperate not to lose millions if Zurin pulls out of The Metropolis. There is so much shit going on you can't imagine. Jenny Gray told me that the former head of zoning quit because he'd been blackmailed. Somebody set him up with a prostitute and took pictures. Maybe Larry was behind it, but is your father that ignorant? I mean, wouldn't he *suspect*?"

"I've heard those rumors," Allison said, "and I wouldn't have trusted Jenny Gray to tell me the day of the week."

"Stuart was having an affair with her. He paid her five thousand dollars to leave him alone and threatened to call Immigration if she opened her mouth."

"That is the most despicable, pathetic lie."

Tom opened his mouth, and it stayed opened for a second before he said quietly, "I'm sorry. I shouldn't have told you." He reached for her hand.

She backed away. "Don't come near me right now, Tom."

A knock sounded on the door, then a voice, as though someone was putting his lips near the crack. "Hey. You guys in there?"

"That will be Eddie. We've got his room key." Tom shouted, "Just a second, man." He looked at Allison. "I need to know. Will you help me?"

Her nerves were so tight she felt as though she might scream. She took a couple of breaths.

Tom came close but didn't touch her. "If you want Eddie to take the photos of Suarez, I'll show him how, but I really need you to talk to Stuart for me. I have to go to Champorcher when he delivers the map to Zurin."

Allison turned her head toward the door, then said, "No, I'll take the photographs. And I'll talk to Stuart. Show him the map first, though. You have to do that."

"All right. I'm sorry. I don't have the answers for you, Allison. I don't." Tom put his hand on her arm, and she didn't draw away. "When you talk to him, you shouldn't mention anything else."

"Not damned likely," she said.

At exactly ten AM, Manny Suarez strode into the piazza from the southern end, a man about medium build, dark hair, carrying a newspaper and a paper cup. The wind opened his black coat and flipped it around his knees as he walked. He paused to take a sip from the cup. Allison put the viewfinder to her eye and followed Suarez as he moved toward the church on the opposite end. He stopped at the bench under the obelisk.

Tom was already there, facing the hotel. Navy blue jacket, no hat. Taking his hands out of his pockets. Suarez standing, his back to the camera, Tom half hidden.

Tom started to stand up, then sat down again. There was some conversation.

Allison heard Eddie murmuring, "Turn around, you son of a bitch. Turn around. Let's see that face."

Tom shifted. Suarez turned, and for an instant, as his eyes moved over the hotel, Allison was tempted to pull back, but she remained perfectly still except for her index finger on the shutter. Suarez was handsome, about thirty-five, with curved eyebrows and a widow's peak. The wind ruffled his hair.

Suarez sat beside Tom and put the newspaper between them. He drank from the paper cup. There was a little more conversation. Then Suarez got up with his newspaper and moved toward the lower right of the viewfinder. Allison started to follow, but swerved the lens back toward Tom.

Tom sat there with his hands in his pockets for a while. The cup was beside him. He picked it up, looked inside, then put his fingers across the top and slowly turned it upside down. No coffee. Tom removed a black object.

"That's it," Eddie whispered. "Allison, do you have it?"

"I think so. Yes. But his coat is so dark."

When Tom held the object in front of the paper cup, it became a plastic bag with something inside, but the details were too small to make out. Tom put the bag into the paper cup, stood up, and walked out of sight at the bottom of the screen.

Releasing a breath, Allison stepped away from the window and looked at the camera. She had hit the shutter 173 times.

CHAPTER 31

At four PM, Stuart, a thin, gray-bearded figure in a tan cashmere coat and polished shoes, stepped into the lobby of the Hotel Mercurio. Allison met him and took him upstairs. Tom was waiting. He opened the map tube and rolled out the *Universalis Cosmographia* on the table in their room and handed Stuart a magnifying glass. Allison glanced over at the door to the adjoining suite. It was cracked open. She could guess why: Eddie Ferraro would have a way in if Stuart grabbed the map and tried to run with it. Allison didn't expect that, but Tom was becoming obsessive. He had even taken the map tube into the bathroom when he showered.

At last her father set down the magnifying glass. "Excellent. It's exactly what I wanted. This is mind-bending." He ran his fingers along the margins. "I could swear it's the same map with the blood magically lifted."

"When do we deliver it?" Tom said.

"*We* do not. That wasn't part of our bargain. I owe you fifty thousand dollars. We can go to a bank in the

morning. It's too late now, but in the morning I can transfer the funds, and our business is concluded."

Tom rolled the map back into its tube. "Give me directions to Champorcher. I'll meet you there and collect
payment after."

The Hotel Cellini was a ten-minute walk, but Stuart
seemed determined to do it in five. Allison kept up with
her father's long strides as they went south on Via dei
Fossi toward the river. To avoid a slow group of shop-
pers, he stepped off the sidewalk to the street, which was
made of square gray bricks aligned in fan-shaped curves.
The windows of the small shops seemed to blur past.

Allison said, "Tom wants to see Mr. Zurin's reaction.
He says there might be questions about the restoration."

"Do you expect me to believe that? He deliberately
waited until after the banks were closed to show me the
map."

"You know the reason," Allison said. "Tom wants to
be there when you show the map to Leo Zurin."

"We'll go to a bank in the morning."

"He won't do it. I'm sorry. I suppose that after so
much work, he wants to see how the map is received. It's
not much to ask, is it?"

They had reached the street that ran along the river.
Allison took his arm. "Come on, let's go across." They
headed east on a broad sidewalk that in summer would
have been teeming with visitors. A wall separated the
street from a grassy slope and the river at the foot of it.

"He wants to be there," she said. "Maybe it doesn't
make sense to you, but it's what he wants. Why are you
opposed?"

"Tom Fairchild is unpredictable. He might say the wrong thing to Leo Zurin. And he shouldn't be anywhere near Rhonda, after what he did to Larry."

"He had cause."

"So he says. Larry has another version."

"I'm sure," Allison said.

"Where is Larry? Have you seen him?"

"No. He's not likely to show up around Tom, is he?"

"Rhonda's concerned. She hasn't heard from him since yesterday."

"One day? He's probably drunk somewhere."

"Could be, if I know Larry," he said.

A narrow boat skimmed the surface of the Arno with four men inside, like some kind of eight-legged water bug. The water was gray glass except for the rippled V of the boat's wake and the circles left by the oars.

Allison brought her eyes back to her father. "What about me? Do you know who I am?"

"What do you mean?"

"Nothing. It's just—nothing." She rested her crossed arms on the wall. "Sometimes I feel like we're strangers. Do you ever feel that way?"

"Of course I don't. You're my daughter."

"When did you stop smiling? I remember you used to laugh a lot. I remember that."

Stuart held his palms up and grinned like a clown in greasepaint. "How's this?" When she failed to react, he resumed his gaze across the river. "Now who's the sour-puss?"

Allison said, "I'd like to go along, too, if you don't mind."

"Go where?"

"To Champorcher. I'm curious who this Mr. Zurin is."

With a short laugh, Stuart said, "We'll have a regular party of it."

"Tom and I can fly to Milan in the morning. Actually, he doesn't want me to go, but I'm going anyway."

"All right, then. I'll square it with Rhonda. We'll rent a car at the airport. Best if you and Tom make your own arrangements. I'll get directions to you." Bracing his hands wide on the cracked top of the old wall, he took a breath as though he'd been walking up a steep hill. "Mary and Joseph and the angels. I didn't think it would happen, and now it's almost over. This time next month, we'll be all right. That damned building will go up. I'll see about getting some of the legal work to you."

Allison shook her head.

"No?"

She pushed her hair behind her ear. "I'd rather not be involved with The Metropolis." She looked at him steadily, then said, "When Tom was in London, he saw Jenny Gray. I told you about her. She used to work for Larry at one of his restaurants, sort of a hostess. She told Tom that Larry was paying bribes to public officials. He had somebody on the zoning board photographed with a prostitute. I believe her. That's so like Larry, and I don't want to have anything to do with him anymore. I'm going to assume that you didn't know about it."

"Is that a question?"

"Maybe it is," she said.

He took his hands off the wall and dusted them. "If and when you are my lawyer—and you've just indicated that you've no interest in it—then you may ask me about my business. I will tell you this much. The

Metropolis is the last project of its kind that I'll be involved with."

She laughed without amusement. "Have I just been fired?"

"Don't be silly. Of course you haven't."

"By the way, Jenny is dead. She was strangled to death in her house the day Tom and I left London." The shock that passed over his face told Allison the truth. Jenny had been his mistress. Not for long, not happily, but he had slept with her. Allison felt as though she were trying to balance on top of the wall.

He said, "That's too bad. Do they know who did it?"

"No. What a strange thing, too. She was the one who found Royce Herron dead."

Stuart squinted slightly in the dull winter light. "Was she? Yes, I believe you mentioned it. Well. What time is it getting to be?" He pulled back his coat sleeve to see his watch. "Nearly five. Rhonda's expecting me. She's afraid the map is no good. I'll be happy to disappoint her."

"Wait. Before you go—" Allison opened her bag and felt inside for the small, leather-covered box she had put there earlier. The edges of the brown calfskin were scuffed, and most of the gold embossing had worn away. "Do you know what this is?"

"Should I?"

"You don't recognize it?"

"Is this a riddle?"

"In a way. A couple of weeks ago, when I came to your office—it was the Sunday of the map fair, and Tom had just left—I asked if you remembered the gift you'd brought me from Dublin when I was about three years old. This is it. It's in here."

"Is it?"

"You said it would always tell me where you were."

A helpless smile appeared as he shook his head. "I'll need a hint."

"You don't remember, do you?"

"That was a long time ago, Allison."

She pressed the brass catch on the front of the box. On faded red velvet lay the miniature globe on its brass stand, blue and ivory, each continent outlined in gold.

He took it from her. "Yes! The globe. I remember now." He gave it a spin.

"Where'd you get it? Do you remember the shop?"

"Oh, my goodness, no. I probably paid fifty pounds for it, though. Nice little piece, isn't it?" When he handed it back, he tilted his head and looked at her sideways. "Was there a trick question in there someplace?"

"No, I was just wondering how much you remembered. That's all." She tried to put the globe inside its nest, but her hands were shaking, and it slipped to the pavement and rolled. "Oh!" She picked it up and wiped away some dirt.

"Careful," he said. "Is it broken?"

"It's fine." She straightened her glasses, glancing up at him, and their eyes held.

"Well. See you tomorrow, then," he said.

Rhonda heard him come in. The heavy door of their suite slammed, and she looked up from the bench at the end of the bed to see Stuart throw his coat over the sofa. She had been buckling the strap on her shoe.

She walked to the wide opening between the bedroom and parlor. "My God, Stuart. Was it that bad?"

"Was what that bad?"

"The map. What did you think I was referring to?"

He pursed his lips, and pressed his hand over his beard, then went to the bar and lifted the lid on the ice bucket. "The map is perfect."

"Are you sure?"

"I said it's perfect. It's a fucking masterpiece. Leo will love it. Tom Fairchild earned his money." Stuart twirled the lid and caught it. "He wants to go with us, he and Allison. To deliver the map."

"Why?"

"To celebrate the moment. To toast Gaetano Corelli's immortal skill as a cartographer."

"They're not going with us."

"Tell them that. Fairchild won't give me the map unless he personally delivers it."

"I don't want him to go. I don't want to see him."

"He's going. So is Allison."

She pulled Stuart around and stared at him. "What's the matter? What's happened?"

"Allison knows," he said.

"What do you mean?"

"She was asking me questions. She knows, or she soon will."

"How could she possibly know?"

With a shrug, Stuart dropped the lid on the ice bucket. "It's amazing we've gotten away with it for this long. For thirty years I've been expecting the ax to drop. Don't you feel the rush of wind on the back of your neck?"

"Stop being so goddamned morbid. What do you want to do?"

"I'm going to have drink. I suggest you do the same."

CHAPTER 32

The blood and the three bullet holes in the original *Universalis Cosmographia* vanished as Tom slid the folded map between layers of cardboard. He placed this inside a large envelope stiffened with more cardboard and handed the package to Eddie Ferraro.

"When you get to the shipping office ask for a box."

"Yeah, I know, and plenty of bubble wrap."

"I gave you Rose's address?"

"You did." Eddie smiled. "Don't worry, it'll get there."

Tom clapped him on the shoulder. "Thanks." The map would go to The Compass Rose, special delivery, express mail, or however the Italians handled such things. Keeping the original around wasn't smart. The computer would also be shipped. Tom had already erased every file relating to the map and thrown away his papers.

Eddie picked up the messenger bag. "Well, I'll grab my hat and be back in a few." He went through the connecting door, which closed behind him. Eddie had said he didn't mind waiting a few days for his half of the remaining fifty thousand dollars. He had even said it was too much, but a deal was a deal.

They would be leaving at dawn tomorrow. Eddie would drop them off at the airport and go back home to Manarola. Allison had already bought two tickets on a nine AM flight to Milan.

Whether Tom could get back to Miami in his lifetime was another question.

Sliding a hand down his thigh, he felt his pocket for the bag that Suarez had given him. It contained four small black transmitters that together would have fit into a candy bar wrapper. Each had a tiny toggle switch and a sticky back under a peel-off square of paper. Three to plant in Leo Zurin's house, and one to practice on. Thinking about it made Tom's hands sweat.

He put his backpack on the bed and took out his hiking boots, which he thought he might need in the mountains. Snow was predicted. He tossed in his camera, some T-shirts, and his underwear. Allison was traveling with a thirty-inch suitcase, a shoulder purse, and a tote bag. She had thrown away her ten pounds of bar exam outlines back at Eddie's place.

Tom heard the click of the locking mechanism on the door and glanced across the room. He saw the red beret and Allison's face. In the next instant he saw an arm in a dark sleeve around her throat, and her terrified eyes.

"Allison!"

Marek Vuksinic came in with her and kicked the door shut. "Hello, Tom. Stay where you are. I can break her neck before you take two steps."

"He was in the hall—" The words were cut off when Marek tightened his grip. Allison held on to his arm, and her toes dragged the floor.

"Marek, let her go!"

He wore a rough gray jacket and sweater, and the collar of a Hawaiian shirt showed at the neck. His heavy mustache shifted when he spoke. His mouth was hidden under it. "She's okay. I didn't do anything to her. We met in the hall, and I introduced myself. Bring that chair. Bring it."

"What do you want?" Tom demanded.

"The chair. Put it here." He motioned with his chin. Tom brought it over from the small table by the window, and Marek told Allison to sit down. He took off her beret and tossed it to the bed, then stood behind her with a hand on her shoulder. He reached into his jacket and when his hand reappeared, he pressed a button, and a slender blade clicked upward.

"You shit-eating bastard."

"Tom, I'm okay." Allison's voice shook.

Marek patted her cheek. "Sit there and don't move. Your boyfriend and I have some business. Where is the map?"

Tom said, "What map?"

The blade flashed in front of Allison's face, then delicately lifted the hair at her temple. She stifled a cry, and Tom said, "The Corelli world map."

"Do you have it? Did you give it to Stuart Barlowe? Where is it?"

"It's here," Tom said. "I have it."

"Show me."

Gesturing toward the corner between the wall and the bed, Tom said, "It's in the map tube."

"Get it. I want to see it. Move slow." His close-set brown eyes followed Tom as he went to the corner of the room and back. Tom took off the end cap and reached in with two fingers. The map, rolled in its Mylar covering, slowly came out.

"Show me. Come closer."

Holding it in both hands Tom moved forward until his knees nearly touched Allison's where she sat in the chair. He thought of Royce Herron holding the map, bullets going through it, and sweat broke out on his neck. He took a breath to steady his heart, whose rate had shot up so fast he could feel it vibrating in his hands. The edges of the map trembled.

Marek's eyes moved over the map. "Is it real?"

"What do you mean?"

"Is it real or did you make it?"

"Make it? I didn't make it. Why are you asking me that?"

A smile revealed a quick flash of stained teeth under the graying mustache. "Somebody told me you made it on a computer."

"Who said that? Do you see a computer anywhere around here?"

"Closer. Hold it closer."

Allison turned her head and stared up at him as he leaned toward the map. "Larry told you Tom forged this map. He told you that, didn't he?"

Marek used the point of the blade to slide Tom's fingers away from the cartouche. "He told me that Stuart Barlowe paid Tom Fairchild to make a copy. Is this it?"

"Larry is a liar," Allison said.

"Maybe no, maybe yes. This doesn't look so old."

"It's five hundred years old," Tom said. "Did Leo Zurin send you to look at it? I'm going to take it to him tomorrow. Mr. Barlowe paid me to restore it. I fixed a rip in the fold. Look." Tom turned the map over.

"Where is Larry?" Allison asked.

"Larry? He left on a boat. He likes boats." Marek squinted at the map. His big hand lay on Allison's shoulder. The mutilated left thumb was touching her neck. "The old man fell on a map when he died. Larry said it was this map."

Allison's lips parted. She said softly, "Oh, my God. It was you. You shot him."

Tom widened his eyes at her, a mute signal to be quiet.

Marek leaned over slightly and looked at her. A strand of wavy hair fell over his forehead. He splayed his left hand on her face and put his mouth by her ear. "If I say yes, what will you do about it?"

"He was a good man! He didn't deserve to die!"

"You're a little skinny for me, but I could show you things."

"Fuck you." She tried to jerk away, but his fingers were clamped onto her face.

Tom ground his teeth together. "Marek, let her go."

Marek laughed. He looked back at Tom. "Larry said the Corelli was destroyed, and you made a forgery."

"No! Royce Herron was holding another map," Allison said. "Larry hates Tom for beating him up. Can't you see that?"

"Allison, shut up. Don't piss him off. I was cleaning the Corelli, not forging it. Larry got it wrong."

Marek's eyes shifted to the map again. "Okay. Put it back in the tube."

"What?"

"Put it back."

"Why?"

"Because if you don't I will cut her throat."

Tom rolled the map and slid it into the tube. Marek motioned for it with his left hand. "Give it to me."

"I have to deliver it to Leo Zurin tomorrow."

"I'll take it. I'll save you the trip."

"But I have to—" Tom stood frozen. When Marek moved around Allison with his hand out, Tom swung the map tube toward the knife. In the instant before the knife flew out of Marek's hand, Tom realized how stupid this had been, and in the next instant, he leaped back on one foot and put the other into Marek's stomach.

Marek staggered to catch his balance. Allison threw herself off the chair and grabbed Marek's face with her nails. He lifted his elbow and caught her under the jaw. Her head snapped back, and she slid to the floor.

He looked around for his knife, then grunted as Tom's left foot caught him on the outside of his meaty thigh. Tom had his fists up. He shifted and aimed another kick at Marek's knee, but the bigger man turned quickly, ducked, and came at Tom sideways. Marek pinned Tom's arms to his sides. His face was so close Tom could smell cigarette smoke.

A foot went behind Tom's, and Tom fought to keep his balance. Marek went back, taking Tom with him, and they hit the bed. As they bounced toward the floor, the flimsy wooden headboard clattered against the wall. Marek straddled Tom and went for his throat. Tom braced his foot beside Marek's, lifted his hips, and tried to throw him off, but Marek knew the moves better.

He got an arm across Tom's neck and pressed down. Tom noted the calm intensity on the other man's face as he went about his work, which was to kill Tom Fairchild. Bright dots of light appeared at the edges of his vision. Marek's face grew larger and went out of focus. Then in the distance he thought he heard a tremendous crash.

Marek collapsed on Tom's chest.

As Tom's vision returned he saw Eddie standing over him with the remains of a chair. Eddie threw it aside and pulled Marek off him. "Tom! You okay, buddy? Hey!"

Coughing, Tom rolled to all fours. Allison knelt and put her arms around him, holding him tightly. "Are you all right? Let me see you. Tom!"

"Yeah. I'm okay." He got to his feet. "Is he dead?"

"No," Eddie said.

"Try again." Tom took a couple of breaths, hands on his knees. He thought he might retch.

Eddie found the knife by the bathroom door. "Wicked-looking thing." He pushed the point against the wall, and the blade clicked into the dull black handle.

"Cosa succede?" There were voices in the hall and shouts in Italian. *"Cosa sta capitando là dentro?"*

A fist pounded on the door. The guests, or the management, wanted to know what was going on in there.

"Chiamate la polizia!"

"They want to call the police," said Eddie.

"No! Tell them to go away," Tom whispered. "No police!"

Allison got to the door before Eddie and opened it a crack. *"Va tutto bene! Non vi preoccupate. Ho scoperto il mio ragazzo con un'altra donna—"*

Eddie moved back. "Let's get him out of sight." He took one of Marek's arms, and Tom took the other, and they dragged him around to the end of the bed, two hundred pounds of dead weight.

"What's she saying?"

"She said she's sorry for the ruckus. She just found

out her boyfriend was cheating on her and beat the crap out of him."

"Jesus." Tom stared at her. The voices had quieted. Allison closed the door and leaned on it.

"They're gone," she said.

Tom saw the green cardboard map tube protruding from under the bed. He picked it up. It was dented but otherwise unharmed. He walked over to Marek Vuksinic, looked down at him a second, then kicked him in the leg. This produced a low groan.

"Take it easy." Eddie crouched beside him and rolled his head to the side. His fingers came away sticky, and he wiped the blood on Marek's chest. "He'll live. What are we going to do with him, Tommy?"

It took fifteen minutes for Manny Suarez and his friends to arrive and another five for them to take Marek Vuksinic down the fire exit and put him into the trunk of their car. He had come to by then, but they had brought a roll of duct tape.

They had put their car next to a panel van behind the hotel, which at least partially hid them from view. The parking area dead-ended at the back entrances to some shops. Daylight was fading.

Suarez slammed the trunk lid just as a kitchen helper came out the back door and tossed a box into the trash bin. He gave them a long look and went back inside. Walking past Tom, Suarez said, "This is the second time in a week somebody's tried to kill you, Fairchild. You should be more careful."

Tom stopped him before he reached for the door of the car. "Marek Vuksinic admitted that he shot Royce Herron. The map collector in Miami—"

"I know who you mean. Judge Herron was a friend of Stuart Barlowe, so I have an interest. Why did he kill the judge?"

"He didn't say. We didn't have much of a chance to talk up there. Do you know anything about Jenny Gray? Did you hear anything from Scotland Yard?"

"The girl in London." Suarez shook his head. "Do you think he did it?"

"I'd like to find out," Tom said.

With a slight smile, Suarez said, "I'll ask him."

"I have another question. Jenny had a roommate named Carla Kelly. Carla worked for Larry Gerard, too. She was sort of a part-time call girl, I guess. Jenny told me Larry Gerard used Carla in getting The Metropolis approved. They found her body in the Everglades a couple of weeks ago."

"And?"

"And I thought you might've heard something."

After a brief debate with himself, Suarez said, "Her neck was snapped. I'm about ninety-nine percent sure it was *not* because she'd been screwing a few politicians. In Miami? Come on. No, it was Vuksinic. I'd been talking to Carla about Oscar Contreras. I think he found out."

"Where are you going to take him?"

"Don't worry about it."

"Ask him about the ship leaving Genoa. He's my gift to you. That ought to let me off the hook, don't you think?"

"If I knew he would talk, it might. I expect he's going to tell us 'up yours' in five different languages. Good luck tomorrow. We'll be nearby. You have the number."

"Hold it. I nearly got killed, and you can't cut me a break?"

"When you've done your job, then we'll talk."

Tom straight-armed the door to keep Suarez from opening it. "Right. I had a feeling you were going to say that. I've got something I want you to listen to." He spoke quietly. "Just you. Not your friends."

"What is that supposed to mean?"

Tom walked a few yards toward the street, a narrow, cobblestone way that ended on the piazza. Suarez leaned down to say something to Ricker, then came over. "All right, what?"

"I was going to use this in case you tried to screw me over, but now's as good a time as any." Tom took his cell phone out of his pants pocket and dialed a number.

"What is this?"

"Wait. I'm calling a number in New York. It's an automated message. A friend of mine set it up." He pressed the button for the speaker and turned the phone toward Manny Suarez.

"Is this a joke?"

"Not to me."

Suarez's voice came out of the phone. *"Put the devices in as many different rooms as you can, preferably close to a telephone. Hopefully Zurin doesn't do sweeps every day."*

Suarez stared at him. Tom held up a hand and heard his own voice.

"Tell me something, Suarez. You don't have jurisdiction out of the U.S. Why'd you come all the way to Italy to get Oscar Contreras? Is it a personal thing between you and him?"

A long pause. A car going by. A dog yapping. Another car. Then Suarez again: *"My brother was a police officer in Lima, a good guy. An honest cop. One of Con-*

treras's men comes to him and says, '¿Plata o plomo?'
That means do you want to take the bribe, or do you want
a bullet? My brother wouldn't play along. They shot him.
He had a wife and three kids. Understand?"

Tom disconnected. "It goes on. I had the telephone in
an upper pocket with an open line to my buddy in New
York. He recorded the conversation. I had someone shoot
some pictures of you leaving that paper cup full of electronics on the bench, and I took some close-ups when I
got back to the room. This afternoon I uploaded about
thirty photos to a Web site."

The glitter in Suarez's eyes had turned dangerous.

Tom said, "It's inaccessible unless you know the
URL and the password." He put the phone away and gave
Suarez a piece of paper. "This is what you need to get in.
Don't try shutting it down. You can't. At any time, the in-
formation can be sent to anyone. Your boss. The CIA.
The United States Attorney General. CNN. *Entertain-
ment Tonight*—"

"What do you want?"

"I want you to do what you said. And I want you to
make it all right for Eddie too."

"You think I'm God? I can't do that. I don't have that
kind of power."

"Eddie saved my life. You think about it. You think
what that might be worth to me."

When Tom went back upstairs, Allison was packing her
suitcase. She looked around, startled, as if she thought
that Marek Vuksinic had come back. Tom held out his
arms, and she came into them.

"Are you okay?" he asked.

"I am now." Her kiss was soft and sweet and it lasted a long time, but not long enough.

"I want you to stay with Eddie," Tom said. "Go to Manarola and wait for me."

"You can't get rid of me that easily."

"I don't want to get rid of you at all, but would you please go with Eddie?"

"Why? Marek's not a problem anymore."

"What if Zurin asks me what happened to him?"

"Tom. Do you really think Zurin knew he was coming here? It was Marek who destroyed the map. He wouldn't have told Zurin about it."

"That's true, I guess, but still—"

She smiled and shook her head. "I have the directions and you don't."

CHAPTER 33

The warehouses and industrial buildings and cheap apartment blocks outside Milan slid away as Allison headed west on the autostrada that would take them to the mountains. Tom sat in the passenger seat reading the instructions for the color monitor on the console, which featured a GPS, along with the sound system and temperature controls. The car was a sleek silver Alfa Romeo with a 3.2-liter engine and V-shaped air intake. It could take a Fiat between its teeth and shake it. Allison wanted the Alfa for the four-wheel drive, in case they ran into some snow. Tom told her he wouldn't mind snow; he hadn't seen any since he'd left New York.

The GPS indicated that the distance to Champorcher was 140 kilometers. Past Novara, they would take the A-5, which came up from Turin and went through the province of Valle d'Aosta to Chamonix on the French side of Mont Blanc—Monte Bianco on the Italian side. Backing up, Tom followed a smaller road to Champorcher on the southern slopes of the Alps.

Allison's father had faxed the directions to their hotel

this morning. The Barlowes had left for Milan last night. Allison said she didn't know if Leo Zurin had been told that she and Tom were coming, too. She had tried to get Stuart on her cell phone, but he hadn't answered. The mountains could be blocking the signal, she said.

Gradually the landscape became hilly, and snow lay in patches on the north sides of farmhouses and in gullies and among the trees at the edges of fields. Allison pointed, and Tom saw the silhouette of a crenellated castle tower before the road turned and put it out of view. The grade of the highway became steeper. Allison accelerated around a tanker truck and blew past a Mercedes with a Swiss license plate.

By tapping the monitor screen Tom could turn on the radio and adjust the volume. He scrolled through the stations and heard a slow ballad in French and rock and roll in German. An Italian announcer said, "*Sono le undici e un quarto. Adesso la nuova in rap Americana*—"

"They're playing hip-hop," Tom said.

"Could you turn that down?" Allison glanced over and said, "Not right now, okay?" She went back to frowning through the windshield.

He turned it off and shifted to get into the right side pocket of his pants. Showing her the three small black microphones in his palm, he pressed the window button. The cold air swirled into the car. Tom pitched the things out and closed the window.

Allison stared at him. "What did you do that for?"

"Does it make you feel better?"

She laughed. "Well . . . yes. Tell Manny Suarez you left them at Zurin's house. He can't go ask him, can he?"

"I should've done that before." Tom interlaced his fingers and stretched out his arms, cracking his knuckles.

"I was thinking. It doesn't matter if Leo Zurin sees the Corelli is a fake. Know why?"

"Why?"

"Because your dad could have bought it that way. Couldn't he? The old lady he bought it from didn't have papers to show the provenance."

Her face became serious again. "You were right about him. He was having an affair with Jenny Gray."

"Sorry I told you."

She shrugged. "I don't care. After this, I'm cutting off my ties with him and Rhonda. I told him I didn't want any business from his corporation. Just let me be an ordinary lawyer with ordinary clients. I want that. And I want you to be all right. Whatever you need to make it happen, I'll do it, Tom." She reached over and held his hand.

The highway split and curved into a tunnel, then out again.

The land had turned hard and gray. Bare outcrops of rock interrupted wide swaths of white. The peaks of the mountains merged with the heavy clouds.

"It's snowing up there," Allison said.

Following a river valley, they crossed the line into the bilingual province of Valle d'Aosta. Tom unfolded the fax and looked at Barlowe's handwritten directions. He told Allison the sign for Champorcher would be another ten kilometers on, near a town called Hône. The S-2 would lead west to Pontboset, then they would look for the turnoff. Tom tried the radio again to see what was there, but only static came through the speakers.

The road had been cut along the banks of a small river, following the folds of the mountains. Tom felt his body press into the leather seat as the car went up a steep grade. Downshifting, Allison took a sharp turn, then another. The Alfa held to the curves like a slot car. Snowflakes moved horizontally past the windows.

They slowed going through toy villages with steeply pitched roofs. Coming out of Pontboset, the road made a long series of hairpin turns. Tom felt dizzy from the constant side-to-side motion, and his ears popped. The snow was falling steadily, and Allison turned on the wipers.

Pine trees pressed on them from both sides as the road twisted up and up. Tom told her that the road to Zurin's house would be the next left. Allison slowed and looked through the windshield at an unmarked one-lane road that vanished around an outcropping of granite.

"Tom, are you sure this is right?"

"Absolutely. I've been looking at the odometer. The GPS is useless up here."

She swung the wheel left and the car picked up speed. "If we don't get there soon, I'm going to turn around and call from the nearest town."

"Do you have Leo Zurin's number?"

"I didn't think to ask. I'll try Stuart again."

Tom looked out his window. There was no guardrail, and the drop to the valley below was so precipitous he couldn't see the bottom. "Slow down. This is making me nervous."

"Do you want to drive?"

"No, thanks."

The tires rumbled over a patch of ice. A waterfall had frozen to the cliff above them, and immense boulders extended over the road. Allison's eyes went to the rearview mirror. "Someone's behind us."

"I guess it means this road goes somewhere," Tom said. He looked around into the headlights of a dark SUV with a roof rack and big tires. The truck followed them down a hill, then around a switchback. The valley spread out before them, then was lost when they went into the trees. Allison muttered, "Get off my bumper, damn it."

The headlights closed in, and Tom read the word NIS-SAN on the black grille. "Let them get around."

"How? The road is too narrow."

She downshifted around a sharp curve, putting the two vehicles momentarily parallel to each other. Tom could see the driver's window, but it was fogged, and he couldn't see who was inside. When the road straightened, the truck quickly came up behind them again. He felt the jolt of the bumper tapping the rear of their car.

He shouted, "Are they crazy?"

"I'm not going to find out." Allison pressed the accelerator, and the car shot up the hill. The truck fell behind. The Alfa's tires skidded, then caught, as she made a sharp turn to the right.

"Be careful, dammit!"

"I am! Stop yelling at me."

The Nissan disappeared behind a curve, then came back into view. Snow swirled behind them, and gravel clattered on the underside of the car. They topped a hill, and the road veered left. Tom braced his feet and grabbed the handhold over the window.

"Allison, slow down."

"Where are they?"

"I don't see them. Yes, I do. Shit. They're right behind us."

"Help me look for a side road." She leaned forward to see through the windshield. The wipers moved quickly across the glass. Trees came at them and blurred past.

Tom shouted, "Look out!"

The road ended at a gate. Two low stone columns

supported a long triangle of rusty pipe. The headlights picked up a red circle with a horizontal black line. The car skidded sideways, plowing through the snow. It came to a stop with Tom's door jammed against one of the columns. He could see nothing through the windshield but the tops of trees and the peak of a mountain in the distance.

Allison threw the car into reverse. The wheels spun. Tom looked past her and saw the Nissan a few yards away. Its wipers were going, and the headlights were on. It sat there a few seconds, then the doors opened. A woman in a white fur coat and hat and black high-heeled boots got out of the driver's side. She walked toward their car and tried the door, then tapped on the glass with a gloved hand. "Are you all right? We tried to stop you. You took the wrong turn!"

"My God. It's Rhonda." Allison put the car into park.

"Don't open the door!" Tom yelled.

But Allison had already pulled on the door release. "Were you trying to run us off the road or what?"

Stuart Barlowe leaned in, a face with a graying beard and dark-circled eyes. Snow was falling on the brim of his fedora. His eyes quickly went over the interior of the car. "Nobody's hurt?"

Tom shoved on his door. It opened a few inches and hit the stone pillar holding the gate. He felt for the buckle on his seat belt.

"Do you have the map in the trunk? Is it safe?" Barlowe searched the dashboard for the trunk release button.

"He can't have the map!" Tom pushed Allison out of the way to squeeze through the seats and get to the rear door. When he opened it, he was staring into the barrel of a gun.

Barlowe said, "I'm sorry. Get back in the car. Both of you."

Allison shouted at him, "Just take the goddamn map! Take it!"

Barlowe pushed her door shut, then Tom's, and stood outside to make sure they stayed closed. Allison turned in her seat. "Tom! Let them have it."

He felt the vibration of things shifting around. The trunk lid slammed shut.

Snow obscured the back window. Tom looked out the side and saw Rhonda walking to the Nissan with the map tube. The engine was still running. She opened the driver's door and climbed inside.

Tom slid across the backseat and slammed a shoulder into the passenger side door. It came open a few inches and clanged into the metal gate.

"Allison, your seat belt! We have to get out of the car!" Tom dove into the front and turned the key in the ignition. Allison was still staring through her window at Barlowe, who held the pistol. "Allison! We have to get out!"

The engine noise grew louder, and the wheels of the truck turned. The headlights aimed directly at them.

Tom hit the button to lower the passenger side window. It slowly slid down. He dove out headfirst as the Alfa skidded toward the edge. He reached back through the window, grabbed a fistful of Allison's sleeve, and screamed her name.

She scrambled over the console and put her head and arms through. He grabbed her wrists and pulled. The car teetered. The rear lifted off the ground, and the car slid out of sight. The crashing and screaming of metal went on and on.

Sprawled on the ground, Tom was staring at the mud-spattered side of the Nissan. He helped Allison to her feet as the big wheels spun on ice, then caught. The truck lurched backward and revealed Stuart Barlowe. He lifted the gun. "Stay there!"

Allison yelled at him, "Why are you doing this?"

Rhonda's fur coat opened as she ran toward them.

Barlowe stood at the edge of the road with the gun extended. Tom put Allison behind him. The gatepost blocked their retreat. When Tom shifted, stones slipped from under his foot and went over, clattering against the rocks.

"Shoot him!" Rhonda's voice was shrill, panicked. "I'll take care of her!" She tried to push past Stuart, and he shook her off.

The heel of her boot caught, and she lurched sideways toward the edge. Her arms whirled, and the heavy white coat made her awkward. She balanced for an instant, grabbing for his arm, for air.

"Stuart!"

He might have stopped her, but he watched her go down. There was a scream, cut short by the cracking of branches.

He stepped to the edge of the cliff, and the snow covered his polished black shoes. He looked over, and his arms lifted as if he might throw himself after his wife.

Allison buried her face in Tom's chest.

Then Barlowe dropped his arms. He swung the gun gently back, then forward, letting go. The gun vanished over the side. As if the string holding him up had been cut, he collapsed and sat in the snow with his long legs straight out in front of him.

There was no sound except for the wind in the tops

of the pines and a soft tapping of snow on Barlowe's hat.

Tom finally breathed. "This is how they killed Nigel. They murdered your uncle. They put his body in his car and shoved it off the road in a snowstorm—"

"No. You don't get it. This is Nigel." Allison ran over and grabbed the shoulder of Barlowe's coat in her fists. She shook him, and in the still, cold air, her voice echoed on the mountains. "You killed him, didn't you, you bastard! You murdered my father! I knew! Somewhere inside me I knew!"

He held up his hands. She flailed at him with her fists. His hat fell off, and his hair fell across his forehead.

"Allison, that's enough." Tom pulled her away from the edge and held her as she sobbed. He looked at the man who sat staring blankly out over the ravine. "Nigel. You're Nigel Barlowe."

His brows lifted as though he had just realized it, too. "Yes, I suppose I am."

CHAPTER 34

Tom backed the SUV up to where Nigel Barlowe was sitting, went around, and opened the back door. He threw a couple of suitcases out and found some bright yellow rope in an emergency kit. Barlowe seemed docile enough, but Tom tied his hands behind his back and said he was ready to send him where Rhonda had gone if he moved.

Allison was leaning against the front bumper with her back turned and her arms crossed tightly over her chest. Her red beret and her coat were in the car at the bottom of the ravine, and she was cold, but she didn't want to be anywhere near Nigel Barlowe. She had suggested they tie him to the roof rack.

Tom helped Barlowe sit on the rear floor and swing his legs in. He tied his ankles, pulling the rope tight. "Who killed your brother? You or Rhonda?"

"Stuart was already dead. They had argued. He fell down the stairs. She said it was an accident. Rhonda wanted me to help her, and I did. I drove to Chamonix from Geneva."

"You believed her?"

"I did then. We were in love. She was the most beautiful, intelligent, *vital* woman."

"So you shoved your car off a cliff with him in it."

"Yes."

"And you took his place."

"We put my identification in his wallet. Stuart and I looked similar enough. I hadn't been to Canada in so long. I never went back. I grew out my beard, like his, and I became him."

"Why? You could've had Rhonda. You could've married her as Nigel."

"Well, there was Allison to consider. She would have inherited. Stuart controlled the family business, you see. I was deeply in debt. No, it made more sense if . . . Stuart remained alive."

"Jesus. You people." Tom put another length of rope through a metal loop in the floor and fastened that to the rope around Barlowe's wrists and ankles. "Royce Herron found out. Is that how it went? You hired Marek Vuksinic to kill him."

"I didn't know until afterward. Rhonda told me she'd asked Larry to take care of it. Larry didn't know the truth. She told him it had to be done if we wanted to keep The Metropolis going. I'm sorry about Royce. I liked him."

With a harsh laugh, Tom jerked on the rope to test it, and Barlowe winced. "Which one of you killed Jenny Gray?"

"Rhonda. She said that Jenny had found out about me from Royce. She went to London to talk to her. It got out of hand."

"Out of hand?" Tom tied the rope around Barlowe's

ankles to a metal cargo hook in the floor. "Jenny knew nothing. She pretended to, so you'd pay her."

"Rhonda said Jenny knew."

"Well, she didn't."

"I'm sorry."

"Sure. How could you do that? How do you live with it?"

"I loved my wife."

"Not enough to save her."

Barlowe shifted his shoulders and put his head against the back of the rear passenger seat. "I don't mind going to prison. I think it will be very peaceful."

"You think so?" Tom backed out of the rear of the truck. "You should have jumped."

The village of Champorcher lay in a long valley. From the road approaching the town, Tom could see roofs of red tile, a church, a stone clock tower. He drove in slowly past an old Roman arch that must have been standing there two thousand years. Snow had collected on top of the arch and on the dark green branches of the pine trees along the road. Only a few snowflakes were drifting across the windshield, but the sky was still gray.

Tom heard Allison sniffle. She had been crying all the way down the mountain, and she'd run out of tissues. Now she was lifting her glasses to wipe her eyes on the hem of her cotton turtleneck. Tom pulled off the road and left the engine running and the heater blowing through the vents. He hunted through the glove compartment and found a paper napkin. "Here."

She grabbed it and shoved the door open.

"Allison, don't—"

But the door slammed, and she began to trudge

quickly along the side of the road toward the village. Tom checked the rearview and saw the gray top of Barlowe's head. The man was off in his own world. Tom drove forward to catch up with Allison, then skidded to a stop outside a small food market and ran to intercept her.

"I refuse to breathe the same air as that son of a bitch," she said, tight-jawed. "It would contaminate my lungs."

"Okay." Tom held her hand.

"Thirty years of lies! My whole life is a lie!"

"No, it's not. You're not a lie, Allison. I couldn't love you as much if you were."

She started crying again, and he put his arms around her. Her hair and face were cold. "I feel like my father died *twice*. It's not fair!"

"Hey, look how close we are to the center of Champorcher," Tom said. "See that church steeple? The main piazza has got to be just over there."

Allison glared at the SUV. "I'll walk."

"Come on, babe."

She hiccuped another sob, and her face crumpled. "What am I going to do, Tom?"

"We're going to find a café with a fireplace and get some hot chocolate or something. I need to call Manny Suarez anyway. He said he'd be close by." Tom took off his jacket and put it over her shoulders.

She looked at him through a glimmer of tears. "Aren't you the practical one?"

"Yeah, well, something I've learned is, there's nothing you *can* do, except go on." Tom pressed his cheek to hers. "If it makes you feel better, we'll let Nigel stay in the truck and freeze his ass till Suarez gets here."

She used the last scrap of tattered napkin to wipe her

cold-reddened nose. She let out a breath. "I'm okay now. Let's go."

He held on to her. In the village he had noticed the clock tower rising above the buildings around the piazza. Ten minutes past two. "Allison, I need to take the map to Leo Zurin."

"Screw the map. I wish it had gone over the side with that bitch."

"Suarez expects me to. He still thinks I'm going to plant the microphones." Allison was staring at him. "I have to talk to Zurin."

"No, you don't. Surely not. After what happened with Nigel and Rhonda, how can Suarez demand *anything* from you?"

Tom shook his head. "I need your help, babe."

Slowly, she replied, "Help with what?"

"Going home. Getting myself out of the pit I've been in for most of my life. And getting Eddie out, too, if I can."

CHAPTER 35

Tom had taken Nigel Barlowe's cell phone away before securing him in the back of the SUV. He looked up the number for Leo Zurin as he walked under the sheltering colonnade of the market. With Allison standing beside him biting her lips, Tom dialed the number, then handed her the phone.

She spoke in Italian, and Tom knew enough of it to guess she was saying what he'd instructed her to say: *I'm Stuart Barlowe's daughter. He couldn't come himself to give you the map, but the map restorer is with me, and he wants to deliver it. His name is Tom Fairchild. We're on our way to Champorcher. Could you give me directions?*

She scribbled in Tom's notebook.

"*Grazie mille.*"

When she disconnected, her hands were shaking. "He said it would be a pleasure to meet us."

"Us? You're not going anywhere." Tom dug his own cell phone from his pocket and scrolled through the numbers.

"Who are you calling?"

"Our pal Manny Suarez."

Zurin lived at the end of a private road halfway up one of the mountains overlooking the valley. Set in a copse of towering fir trees, the house was constructed of rock and heavy timbers. Icicles hung from the eaves of the sharply pitched roof. There were a couple of outbuildings, a garage, and an eight-foot-high stone wall. Driving closer, Tom could see that the back of the house extended over a steep incline. The front faced the side of the mountain, a smooth blanket of white broken by rocky ledges and clusters of fir trees. The peak was lost to the clouds.

Tom drove through the open gate and parked in the yard. A stone patio led to an entry door painted bright red. A long glass panel revealed the figure of a man standing there, looking out.

As Tom got out of the truck, two men in heavy jackets and knit caps walked over to check him out. One had an automatic weapon on a strap over his chest, and the other held the leash of a German shepherd. The dog gave a low growl, showing its teeth.

Tom didn't move.

The guards closed in. *"Cosa vuoi? Chi sei?"*

"Sorry. *Non parlo italiano."* Tom lifted a hand toward the house and called loudly, "Mr. Zurin, hello! I'm Tom Fairchild." The vapor from his breath drifted out ahead of him.

The dog began to bark wildly, and Tom stepped back.

The front door opened. A man in a fur hat and a black turtleneck sweater walked onto the patio. He clapped his hands once. "Bruno!" The dog went silent and sat in the snow with its tongue lolling out. Zurin's voice carried to the yard. *"Perquisitelo."*

The guard with the weapon motioned for Tom to hold his arms out. He patted him down thoroughly, under his jacket and down his legs. *"È pulito."* He pushed Tom toward the porch. *"Vai."*

Shorter than Tom by several inches, Zurin had a sharp triangle of a nose, deep folds to the corners of his mouth, and thin lips. Under heavy black brows, dark eyes examined the visitor with open curiosity. The fur hat was the pelt of a wolf.

"I am Leo Zurin." Hands on hips, he stood just beyond reach of a handshake. "I admit I couldn't understand completely Miss Barlowe's phone call, but it appears that my friends have decided not to come." He had a slight accent that Tom guessed was Russian.

"That's . . . about it. It's a little more complicated, but I have the *Universalis Cosmographia.* They asked me to deliver it." The cold was numbing Tom's lips.

Zurin looked past him to the truck, but he said nothing.

"Stuart Barlowe hired me to restore it. I had to clean it and fix a few things. Some age spots. I have it, but not with me."

The eyes snapped back to Tom.

"The map is in Champorcher. I'd like to work out a trade. Not money. I don't want anything like that. The map is yours. I just need a favor." He started to reach into his pocket. "I want to show you something on my cell phone. A picture. May I get it?"

"Please. This is so fascinating."

With frozen fingers, Tom managed to hit the camera function on his phone. He pressed another button and turned the screen toward Zurin. "Can you see it?"

Zurin squinted. "I see . . . a young woman. She's holding . . . what is that?"

"It's your map. That's Allison Barlowe. She has a cigarette lighter in her hand. It's under a corner of the map."

"Ehi!" Zurin breathed. His eyes widened.

"You see the clock tower in Champorcher. This was taken at three fifteen. If I'm not back there in an hour, she'll light the map."

A strange laugh gurgled from his throat. Zurin said, "If the map is not here in half an hour I will instruct my men to each grab one of your legs, make a wish, and pull. Bruno can have the remains. Why should I not do that?"

"Because you want the map. It belonged to your great-grandfather. It was stolen out of a museum in Latvia, and you have all the other maps in the atlas except this one. It's beautiful. It's perfect." The cell phone was shaking. "Look at it."

Zurin stared down at the small screen.

"If anything happens to me, she'll burn it."

Gradually Zurin's lips curved, and his eyes lifted to Tom's. "And what is it you want, Mr. Fairchild?"

"I want my freedom. You're the only one who can give it to me."

On his way down the mountain an hour later, Tom called Allison to reassure her he was still alive. In Champorcher, he found her where he had left her, at a table near the fire in a small *osteria* just off the plaza. Suarez and Ricker were seated nearby, pretending to be tourists. The other guy, Ianucci, was keeping Nigel Barlowe out of sight for the time being in a hotel around the corner.

Suarez went to the window and looked out. Walking past him, Tom said, "They didn't follow me."

"Did you get inside?"

"Back off, will you?" Tom sat down and put a hand over Allison's. "You doing okay?"

She puffed out some air. "Are you?"

"So far, so good. Where's the map?"

"I'm going with you."

"No freaking way. Where's the map?"

"Manny Suarez thinks it would be less suspicious if I went along, too."

"Oh, he does, does he?"

Tom swiveled around. Suarez sent a shrug his way. When he turned back, he saw that Allison was sliding her arms into a black wool overcoat. Suarez's coat. It came nearly to her ankles. "I'm going with you, Tom."

As Tom turned through the gate at Zurin's place, the guards and the dog were nowhere in sight, but a small gray car was parked near the front steps.

"Who's that?" he wondered aloud. "The car. It wasn't there before."

"The license place is from Firenze," Allison noticed.

The door of the chalet opened before they reached it, and Leo Zurin took them inside. His eyes went quickly to the map tube before he turned to Allison. "The lady of the flame," he murmured.

She pushed back the cuff of the coat and offered her hand to Zurin. "It's a pleasure to meet you. My father is sorry he couldn't be here. There was a personal matter to attend to, so he sent me instead."

"This is in no way a disappointment." Zurin brought her hand to his lips. "Springtime has come to these icy slopes."

Without looking around he motioned to his houseboy,

the same guy who had brought Tom some hot tea an hour ago to help him thaw out. He was about five feet tall, with straight black hair and a collarless green shirt that buttoned at the neck. When he offered to take the map tube, Tom pulled it away.

As Tom had done before, Allison wandered over to the fireplace, but it was the view that grabbed her attention. A leather chair was positioned to look out over the valley. At the same time she and Tom noticed the man standing next to it with a glass of wine. He had neatly combed gray hair, a short beard, and glasses. He smiled at them expectantly.

Leo Zurin extended an arm. "Miss Barlowe, Mr. Fairchild, you must meet a friend of mine from Firenze who has just arrived."

Allison exchanged a glance with Tom, who sucked in a quick breath through his teeth. Then she was crossing the room, offering her hand. "Why, it's *Dottor* Grenni. We've already met, haven't we, Tom?"

"Ah, yes!" Guido Grenni set down his wine. "I know them, Leo. We meet at the Biblioteca Nazionale. *Buon giorno, signorina.*"

"Please call me Allison. This is Tom Fairchild, the curator of my father's map collection."

"How do you do?" Tom shook Grenni's hand.

Nodding, smiling, Grenni said, "I am so happy to see this map that you bring from America. Gaetano Corelli's atlas is rare, very rare. He made only one, you know, and to find the map of the world, the . . . centerpiece, no? Very exciting. But Leo wants me to give an opinion. Is this the map from the atlas? Without the papers for the provenance, we have to be sure. It is customary in America also to have an opinion, is it not?"

"Absolutely," Tom said.

Zurin's eyes wandered again to the map tube.

Grenni said, "If the map is what we think it is, we will make a new atlas. One of the best artisans in Firenze will make the binding from the best leather."

"I would love to see it someday," Allison said.

"Yes, why not?"

Zurin's hands were clasped as if he couldn't trust them not to rip the top off the tube. "My cook has prepared some regional specialities for us, and we'll open a bottle of wine, but first . . . the map. Mr. Fairchild?"

They followed Zurin to the other side of the room, where a hanging lamp made of deer's antlers illuminated a polished plank table. The chairs had been moved, and a white cloth lay across one end of it.

"Mi faccia vedere." Grenni smiled at Tom. "May I see it, please?"

Tom removed the cap and tugged on the plastic sheet inside. He unrolled it on the white cloth and slid the map out.

Zurin and Grenni stepped closer.

The paper was the color of old ivory, and the lines were crisp and black, except where age had worn them away. The missing corner, Tom explained, couldn't be replaced, but he had done the best he could with the stains, and he had repaired the tear in the fold so that it was hardly noticeable—

Grenni pulled a magnifying glass from his pocket and leaned over the map. *"La carta è certamente molto antica . . . quattrocento o cinquecento anni."*

Allison whispered, "He says the paper is obviously very old, four or five hundred years. . . ."

"La mappa è del tipo di quelle del sedicesimo secolo."

"And the map appears to be from the sixteenth century."

"Appears to be?"

"Shhh."

At last Grenni straightened and said to Zurin, *"Sì, si tratta di una Corelli."*

"What?" Tom said.

"It's a Corelli." Allison's fingers tightened on his.

"Ne è sicuro?"

"Zurin is asking him if he's sure."

"Certamente! Non ho alcun dubbio." Grenni put down the magnifying glass and turned to Tom and Allison. "I have no doubt. It is the map from Gaetano Corelli's atlas."

Zurin put his hands to his face and whispered, *"Slava boghu!"* He glanced at the others. "Forgive me. Such emotion!"

Tom had to sit down on the nearest chair. Turning her back to the table, Allison widened her eyes at Tom and mouthed, *Oh, my God.*

Through a fog, he heard *Dottor* Grenni asking Allison if she agreed with him that Zurin should not fold the map again but frame it. Then Zurin wondered what to put in the atlas if the original were in a frame, and Grenni suggested that he have a copy made. Zurin asked if he knew someone who could do this.

Allison leaned close to Tom and whispered, "Don't even think about it."

"I wasn't," he said. "Trust me, I wasn't."

Leo Zurin gazed at the map awhile longer, caressing its borders. He laughed out loud, then went around the corner and yelled, "Alexei! *Il vino!* Open the wine!"

CHAPTER 36

With all the red tape, it was the middle of July before Eddie Ferraro could get safely back into the United States. The first weekend Tom could round everybody up, he took them out on his sailboat. It was typical summer weather, low nineties, with humidity you could eat with a spoon. Rose and Allison, slathered with sunscreen, stretched out on the bow. The twins in their life vests sat in the cockpit, leaning over the side throwing potato chips into the water to watch them float backward. Eddie had just gone below to find them something to drink.

The boat was heading south in Biscayne Bay, doing about four knots in a steady east wind. Astern, the shimmering buildings of downtown Miami seemed to float on glittering turquoise.

When the boat got about even with Stiltsville, Tom's plan was to tack northeast toward Key Biscayne, then northwest under the Rickenbacker Bridge, then west. He would furl the sails and motor up the river. Martha Framm was letting him use her marina for nothing, and if he needed any boat repairs, they were on her, too. She was that happy about The Metropolis biting the dust. When Barlowe's group went under, other major investors pulled out, and the entire project folded.

Allison had decided not to hide the truth, and the story about Nigel Barlowe had been international news for weeks. She had turned down dozens of requests for interviews and about as many proposals of marriage.

It would take a while to untangle the legal issues involved in her real father's death, but it looked like Allison would be getting everything Nigel Barlowe owned. Nigel would be prosecuted in Italy for kidnapping and assault, the best they could do given the fact there was no proof he'd been involved in any of the other crimes. Allison wasn't happy about having to see Nigel again when she testified at his trial, but it had to be done.

In the spring, she had gone up to Toronto to visit her father's grave and see about changing the headstone. The grief she'd been too young to feel at age three was hitting her almost thirty years later.

The mystery of Larry Gerard's disappearance had been solved. When the Peruvian police seized the shipment of illegal weapons destined for Oscar Contreras, they found Larry's body in the container. He'd been shot with three bullets, a match for the ones that had killed Royce Herron. There was no chance Marek Vuksinic would ever be arrested, but it didn't matter. Manny Suarez had turned Vuksinic over to some Bosnian war-crimes survivors who had been looking for him.

Suarez had asked Tom why Leo Zurin had been so willing to turn on Oscar Contreras, giving up not only the shipping information but the evidence that the Peruvian government needed to arrest Contreras and his associates. Tom didn't know the answer to that, but Suarez was grateful as hell. Allison had suggested that as long as Suarez was so grateful, he could arrange to have George Weems transferred to do counseling at a maximum security prison. Tom had been content just to have the Weasel off his back. He had sent him a photo of himself in Florence with the Ponte Vecchio in the background, but he hadn't received a reply.

Eddie came back topside with a couple of cans of apple juice, and he sat next to Megan and Jill to open them. He and Rose were getting reacquainted, and it looked like a wedding might be in their future. Eddie hadn't asked her yet, but Rose said he probably would, and she would probably say yes. He would be going back to Manarola soon, this being high tourist season. He could make decent money selling his watercolors. Rose was thinking of going back over with him for a week or two, if Tom could watch the girls. They would work it out somehow.

Tom stood up at the wheel and gave Eddie the winch handle for the jib. He cupped his hand at his mouth and shouted toward the bow, "Ladies! Coming about! Turning to starboard, watch your heads!"

Allison and Rose ducked as the jib let go, fluttered over the foredeck, and snapped tight on the other side. The boat swung around. Holding on to the stainless tubing that supported the Bimini top, Allison made her way to the cockpit, where she traded places with Eddie, who went to join Rose on the bow.

Allison's legs had picked up a nice honey-gold tan. She bumped Tom's hip, and he scooted over and let her take the wheel. Her brown hair, in a long ponytail, stuck out the back of her ball cap. He gave it a little tug. She smiled at him. "Where am I supposed to be steering this thing?"

"Just keep it pointed toward the lighthouse on Key Biscayne." Tom opened a beer and leaned back on the bench seat, feeling the warm salt air on his face.

What would happen with him and Allison, he didn't know, but so far it was working out. She had passed the bar, and he still had his graphic design business. Now that his record had been cleared, it was easier to find work. He didn't mind having a rich girlfriend as long as she didn't remind him of it too often.

"You want to take the wheel back?" she asked.

He shook his head and closed his eyes. "You drive."

ACKNOWLEDGMENTS

Authors seldom know where the next idea is coming from, so we keep our antennae up. Over lunch one day, a new friend mentioned that she and her husband collected antique maps. She told me about a 1507 atlas of the world recently purchased by the Library of Congress for ten million dollars. As a mystery writer, naturally my first thought was, "Well, that's something worth killing for." My friend continued to talk about maps, and I felt the familiar flutter in my chest that signals a story just over the horizon.

For setting me off on this voyage of exploration, I must thank Lorette David. She invited me to the Miami International Map Fair, where I met her husband, Bob David, who is even more of a map fancier. They introduced me to an eminent map expert in Miami, Dr. Joseph Fitzgerald. He helped me invent an Italian Renaissance cartographer, Gaetano Corelli, then sent me to the Historical Museum of Southern Florida, where curator Rebecca A. Smith and her assistant, Dawn Hugh, let me go through the map collection.

With my plot still unformed, Bob and Lorette arranged a visit to the Library of Congress in Washington, D.C., where Dr. John R. Hèbert, chief of the Geography and Map Division, generously shared his time. Dr. Hèbert set me straight on my plan to have someone in the story sell a forgery to the LOC. "Very unlikely," he said, and sent me to talk to Heather Wanser, an expert in the Library's Conservation Division. Heather then introduced me to Cindy Ryan, a scientist in the document testing laboratory. I quickly realized there wasn't much chance of fooling any of them with a fake.

At the Library, I was taken on a tour inside the vault, the fortified room where our nation keeps its most precious cartographic treasures, including globes hundreds of years old and rare maps of unique beauty, printed onto vellum or laid paper, hand-painted in full color, and touched with real gold. John W. Hessler, a brilliant cartographic technician, turned history into suspense stories, sparking my imagination.

It took several more weeks to get my story under full sail. I corresponded with Kirsten A. Seaver, who had written a nonfiction book about an infamous fake, the so-called Vinland Map. Deciding that a hand-drawn map would be too difficult for my purposes, I researched copperplate techniques online and found Evan Lindquist, an artist and expert on intaglio engraving and printing. He supplied details of the antique printing press, the ink, and the technique for re-creating Corelli's 1511 masterpiece, the *Universalis Cosmographia*.

But first the original map had to be transformed into a digital image, and for that, credit goes to my son, James Lane, who works in graphic design in New York City. He gave Tom Fairchild his ability to join modern computer technology with Renaissance cartography.

I am also indebted to John Prather for his comments on the Department of Corrections in Miami; and to attorney/mystery author Milton Hirsch for suggesting Leo Zurin; and to Sallye Jude and Jane Caporelli for their observations about overdevelopment along the Miami River.

If Allison Barlowe speaks Italian, she learned it from my friend in Italy, Grazia Guaschino. Grazia's charming husband, Guido Grenni, supplied photos of the train station in Turin and played the part of the curator of maps from the Biblioteca Nazionale Centrale di Firenze. *Grazie mille* to Loredana Giannini, who lives in Florence, for a glimpse of the interior of the library.

Writer Christine Kling, who knows her way around a boat as well as a mystery novel, gave Tom Fairchild his sailboat and made sure he could handle it.

A final thank-you to my editors at Penguin, Julie Doughty and Brian Tart, and to my agent, Richard Curtis, for encouraging me to take a vacation from my long-running series and chart a new course.

For more information and links about the fascinating world of rare maps, please see the links on my Web site, www.barbaraparker.com.